MYSTIC BRIDGE

MYSTIC BRIDGE

Janis Bogue
and
William Keller

This is a work of fiction. The characters, places and organizations are either fictitious or used fictitiously.

ISBN-13:978-1481049986

To Lyn and to Dad

ACKNOWLEDGMENTS

Thanks to Steve Hamilton and Frank Hayes, for their advice and for their patience with the woo woos. Thanks to Lyn Desautel, for her support and for her real estate expertise. To Rick Bryant, Executive Director, Central Pennsylvania Festival of the Arts, for help with some architecture questions. To the sharp-eyed Sara Keller. To Mom and Dad, for their encouragement. And to Zoe and Maisy, for too much to list.

CHAPTER 1

The last time they patrolled together, AJ and Tony drove under the highway into a forgotten part of the city.

"Look at it," Tony said, "the new American ghost town."

The street had been commercial, once, but no one shopped or worked or lived here anymore. The rusty rolldown grates covering the storefronts hadn't budged in years. There was no curtain-softened light in the upstairs windows—they were blank, some patched over with plywood, some empty and bearded with soot. There was no traffic in the wide lanes. No cars were parked at the curb. Nothing moved.

Two young men came around the nearby corner. They staggered up the sidewalk, laughing.

"Here we go," Tony said. He had a rough voice and a jowled, stubborn face. "Some signs of life."

"They look like college kids. What brings them down here? Drugs?" Though AJ was new to the job and not yet thirty, there was a wariness in his deep-set eyes.

"Nah, they don't need to leave campus to buy drugs. They like to hit the local dive bars—makes them feel tough. They probably just took a wrong turn. Or forgot where they parked the car. Which, given the state they're in, would be a good thing."

Tony pulled up to a red light. He waited for it impatiently, tapping his wedding band against the steering wheel. AJ kept his eyes fixed on the young men. Weaving, trading places, they approached an old theater, once grand, now derelict, its sagging marquee held up by a thicket of two-by-fours.

The light changed and Tony pulled forward. Under the marquee, the columns of shadow seemed to merge into a gray shape that could have been a figure with a haggard face.

AJ stiffened. "Shit," he said quietly.

"What?" Tony leaned across the seat to get a better look.

The men had reached the theater. They laughed, stumbled, laughed some more. The darkness under the marquee was still.

"Nothing, I guess." AJ sat back.

"All right. I want to talk to these guys. Point them in the right direction."

Tony pulled alongside. When the men took no notice of the black and white, he gave a single whoop on the siren. The men glanced left, straightened up a little, but kept walking.

"Jesus Christ." Tony put the car in park. He opened the door.

Just then a call came over the radio.

"You take that," Tony said. "I need a quick second with our friends."

As AJ talked to the dispatcher, he saw Tony block the sidewalk, then gesture back toward the highway. One of the men gave him a sloppy, mocking salute, but they turned around, walking more purposefully now.

"That was easy," AJ said, as Tony dropped into his seat again.

"A couple of wise asses. They pretended they knew exactly where they were headed. I sent them to the bus stop on the other side of the overpass. So what did Dispatch have for us?"

"Another domestic disturbance. On Linden."

"Shit. That's our third one tonight." Tony swung the car out into the empty street, then spun the wheel, executing a tight U-turn, already accelerating. "Number three. I don't like that. Not good, not good at all."

"The last two didn't amount to much," AJ said. "What—you think we're due for a bad one?"

"No, rookie. That's not it."

The car was dark but AJ could see the clench of Tony's jaw. "So what is it, then?"

"I just don't like things in threes."

There were no other cars on the street, and not a soul on the sidewalk except the two lost college students receding in the rearview mirror.

When they'd passed under the highway again, AJ said, "You're serious?" He let a hint of a smile show. "About stuff coming in threes? I wouldn't have taken you for the superstitious type."

Tony's hands held tight to the steering wheel. "I'm not. Black cats, broken mirrors, whatever—they don't bother me. It's only the number three that does it. Crazy, I know. You don't have any crazy shit like that?"

AJ looked out the window and said nothing.

"Nah," Tony said. "Not you. You're a feet-on-the-ground, rational, practical guy, right?"

"I don't know about that. But I do know that three in a row, four in a row—it doesn't matter to me. They're keeping us busy. And I like being busy."

"Oh, we're going to be busy, all right." Tony relaxed his grip a little. "Wait until the first summer heat wave comes—then you'll see some fireworks. Think you can handle it?"

"No problem," AJ said. "If I can handle Mystic in August I can deal with anything this town throws at me."

"Yeah? What goes on in Mystic in August?"

"Height of the tourist season."

Tony laughed. "Right. Height of the tourist season." He laughed again, making a thick sound that caught somewhere deep in his chest. "A sense of humor is a good thing for this job."

He took a left and sped through a neighborhood. The houses on either side were random and rundown, losing shingles and downspouts. A few looked unlived in, or like they should be.

AJ read the numbers out loud. "The next one," he said after a while.

Tony stopped the car under a dying streetlight. They sat there, checking out the house. It was narrow across the face, with dingy aluminum siding and mismatched windows. The lawn was a strip of weeds behind a wire fence. The porch was dark.

"Seems quiet," AJ said.

"Not necessarily a good sign."

As AJ and Tony got out of the car, a young couple emerged from a house across the street.

"We're the ones who called," the woman said. She was short and skinny and maybe nineteen. "I don't hear them now, but they've been going at it all night."

"Are there any kids in the house?" Tony said.

"No. It's just Gina and her latest boyfriend. I told her he was no good."

"Do you know the boyfriend's name?" AJ said.

"Kevin," the man said. He wore a Cavaliers jacket that hung loosely off of him.

"Okay." For a moment, Tony seemed to be working on taking a good, deep breath. "Thanks for your help. You two should go back inside."

The woman glanced at the house. "He said he was going to kill her. I mean, Gina's been telling me right along that he says that, whenever they fight. Tonight, we heard it. He just yelled it out—'I'm going to kill you, bitch.' That's when we called 911."

"Okay. You go on home," Tony said.

The couple retreated as far as their front door.

"Let's get this over with." Tony led the way up the soft, slightly skewed stairs onto the porch. He banged the door with his palm. "Bridgeport police! Kevin! Gina! We need to talk to you!"

There was no response.

"Everyone all right in there?" AJ leaned closer to the door. "Why don't you open up so that we can see that everyone's doing all right?"

Silence.

Tony turned the knob. "Bridgeport Police!" He swung the door open. "Kevin? Gina? We want to talk to you. We're here to help."

In the dim room was a ripped-up couch, a tilted easy chair and a little flakeboard table, smashed to pieces. There were stacked pizza boxes and socks and soda cups. There was no sound.

Guns drawn now, AJ and Tony crossed the room.

"Kevin," Tony called out again. "Come on. Let's talk."

AJ went left, into the kitchen. Tony went right, into the hall. They met up again and took the next door, into a bedroom. Exposed bulbs on the ceiling gave a harsh glare. There was a queen-sized bed with a quilted headboard. On the left were two doors, half open. On the right was hell.

A woman knelt on the carpet, an otherworldly shine coming from her bare back. She was tending to something, something red and sparkling with silvered glass. It was a body—the body of another woman, lying on her back, naked, her skin shredded and covered in blood.

"Jesus." Holstering his gun, Tony brushed past the kneeling woman as if he didn't see her, going straight to the victim. He tugged the jagged shards of broken mirror from her face, spoke to her. AJ stayed put, his weapon sweeping from one door to the next.

The kneeling woman backed away. She watched Tony but kept silent, and he said nothing to her, all of his focus on the broken body, his fingers on the neck, first one side, then the other, searching for a pulse.

As Tony worked on the victim, the other woman turned toward AJ. She was young, bare from head to toe, her skin unscathed and radiant. Though she was slender, almost frail, her eyes were fierce with terror. Her arms reached toward him. Her mouth hung open. She and AJ stared wordlessly across the room at each other. Then she began to scream.

AJ lowered his gun. He motioned with his hand—*Calm down, quiet.*

The woman came at him, her gaping mouth making a sound that was sharp with rage and fear, impossibly loud. When she was directly in front of him, AJ finally spoke. "It's all right. It's all right."

But the woman kept on screaming, an endless scream without breath.

Tony didn't turn around. He cocked his head and leaned forward, listening, as if, despite the bedlam behind him, he might hear the faint whisper of air escaping her lips. He sat back. "She's not breathing." For the first time, he looked up.

Across the room, in one of the empty doorways, there now stood a man. No one had noticed him take up a position there. No one had noticed that he held a gun. He raised it. In that instant, Tony found him.

"AJ!" Tony yelled, throwing himself behind the bed.

The man fired. The bullet disappeared into the wall. AJ spun and shot and the man went down.

***

They watched the body bag slide into the ambulance. Tony dropped a half-smoked cigarette. He ground it into the blacktop with his shoe.

AJ kept watching the ambulance. It glowed red, then blue, then purple in the swirl of emergency lights.

"You did good," Tony said. "If he'd gotten off another shot, one of us would be in a bag right now."

AJ finally looked his partner in the eye. "He shouldn't have gotten off even one shot. I should have been watching for him. That was my job, to watch for him."

"Yeah, well, and I should have checked the bathroom. Or I should have told you to do it." Tony coughed a gurgling cough. "I'm the one with the experience here. I've got no excuse."

AJ stood there, his arms crossed, not saying anything.

"Look, guys like us, we take this job because we want to protect people, save lives, be the hero. At some point, usually sooner than we're ready for it, we find out that sometimes, in order to do that, to save one life, we have to take another one."

"I know that," AJ said.

"Do you? Because you look like you're not getting past the fact that you just shot a guy. You need to see things different—"

AJ's hard stare stopped Tony cold. "I do see things…differently," he said.

Forcing a smile, Tony took AJ's shoulder in a firm grip. "It's all right, kid. You stick with me, you'll be okay."

"It's not me I'm worried about." AJ turned to the house, which was bright now, every light bulb burning. "You stick with me, Tony, you're going to end up dead."

CHAPTER 2

Three men in their twenties occupied a front table at the Honey B Dairy in Mystic, Connecticut. Between bites of his clam roll, Ben Shortman kept watch. He had a good view of Mystic's main street, which was lined with shops under painted wooden signs.

"Do you see him?" Sela asked, dipping a french fry into ketchup.

Ben raised a hand to cut the glare. His muscular arm was almost completely covered with a colorful, supernatural-themed tattoo. "Not yet."

DaSilva—leaner, fidgety—squinted toward the glass. "Do you think he won't show?"

"I don't know what to think," Ben said. "He's so different lately."

"You mean, since he came back from Bridgeport." Sela popped a fry into his mouth.

"Yeah, what's with him?" DaSilva said. "It's like he's not even there sometimes. He's like the walking dead."

"It's true," Ben said. "He's a zombie."

DaSilva held his arms out in front of him and moaned, in imitation.

"I wish he'd talk to us," Sela said. "Has he said anything to you, Ben?"

"Nah." Ben sat back. He plumbed his milkshake with his straw. "But I don't think it's any big mystery why he's so miserable right now. Going from a beat cop in Bridgeport to a part-timer in Stonington is a huge comedown. He's got to feel like a fuck-up."

They dug into their meals, then. The restaurant was noisy with laughter and the clatter of dishes.

"How do you kill a zombie?" DaSilva said, after a while.

"What the hell, Dave?" Sela lifted his Red Sox cap, revealing wavy, black hair, cut short.

"I'm just trying to remember. With werewolves, it's the silver bullet. With vampires, it's a stake through the heart."

"You shoot them in the head."

"Yeah. Or do you have to cut their heads off?"

"The better question," Ben said, "is how do you make a zombie? Right? That's what we really want to know." He turned to the window again. "Ah. Here he comes now. We can ask him."

Just behind the table, the door opened and AJ Bugbee stepped inside.

"Hey, where've you been?" Ben said, his tattooed forearm reaching over the back of the booth. "Everything all right?"

"The chief was in a mood," AJ said. "Budget problems. He had me trapped in his office, ranting about it. I thought I was going to die. I hope you guys are talking about something more interesting."

"Zombies," Sela said.

"Perfect." AJ slid onto the bench next to DaSilva.

"We were wondering how you make one," DaSilva said. "We thought you might know."

"What?" AJ rubbed his eyes with his fingertips.

The waitress appeared at the end of the table. "What'll it be, AJ? You want the clam roll special that your friends are having?"

"What, the tourist platter? No, thanks, Doreen. I'll stick with the usual."

"Burger, onion rings and a shake, coming up." She paused for a second. "You want coffee instead of a shake? You look like you could use a little pick-me-up."

"I'm fine, thanks."

The table fell quiet again as the waitress headed toward the kitchen.

Sela looked at Ben with raised eyebrows.

"We were saying the same thing," Ben said. "That you've seemed a little tired or something lately. Everything okay?"

"Can I just enjoy my dinner?"

"Sure, sure," Ben said.

No one spoke for a while. DaSilva slurped some ice from his soda and began chewing it.

"So, I have some good news," Ben said. "I've been sitting on it until AJ got here."

"All right," Sela said. "Pull it out of your ass and let's hear it."

"I met with Mike Taylor today."

"No way," Sela and DaSilva said together.

AJ stole a fry from Sela's plate. "Who's Mike Taylor?"

"C'mon, AJ," Ben said. "The guy from the Mystery Channel? I've only been talking about him for the last two months. I finally got a meeting with him. Took the train down to New York and everything."

"Jesus," Sela said. "And you didn't tell us any of this?"

"I didn't want to get your hopes up."

"All right. So?"

"He wants to do it. He wants to build a show around a group of paranormal investigators."

"And he's interested in us?" DaSilva said. "In you? In *Mystic Afterlife?*"

"Us. Us. But here's the thing. He's definitely looking at us, but he's looking at a group in Rhode Island, too."

"Well, we can't let that happen," Sela said. "We can't lose out to Rhode Island."

"That's what I said. We've got to beat them out, guys."

"Has he seen our show?" DaSilva said.

"Are you kidding?" AJ said. "It's on Channel 12. Nobody has seen the show. Your own mothers haven't seen it."

"That's what you think," DaSilva said. "We have a following."

"I sent him a couple of clips," Ben said. "He liked them. But he's got a different concept for this, because it will actually have a budget. No more just sitting around a table talking about ghost stories or local legends or whatever. We're going to be out in the field every episode."

"Sounds awesome," DaSilva said.

"Yeah. You would have been proud of me. I had a little pitch prepared. I said there were two keys to success." Ben tapped the lacquered tabletop "Number one, you've got to get video. Audio is great—a good whispery voice, sure, but that's radio. Television is a visual medium. You've got to show it to them.

"And number two—people want to believe in an afterlife. They're hungry for proof that it exists. But they won't put up with being jerked around. So everything you show has to be totally believable, without question. If anything looks like a camera trick or lighting effect, you lose your audience. And you'll never get them back."

Seeing that AJ was staring out the window, Ben said, "What's so interesting there, AJ?"

"Bridge is about to go up."

"Good," Ben said. "I know I'm not as entertaining as the traffic, but if it stops, maybe I can get your attention. You know, this meeting with the producer is the break I've been working toward for, like, five, six years. You could pretend to be interested for two minutes."

"I'm listening."

"Yeah? So what did I just say?"

"Get video."

"Yeah, that's it." Ben leaned back against the booth. "You think it's a bunch of crap, don't you? So there are no ghosts, no spirits of any kind. No afterlife."

"I think there's plenty going on in this life, that's all. I've got enough to worry about."

"Uh huh. I understand. Cop like you, he's got to focus on the here and now. Keeping us safe from the bad element in Mystic, the jaywalkers and the double-parkers—that demands constant vigilance."

AJ stared back at Ben, his eyes coming to life a little.

"Sorry," Ben said. "But look, if you'd seen the show even a couple of times, we wouldn't be having this conversation."

"We didn't get your show in Bridgeport. They have a whole different amateur hour down there."

"Yeah, that's funny. But you've been back here for a while now."

"Maybe you can give me the highlights."

"Forget it," Ben said.

"The inn in Old Mystic," DaSilva said. "We got some awesome audio there. You could almost make out the words."

"It was *Get out*," Sela said. "Really clear."

"Uh huh," AJ said. "You sure that wasn't the innkeeper?"

"Or the girl in the window," DaSilva said. "That was my favorite."

"Yeah?" AJ swiped another french fry.

"There's this house in Groton," DaSilva continued, the words racing out of him. "A creepy old place, empty, all boarded up. It's near where my grandparents used to live. Anyway, it's one of those houses that's all vertical, you know what I mean? People have seen a girl in a window way up on the third story. In this old fashioned dress of white lace. When Dewey did the research, he found out that an eight-year-old girl had died there in, like, 1875. She was kicked by a horse. Died in her bed, a few days later."

"Yeah?" AJ said. "Did you get video of her?"

"No. But when we were standing there looking up at that window, I sensed something. This really bad feeling came over me—like dread, or hopelessness."

"Like what I'm feeling right now," AJ said, "listening to you."

"Fine," Ben interrupted. "You're going to tell me you don't even believe the event that started all this? The thing that Sela and DaSilva and I all saw, together?"

"The famous eeling adventure."

"Right."

"Yeah. How could I have any doubts about that? Let me see. You're out poling around the shallows in the dark, with only the lantern at the waterline to see by—in other words, you can't see shit. And you're passing around some Maui Wowie that DaSilva stole from his big brother, that was ten times stronger than anything you'd ever scored before. You guys were so wasted, I'm surprised you didn't see the ghost of Kickin' Jack Williams himself. So, yeah, forgive me if I'm not as certain as you are of what happened out there."

9

"We all saw it," Ben said. "There was a girl, a teenager, standing on the shore, watching us. I waved to her. She started to come toward us. When she got close to the water I tried to wave her back, but she just kept coming. Then she was *on* the water. Swear to God, on top of the water, just gliding across it like it was frickin' ice or something. And then she disappeared."

"That's exactly what I saw," DaSilva said.

"Me, too," Sela said.

"Great," AJ said. "Corroboration from Smoke and Toke."

"What is it with you?" Ben said. "What makes you so damn hard-assed about this?"

"Just trying to hold on to a little bit of reality, that's all."

"Okay," Ben said, "deny it all you want. We'll lead you to the truth eventually. We'll turn your neat little reality upside down." He finished his shake and stood up.

"Where you going?" AJ said.

"To tell Melody the big news."

They all looked across the dining room to where a waitress was doling out shakes and lobster rolls.

"Oh, give it up, man," DaSilva said.

"Yeah," Sela said. "At least wait until after you have a deal for a show. Then you'll have something new to work with."

"Are you kidding me? I have plenty to work with." Ben swept his hands across his torso.

"You could show her your new tat," DaSilva said. "You've almost got the full sleeve now."

Ben touched the spectral face, pinkish and still a little raised, on his forearm. "I think I will." He started across the room.

"That's just sad," Sela said.

It was quiet at the table for a while. They all watched Ben and Melody, a slender, pretty woman with dark hair, talking by the door to the kitchen.

"You working tomorrow, AJ?" Sela said.

"Yeah. The chief has me down for tomorrow and Sunday. You?"

"Your dad wants us for the afternoon tomorrow, is all. He's got a clambake special going that he thinks will bring 'em in."

"Do I need to talk to him about easing up on you guys a little?"

"It's fine. I can use the money."

"Still, he could stand to hire someone."

"Well, he hasn't had much luck with that."

They talked about the few attempts over the years—a kid who lasted two days, a girl who filled the place with cigarette smoke, a lunch guy who showed up in the deadest lull of late afternoon.

AJ glanced toward the kitchen again. No sign of Ben. The doors with the porthole windows swung open and Melody appeared. She crossed the room towards them, carrying a tray.

"Hi, guys," she said. "I didn't see you come in, AJ. How are you doing?"

"Good, despite what everyone seems to think."

"All right." She put his plate in front of him, then handed him the tall glass.

He took a sip. "Best milkshake in the world."

"Well, I can't vouch for the whole world, but definitely the best in town. Who wants the check?" Melody waved a slip of paper.

"Give it to Ben," Sela said. "Since he's a TV star and everything."

"Too late for that."

"What do you mean?"

"He left a couple of minutes ago."

"Wow," Sela said. "He must have been taking it kind of hard tonight. Guess you didn't let him down as easy as you usually do."

"Nah. He doesn't even mean it anymore when he asks me out."

"So he just bolted?" Sela said. "Did he say anything before he left?"

"You mean, to tell you guys? No. Nothing."

"What did he say?"

"Actually, he told me not to tell you, but..." Melody hesitated. "We were talking about the old Westbury place."

"What about the Westbury place?" Sela said.

"It's been sold."

"What?" DaSilva leaned forward.

"I didn't even know it was for sale," Sela said. "I never saw a sign."

"I don't think they put out a yard sign for a property like that," Melody said. "Apparently, Schwartz Realty had been showing it quietly."

"Do you know who bought it?" AJ said.

"Yeah, I do, actually. She came in here a couple of days ago. She told me the whole story. I guess she picked Schwartz Realty pretty much at random out of the phone book, and the Westbury house was the first one she looked at. She's pretty excited about it. I liked her. Her name's Claire Connor."

"Did you say anything to her?" Sela said. "About the place being haunted?"

"You guys know I don't believe any of that stuff. No offense."

"You don't have to believe us," DaSilva said. "The cleaning lady we talked to saw the ghost of a woman on the stairs. We interviewed her on our show. She said she saw it, plain as day."

"I know. And I'm sure she believes it."

"There are historical records, Melody. Dewey did the research. He found some great stuff."

11

"It's true," Sela said. "This goes way back. Seven people died in that house, and not all from old age."

"Yeah, I know," Melody said. "Ben told me the stories."

"Okay," DaSilva said. "The buyer should at least know that much."

"Why? Unless you want to scare her."

"She'll hear it sooner or later," Sela said.

"Well, not from me."

"That place has been empty a long time," AJ said.

"Since I moved here," Melody said. "That's six years."

"It's been empty most of my life," DaSilva said. "Must be twenty years, right, Sela?"

"Close to it. I bet Schwartz didn't tell her about that whole mess. The missing girl, Jacques Westbury running off to France, the parents moving away in disgrace. Melody, did you say anything?"

"No," Melody said. "That was all before my time. I don't really know what happened."

"No one does," Sela said.

"So how did Ben get by us?" AJ nodded toward the door that opened to the street. "I didn't see him go."

"He asked me if he could go out the back," Melody said. "He thought he could beat the bridge that way."

"Why was it so important that he beat the bridge?" AJ said. "He didn't say where he was going?"

"No. Just that he hates waiting for the bridge."

"Maybe he's not such a sucker, after all," Sela said.

"You don't think—" DaSilva stopped himself.

"I'll take the check, Melody," AJ said.

"What about your dinner? You barely touched it."

AJ took a big bite of the burger, then reached for his wallet.

"How about I put the shake in a paper cup," Melody said.

The traffic was still backed up on Main Street when they left the restaurant. Ahead, the raised drawbridge made a black tower in the twilight. The masts of sailboats heading in for the evening slid behind it.

AJ stopped where a walk cut between stores to the parking lot. "He's on his way over there, isn't he? To the Westbury place."

"Man," DaSilva said. "How'd you figure that out? Guess it comes from being a cop."

"It comes from not being an idiot."

"He always wanted to investigate that place," Sela said. "When he talked about getting video, he had the Westbury house in mind. You know, with so many sightings over the years."

"So why didn't you guys ever check it out?" AJ said.

"We tried," Sela said. "Ben liked to do everything above board. He wanted to get permission, and we couldn't even find anyone to ask. We talked to Henry Jacobson, the guy who was the caretaker all those years. But he couldn't give us the okay. Or he wouldn't."

"Ben doesn't have permission now."

Sela turned his cap so the bill pointed backward. "I'm sure it's that TV thing. He wants something to show the producer. He's desperate."

"So desperate that he just took off without you guys?"

"Well, we were with you. If he had said anything, you might have stopped him."

AJ sucked milkshake through a straw and watched the cars stack up behind the bridge. "We might as well get in line. He'll have half an hour on us."

"You're not seriously going after him, are you?" Sela crossed his arms. "Just leave him alone. He's not hurting anyone."

"Yeah," DaSilva said. "We'll all just, you know, head home, call it a night."

"Jesus, you're a bad liar," AJ said. "You don't think I know you're both going straight over there?"

Sela punched DaSilva on the shoulder.

"You guys are quite a team," AJ said. "No wonder they want to put you on television."

One of Sela's pockets beeped.

"You going to check that?" AJ said.

Sela dug the cell phone out. "It's just my sister." He typed something.

"Yeah?" AJ said. "What's your sister want?"

"Nothing much." Sela finished typing.

Almost immediately, there was another beep. As Sela glanced down at the little screen, AJ, smoothly and without warning, swiped the phone from his hand.

"That's funny," AJ said. "This one's not from your sister, it's from Ben."

Sela made a feeble grab for his phone. AJ blocked him.

"What's it say?" DaSilva said.

"Let's find out." Tilting the screen, AJ read the text out loud. "'Just get over here. If you can't get rid of AJ, bring him along. We'll make him a believer.'"

CHAPTER 3

They took Pequot Trail, a road narrow and bumpy enough to live up to its name.

"So what's the plan?" Sela said. "You're going to arrest your best friend? Put him in handcuffs?"

"I just want to get there before he breaks in," AJ said. "I can't let him commit a crime right in front of my face. Whether you want to believe it or not, I'm an actual cop."

DaSilva leaned forward from the back seat. "Forget it, AJ. Ben's already in by now."

The Jeep bounced over a particularly large patch in the asphalt, sending DaSilva's head into the rollbar.

"Ow!" DaSilva sat back.

Ahead, a slow pickup truck straddled the middle of the road.

"Great." AJ flashed his headlights, then tapped the horn.

The driver didn't move over or speed up. He just kept rolling down the road like it was his driveway.

AJ cursed under his breath.

"We're almost there," Sela said. "Just around this corner."

On the right, a dirt lane bore away into thick woods. AJ took it. They drove over a chain that had been dropped to the ground. The way forward was a tunnel made by stone walls and briars and trees cloaked in Virginia creeper and poison ivy. Saplings had encroached on the dirt track, some even in the dead middle of it. A tree limb as thick as an arm scraped the door.

"Turn off your headlights," DaSilva said.

"What?" AJ said.

"If there's an intelligent haunting, it might be scared off. We'd never see it."

"An intelligent haunting?" AJ said. "I can buy that. If there's anything intelligent in that house, it would be the ghost, not Ben."

"Lights, please?" DaSilva said. "You don't really need them."

AJ switched off the high beams. "That's as far as I go."

The headlights caught plumed seeds fleeing past them, then the shine of glass and chrome.

"That's Ben's car," DaSilva said.

It was stopped in front of a tall garage. Beyond that, the house loomed, silent and black.

AJ killed the engine. "You guys wait here." He reached into the glove compartment and retrieved a flashlight. "I'll go get him."

"Sure, boss." Sela was already opening his door. DaSilva, too.

AJ paused there in the shadow and the dying daylight, considering the two men. "Stay with me."

He pointed the flashlight at the garage, then swept the beam across a low addition connecting the garage to the house. The light found a window, then a door. He headed for that. There was no path or stone walk, just weeds and wild grass.

Sela hesitated by the Jeep. "Do you have any bug spray?"

DaSilva rolled his eyes. "Man, give it a rest."

"There's got to be ticks in that grass."

"If there are, AJ and me will get them."

"What was that?" Sela pointed at an upstairs window. "Did you see that?"

DaSilva looked toward the house. "See what?"

AJ aimed his flashlight higher, turning the windowpanes white. "What'd you see?"

"I don't know."

"Was it Ben?"

"I don't know. Some sort of glow. I guess a flashlight?"

"Could be just a reflection," DaSilva said. "This changing light is the worst."

They continued to the door, Sela lifting his feet in an exaggerated way.

DaSilva turned around to watch. "You look like a freakin' marionette."

"Shut up."

There was a low concrete step. No screen door, just the windowless, six-paneled wood. In the middle of it was a laminated sign.

NOTICE. *Trespassing is Prohibited. Violators will be Prosecuted.*

"How do you think he got in?" DaSilva said. "A window?"

AJ reached for the knob. It turned.

"Is it still trespassing if you're with a cop?" DaSilva said.

They crossed the threshold into darkness. The flashlight showed a big empty space, wide plank floors, blistered paint. On the right was a large fireplace and a door. To the left was the main part of the house.

"Ben!" AJ yelled.

There was no response.

"He's going to make us look for him," AJ said.

"Can you kill the flashlight?" DaSilva said. "We usually do this in the dark."

"I'm not ghost hunting," AJ said. "I'm looking for Ben. And I'm pretty sure he'll show up in a flashlight."

Sela had started across the room. "I'll take the second floor. The stairs must be this way."

"You can see where you're going?" AJ pointed the flashlight at him.

"Like the man said, we work in the dark. I just have to let my eyes adjust."

"Be careful."

"You bet." Sela was already around a corner.

There was a crash, then Sela's voice. "What the—"

"Sure, you work in the dark," AJ said, moving after him. DaSilva followed. As they passed through a kitchen into the front hall, they could see Sela scrambling like a crab, backing toward the door. He was tangled up in a wooden chair.

"Jesus. You're pathetic." AJ came around to the landing. He swung the light from Sela to where he was looking, at the foot of the stairs. The beam hit a pair of legs, then a tattooed arm, then a face. The mouth hung open. The eyes stared upward into the glare, indifferent to the light, indifferent to anything. AJ leaned in close. "Ben?"

CHAPTER 4

AJ put his ear to Ben's mouth. "Call 911."

Sela already had his cell phone in his hand. He began talking to the operator as AJ tilted Ben's head back. "I don't know the address. Pequot Trail—the old Westbury place. Yes, the Westbury place."

AJ was pressing on Ben's chest, counting.

"Fell down the stairs, I think," Sela said. He looked up at the banister.

DaSilva tried to straighten Ben's legs.

AJ waved him off. "There's nothing you can do. Just stay out of the way."

Sela ended the call. "They'll be here soon. Just a couple of minutes." He watched AJ dip his head toward Ben. "Jesus Christ," he said. "Jesus H. Fucking Christ."

The flashlight lay on the floor, pointing at AJ and at Ben's body, making a giant tandem shadow on the wall. Beyond them, a chair lay on it side, a frayed hole where the cane bottom should have been, one of the legs broken.

Sela knelt by the chair. When he stood up, he was holding a compact video camera with an infrared illuminator attachment. "Ben must have had it propped up on the chair," he said.

DaSilva stared blankly at Sela, his Adam's apple jerking up and down.

"It's going to be all right," Sela said. "Ben's going to be all right. AJ knows what he's doing."

AJ pushed down on Ben's chest, counted *one, two, three*.

"Jesus," DaSilva said. He went to the front door. He fumbled with the deadbolt, cursing, then opened the door and peered out into the darkness. "Where the hell are they?"

"They'll be here soon," Sela said. "There's going to be a lot of people here. Cops, ambulance guys. I don't want anyone touching Ben's stuff."

He picked up the flashlight. "He might have had the still camera. And the voice recorder."

AJ pressed Ben's chest, counted, checked the throat, all the time muttering, "C'mon Ben. C'mon Ben."

Red flashed across the wall, disappeared, then flashed again.

"They're here!" DaSilva said.

A blinding light shot through the open door. An ambulance was racing across the yard, straight at them, as if it would crash into the house.

"Hey!" DaSilva yelled, as the driver cut the engine. "In here!"

The EMTs brushed past with their medical kits. They took AJ's place next to Ben. One resumed CPR.

"They were quick, right?" DaSilva said to AJ.

"Yeah." AJ seemed to be counting, still, as he watched the EMTs. The light coming in the open door churned white and red. One of the men, shifting his position around the body, kicked the flashlight. It rolled to a stop at the stairs, its beam overwhelmed now by the ambulance.

"Sela was using that flashlight a minute ago," DaSilva said. "Where'd he go?"

An EMT was pressing a wired pad onto Ben's exposed chest. Next to him was a case, the lid open.

One of the EMTs turned to AJ and DaSilva. "Stay clear."

Ben's legs jerked.

There was the sound of a car door slamming, then a man appeared in the doorway. He was big and bald. He measured the scene with a scowl.

"I thought I was done with this place," he said. "Officer Bugbee, and your friend—you don't need to be in the middle of this. Come on outside."

The three men went out into the frenzy of flashing lights and high beams. They stopped on the concrete step. From there, they could still see into the hall.

"You're DaSilva, right?" the man with the bear T-shirt said.

"Yes, sir. Dave DaSilva."

"What the hell happened?" The man was looking at AJ, now.

"We don't know, chief," AJ said. "That's how we found him. It looks like he fell down the stairs."

"You started CPR immediately?"

"Yes."

"Good. How'd you know he was here?"

"I got a text message. Actually—" AJ glanced back into the house, then seemed to change his mind. "A text message. He said he was coming here."

"So you came after him."

AJ nodded. "I thought I could stop him from doing something stupid."

The chief's stomach growled underneath the printed bear. All three of

18

them stared through the doorway into the hall, where the EMTs crowded around the body. Another car pulled into the yard, a single emergency light flashing on the driver's side. The man who got out wore a cap with the letters WFD. Nodding to the chief, he went inside.

"Those are good guys in there," the chief said. "They'll do what they can."

AJ ran a hand through his short, dirty blonde hair, pushing it back from his forehead.

"I guess I don't have to ask what Ben Shortman was doing here," the chief said.

"He was investigating," DaSilva said.

"You were with him?"

"No," DaSilva said. "We were all at the Honey B Dairy, and he heard about the new owner moving in here. This place was like the ultimate for him. So, he gave us the slip and came over. He knew AJ would never go for it."

An EMT pushed past them from inside the house.

"How is he?" AJ called after him. "Is he going to make it?"

"We're going to get him to the hospital," the EMT answered, without turning around. "They'll know better there."

"But did you get his heart started? Is he breathing?"

The EMT paused, then continued toward the ambulance.

The chief put a hand on AJ's shoulder.

"The damn bridge," AJ said.

"What?"

"He got the jump on us. He beat the bridge. We didn't."

"C'mon. We're in the way here." The chief led AJ and DaSilva from the step into the overgrown yard. DaSilva sat down. He was shivering.

"What the hell happened in there?" AJ said, to no one in particular. "He just fell down the stairs? That's it?"

"More people die from falling down stairs than from drowning," DaSilva said, looking up from the weeds. "My brother-in-law's an actuary. That's the kind of stuff he talks about."

"Would he even have been carrying a flashlight?" AJ said. "Or would he have been like Sela, stumbling around in the dark, crashing into things?"

"Sela?" the chief said.

"Dave Sela," AJ said. "He was with us. He's still inside."

"Doing what?" the chief said.

The EMTs were working the stretcher through the door. Ben was strapped to it, his face pale and blank.

"Let's go," AJ said. "We'll follow them to the hospital."

DaSilva stood up. "We need to get Sela."

"You sure as hell do," the chief said.

There was a shout from inside. The volunteer fireman ran out the door and jumped from the step, landing six feet out in the yard. He stood there, crossing himself. "Holy mother of God," he said.

"What is it?" the chief said. "What happened?"

"I knew it was true," the man said. "There is a ghost. I knew it."

"What did you see?" The chief looked back into the house.

"It came down the stairs. Right at me."

Just then, Sela stumbled out the front door, blinking in the glare. He raised his hands in front of his face.

"Is that the ghost?" the chief said.

The fireman took a couple of deep breaths. "Yeah, I guess it is. Sorry."

Sela was looking around but he didn't seem to be taking in the vehicles and the emergency lights or the doors closing on the back of the ambulance. He didn't seem to be seeing anything.

The ambulance began to move.

"We've got to go," AJ said.

"Sela," the chief said, "what the hell were you doing in there?"

"Roland," AJ said. "Please."

"All right. Go. But I want you all in my office tomorrow morning."

The three men climbed into AJ's Jeep and took off after the ambulance. Once they were on pavement, they flew, leaning around the turns, weightless as they crested a steep rise.

When they joined up with Route 1 in Pawcatuck, DaSilva said, "What if his neck was broken. I moved him. What if he ends up paralyzed because I moved him?"

No one said anything. Ahead of them, the ambulance parted the traffic.

"AJ," DaSilva said, "when you were in Bridgeport, you saw dead people, right?"

"What?" AJ checked the rearview mirror, but DaSilva was tucked close to the door, out of sight.

"You saw dead bodies," DaSilva said.

"Yeah. A few."

"Ben didn't look... He was just knocked out, right?"

Sela turned around. "Yeah. He was just out cold."

AJ didn't say anything. He kept his eyes forward and his foot on the gas, aiming straight at the red chaos of the ambulance lights.

CHAPTER 5

A sedan with a blue flashing light came up fast behind them.

"That's Dewey," AJ said, checking the mirror.

DaSilva looked out the rear window. "Shit. I should have called him."

"It's okay," Sela said. "He must have heard through the fire department."

They crossed the bridge into Rhode Island, then followed the ambulance down Main Street toward the Narragansett Bay and the hospital. The whole way down Beach Street and up Wells, the three vehicles made a speeding convoy, red and blue lights mixing in the air and on the houses and shops and the leaves of trees.

As the ambulance backed toward the emergency entrance, AJ pulled over to the curb. The car with the blue light stopped behind him.

"Hey," AJ said to the driver of the other car, when they were standing on the pavement.

"Hi, AJ." Dewey Allan was a thin man with a long salt-and-pepper ponytail and drooping eyebrows. "I talked to Tom, the guy who was out there. Jesus."

"Yeah."

They watched the stretcher go through the swinging doors, then AJ led them down the walk toward the big *Emergency* sign.

It was the shortest wait any of them would ever have in a hospital waiting room. A doctor appeared within minutes. He wore scrubs and had a five o'clock shadow. His wristwatch dug into his arm. "I'm sorry," he said. "There was nothing we could do. He was already gone when he got here."

Sela smacked the wall with his hand.

"This can't be happening," Dewey said.

"I'm so sorry," the doctor said. "Has anyone contacted his family?"

21

"I'll talk to his sister," AJ said. "And his parents."

"No," Dewey said. "I'm supposed to call Chief Brown. He'll take care of all of that."

The doctor shook AJ's hand, then went back through the door he'd come out of. The four men stood in a loose group under the wall-mounted television, which showed a map of the country dotted with yellow suns—a weather forecast for travelers.

DaSilva looked from one face to the next. "I can't believe it."

"What was he doing out there?" Dewey said. "Did he finally get permission to investigate?"

"He didn't have permission," Sela said.

"He broke in?" Dewey said. "Wow. I didn't think he would ever do that."

"It doesn't matter," Sela said.

"I know. I'm just trying to understand what happened."

On the television, the weatherman worked his way around the map to the Northeast, which was supposed to have a perfect weekend.

"Let's get out of here," AJ said.

Outside, the ambulance was still backed up to the big doors, the lights still flashing.

"Where are we going?" DaSilva looked over the top of AJ's Jeep.

"My place is closest," Sela said.

"You have a couch yet?" AJ said. "Or anything that could be called furniture?"

Sela shifted his cap but said nothing.

"My house, then. See you there, Dewey."

Dewey stared off into the night for a moment. "Thanks. I think I need to be alone. I don't know. Maybe I'll work on the obituary for a while."

"You want to do that now?" DaSilva said. "How can you even think straight?"

"Yeah, come with us," Sela said.

Dewey smiled weakly. "Thanks. I just want to head home. I'll see you guys soon. Take care of yourselves."

"You, too," AJ said.

DaSilva hugged Dewey awkwardly, slapping his shoulder blades. "Good night."

As they headed back to Mystic, there was little conversation in AJ's car. After several dark and empty roads, AJ pulled into the gravel driveway of a small house. A creek ran past one side. Beyond the house, a thin finger of the bay glimmered. The house was black.

AJ opened the front door. "Hey, Buck," he said.

A greyhound lay across the entryway. He stayed there as the men, one after the other, stepped over him.

"Anyone want a drink?" AJ said. "I have beer, and there's scotch, too, if I can find it."

The living room was as neat as a ship's cabin, except for a bedsheet and pillow on the couch. AJ scooped them up and put them on the stairs. Sela stood by the window, looking back toward the road. He didn't answer.

DaSilva asked for some water. He dropped on the couch.

When AJ came back into the room with a couple of glasses, Sela was still at the window. DaSilva was sitting quietly on the couch with tears streaming down his face.

"Jesus, AJ," DaSilva said. "I can't get my head around it."

AJ put one glass down on the coffee table. "Me, either."

"I've known him since I was, like, five years old. We were in the same freakin' kindergarten."

AJ sat down. They drank without saying anything, looking at their drinks, at the floor, at Sela's back.

"It's bullshit," Sela said after a while, without turning around. "I keep thinking if we just go back there now, that he'll be there. We just got it wrong, the last time, you know what I mean? We get in the car, and drive over there, and it's all right."

"Yeah," AJ said. "I've had the same thought." He stood up. "I'm getting another one of these." He held up his glass. "Sela, you want something?"

Sela shook his head.

AJ left and then came back with a refill. No one spoke for a long time.

"We should have been with him," Sela said. "He shouldn't have died all alone in that house." He came over from the window and squeezed in next to AJ. He let his head tip back. AJ gently rolled his glass in his hand. DaSilva cried quietly. They were unchanged a half hour later. Then another half hour. Once in a while, AJ or Sela spoke, nursing their regrets. In the long silences, a buoy clanged somewhere out in the sound.

DaSilva, his voice breaking, said, "His parents are going to blame me. They were always telling him to give up the paranormal stuff and make a real life for himself. I know they were going to kick me out eventually, for being a bad influence. Maybe I was."

"They won't be thinking about anyone but Ben right now," AJ said.

"They thought we were both a bad influence," Sela said. "But you know Ben. He did what he wanted to do."

"Yeah."

"You can't stay at the Shortmans's anymore, Dave." Sela looked past AJ. "You can crash with me for now."

"You don't have room for all of my shit," DaSilva said.

"This can all wait," AJ said. "We'll work it out."

"Okay." DaSilva bent toward his knees. His shoulders bounced as sobs overtook him.

"Dave," AJ said. He put a hand on DaSilva's back.

The sobbing did not stop.

AJ said, "If you're going to be ready to face Ben's parents tomorrow, you should get some sleep."

DaSilva nodded but remained folded up on himself, crying. The greyhound roused himself from the floor and approached, carefully. He rested his head against DaSilva's thigh.

Thunder boomed in the distance. AJ listened to the storm coming, watched the windows for the first lightning, tried to wait out DaSilva's crying. The thunder moved overhead, rattling the windows. Still no rain. DaSilva showed no signs of stopping.

"I have some sleeping pills," AJ said. "They could help you. Would you take one?"

Sela gave AJ a hard look. "Good idea," he said.

DaSilva didn't respond.

AJ climbed the stairs. He came back a few minutes later with a glass of water and a pill in his hand. "Here you go, buddy."

With Sela's help, DaSilva sat upright. He took the pill, then folded up again.

"C'mon, let's get you lying down," AJ said. "There's no fooling around with this stuff. You will sleep."

DaSilva allowed himself to be led upstairs. He lay on AJ's bed, stiff, unwilling to let go. AJ pulled a blanket over him. Inside of ten minutes, he was dead to the world.

"He's out," AJ said, when he returned to the living room.

"Already? What'd you give him, a horse tranquilizer?"

AJ let that go. "We'll see the storm better out back."

They went into the kitchen and sat down at the table by the window. A brilliant flash of lightning illuminated the water. The banks on either side looked, for that instant, shockingly green, as if color were something new and unsustainable. The scene went black again.

After a long silence broken only by thunder, AJ said, "I should have stopped him. I became a cop to protect people. But I can't even protect my own friends."

"Forget that, AJ. There was no stopping him. When he wanted something, he was going to get it." Sela pointed toward the refrigerator. "I think I'll take a beer now."

AJ got up and fetched a cold, long-neck bottle. As he closed the refrigerator, Sela was pulling something from a pocket. A video camera.

"Is that Ben's?" AJ said. "The one from the house?"

"Yeah."

"Shit," AJ said. "Do you have anything else? Any of Ben's other

24

equipment? What was it, a voice recorder?"

"Digital audio recorder. And a still camera. Usually we'd have both of them. I didn't find either one."

"Okay. The chief will find them."

"Maybe Ben didn't have the still camera. Since he got the DVR, he doesn't use the still camera that much."

AJ put the bottle down in front of Sela. "I think I'll join you." He got his own bottle from the fridge, then sat down on the bench again. "We're going to have to watch that video," he said. "The chief's going to want us to."

Sela opened his bottle and took a swig. "Listen, I know you don't believe in this stuff, but when I went upstairs, at the Westbury place, I saw something. It looked like... I don't know. Anyway, I had the camera going. I think I got it on video."

"Oh, Christ."

"Right, I'm full of shit," Sela said. "But I'd like to check it out before we have to turn the camera over to the chief."

AJ stared into his bottle. "All right. What do we need to do?"

They talked electronics for a minute—cords and ports—and AJ fetched a laptop computer. Sela connected the camera and positioned the computer so that they could both see it.

On the screen, a gauzy gray blob bounced erratically. A voice came from the tiny speaker. "Ben Shortman. Approaching the Westbury house." Lines appeared in the gray—a door. The camera found the *No Trespassing* sign and lingered over it. "Guess I'll have to edit that out," Ben said. There was a metallic sound. "This lock doesn't look too bad." The view blinked black for an instant. They were in the house, then, the camera panning slowly.

AJ reached for the camera. "Let's fast forward past this. We just want to see what you got."

Sela blocked his hand. "No. Leave it."

"This is so awesome," Ben was saying. "Something is going to happen tonight. I just know it. In fact, I'm starting to feel bad about being so far ahead of you guys. That bridge is a bitch, isn't it?" Ben breathed audibly. Then they were moving past the dark hanging shapes of cabinets. "The kitchen. I'm heading toward the front door." The camera whipped along a wall and found stairs, rising into shadow. "This is where the ghost has been spotted. The cleaning lady was coming down the stairs from the second floor when she saw it, standing right there." The video paused on the lower steps. "I'm going to set this camera up here. There should be another set of stairs in back of the house. I'll go up that way, do a sweep of the second floor, then come down here, like the cleaning lady did. I just need something to set the camera on. One sec." The image blinked, bobbed, spun. They were looking up the stairs. Everything tilted left, giving it a funhouse look. "Okay. That will work." Ben's face appeared, in close-up. "This is so cool, guys. Be back in a couple of minutes." Ben moved out of view. The stairs tilted silently.

A flash of lightning from outside AJ's kitchen window overpowered the screen for an instant. Then the stairs reappeared. Sela and AJ watched them in silence.

Ben's feet and legs emerged from the darkness. He descended a few steps, came fully into view, stopped, turned around, then climbed out of sight.

AJ let out a long breath.

Then Ben pitched suddenly into the frame. He crashed toward the camera with speed and violence. He struck the banister, tumbled on. The stairs dissolved into swirling gray. The camera hit the floor. Something filled the screen. The lens, obliging, pulled back, and the fuzzy shape came into focus. A slack mouth. Sightless eyes. Ben's face.

Sela jumped up, crossed the room and threw up into the sink. He stood there for a while, letting the water run.

AJ closed the lid of the laptop, then switched off the camera.

"You were right," Sela said. "I wasn't ready for that." He wiped his mouth with a paper towel. "I shouldn't have even picked up the camera. That was stupid. No, wait—I'm glad I did. Because we can erase that right now. No one should ever see it."

"We can't erase it," AJ said. "But we will turn this in tomorrow."

"Yeah," Sela said. He shut off the water. "I should head home. Can you take me to my car?"

"No way. Neither one of us needs to be driving right now."

"Well, I'm not taking your bed."

"No, you aren't. DaSilva already did that. You take the other bedroom upstairs. I'll use the couch."

"Okay," Sela said after a while. "I'll see you in the morning."

When Sela's footsteps had receded, AJ took the bottles to the sink. He ran more water, splashing it around with a cupped hand. From upstairs, there was the sound of a toilet flushing, then a door closing. AJ sat down at the table again. He looked out the window. The storm was moving off. A moon emerged briefly between clouds, then disappeared again. AJ sat for a long while, as if waiting for the moon to return. Then he opened the computer and switched on the camera.

Ben's frozen face. Voices came from the speaker—Sela's, his own. They had arrived at the house. The voices got louder. He was telling Sela to call 911. Ben being rolled onto his back. Soft, steady thumps—that was the sound of his palms on Ben's chest, trying to trick the stilled heart into copying the rhythm. DaSilva and Sela talking—DaSilva already losing it.

Climbing the stairs, then. Darkness closing in on the turn. A bounce as Sela stumbled, saying, "Jesus. No wonder Ben fell."

At the top, a long hallway. Taking the first door, entering a square, empty room. A swift circuit, traveling along one wall, then the next. One more wall. Before anything showed on the screen, there was the sound—the hiss of Sela's quick, sharp breath. The camera swerved, stopped and held on its target.

In his kitchen, AJ leaned toward the computer. He paused the movie and edged a little closer. He shook his head. "I'll be damned."

CHAPTER 6

Early on Saturday morning, Claire Connor sat down near the window at the Honey B Dairy. She placed a trim leather briefcase on the bench beside her and opened her cell phone. "Damn," she said, loud enough to bring the waitress to her table.

"Are you ready to order?"

Claire flicked her blonde hair away from her forehead. "I'm not going to be able to stay. My phone died on me and I have calls to make. I'll have to charge the thing up in the car. Can I just get a muffin and a coffee to go?"

"You have a charger with you? One that you can plug in?"

"I actually do. I carry it with me because the stupid battery on this phone is always dying."

"Good. There's an outlet right here. But you better let me do it." The waitress held out her hand.

Claire produced a charger from her bag. Taking it, the waitress slid across the bench and, ducking quickly under the table, pushed the plug into a socket. "You just can't be too obvious," she said. "The owner is a real tightwad."

"Okay. Thanks." Claire put the phone into the bag and the bag on the bench and no one higher than two feet off the ground would have known anything about it.

"Would you still like the muffin, or can I bring you something else?"

Claire flashed a bright smile, rounding her cheeks. "Well, since I'm staying, let me get something more substantial. I have a big day ahead of me." She ordered eggs and toast and sausage.

She was digging into the meal when she noticed three men at a nearby table, glancing furtively at her, talking low. Turning toward the window, she watched the cars for a while. She checked the battery indicator on her phone. One bar. When she looked up, Melody was standing at the end of the table.

"Hi, Claire." Melody had a pale, open, unadorned face.

"I was wondering if you'd be here this morning."

"You were?"

"Yeah, well, you're the only person I know in the area. Can you sit for a minute?"

"Sure." Melody slid her oversized, orchid-colored bag across the bench and then followed it. "So how's it going? I was thinking today might be your moving day."

"I'm starting," Claire said. "Some things are arriving today. I have to meet a painter in a little while, and then an electrician after that."

"You must be excited. And maybe a little nervous."

"I should probably be more nervous. It's a lot to take on. But there's something about that place. It's hard to explain. As soon as I walked into it the very first time, I felt like I belonged there." Claire shook her head. "Listen to me. Geez."

"No, that's great."

"Once I'm in the house and make a list of the things I want to do, or have to do, I may be singing a different tune."

"I think you're going to really like it there."

"Thank you. I think so, too." Claire took a sip of her coffee. "It is a little isolated. Especially when you're starting fresh, not knowing anyone…"

"Well, like you said, you know me. So there's one person."

"Right." Claire smiled again.

"It was the same for me when I moved here," Melody said. "People will tell you that New Englanders aren't friendly, but I've made a lot of friends. Of course, this job helps. I'm always out there."

"Yeah. My job, not so much. There's a lot of sitting alone in my room. That didn't seem so weird when my room was in an apartment building full of people. But I think about being in that big house, with no other houses even in sight, and I wonder, what the hell was I thinking?"

"Maybe you should take a shift here."

"Maybe I should." Claire looked across her coffee cup. "Could you be a little more subtle?"

"What?"

"Some guys over there have been giving me the eye since they sat down. I thought maybe with you here they'd stop, but instead it's worse. Wait, one of them's coming over."

Melody turned. "That's half of the Wequetequock volunteer fire department, right there. The one who's coming over is Joe. He's a nice guy. He could be the second person you know in Stonington."

"Wicketygwag? You're going to have to teach me how to say that."
Melody smiled. "Close enough."
The man reached the table. He clasped his hands in front of him.
"Hi Joe," Melody said. "This is Claire."
"Hi." Joe barely glanced at her. "Mel, I need to talk to you."
"Sure. What's wrong?"
"Outside?"
Claire watched them go out. They stopped on the sidewalk just beyond the window. Melody put her hands on either side of her face and begin to cry.
In the dining room, the waitress had come to the table. She stood there with the coffee pot in one hand, looking out.
"Excuse me," Claire said. She slipped past the waitress and went outside. "Melody, what happened? Can I help?"
Joe didn't seem surprised to see her. "Actually, it concerns you, too."
"What do you mean?"
"You bought the old Westbury house?"
"Yes."
"Something happened there last night. I thought you would know by now. Hasn't anyone from the police department contacted you?"
"Well, no. I've sort of been in transition. And my cell phone's dead."
"This really should come from the police, but... A man was in your house last night." Joe looked like he'd rather be anywhere else on Earth. "He took a bad fall. He died."
"Oh my God."
"Yeah. I guess some of his buddies found him. By the time the ambulance arrived, it was too late."
"What was he doing in my house?"
Joe shook his head. "You really should talk to the police."
Claire went to Melody and put her arms around her. "Was he a friend? A boyfriend?"
"I can't believe this," Melody said. "It's all my fault."
"Ma'am," Joe said. "Claire, was it? You could just drive over to the police station. I mean—it's not far."
"Okay. I'll do that. Melody, I'm so sorry. Can I take you home?"
Melody didn't respond.
"Come on," Claire said. She put her hand on Melody's elbow. "Let's just get our things."
Inside, the waitress was standing by the table, holding a white box tied with string. She handed the box to Claire and gave Melody a long hug.
"What's this?" Claire said, weighing the box.
"Blueberry muffins," the waitress said.
"Thanks. I just need the check."

"No you don't."

This conversation was the only sound in the place.

"Thank you," Claire said. When she unplugged her phone, now half charged, she saw that she had missed calls.

Claire's compact SUV was in the big parking lot behind the shops. Melody sat in the passenger seat. "I could drive myself," she said. "I'm all right."

"No way. Just tell me where you live."

"Near the reservoir. I'll show you."

Melody had Claire take a route that twisted up a hill. The village disappeared. On either side, the woods were thick and divided by rough stone walls.

"It's my fault," Melody said. "I could have prevented it."

"What do you mean?"

"I told him about the house. That it had been sold. That you were about to move in."

"I don't understand," Claire said.

"He asked me out, for the thousandth time, and I said no, again. I could have just gone out with him." Melody wiped tears from her cheeks.

After a while, Claire said, "Why was he in my house? There's nothing to steal. Not yet, anyway."

Melody shook her head.

The road dipped where a creek passed under it.

"Wait, stop!" Melody said.

Claire put on the brakes.

Melody was rolling down the window. "Dave!" she yelled.

Dave DaSilva was standing beside AJ's house, looking out at the narrow reach of water.

"Can you pull into the driveway?" Melody said.

Claire backed in, coming to a stop behind AJ's square, well-worn Jeep.

"Just a minute," Melody said, opening her door.

Dave Sela and AJ came out of the house, followed by the greyhound, which immediately sprinted across the yard, freakishly fast on its lean legs.

From her car, Claire watched in the rearview mirror. She saw Melody embrace each of the men. When Melody began to cry again, Claire looked away. She took her phone from her purse. There were three missed calls from her real estate agent and one from a local number she didn't recognize. When she checked the mirror, AJ was holding Melody's hand and talking to her. Of the three men, he was the only one wearing long pants and a shirt that had been recently ironed.

"This must be his house," Claire said under her breath.

Just then, his eyes went straight to the rearview mirror, taking her by surprise. She opened the car door and stepped out. The dog bounded past her, juked left, then raced the other way.

"Hi, I'm AJ," he said, approaching her. There was a sort of tired strength in his face.

"I'm Claire."

They shook hands.

"I guess we're all headed to the station. Melody is going to come along. You can just follow me."

"Okay."

"You sure you want to go?" Claire asked Melody when they were both seated again.

"Yeah. I would feel weird just going home, now."

From the open door to the house, AJ called the dog. It ran back inside as eagerly as it had run out. Then AJ got into his Jeep, swerved around Claire and led the way down Mistuxet.

"Are these the guys—" Claire said.

"Yes. I'm sorry, I'll introduce you. I don't have my head on straight."

"They don't look like the kind of people who would break into a house."

"They aren't. AJ, the one who you talked to, is a cop."

"Oh. So what were they doing there?"

"I think they were trying to stop Ben."

"Stop him from doing what?"

"I just need to close my eyes a minute," Melody said. "Do you mind?"

"Sure."

After winding through the countryside—gray rocks and stone walls and greenery, now and then a slight fog—they turned onto Route 1, and finally into the parking lot of the Stonington Police station. AJ led them all inside, then through the inner door and down a short hall to Chief Brown's office.

The chief stood up behind his desk. "Rough morning."

The others huddled by the doorway, silent.

"I'm Roland Brown." He came around the desk and shook Claire's hand.

"Claire Connor."

"I'd say welcome to Stonington, but I'll save that for a better circumstance."

"Thanks."

"Okay." He ran his hand across his smooth scalp. "First, let me say how sorry I am. I know how much Ben meant to you. I didn't know him maybe as well, but I know he was a good guy and an asset to the community. Really, a kind of local celebrity, with his TV show. He touched a lot of lives with that. My wife's a big fan, and she's devastated this morning."

Claire gave Melody a puzzled look.

32

"All right," the chief said. "We'll just take care of business as quickly as we can."

He called an officer to take statements from AJ, Sela and DaSilva, and to set Melody up with some coffee.

"Ms. Connor," he said, when the others had been led away. "I just need a minute of your time." Pointing to a molded plastic chair, he sat down behind his desk.

Claire had turned toward the small combination TV-VCR against the wall. A bright red CNN logo spun to an electric rhythm.

"Sorry." The chief picked up a remote control from his desk and muted the sound. "I got hooked on the news during the last election. I'm trying to quit, but it's tough. Almost as bad as cigarettes, which is going on five years now." He put the remote down but continued to look at the TV for a second. "I was surprised to see you come in with Officer Bugbee. Last I heard, no one had been able to reach you."

"Sorry, my phone was dead. I was at the Honey B Dairy, with Melody. A volunteer fireman, Joe something, told me about the accident, and said I should come here. I'm confused. Why was their friend in my house?"

"Have you had a chance to watch our local cable channel? Channel 12?"

"No. Why do you ask?"

"Well, Ben Shortman and his two friends that are in the other room now, Dave Sela and Dave DaSilva, have—had—a show they called *Mystic Afterlife*. It's about the paranormal. Ghost stories, that kind of thing. It appears that he was doing research for the show at your house."

"Research? You mean he was looking for a ghost?"

"Yes. And in trying to get around in the dark, he apparently fell on the stairs."

"Oh, God." Claire tucked her hair behind her ears. "If I had had the power turned on—"

The chief stopped her. "It wouldn't have mattered. I've seen enough of the show to know that these guys like to work in the dark. Those stairs—at the top, on the turn, where they're little wedges, little pie slices?" He made the shape with his hands. "That's probably where he lost his footing. I'd forgotten how treacherous they are." He let his hands fall to the desk. "If I were you," he continued, "I'd see about having something done there."

"Right. I'll look into it."

"Good, good." The chief spread his hands on the desk. "The woman at the Schwartz Realty office said you closed on the property a couple of days ago."

"Yes. This past Wednesday."

"But you haven't moved in."

"No. Wednesday night I stayed in a motel. Thursday, I met with an electrician and a painter. Then I had to go to my sister's in Massachusetts—she's been storing some furniture for me—to make arrangements with a mover. I wasn't back in town until this morning."

"Who's doing the electric, Thibeau? Or Simons?"

"No, it's Stan's Electric. My real estate agent recommended them. The painter's name is Pierce. Mike Pierce." She checked her watch.

"Stan's good. I don't know Pierce."

"I don't want to be insensitive," Claire said, "but will I be able to move in today? The truck is probably already on its way. I'm supposed to open the house for the painter in about forty-five minutes. Will I even be able to get in? Is it taped off or something? Is it a crime scene?"

The chief shook his head. "No, it's not a crime scene. But before I give you the go-ahead, I need to speak with Officer Bugbee."

"I guess I should call the painter, then. Tell him not to come."

"Yes. I'm sorry about that. One other thing I have to mention, Ms. Connor—have you given any thought to any charges?"

"I'm not sure what you mean."

"Technically, Mr. Shortman's friends were trespassing. Of course, they were only trying to keep him out of trouble. There was a chair that was broken. It looked like an antique..." He let his voice trail off.

"I don't want to see anyone charged with anything. They're suffering enough. That chair—it's not even mine. It was left by Jacques Westbury. He said he ran out of room in the moving van."

"By *he*," the chief said, "you mean Mr. Westbury's lawyer? Or maybe his real estate agent?"

"No, Jacques. I met him at the closing. He said that anything that was still in the house I could have."

"Jacques Westbury was at the closing? Here in Stonington?" The chief was sitting very erect now, his hands no longer resting on the desk but pressing there with force.

"Yes. I guess he flew in on Tuesday and cleared out the house in time for the walkthrough."

"Huh," the chief said. "Scott Schwartz didn't tell me that." He stood up. "Thanks again for coming in. If you want to wait a few minutes while I talk to Officer Bugbee, I'll know more about how we stand with your move."

The chief led Claire out front to where Melody was sitting, staring into space, her arms around her oversized bag. He asked an officer at the desk to give them anything they needed. Then he went back through the heavy locked door. He stuck his head into a conference room. "Officer Bugbee?" He waved at Sela and DaSilva to stay seated.

In his office again, the chief sat behind the metal desk. AJ stood against the wall, next to the television.

"You all right?" the chief said. "You look like you didn't get much sleep last night."

AJ shrugged. "I'm okay."

"How about Sela and DaSilva?"

"Hanging in. DaSilva is taking it pretty hard."

The chief nodded. "They go back a long way."

"Yeah. He's been living at the Shortmans' house. His world's sort of upside down right now."

"I bet it is." The chief gestured toward the molded chair. "You know, you can take a seat."

AJ sat down heavily.

"That Claire Connor is a nice person," the chief said. "She doesn't want to make it worse for any of you."

AJ didn't respond.

"Okay. Is there anything else I need to know about what happened?"

AJ sat silently for a moment. "I should have called it in."

"What?"

"I should have called here. As soon as I knew that Ben was going to break into that house, I should have called it in. But instead I waited for the bridge, and then I went after him myself. If I had called, maybe he'd be alive."

"Well, let's see," the chief said. "Lundy was tied up with a fight down at the point, and Osborne was out with Jenkins trying to round up that damn horse again. That thing's smarter than its owner. So if you had called, Brenda would have told you to take care of it yourself. It wouldn't have changed one damn thing."

AJ slipped lower in the chair. "I just can't stop thinking about it."

"I know how you feel. I've been there."

The two men looked quietly across the room at each other.

"You know what?" the chief said. "Why don't you take a few days off? Get some rest. Spend some time with Sela and DaSilva. It'd be good for all of you."

AJ didn't answer right away. "Yeah. I should do that. At least until I can think straight."

"Good. How about we talk on Monday, take it from there?"

"Okay. Thanks." AJ got slowly to his feet. "I have something for you. Or, Sela does. A video camera. He found it at the scene and pocketed it."

"And he just told you about it?"

"Last night. Late."

"Uh huh. So you watched the tape already."

"It's digital, so there's no tape. But yeah."

The chief drummed his hands on the desktop. "You really should have handed that camera over last night."

"I'm sorry, chief. I didn't know about the camera until we got back to my house. Then… Like I said, I'm not thinking straight."

For a second, the chief watched the TV screen, where a forest fire raged across a hillside. "On the show, Ben always has a regular camera, too. A little thing, for taking snapshots. I looked for it last night. In fact, Jenkins and I spent half the night looking for it. All we came up with was a recorder. Tiny thing, like one of those music players."

"Sorry," AJ said. "Why didn't you call me, to see if I had the camera?"

"Maybe I wasn't thinking straight myself. That house… Let's just say it's not my favorite place in the world. It doesn't exactly bring back the best memories."

"I'm sure it doesn't."

"Anna Marie Rose. The first big case I ever worked, and still the biggest, all these years later. This pretty, popular girl. Seemed like the whole town loved her. Jacques Westbury, my main suspect, was local royalty. He had all the power, really. So of course it ended with no conviction, no charges even being filed, no nothing. That spoiled playboy took off for France, and I couldn't do anything about it."

"The body was never found?"

"No. All we found was some blood in the woods behind the house."

"How did Westbury explain that?"

"He didn't, really. He was giving her sailing lessons. He used to drive her to the marina. She'd cut through the woods to get to his house. He said she must have fallen back there. Skinned her knee, or something."

"You don't believe that."

"No. No, I didn't, and I still don't. If you had heard the way he said it, seen the look in his eyes, you would have thought it was bullshit, too." The chief pushed away from the desk. "I can't believe he came back here."

"Who, Westbury?"

"Yeah. Miss Connor said he was at the closing."

AJ's eyes narrowed. "That was a few days ago. Do you think he's still around?"

"I hope so."

"Why?"

The chief didn't answer right away. "I'd like a second chance at him."

"I bet you would. But unless you had new evidence, what could you do?"

"I don't know. There's got to be something."

The chief sat there with his hands on his knees, staring in the direction of the television. Then he stood up. "So tell me, when you looked at the video on that camera, did you see anything?"

"His fall. You see Ben fall."

"So it's cut and dried. An accident. A damn tragic accident." The chief started to the door. "Let's go get the camera."

The two men went down the hall.

"You have something for me?" the chief said, when they caught up with Sela.

Sela pulled the video camera from a pocket of his baggy shorts.

"Anything else?"

Sela pulled the infrared attachment from another pocket.

"You're a regular Captain Kangaroo with those pockets, aren't you?" the chief said.

"What?"

"Never mind."

They all went to the waiting area, where they found Melody standing in front of a bulletin board, staring at a photo of a missing child. Claire was flipping through a brochure about boating safety.

"Thanks for your time, Ms. Connor," the chief said. "I'll be talking to the medical examiner a little later. Unless things change, you should be able to start moving in this afternoon. Will I be able to reach you?"

"I'm not sure I trust my phone. Maybe I should call here, if I haven't heard from you?"

"That will work," the chief said. "Good luck with everything. All of you, take care." He patted AJ on the back. "Call me in a couple of days, and I'll put you on the schedule."

In the parking lot, Sela and DaSilva shook hands with Claire. She said how sorry she was. AJ, watching this, put his keys back in his pocket and came to her. "So you're moving in today?" he said.

"Getting started, at least."

"That's a lot of work."

"Yeah." She gave him a noncommittal smile.

Overhead, seagulls squabbled over a light pole.

DaSilva spoke to Sela. "I should go to the Shortmans' house, get my stuff."

"I'll go with you."

Another silence.

"Look, I'm not going in to work now," Melody said. "I bet everyone could use a little time to regroup before they face reality. Why don't we head over to my house and I'll make us some breakfast?"

"That would be great," DaSilva said immediately.

"We haven't eaten since yesterday," Sela said. "Since before…"

Melody touched AJ's shoulder. "It sounded like the chief isn't expecting you to work today."

"Right."

"Well, you have to come, then. Claire, how about you?"

Claire hesitated.

"You really should," Sela said.

"I don't know." Claire glanced at AJ.

"Come on," he said. "We'll tell you all about Ben."

***

Meody's house was a one-story cottage, barely wide enough for the front door and two windows with green shutters. They gathered in the kitchen, filling it. Melody scrambled eggs. AJ and Claire teamed up to reassemble the coffee maker and brew a pot. Sela handled the toast. Bumping into each other, they apologized quietly.

They sat at a round table with steaming plates and mugs and droplet-covered jars of jelly and a cool stick of butter on a plate. For a while, the only words spoken were compliments directed at Melody.

"I'm sorry," she said, in a long pause, crossing her arms. "I'm so, so sorry."

"You don't have anything to apologize for," AJ said.

"Yes, I do. When he asked me last night, I could have said yes. Why did I turn him down? It would have been fun. He's—he was—a great guy. Any woman would be lucky to have him."

"I was doing the same thing a few minutes ago," AJ said. "Getting stuck on what I should have done. The little ways I could have changed everything. It doesn't help."

"You're right, AJ." Sela tapped his fork against his plate. "But I have to ask Claire something."

"Oh," she said, apprehensively.

"Would you have let Ben do an investigation at your house? If he had asked you, what would you have said?"

"No. I would have said no."

A look of relief flashed across Sela's face. "Okay."

"Wait," DaSilva said. "You'd say no because you think it's a waste of time, or because you're afraid of what we'd find?"

"Neither. If I said yes to your friend, and he put it on your TV show, then it would be like hanging out a sign, wouldn't it? I'd have all kinds of requests to come check the place out. One of the reasons I bought this house was so that I could have some peace and quiet."

"You didn't answer the question, though," DaSilva said. "Do you believe in ghosts, or not?"

"Honestly, I haven't thought about it. What do people say they've seen at my house? What was Ben so sure he'd find?"

"Well, some people are supposed to have died there," DaSilva said.

"Considering how old the house is," Claire said, "I'm not surprised."

"Exactly," Melody said.

DaSilva sat forward, his right knee bouncing up and down. "We're not talking about dying in their sleep. We have a guy, Dewey Allan, who does historical research for us, for *Mystic Afterlife*. He found out that sometime in the 1800s—he could tell you the exact date—a woman fell down the stairs and died. Some people thought it was murder."

"Why did they think it was murder?" Claire said. "Those stairs are treacherous. We've seen that."

"I guess right after she died, the rest of her family took off. Nobody knew where they went or ever heard from them again. It looked suspicious."

"All right," Melody said. "I don't think Dewey found all of that in the historical records. It sounds more like local folklore to me."

DaSilva's held his knee still with his hand. "There have been lots of sightings of what people think is her ghost on the grounds and in the house."

"Melody's right," Sela said. "Some of that's just people making stuff up. Ben's thing, what *Mystic Afterlife* was all about, was to find out the truth. To collect real evidence."

"This is going downhill fast," AJ said. "Anyone want more coffee?"

Claire put her hand over her mug. "No, thanks. I want to hear about the ghost in my house."

"Claire," AJ said, "this isn't helpful. C'mon, guys. Enough. Story hour's over."

"I like stories," she said. "It's sort of my business."

"What do you mean?" AJ said.

"I'm a writer. I do a series of novels for teens."

"Your books must sell pretty well," DaSilva said, "if you can afford that house."

"I hope I can afford it. Anyway, I had some help from my sister. She's the one with money."

"Really?" Sela said. "Is she single? Can you introduce me?"

Claire smiled. "Sure. She probably won't be visiting too much, though, at least not right away. She's a workaholic trying to make partner in a law firm. But I'm not going to be distracted so easily. I want to hear more about the ghosts. Who am I sharing the house with?"

"Actually, there is another story, a more recent one—" DaSilva stopped, a look of pain on his face.

Sela scowled at him across the table.

"Hey," DaSilva said. "She's going to hear this eventually. Better if she hears it from us." He turned to AJ. "Am I right?"

AJ stared into his coffee mug. "Okay. How much do you know about the Westburys?"

"Not much," Claire said. "Let's see. They were a prominent local family. The only one living is Jacques. He left here a long time ago, for France. I guess he didn't want the family homestead."

"There's a little more to it than not wanting the house," Sela said.

"He took off right after a young girl disappeared." DaSilva shifted in his chair, pulling his feet back. "Some people thought he murdered her."

"Wait." AJ raised a hand. "There was no body, so the girl would have been officially a missing person. And Westbury was never charged. He would have been a person of interest, that's all."

"Who was she—the girl?" Claire said.

"Her name was Anna Marie Rose," DaSilva said. "She was only fifteen years old. Jacques was, what, in his early thirties at the time? He was her sailing instructor at a local yacht club, the Quanaduck. There was some kind of relationship between them. We were just kids, but I remember a lot of talk about it. My parents were sure he did away with her, but, like AJ said, the cops couldn't prove it. I guess it got so Jacques couldn't stand the way people looked at him, and he ran off."

"Okay, that's enough," AJ said.

DaSilva shrugged but continued. "Personally, I don't think he would have killed her at the house. If he did do it, it would have been out on the water, in a boat. Then it would have been so easy to just dump the body. No one would ever find her."

"DaSilva!" AJ said.

Claire's eyes had widened. "Now I know why Chief Brown reacted the way he did when I mentioned meeting Jacques."

"Hold on," Sela said. "You met him? Jacques Westbury?"

"Yeah, at the closing. I have to say, he didn't seem like a murderer."

"They never do," DaSilva said.

"Jesus. Jacques Westbury, back in Stonington," Sela said. "Did the chief say anything to you, AJ?"

"Yeah. He was pretty wound up. He actually started talking about the case. It's the first time he's ever mentioned it to me. The whole subject is taboo."

Melody left the table and opened the window over the sink. "It's going to be hot today," she said. "Is there air conditioning in your house, Claire?"

"Crap!" Claire said. "If I don't make the call soon, there won't even be electricity. That's just what I need, to be there tonight with no lights."

"You can use my phone," Melody said, but Claire was already digging her cell phone from her purse.

She made the call, punched some more numbers, waited. She spoke to someone about turning on the power and gave the address. She closed the phone. "Well, at least I'll have lights. It's going to be a long night."

"Now we've made you afraid to stay in your own house," Melody said, giving the guys a look. "I'm sorry."

Sela and DaSilva glanced at each other across the table.

"We could stay with you," Sela said.

DaSilva's knee was going again. "Yeah, so you wouldn't be all alone in the house."

"Easy, guys," AJ said.

"You could stay with me for a couple of days," Melody said. "Give yourself some time to get used to the new place. The couch pulls out. It would be fun."

"That's really generous. But I have to spend the night there eventually. If I put it off, it will just be that much harder later."

"I could stay with you, then," Melody said. "I have a sleeping bag."

"Right," DaSilva said, his knee bouncing again. "Like two beautiful women alone in a haunted house is a good idea. Have you guys ever seen a horror movie?"

Melody gave DaSilva a swat. "Stop!"

"Seriously, Melody," DaSilva said, "you're good company, but with Jacques Westbury in town, what Claire really needs is—"

"If you're about to say protection," AJ said, "then I'm the one who should stay with Claire." He looked across the table at her. "I have a sleeping bag, too. What do you say about some unofficial police protection?"

CHAPTER 7

They crossed the hard-packed dirt toward the barn, two men matched in size, tall and square shouldered, though Henry Jacobson was older by almost twenty years and his arms were spotted and scarred. Jacques Westbury's hair was gray but his face was still smooth and ruddy, as if he'd just stepped off the squash court, and everything about his clothing was soft, down to the slipper-thin leather of his shoes.

"I'm guessing you haven't heard," Henry said. "Since you haven't said anything."

"Heard what?"

"There was an accident in your house last night. A man died." They'd reached the barn. Henry put his hand on the heavy latch. "Name's Ben Shortman," he added, softening the *r*.

"Jesus, Henry. What kind of accident? How'd he die?"

"Fell down the stairs."

"That's terrible." Jacques shook his head. "I guess I did the right thing, getting out from under that place. There seems to be some kind of curse on it."

"Well, at least they won't be trying to pin this one on you."

"We'll see."

The old man shoved the big door to the side, leaning on it, laboring, his boots pushing against the dirt. The cloud-dulled sunlight slipped through the opening and showed a cluster of furniture and boxes.

"I really appreciate this," Henry said.

"It's a fair trade. You helped me out by providing the storage on short notice. How did you want to mark the pieces?"

Henry lifted a roll of blue painter's tape from a table. "Just lay a strip on whatever my daughter can have."

"It'll be easier to mark the pieces I want to keep." Jacques accepted the tape. "There won't be so many."

"Okay with me, if you're sure. Like I said, you can leave your things here as long as you want. The roof is good. I have no other use for the barn. It's been a long time since I had a horse."

"I hear you. I doubt I even remember how to ride."

"Oh, you do. I taught you too well. You won't ever forget that."

Jacques put his hand on the old man's shoulder. "You're right, as always. And I bet you're still great with a fast mount."

Henry smiled. "Now there's a crazy idear. You won't get me on anything faster than a lawn tractor these days."

Jacques let his hand drop. "Are you going to need help getting the furniture to your daughter's house? Do you still have that trailer to haul things?"

"I haven't had that trailer for a good long while." Henry looked hard into the other man's eyes. "You seem to have lost track of time, Jacques. It's like you're Rip Van Winkle waking up from his nap. Just because you were in France for those twenty years doesn't mean they didn't pass here, too."

"Believe me, I know. It's nineteen, by the way. Don't steal that year from me."

They were quiet for a moment, staring at the furniture, dark wood in shadow.

"My son-in-law is going to provide a truck," Henry said. "He'll be here later today."

Jacques put his hands on a gateleg table. "Can you help me move this?"

He took one end of the table and Henry took the other. They carried it a couple of feet. Jacques stepped into the empty spot. He bent over a trunk, square and large, with metal corners and an enormous latch. He tore off a length of tape.

"The trunk, huh," Henry said. "That's what you go for first?"

"Does that surprise you?"

"A trunk is for a man who's traveling. Are you still traveling, Jacques?"

Jacques pressed the tape flat. "I don't know. It's been a long time since I felt like I had a home."

"Maybe I should ask what you got in there."

"What do you mean?" Jacques applied another strip of tape.

"Well, it's about right for a body, isn't it? Is that where you been keeping her all these years?"

Jacques straightened. For a long moment, he studied Henry's face. "No," he said. "I left the skeleton in the house. In the closet, you know."

"Uh huh. No use carting around a bunch of old bones, I guess."

"Exactly." Jacques surveyed the furniture again. He put tape on a short, glass-doored bookshelf. Coming around to the other side of the collection, he taped a wooden, swivel desk chair. "There. That's all I want."

Henry scratched his weathered chin. "That's some selection you made. The trunk, the bookshelf and the desk chair. Looks like you're setting up the library again."

"I guess I am. I have fond memories of the library." Jacques pulled another length of tape free and stuck it to the one cane-bottom chair that still had a seat. "There. Something that's not from the library."

"You sure you want to break up the set? There's four more." Henry pointed. "Recane them, put them together with that table, you'd have something."

"You know someone who could recane the chairs?"

"Sure. Known him every minute of my life."

"I see. What would he charge for a job like that?"

"For an old friend? Nothing. Not a cent."

"Well," Jacques said. "I might be interested in that. On one condition."

"What condition?"

"That when he was done with the chairs, he gave them to his daughter." Jacques peeled the tape off of the cane-bottom chair. He handed the roll to Henry.

"All right. That could be arranged."

"There's one more chair, the sixth, still at the house. I couldn't fit it in the truck. We'll have to see about getting that one sometime."

They went out of the barn. Henry slid the door shut. "Let me show you where I leave the key for Ellis."

"Why?"

"So you can get at your stuff when I'm not around."

"Why would I need to get at my stuff?"

"In case you're moving into some place that's not furnished."

"Moving in? What makes you think I'm even looking for a place here? I just sold one, remember?"

"You don't fool me," Henry said. "You never have and you never will."

"All right. If it makes you happy."

The key was in a can tucked under the side of the barn.

Henry and Jacques shook hands, then Jacques drove slowly down the rock-walled road to Route 1. The cloudy sky and lingering dampness produced a soft glare. He lifted a pair of sunglasses off of the rearview mirror and put them on. After a while, he went left toward the water and Lords Point. Once he had reached the houses—well-kept cottages and Capes—he worked his way deliberately through them, as if to try each street—James and Ashworth and Langworthy, then Boulder, which ran along a cove. There was a sandy spot big enough for a couple of cars, and he pulled off. A half-dozen single-masted sailboats were anchored in the water. Along the shore, smaller vessels were tied up at a wooden dock.

A girl passed on a bicycle, then swooped across the road in front of him. She left her bike on the side of the road and continued on foot toward the water's edge. She was maybe thirteen or fourteen, with spindly, bare, slightly tanned legs and slender arms and, when she removed her bike helmet, straight blonde hair that seemed to give strength to the weak sun. She went straight toward a Sunfish that was nearest the water. A boy was climbing into it, something square in his hands—a cooler, which he placed in the footwell that was the boat's only cargo space. She approached him, said something. He was older than her, an upperclassman in high school, probably, with brown curls and a quick smile.

Jacques watched the girl's head dip as she talked to the boy. The boy laughed. The girl pointed one foot into the sand. She stepped onto the dock and then sat down there, her legs dangling toward the water. The boy sat next to her. They went on talking. After a few more minutes, the boy looked in Jacques's direction, making a visor with one hand. Jacques started the car and pulled away.

He went back out to Route 1, toward downtown. Just before the train station, he pulled into the parking lot of a rectangular building with a flat roof and a wooden sign that read Schwartz Realty.

"Is Scott here?" he asked once he was inside.

"One second, Mr. Westbury," the woman at the desk said, punching a button on the phone with a red fingernail.

Scott was already shaking Jacques's hand. He ushered Jacques into a cramped office papered with maps of New London county.

"I assume you heard," Scott said. "Terrible thing. I'm so glad you sold that place."

"Yes. I feel like I've thrown off a curse."

Scott went around the desk to his faux-leather chair. "So what can I do for you? Are you thinking of staying in the area for a while? It's a buyer's market, as I'm sure you know. You can be on the right side of it this time."

Jacques had turned to one of the maps. "I'm not buying. But I might be renting. Do you have anything on the water?"

"I bet we can come up with something."

"Good," Jacques said. He faced the realtor again. "Maybe you can help me with one other thing."

"I'll try."

"A boat," Jacques said. "I'm going to need a boat."

CHAPTER 8

AJ turned off the paved road. All the way up the narrow lane to Claire's house, there were stone walls on either side, and beyond them, thick woods strewn with rocks, an endless supply of all sizes, as if this place had been pelted by some relentless, obliterating storm.

He parked in front of the garage. For a long while, he sat there, listening to the ticking of the engine, not even looking at the house.

"AJ!" Claire called to him from the nearest door, the one that just the night before had had a *No Trespassing* sign. The sign was gone now. "Can I carry something?" She crossed the weedy yard, her hair teasing her bare shoulders.

"Hi," he said, getting out of the car. "You want to take this?" He handed her a small cooler, then grabbed another cooler and a six-pack of beer.

Before they could go inside, there was the soft rumbling of tires on dirt. Melody's rusted sedan came up the lane. It stopped next to AJ's Jeep and the engine died reluctantly, with a rattle. When she slid out of the front seat, Melody had a bottle of wine in one hand. The other hand gripped a package of toilet paper. "How's this for a house-warming gift?" she said, holding up the toilet paper. "I wanted to bring something that you would need right away, and this is what I came up with. Brilliant, huh?"

"It's great," Claire said. "Thank you." She started toward the house. "I set up out back, on the porch. We'll just go right through."

AJ stopped in the middle of the room that connected the garage and the house. With sunlight coming in the windows on either side, and the pine floors, the room was warm and bright—nothing like it had seemed the night before. AJ stood there looking toward the kitchen.

Melody came back for him. "Come on," she said, taking his arm.

The large, screened-in porch was bare except for a dining room set that looked out of place surrounded by rough wood.

"Everything can go on the table," Claire said. She hugged Melody and AJ quickly. "I really appreciate your being here to support me. With what just happened, I feel selfish, but mostly, really grateful. So, thank you."

"It's not selfish," Melody said. "I'm glad we can help."

"Ben would want us to be here," AJ said.

Claire accepted that with a closed-lipped smile.

"So what did you bring, AJ?" Melody said, lifting the lid of one of the coolers.

"I don't actually know. My parents had it ready for me."

"Oh, God," Melody said, having dug through a layer of paper plates and napkins. "Lobster rolls. Claire, they make the best lobster rolls." She opened the other cooler. "And chowder. I love their chowder. It's New England style, Claire. You don't mind that, I hope, being from Manhattan?"

"Are you kidding?" Claire said. "Manhattan style isn't even chowder. It's clam soup."

"This table is nice," Melody said, sweeping her hand across the slick surface. "Do you want to cover it?"

"One sec." Claire fetched some placemats from a box in the kitchen. "The porch will be my dining room for now. I figured it would be easier to paint in there with the table out of the way." She passed out the plates. "Anyway, I like being out here. After the movers left, it seemed so quiet in the house."

"You just need to get used to it," Melody said. "And you will."

"Tom Schwartz said the crime rate is practically nil in Stonington." Claire looked at AJ. "Is that true?"

"We do our best," he said.

"So what keeps you busy?"

"The usual small town stuff. DUIs, bored teenagers fooling around."

"Lately," Melody said, "they've been spending a lot of time rounding up a horse that's determined to be free."

"It's true," AJ said. "The chief's about to have it stuffed and mounted."

"Would you ever want to work in a bigger town?" Claire said.

"He tried that already," Melody said. "I don't think he liked it."

"Really?" Claire said. "Where?"

"Bridgeport." AJ spun a bottle in the six-pack

"What didn't you like about being a cop in Bridgeport?"

AJ watched the bottle and it seemed that he wouldn't answer. But he met Claire's eyes again. "Bridgeport has all of the problems of a big city but not many of the perks."

"Right," Claire said. "Anyway, Stonington is such a beautiful town. I can see why you'd want to stay here. And what we're doing—this would never happen in a city. You know, having someone you just met offer to stay the night." She made a face. "To just stay, I mean. To help out." She laughed, blushing.

"Wow, Claire," Melody said. "When your face turns red, it turns red. You're like a chameleon."

"Thanks," Claire said. "Perfect if I want to hide next to a fire truck." She took a deep breath and the color faded. "Look, all I'm saying is that if anyone tries to tell me that New Englanders aren't friendly, I'll tell them they don't know what they're talking about."

"Remember, I'm a transplant," Melody said. "Midwesterner. But AJ, he's the real deal."

"Yeah. My family has been in this area for a long time," he said. "My mother could take you on a cemetery tour, show you where all our ancestors are."

"Nice, a cemetery tour," Melody said. "See, Claire, New Englanders know how to have fun, too."

As they ate, the sun went down behind the trees. The air cooled. Though there were rips in the screen, the mosquitoes were slow to find them.

"It's nice back here," AJ said, looking down the long sweep of weedy yard.

"Yes, it is," Claire said. "I only walked some of it with the realtor. He said there are old trails that crisscross the woods. I'll have to check them out sometime."

"You should," Melody said. "Who knows what kind of remains you'd find."

"Remains? God, not that again."

"No—I meant foundations, or old farm tools. I bet there's something interesting back there. People have lived here almost three hundred years."

"The Pequots would say that number's a little low," AJ said.

"And they'd be right," Melody said.

For a while the conversation was about the local tribe's success with a casino. AJ started a second beer. By then, with stars beginning to show in the sky, the mosquitoes had discovered the way in.

"Anyone else getting bitten?" Claire said.

After they'd brought the plates and the drinks into the kitchen, Claire showed them the dining room. "Now I just hope I can get the painter out here," she said. "When I cancelled this morning, he said he would have to start somewhere else. So it may be a while."

AJ turned back toward the porch. "You don't want to leave that furniture out there for long. If we get a bad thunderstorm, with wind, it could get drenched."

"I know," Claire said, looking frustrated.

"I could help you," AJ said.

"Thanks. You mean, move the table?"

"No, I mean with the painting. I have some free time. And I kind of like painting, anyway."

"Really? Are you serious? Because that would be fantastic. This just seemed like too big a job for me. But if we could work together…"

"Sure." AJ pointed across the room at a mound of drop cloths and roller trays, partially tucked under a stepladder. "I see you have the materials already."

"Yeah. I brought it here in a burst of enthusiasm right after the closing. I really want to do the whole house, eventually. But, you know, whatever you can do would be great. I can pay you what I was going to pay the other guy."

"We'll talk about that after you've seen my work."

"Okay." Claire stood looking at AJ for a moment. Then she seemed to catch herself. "Should we go back to the kitchen? It's the only room that feels lived in. We can bring chairs in from the porch. There's some wine left."

AJ asked for directions to the bathroom.

"Just here to the right," Claire said, pointing.

When he was alone, AJ ignored Claire's directions and circled around to the front hall. The chair that Sela had gotten tangled up in was gone. There was no sign that anything had happened there. AJ stood by the door, his arms crossed, looking up the stairs, studying the climb and the turn. After a while, he looped back the way he had come. He found the little bathroom that was squeezed under the stairs, flushed the toilet and ran water in the sink for a few seconds. Then he joined the women in the kitchen.

When the wine was gone and the windows had long been black, all three of them went out to the cars to get their sleeping bags. A quarter moon made no dent in the darkness.

"Jesus," Claire said. She waved her flashlight in front of her.

"Something wrong?" AJ said.

"It's so damn dark."

"I can help you replace the floodlight on the garage."

"That would be great," Claire said. "It's so quiet, too. I don't know what I can do about that."

"You should get a dog," Melody said. "I think I'd want one if I lived out here. Or a man. They're not as much fun, but you don't have to take them out in the morning to pee."

"Can you train a man to fetch the newspaper?" Claire said.

"If you got an especially smart one."

"You know, I can hear you," AJ said.

Claire laughed. "I like the idea of a dog. But I couldn't have a dog that barks every time it sees a squirrel. That would just make me more on edge."

"Then you need what I have," AJ said, slipping his arm through the strap of a backpack.

"I saw your dog yesterday. Is it a greyhound?"

"Yes. He's a retired racing dog. Greyhounds only bark when they really mean it."

"But aren't they kind of hyper? The way he ran around your yard, I don't know…"

"They love to run, but when they aren't running they're sprawled out on the floor. They're the perfect dog, really. Gentle, great with kids, beautiful animals. They do well here in the country, but they do well in apartments, too. The racing business just chews them up. When a dog can't win, or can't win any more, that's it."

"I wish you had brought him with you," Claire said.

"Maybe next time."

"Good. That would be fun."

They carried everything in one trip. Claire and Melody pulled out the sofa. AJ unrolled his sleeping bag in the dining room. After Claire headed upstairs, AJ stood in the middle of the room, as if waiting for something. From the pocket bathroom there were the sounds of Melody brushing her teeth. AJ went to the front hall and stood at the base of the stairs, looking up.

"All yours." Melody appeared from the shadows. "Are you okay?"

"Yeah."

"So you're a painter now," she said.

"I just thought I could help her out."

"Right. I think it's cute." She grinned.

"Good night, Melody."

"Good night."

He finished getting ready for bed. Barefoot, in shorts and a T-shirt, he sat down on the sleeping bag, his back against the wall, taking deep breaths. Even with the windows open, it was quiet. In his hand was an orange pill bottle. He unscrewed the white top and looked in at the pills. Then he replaced the top. He tossed the whole thing into the backpack.

He leaned against the wall. He stayed that way for a long time, staring into space, letting his eyelids close now and then, not fighting sleep but not sleeping. In the next room, Melody's breathing made a quick, regular whistle. AJ got to his feet. He went the long way around, avoiding Melody, to the front hall. The house was only a little better lit than the first time he had navigated his way through it. But the light in the upstairs hall was on, making a glow from behind the turn in the stairs. AJ studied the landing, the sturdy banister, the knobbed newel post. Then he returned to his bed.

He lay down on top of his sleeping bag. He checked his watch. It was two a.m.

When he opened his eyes again, it was three a.m. He stared up at the shadows on the ceiling.

There was a clatter from the kitchen, like something falling to the floor and rolling. AJ stood slowly, careful to make no sound. Placing his feet on the planks, lowering his weight deliberately with each step, he crept across the room. He reached the open doorway. He was holding his breath now. He took another step, so that he could see past the cabinet.

Ben Shortman was standing at the counter.

CHAPTER 9

Ben's index finger slid toward a bottle cap. His hand moved gradually, almost stealthily, closing in on the target. His finger reached the jagged rim. It pushed forward. But instead of nudging the bottle cap across the counter, Ben's flesh merged with the metal. The bottle cap stayed put.

"Damn it," he said.

He pulled back and tried again, quicker this time. The bottle cap jumped slightly.

Still in the doorway, AJ sucked a quick breath between his teeth. At the sound, Ben's whole body jerked and the bottle cap went flying. It dropped to the floor, then spun loudly across the tile. AJ stepped forward and silenced it with his foot.

"AJ!" Ben said, moving toward him.

AJ backed up.

"You can see me." Ben waved his hands in AJ's face.

AJ blinked but held his ground.

"Holy shit. Can you hear me, too?" Ben repeated the question, shouting this time. "Can you hear me?"

AJ glanced back over his shoulder, toward the living room, where Melody was sleeping.

"You're worried about the noise," Ben said. "So you *can* hear me. Wow. Wow. No one else—the chief, Claire, the movers—could see me or hear me, no matter how hard I tried. I'd just about given up."

AJ didn't respond.

"I get it," Ben said. "You can't talk because they'll hear you. Come on. Let's go out to the porch."

Ben crossed the kitchen and, after hesitating for a moment, passed through the back door. AJ shook his head, as if trying to clear it. Then he bent down, picked up the bottle cap, and followed Ben. Turning the doorknob as carefully as if it were some kind of hair-trigger detonation device, he went out.

Ben was waiting on the other side of the table. In the dark, every part of him—his face, his eyes, even his clothes—glowed softly. He looked down at himself. "Weird, huh? I'm like a freaking lightning bug." He held his arm out and examined his colorful tattoo. "Don't be afraid, AJ. I'm still me."

AJ's face remained fixed, his jaw clamped shut.

"It's all right," Ben said. "You're not crazy. I'm really here."

AJ was a silent shadow in the dark.

"Say something," Ben said. "Jesus, you're scaring me. Isn't it supposed to be the other way around?"

There was another long pause. Outside, somewhere in the dark woods, a bird let out a raspy cry.

AJ turned the bottle cap in his hand. He put it down on the table. "You do understand," he said, in a voice barely above a whisper, "you're…"

"Dead? A ghost? Yeah, I get that. It's just like I always said it would be. I'm a person, but without a body. Pure energy, Captain." Ben laughed.

The two men stared across the dark room at each other.

"I don't know how I ended up this way," Ben said. "One minute I'm opening the door, all excited about the investigation. The next thing I know, I'm watching you guys driving away behind an ambulance. It's weird. I don't remember anything in between. Total blank. Then Chief Brown was here. I tried talking to him. That's when I started to catch on."

AJ nodded but didn't speak.

"So what did happen to me?" Ben said.

"You fell down the stairs."

"The chief said something about that. Weird. I'm really careful when I'm investigating. I never fall."

"It was pitch black. You were trying to make that turn on those narrow stairs, in the dark."

"Yeah, I guess. Anyway, I said I'd make a believer out of you. Looks like I have, huh?"

AJ said nothing.

"I'm glad you missed my first few hours after… I didn't handle it all that well. When the chief wouldn't respond to me—and I tried everything—shouting at the top of my lungs, punching him—I even poked him in the eye." Ben jabbed the air with his fingers. "Nothing. That's when I really lost it. I spent a good long time screaming and crying and trying to hit something, anything—which only made me more crazy. The sun was coming up before I finally calmed down."

"So you screamed, too," AJ said, under his breath.

"What was that?"

AJ shook his head. "So how do you do it—appear, materialize, whatever?"

"What do you mean?"

"I've been here since dinner and I didn't see you until now."

Ben raised his arms in front of him and seemed to examine them for a second. "I don't know. I wasn't here at dinner. I tried to leave the house again. Every time I do that—try to pass through a window or a door—there's this whooshing sound and then... It's like I disappear for a while. When I come back I'm at the foot of the stairs. I guess I should stop trying to leave. Bad as it is, I'd rather be trapped in this place than just—"

"Gone."

"Yeah." Ben squinted at AJ and edged a little closer. "You know, you're not really acting like a guy who's seeing his first ghost. A full body apparition, no less."

"Yeah?" AJ said. "How am I acting?"

"I don't know. If you're freaked out, you're keeping a lid on it. It's almost like you were prepared for this. Like you expected it." Ben moved still closer to AJ, cutting through the table rather than going around it. "Is there anything you want to tell me, AJ? Were you surprised to see me?"

AJ held his ground while Ben waded through the table as if it were a pond. When Ben was right in his face, he said, "No, Ben, I wasn't surprised."

"I'm not the first ghost you've seen, am I?"

AJ looked back toward the kitchen.

"How many? How long has this been going on?"

"I don't keep count. I was twelve years old the first time."

"So, what, hundreds, thousands?"

"No, nothing like that."

"All this time, and you never told me. In fact, you gave me such shit. You know, I was running a ghost hunting business, you asshole. Did it ever occur to you—" Ben tried to punch AJ's shoulder but his hand only disappeared into its target. He resorted to shaking his worthless fist in his friend's face.

"I'm sorry I held out on you," AJ said. "But for a long time, I thought I was crazy. Even if I wasn't, I was sure people would think I was. I still think that. Be honest, Ben. If I had told you, even you..."

Ben let his hand fall to his side. "Yeah, maybe."

In the distance, a train rumbled through the dark.

"Well, some shit, huh?" Ben said.

"Yeah."

"You want to grab yourself a beer? Because we've got a lot to talk about. It's going to be a long night."

CHAPTER 10

"I hope you're not too disappointed, having to leave the big house. I know how much you like it there. But it's kind of fun, isn't it, to do something different, to mix it up a little bit?

"I guess I don't really expect you to buy that. I'm just trying to look on the bright side.

"Really, and you know this, it couldn't be helped. You couldn't stay there. It was too risky. Imagine if they'd found you. I don't even want to think about that. First off, they would have separated the two of you, for sure. Think how lonely you'd be. And who knows where you would have ended up? In a police station or a morgue somewhere. They'd keep you in a stainless steel drawer, and haul you out to poke you and prod you, cut you up for samples. God knows what all they'd do to you.

"I know change is hard. But change is a part of life and it's a part of the afterlife, too.

"Anyway, this is only temporary. You'll have a better place soon, like I promised. It may still turn out to be the best summer ever.

"Don't give me that look. I know you're giving me that look.

"Okay. I wasn't going to tell you this yet, but since you seem so unhappy... I have something really big planned. So, pay attention.

"I know how much you've always wanted a sister. Well, what do you say I get you one?"

CHAPTER 11

"Talk about out cold." Melody leaned into the dining room, where AJ lay, dead to the world, half out of his sleeping bag, his face flat against the wooden floor. "He must have been up late."

"Yeah," Claire said. "I hope he didn't feel like he had to stay up all night keeping watch."

"He had a good reason for not sleeping."

"You're right. I know he volunteered, but do you think it's a good idea for him to be right back here so soon after what happened?"

"After you went upstairs," Melody said, "he was in the hall for a while, just standing there. I can only imagine what was going through his head."

"It would be impossible not to relive that night. Maybe he was fighting that. Or maybe he *wanted* to relive it, to hold on to his last moments with Ben."

AJ sat up, wiping drool from his mouth. "That's attractive."

"I was just saying how cute you looked," Melody said.

"I'm sure you were."

"Did you get any sleep at all on that floor?" Claire said.

"I did. I slept really well." AJ patted the wood as if it were a mattress.

"There's coffee," Claire said.

"That would be great."

"How about you, Melody?"

"I'll get something at the Dairy. I'm late already."

"Oh. You sure? I could whip up some eggs."

"Sorry, I really have to go." Melody jingled the keys in her hand. "He likes them scrambled, with a little cheddar if you've got it."

Claire turned to AJ, who shrugged.

The two women went to the door. While they were gone, AJ pulled on a pair of jeans and a fresh T-shirt, then stuffed his sleeping bag into its sack.

"Okay," Claire said, returning. "Scrambled with cheddar, like she said?"

"That would be really good."

"Guess she knows what you like."

"Yeah. I've had a few breakfasts at the Dairy."

"Right, of course," Claire said. "She's great, isn't she?"

"Yes, she is."

"She's made me feel like we're old friends. That's a big thing when you're new somewhere."

"Yeah."

"Well, I'll start the eggs." Claire headed toward the kitchen. Her hair was up. She wore a knit top and shorts and her legs gleamed in the morning light.

AJ put his sleeping bag down and followed her. He found the coffee pot while she put a frying pan on the stove.

"Do you want milk or sugar?" Claire said, handing him a mug. "Actually, I don't have sugar. There's sweetener."

"No, thanks, nothing."

"Are you serious? You take your coffee black? I didn't know anyone drank it that way anymore. Is that a cop thing?"

"Only if you have a donut with it," he said. "What can I do to help?"

She pointed to a loaf of bread. "Could you pop a couple of slices into the toaster?"

"Sure." He began undoing the twist-tie.

"Speaking of helping, are you still—do you really want to help with the painting? You sure you have time?"

"Yes. I thought we were starting today."

She smiled. "Great." She cracked the eggs into a bowl and scrambled them. "I hope you don't mind paper plates again. My dishes are still in boxes."

"No, that's fine."

"Before I start these, let me see if the newspaper has come," Claire said. "They were supposed to start delivery today, but it wasn't there when I said goodbye to Melody. I need my paper with breakfast on Sunday—it feels weird without it."

AJ dropped the bread in the toaster. "Are you getting the local paper, *The Day*?"

"Yeah, I thought I'd try it. Be right back." She headed toward the front door.

AJ surveyed the kitchen. "Ben," he said, in a low voice. "If you're around, behave. No pushing bottle caps off the counter. That's the last thing she needs."

From the front of the house, there was the squeak of door hinges. Then a scream.

57

AJ sprinted toward the sound. "Claire?"

He found her standing in the doorway. Beyond her, a man straddled a bicycle. He wore a bright, zippered top and skin-tight shorts.

"Everything okay?" AJ moved past Claire.

"Morning, AJ." The rider grinned up at him. "This is a surprise."

"Dewey? What, are you training for the Tour de France?"

"Just trying to stay in shape. Keeping up with my scouts is getting tougher all the time."

"I bet," AJ said. "Claire, this is Dewey Allan. He was my history teacher in high school. Now he works with the guys at *Mystic Afterlife*. Among many other things. Dewey, this is Claire Connor."

"Nice to meet you," Claire said. "Sorry I screamed. I guess I'm more on edge than I realized."

"Understandable," Dewey said. He shifted the bike underneath him. "Well, anyway, I just thought I'd introduce myself, welcome you to Stonington. This is a beautiful house you have here. You know, I've done some research on this house. If you'd like to see that sometime, I'll bring it over."

"Oh, right," Claire said. "I—"

"Dewey," AJ said, "why don't we save that."

"Sure. You okay, AJ? Sela and DaSilva—are they doing all right?"

"DaSilva's in rough shape."

"I'll give him a call. Maybe I can get him out with the scouts later this weekend. We have something planned that he might like."

"That would be good."

"Well, I'd better get moving if I'm going to keep my heart rate up. Nice to meet you, Claire." Dewey clipped the helmet strap under his chin. "Let me know if you want to see that research. AJ has my number."

"Thanks, Dewey."

Dewey pedaled away down the driveway, his gray ponytail swinging across his back.

"He seems interesting," Claire said.

"Yeah," AJ said. "He's a character."

"So he's part of your friends' ghost hunting group? And a Boy Scout leader?"

"Right. He does all the historical stuff for *Mystic Afterlife*. The scouts are Venture Scouts—it's an older group. And he's a volunteer fireman. And I guess an avid bike rider. Oh, and he writes, too. No doubt you'll be hearing about that at some point. He has a piece in the paper once in a while."

"I'll have to keep an eye out." Claire started toward the kitchen. "We'd better get to the eggs."

They ate on the porch, passing butter and jelly and pepper across the table. Claire described her childhood in upstate New York—the beauty and boredom of living in the mountains. AJ talked about growing up working at a fish market—long days, the tight fit of family. Ben didn't make an appearance.

After breakfast, Claire headed out to get paint and other supplies. AJ went home for a quick shower. When he arrived back at Claire's house, her car was still gone. Carrying a couple of sodas by the plastic yoke, he retrieved the key she'd left for him above the door, then let himself in.

"Ben!" he said.

There was no answer. AJ went to the kitchen and stashed the sodas in the refrigerator. When he turned around, Ben was right in his face.

"Boo!" Ben said.

AJ stumbled backward, his elbow slamming into the handle of the refrigerator door.

"Now that's more the reaction I expected," Ben said.

AJ rubbed his elbow and glared.

"You look beat," Ben said. "Sorry I kept you up."

"I'm fine."

"If you say so. So are you ready now to tell me about the other ghosts that you've seen?"

"Claire may be back any minute."

"I don't think so. She left just a little while ago. It took her a long time to get ready. She changed clothes. She changes clothes a lot."

AJ gave him a sharp look, but Ben continued.

"I wouldn't mind changing just once, you know? I guess I'm stuck with this outfit forever." He looked down at his T-shirt and knee-length shorts. "So, tell me about the ghosts. Where did you see the first one?"

"I'll talk while I spread out the drop cloths." AJ went to the dining room, where he started shaking out a large plastic sheet. Ben watched him, looking impatient.

"The first ones were old," AJ said. "I mean, they'd been ghosts for a long time. I could tell by their clothes."

"Interesting. Did they talk to you?"

"No, like I said last night, I didn't really talk with any of them. The first few, it wouldn't have even occurred to me that they could talk. They seemed like they were in a trance."

"They were probably residual haunts—just energy that keeps repeating some motion over and over, a continuous loop. There's no intelligence. They didn't respond to your presence, right?"

AJ squared a corner of the plastic with the wall. "There was this boy who bounced a ball outside the old Broadway school. He would stop when I was near, but he never made eye contact with me, or said anything. I was never sure if he saw me."

"Huh," Ben said. "That doesn't sound residual, exactly. The ghosts in Bridgeport, did they respond to you?"

"If screaming in my face counts as a response, then yeah, they responded to me."

"Oh," Ben said. "I told you, I did a lot of screaming at first, too. I guess that's normal. Didn't you ever go back to check on them?"

AJ went on smoothing the dropcloth along the floor. "No."

"You're kidding me. AJ, you have to do that. They could be as sane as me, now."

"Yeah? What am I supposed to do then, strike up a conversation?"

"Yes, exactly. You're talking to me, aren't you?"

"What would I talk to them about?"

"You ran into them on the job in Bridgeport, right? Were they murdered?"

AJ nodded without looking up.

"So for starters, if you talk to them, you might catch some bad guys."

"Great. Testimony from the spirit world. I'm sure that would go over real well with the D.A."

"Whatever. It's too late for that, anyway, since you quit that job. Which maybe you wouldn't have had to do if you had told me what was going on. I could have helped you deal with it. You could have stayed in Bridgeport."

AJ brought some paint rollers and a tray onto the dropcloth. He crouched over them.

"You need to do this for yourself, AJ. This ability you have—you've got to face it. Take ownership of it."

"Take ownership of it? What, you're Dr. Phil now?"

"I'm just saying, you can't keep running away from this thing."

AJ slid a roller cover onto a roller.

Ben sighed heavily. "Have you given any more thought to telling anyone about me?"

"Like I said last night, Ben. I can't. I'm sorry. Not yet."

"Last night you said you'd think about it."

"No, said I should think about it."

"Jesus, AJ. It's not fair. With you helping, I could still talk to everyone. I could still have some kind of life."

AJ pushed the roller across the wall, testing it. "They'd think I was crazy. You know they would. Or worse. Your mom—forget it. She is so religious—"

"Yeah, my poor mom. She'd freak. It's better if she thinks I'm in heaven."

They were both silent for a while.

"Just tell Sela and DaSilva," Ben said.

AJ moved toward the front door. "I think I hear Claire's car."

60

"Oh, sure. That's convenient."

AJ opened the door. "If you don't believe me, come take a look."

"Are you trying to trick me into getting too close to the door? I told you what happens."

"Ben."

"Whatever. I'll just hang in the background. I won't bother you."

"Why don't you look for that other ghost? You know, the one you were hunting for—the one Sela got on video? He saw it upstairs."

"I have been looking for her—it's supposed to be a woman. So far, nothing." Ben craned his neck to see past AJ. "I bet Claire would be totally cool, if you told her."

Then Claire was on the front step, in jeans, slope shouldered under the weight of two paint cans and a bulging plastic bag.

"Let me take something," AJ said.

"I'll just put them down," she said, stepping inside. "You look ready for some painting."

"I am."

"I have to change again."

"I'll finish spreading out the drop cloths."

"Oh, thanks." Claire headed for the stairs. "Keep your eye out for painter's tape. I brought it with me from New York. It's blue."

"All right."

In the dining room, AJ sorted through the supplies—roller trays, a wooden handle about a yard long, a screwdriver, a hammer and several stirrers, rounded with dried paint.

"She's nice." Ben's voice was right in his ear.

"Jesus," AJ said, startled.

"She likes you."

AJ grunted dismissively and began unfolding another plastic sheet.

"Okay, okay," Ben said. "I'll make myself scarce." He went toward the kitchen.

Claire came back into the dining room wearing worn shorts and a tee. She had green flip-flops on her feet. A bandana covered her hair. "Looks like you got everything set up," she said. "I like to tape before I do any painting. I'm kind of anal about it."

"I didn't find any tape."

"I'm sure I had some. Maybe it got stuck in one of the drop cloths."

They both scuffed around the room, heads down.

"Weird," she said. "I don't know what could have happened to it."

AJ kept moving.

"This is a pain," Claire said. "I hate to go back to the store. But I don't want to start painting until I have the molding taped. And the corners." She glanced up toward where the ceiling met the wall.

"Maybe we can do without," AJ said. "I can get a pretty straight line along the ceiling with a brush. My dad repaints the market every couple of years. I've been helping him since I was maybe ten years old. And we can pull the drop cloths up over the molding, like this." He demonstrated.

"You really think so?" She reached into the plastic bag and produced two trim brushes. "Here's what I have to work with."

"Perfect," he said, taking one. "I'll cut in a short section, and you can decide whether I keep going or not."

"Okay. Convince me."

When he had painted a four-foot strip of ceiling right along the wall, he looked down at her from the stepladder. "Well?"

"Oh, you're good," she said. "Forget the tape."

They began in earnest. After giving AJ a headstart, she worked behind him with a roller on the long handle. They moved quickly, coordinating their efforts. As he shifted the ladder, he asked, "So if I wanted to read one of your books, which one would you recommend?"

"Hmmm..." she said, eying him. "Mostly, my audience is fifteen-year old girls. So, I'll have to think about that."

"I hope you're not just blowing me off, because I'm serious."

"All right. I think I know the book. It might keep you awake—it's sort of scary."

"I don't really need any help with that."

"You're not a good sleeper?"

"Not really." AJ kept his eyes on the right angle where the wall met the ceiling, his hand steady, the line straight. He slid the ladder a couple of feet along the wall. They went on painting. The plastic crackled under their feet. The roller squeaked as it spun.

"You know, if I had a dog," Claire said after a while, "wouldn't this be a lot harder?"

"Why?"

"Wouldn't he be in the middle of this? Putting his nose in the paint, tearing up the drop cloths?"

"I guess some dogs would. Not Buck."

"You really should bring him over," Claire said, "so I can see him in action."

"I definitely will."

When they had finished the ceiling, Claire stood in the center of the room, admiring their work. "Maybe one coat will be enough."

AJ tapped the lid onto the can.

"While that dries, do you want to look at the room I want to do next?" Claire slipped out of her flip-flops. "I think I stepped in paint. I don't want to track it all over the house." She headed for the stairs. "This way."

AJ tried to peer over her shoulder as they went up, but near the top, where the stairs made a turn to the right, and the treads went from reliable rectangles to unpredictable triangles, he had to watch his feet. He followed Claire into the long hall that he'd seen on Sela's video. They passed an open door, the one that Sela had entered, and AJ turned his head, instinctively. Ben was there, lurking just inside the doorway. As their eyes met, Ben gave AJ a thumbs up. AJ let out a low sound.

Claire stopped. "You okay?"

"Big place," AJ said.

They passed another door, then a third. Claire went left into the fourth room. Before following her, AJ checked the hall again. No sign of Ben.

"This will be my office," Claire said. "It's close to my bedroom, and it's the right size."

"Nice."

She went to the closet. "I need to get this pole out of here, though, so my filing cabinet will fit in here. I tried, but couldn't get the screws to budge."

"Let me see."

Claire stepped aside and AJ leaned in. He put his face right next to the pole, trying to get his bearings in the darkness. "You have a Phillips head screwdriver?" he said.

"Yeah. One sec." Claire left the room.

AJ put his fingertip on the head of a screw that held the bracket in place, feeling the burr from a previous failed attempt to turn it. He was practically all the way in the closet now. Then, right behind the pole, Ben's bright face slid out of the wall.

"You might want some Liquid Wrench for that, if it's rusty," Ben said.

"Jesus!" AJ jerked upright, banging his head.

Ben's face remained there, visible to the middle of his temples, as if it were a mask hanging on a nail. "Just trying to help."

"Yeah, thanks," AJ hissed, just as Claire came back into the room, her bare soles noiseless on the wooden floor.

"What did you say?" She had the screwdriver in one hand.

"Nothing." AJ took the tool and worked on the screws. In a few minutes, the pole was down.

They went out of the room and back down the hall. When they reached the stairs, AJ glanced behind him, as if he'd caught motion out of the corner of his eye. He was just in time. A figure was crossing from the right side, heading away—not Ben, but a woman, wearing a long dress, her hair up, everything about her glowing ever so slightly. She reached the end of the hall, where there was a door. She continued through it and disappeared.

"AJ?" Claire was two steps down already. "You coming?"

"What's behind that last door, down at the end?" AJ said.

"Which door? The one straight ahead goes up to the attic. The one on the side is the back stairway to the first floor. You want to see the attic?" She brushed past him. "It's really a neat space. I've been trying to figure out what to do with it."

After retrieving a flashlight from her bedroom, Claire opened the attic door. Rough, worn stairs rose into shadow. She started up.

AJ followed close behind her.

"It's huge," she said. "I could—Ow!" She stopped, one foot raised.

"You okay?" AJ put his hand on her arm.

"I stepped on something sharp. A piece of glass, I think. That's what I get for going around barefoot."

She pointed the flashlight down. "There it is. Damn."

AJ pried something loose from the wood. "What the hell?"

They looked at the yellowed, misshapen object in AJ's palm.

"That doesn't look like glass," Claire said.

"That's because it's not glass," AJ said. "It's a tooth."

CHAPTER 12

When AJ arrived, with the tooth tucked away in a plastic bag in his pocket, the chief was behind his desk, staring intently at the television. In front of him were a paper coffee cup and a cinnamon roll, but he ignored them, just as he ignored AJ, who sat down on one of the molded chairs.

"What is this?" AJ said, looking at the television. "I didn't know you got anything but the news."

On the screen was a tall, dingy Victorian house. The camera swung up to a third floor window, which, from below, looked completely opaque. After a good twenty seconds of this image, with no sound, everything went black. Then there were two men standing in front of the same house— Dave DaSilva and Ben Shortman. Before either could speak, the chief hit the mute button on the remote.

"Channel 12 is running a *Mystic Afterlife* marathon," the chief said, finally turning to AJ. "My wife's in heaven." He grimaced, as if wanting to take that back. He picked up his coffee cup. "Have you ever seen the show?"

"Not really."

"I know this one." The chief waved toward the television. "There's supposed to be some kind of ghost in that third floor. A girl in a white dress."

AJ kept his eyes straight ahead.

"You see that?" the chief said. "He's using a regular camera there, a little digital job."

The screen showed Ben in a dimly lit room, holding a camera chest-high in front of him, snapping pictures seemingly at random.

"On the tape you brought me, someone says something about the still camera," the chief said. "I guess it's Dave Sela. He says he's going to look for it." The chief pointed. "That's the camera he's talking about."

"Must be."

"Apparently he didn't find it. I didn't see it, either."

AJ waited for the chief to continue.

"Wonder why Ben didn't have it that night," the chief said.

"No idea."

The chief let his gaze go back to the television. There, Ben and DaSilva walked down a path. "The tape from that night—have you watched the whole thing?"

"It's digital. There's no tape."

"Right. I got that," the chief said. "What about the video that Sela took, upstairs? Did you get that far?"

"Yeah, I watched it."

"There's a moment there," the chief said, "when it almost seems like… What did Sela say about it?"

"He hasn't seen it. He's not ready for that, chief."

"Okay. But he took the video. He was shooting something. What did he think he had there?"

"You'd have to talk to him."

The chief smacked his palms on the desk, almost spilling his coffee. "Cut the crap, AJ. What do you think is there? What did you see?"

"I don't know. Shadows, dust in the light, something on the lens. Could be a lot of things."

The chief pushed his chair back, looking defeated. "I know what my wife would see, if I showed it to her."

AJ waited.

"I had a friend who claimed he saw that kind of stuff," the chief said. "Supernatural, paranormal, whatever you want to call it."

"Yeah? Maybe you should show it to him."

"I would if he was still around."

AJ pulled the plastic bag from his pocket. "Can we get on with why I'm here? I told Claire I'd be back before long, with some kind of answer."

The chief pointed the remote at the television and the screen went blank. AJ passed the bag across the desk.

The chief held it up to the light. "I don't know squat about teeth. Do you? They teach you some forensic dentistry down in Bridgeport? What do they call it, odontology?"

"No, I didn't learn anything about that."

The chief pressed at the edge of the tooth through the plastic. "That's a human tooth all right. I already checked with the coroner—it doesn't belong to Ben Shortman."

"If it was Ben's, it would have been on the front stairs. This was on the attic stairs."

"What did you say to Claire?"

"I said that I'd bring it to you, that's all."

"Okay. No need to upset her, make her more uncomfortable."

"If this does turn out to be related to the Westbury case—"

"Hang on," the chief said. "This may not be related to any case at all. My wife has a box of the kids' baby teeth rattling around somewhere in our house."

"That's not a baby tooth."

"My point is, we shouldn't get ahead of ourselves."

"Fair enough. But if this is from the Rose girl—"

"It could be a big break? I'm not even going to think about that." The chief was still squinting at the bag.

"What I'm saying is, if the tooth is from Anna Marie Rose, and it was in Jacques Westbury's house, and he's back in town... Do we know if Westbury's still around?"

The chief closed his hand over the bag. "He is. I talked to Scott Schwartz. Turns out Westbury is looking to rent."

"So he's staying." AJ inched forward on his chair. "What I mean, Chief, is should we be worried about Claire being alone in that house?"

"Because of Westbury? It seems to me if there's one guy Claire doesn't have to worry about, it's him. She's an attractive woman. But she's not his type. He likes them young."

"He's been gone twenty years, chief. How do you know what his type is anymore?"

"Because that's one thing that doesn't change." The chief's eyes drifted back to the dark television. "Okay. First thing Monday morning, I want you to see a man at the state forensics lab, a Dr. Umble. Best one in the state with this kind of thing. You ever been to the lab?"

"No."

"I'll get you directions."

"I can find it."

"Okay. In the meantime, why don't you just keep lending a hand over there at Ms. Connor's house. Keep an eye on things."

"All right."

"I take it that won't be too much of a hardship?"

AJ didn't respond.

The chief pushed his pastry across the desk. "All this talk about teeth," he said, "I don't feel like eating anymore."

CHAPTER 13

Claire came out onto the front step to greet AJ, as if she had been listening for the Jeep. She had changed out of her painting clothes and removed her bandana. Her hair was almost white in the bright sun. "What did the chief say about the tooth?"

"Not much. He said his wife saved a bunch of their kids' teeth."

"Yeah? He didn't think it was weird? He wasn't concerned?"

"Well, he said I can show it to a friend of his in the forensics lab. But no, he's not too concerned."

"Are you going to do that—show it to someone at the lab?"

"Yes, tomorrow. So, can we try to get some more painting done today?"

"Okay. Yeah."

As they went inside, there was a voice from the living room.

"The cable's working," Claire said.

"Good. Now you're officially moved in."

"Right. I'm not really watching anything. I'll turn it off." She started into the living room. AJ went with her.

The television was against the far wall. AJ could hear the voices of Ben, Sela and DaSilva clearly, but even with the large, high-definition screen, he couldn't see them. That's because standing in the way, in all his overcolored splendor, was Ben's ghost.

AJ stopped suddenly.

"I'm sorry," Claire said. She touched AJ's arm. "I didn't mean to upset you. I'll turn it off."

AJ exhaled. "It's okay. You can leave it on."

"This show's really pretty interesting. They're a bunch of characters."

"Yeah, they are."

"They don't find a lot of real convincing evidence. I mean, I'm not sure from watching this that you'd believe there was an afterlife, if you didn't already. But at least they're honest about it. Some of these shows about the supernatural—the trickery is so transparent."

"Thanks, I guess," Ben said, turning around. He assumed the stance of a hockey goalie guarding the net. He blocked the television completely.

"I'm going to turn this off," Claire said. She went for the remote.

Backing up to the TV, Ben disappeared into it. Now his recorded face was visible on the screen, in close-up. While the recorded Ben talked, the face of Ben's ghost emerged slowly from it like some kind of bizarre 3D effect.

Claire pushed the button on the remote and the screen went black. Ben's glowing face remained for a moment, then receded, slowly, as if sinking into quicksand.

"They're doing an all-day marathon of that show," Claire said.

"Now that's a grueling marathon," AJ said. "Beats the running kind all to hell."

Ben's hand reached out from the screen, giving AJ the finger.

"So you think you'll be working a full day tomorrow?" Claire said.

"Most of it, probably."

"Okay." Claire crossed her arms in front of her. She was still clutching the remote.

"The funeral is on Tuesday."

"Oh, all right," Claire said. "I'll be fine here," she added, already looking less than fine. "I really do have to get used to being alone in the house."

AJ gave her a tight-lipped smile. "I was thinking, we could finish that room upstairs today. We'd do the ceiling up there next, then come back down and finish the dining room while the ceiling dries. Then move back upstairs."

"That sounds great," Claire said. "But I'll have to run out to get the paint. And I don't have anything for lunch."

"Have you ever had an Angelo's meatball grinder?"

"No."

"It's a perfect day to try one."

"Where's Angelo's?" Claire said. "Could I stop there after I get the paint?"

"That would work. It's right near the train station, in Mystic."

"You can come with me, or—"

"I'll stay here, if that's all right. I can move the drop cloths upstairs while you're gone. Get everything set up. Maybe even start on the ceiling."

"Okay," Claire said. "Thank you so much."

When Claire went out the front door, AJ watched her from the living room window.

69

Ben came over to him. "She's great."

"Nice prank with the TV," AJ said.

"Yeah? Watch this." Ben found the remote on the television stand. He leaned down on it with his hand.

"What are you doing?"

"I almost got it," Ben said. "These buttons are pretty sensitive. If I can just get a little firmer push…"

"Cut it out. Claire doesn't need a television that turns on all by itself."

"Ah!" Ben said, in exasperation. "I thought I had it." He turned around. "I'm still trying to figure it out. Sometimes I can make contact. You saw me, with the bottle cap."

AJ didn't respond.

"It's pretty painful, isn't it?"

"What is?"

"The show." He shook his head. "I guess we did the best we could with what we had. If we'd only had the chance to try the real thing, with a real studio, real crew, real equipment. I think we could have done something."

"Yeah. You could have."

"So what did the chief have to say about the tooth?"

AJ told him about seeing Dr. Umble at the lab.

"Good. There'll be DNA."

"Maybe." AJ moved to the dining room. He reached for a drop cloth.

"Hey," Ben said, following him, "when are you going to tell Claire about me?"

AJ lifted an edge.

"It would help both of you. You heard her—she's uncomfortable here when she's alone. But the thing is, she's not alone. I'm here. There's no need for her to be spooked."

"Ben, you *are* a spook." AJ folded the drop cloth on itself.

"Very funny." Ben bent down like he was going to help. His hands passed through the plastic. "Damn." He straightened up again. "I'm trying to have a conversation. Do you have to do this right now? I understand that life goes on but—"

"If Claire comes back and I haven't done anything, she'll wonder what the hell I was up to."

"And then you tell her," Ben said.

AJ went on folding the plastic.

"Come on, AJ. I'm dying. I mean, I'm dying again, but slowly this time, and every minute of every day. I'm stuck here. I can't go anywhere. I can't do anything. I can't talk to anyone, except you, when you decide to grace me with your presence, and then, only when there's no one around. Do you have any idea what that's like?"

"Even if I told Claire, you still wouldn't be able to talk to her."

"She could talk to me. And I could—I don't know—signal somehow. Knock once for *Yes*, twice for *No*. If I could learn how to knock. Something. Look, it would make life easier for you, too. When you're around, you wouldn't have to pretend I'm not here. You wouldn't have to keep lying, AJ. This thing you have—you've got to—"

"I know. Take ownership."

"Exactly."

AJ collapsed the plastic, hugging it to his chest. "Have you looked for the other ghost? When I saw her, she went right down the upstairs hall. If you keep watch up there, maybe you'll meet her."

"I can't believe you," Ben said.

"What?"

"Are you telling me to hang out with my own kind?"

"Jesus. I'm just thinking, maybe you could talk to her." AJ put the drop cloth down. He closed the step ladder and leaned it against the wall.

"I just had an idea," Ben said. "I want to see that video. Sela's footage. You've got to bring it over here. And I want you to take some video of me."

"Why?"

"A test, to see if I show up. And if my voice comes through. We'd want the digital audio recorder."

"Why would we want that?"

"Don't you see? All that time I was looking for proof of the afterlife— now I could be that proof. If I can be recorded, why couldn't the show still go on? Why couldn't I still be on it? Never mind a show about ghosts. How about a show hosted by a ghost?"

"Listen to yourself," AJ said. "Does that even make sense?" He went on to the next drop cloth. "The chief was asking me about your other camera. The still camera. I guess you didn't bring it here that night?"

"I'm telling you, I don't know. Everything about that night is still a blank."

"Did you normally bring it on an investigation?"

"Normally, yeah, I would have had it on me. I would have had the video camera, and the audio recorder and the still camera."

AJ squeezed the air out of the folded drop cloth. "I guess nothing about that night was normal."

71

CHAPTER 14

AJ sat in an unmarked car in the parking lot of a low, clean building with a green metal roof. It looked more like a restaurant, the kind with an all-you-can-eat buffet, than a crime lab. He punched a number on his cell phone.

"Chief Brown."

"Hey, Roland, it's AJ."

"Are you at the lab?"

"Just left."

"How'd it go? What did Dr. Umble have to say?"

"I didn't talk to him."

"Why not? He should have been expecting you."

"He may have been expecting me, but he wasn't here. The man at the desk told me he's in court all day."

"Who did you talk to?"

"I filled out a form. The man says there's about a year backlog on property cases. I made it clear we were interested in a homicide."

"A twenty-year-old homicide," the chief said. "I'm sure it will jump right to the top of the list."

"Yeah."

"I'll call Umble. I don't know if it will do any good, but I'll give it a shot."

"So I'm done, then."

"For now."

AJ hung up. He tried Claire's cell phone but got her voice mail.

He started up the car, wound through the outskirts of Meriden, eventually found the ramp to the highway. He headed east, toward Stonington. Before long, though, when a connection with I-91 came up, he took it, heading southwest, toward the opposite end of the Connecticut coast. Thirty minutes later, he was in Bridgeport.

Once off the highway, he turned away from the sound. He drove down an abandoned commercial street lined with boarded-up windows and steel grates. Headless parking meter poles tilted across the cracked sidewalk. He took a left, into a neighborhood of two-story houses. After a couple of blocks he pulled to the curb. Just ahead was the house with the mismatched windows, the house that had been his last stop as a member of the Bridgeport P.D.

"Right, Ben," he said. "Take ownership. Great idea."

The roof sagged over the porch. There were curtains in the big window on the right, now, though the smaller window on the left was still bare. On the railing, there was a yellowing tomato plant in a pot.

Across the street was the house the couple had come out of, that night—the man in the Cavaliers jacket and the woman who looked barely out of high school. Nothing moving there, either.

There was a thud from the house with the mismatched windows. The front door swung open. A boy, maybe five or six years old, came out, struggled to close the door behind him, then ran down to the sidewalk. He began bouncing a dirty, blue ball.

AJ got out of the car. "Hi," he said.

The boy kept his eyes on the bouncing ball.

"What's your name?"

The boy pulled the ball out of the air and raced back to the house. The door slammed shut behind him.

AJ cursed quietly. He stood there for a while, leaning against the car. Then he ducked across the seat and began rooting around in the glove compartment. He produced a tape measure. "That'll work," he said, sliding the tape measure into the pocket of his windbreaker. As he walked toward the porch, the door opened and an elderly woman, barely taller than the boy, peered out.

"Hello, ma'am. Police officer." AJ flashed the badge on his hip, then let the windbreaker cover it again.

The woman spoke over her shoulder in Spanish.

"I just need a moment of your time," AJ said.

The door opened a little more, revealing a young woman with a wide, brown face. She whispered something to the older woman, who walked away, waving her hands.

"I'm sorry," AJ said, approaching the door. "I didn't mean to upset her."

The young woman kept the door half closed. "How can I help you, officer?"

"I'm just following up on an incident of domestic violence that took place here a little while ago. Before you moved in."

"I heard about it. A guy killed his girlfriend, right? And the cops shot him."

AJ's eyes tightened for a second. "Yes," he said. "I'm just doing some follow-up. I was hoping to take a look at the back bedroom. I need to take some measurements."

"Why?"

AJ held up the tape measure. "It's for the report."

The woman shouted something over her shoulder. After a moment, she stepped back from the door. "I guess it's all right."

"Thank you," AJ said.

He went in. He kept going through the living room, which was orderly, now, though sparsely furnished. There was a Mexican soap opera on the television. The young woman yelled something in Spanish. AJ kept going, turning right, into the hall, then taking the next right, into the bedroom. He stopped just inside. The older woman was there, folding a blanket that she squared across the foot of a neatly made bed. She brushed past AJ without looking at him.

AJ's gaze jumped to the spot on the floor where the body had been, then to the doorway that opened to the bathroom, where the killer had appeared suddenly, his gun already pointing at Tony. He took deep, controlled breaths, scanning the rest of the room. There was a cheap dresser with a mirror over it, and a single wooden chair. There was a short shelf mounted on the wall, holding a framed photograph. There was a shoebox, in the corner. There were no ghosts. No screaming.

Behind him, the two women conversed in Spanish.

AJ began to extend the steel measuring tape, at the same time walking to where the body had lain in blood and glass and silver.

The younger woman came forward and took the advancing end of the tape. "Do you want me to hold that?"

"Yes, please," AJ said. "Back up a couple steps. There. Thank you." He read the numbers out loud. "Okay. You can let go."

The tape snapped back into the case. AJ stared at the carpet. He brushed his fingers across it.

"Everything okay?" the woman said.

"Yes. That's it." AJ stood up and slipped the tape measure into his pocket.

The woman followed close behind him as he went back through the hall and the living room to the door. She opened the door and stood aside. When AJ was on the porch, about to take the first step down, the woman stuck her head out. "So you were here the night those people got killed?"

AJ turned. "Yes. Me and my partner."

"Which one of you shot the guy?"

AJ just looked at her for a moment. "I did."

She nodded. "Good. He was a bastard." She pushed the door closed. There was the thick click of a deadbolt sliding shut.

AJ got into his car. He tossed the tape measure into the glove compartment. Then, with a quick burst, he threw off his windbreaker. The shirt underneath was dark with sweat.

He started up the car and switched on the air conditioning. While the vents blasted him, he tried Claire on the cell phone. This time, he left a message. "Hi, it's AJ. I just thought I'd see how things were going. You should keep your phone on. Talk to you later."

He got the car turned around. After driving through more neglected neighborhoods, he parked in a small dirt lot next to a car with plastic for a back window. Across the street was a low building plastered with advertisements for sandwiches and drinks. A black and yellow sign on the roof read *Superette*.

He put his windbreaker back on. "Here goes," he said, as he got out of the car.

Inside, the clerk was slicing and buttering hard rolls behind the counter. He wore a baggy T-shirt with the word *Monster* printed on it. His ears and nose and lower lip were pierced with tiny silver dumbbells.

AJ drifted down the aisle between two rows of metal shelves, past chips and light bulbs and batteries and loaves of bread. He paused every few feet and looked around him. When he reached the rear of the store, he scanned the entire space, including the ceiling.

"Can I help you?" the clerk said.

"No, thanks." AJ opened the refrigerator case and grabbed a soda. He went to the counter with it, his eyes sweeping right and left.

The clerk had gone back to working with the rolls, wrapping them up in little wax paper pouches. "One fifty," he said, without turning around.

AJ checked the big convex mirrors in the corners of the ceiling. He saw movement. He turned towards it.

"You okay?" the clerk said. He was facing AJ now.

"Yeah," AJ said. But he continued to look to the left.

There was a man. He was young, but haggard, exhausted, like a junkie wasted by his habit. The color had been drained from him. More than that, there were holes, spots where it seemed his body had worn away, through which the glass front of the store and its bright signs were plainly visible. The man's hollow eyes met AJ's. He froze.

"Hey, mister," the clerk said. He looked from AJ to the window and back again. "What's going on?"

Before AJ could answer, the man with the hollow eyes began to scream, opening his mouth wide, baring his gray teeth. There were no words, just noise, just inconsolable pain and rage. He reached for a rack of chips, failed to make contact, screamed, tried again. The metal trembled. A single snack-size bag fell to the floor.

"You saw that, right?" the clerk said. "The way that rack shook, then the bag fell? I know you saw that."

"Must be from the traffic," AJ said. "A truck just went by."

"It wasn't a truck. That kind of shit happens all the time. This place is haunted."

"A haunted convenience store? That's a new one."

"I'm telling you, I see things. Weird shit."

"Yeah?" AJ hadn't yet met the clerk's gaze. "Why would a ghost hang around this place?"

And then the ghost spoke, with a voice that was dry, little more than a croak. "I can't get out," he said. He flew toward the entrance. When he reached the door, he bounced backward, then vanished. The glass rattled.

"Did you see the fucking door?" the clerk said. "It was like someone was trying to open it, or break through it. Only there's no one. There's no one there."

"So I guess that was your ghost, too?" AJ said.

"It's for real, man. There's a lady who comes in here who says she's seen him, says it's the guy who was killed here a while back." The clerk pointed toward the beer cooler, where the ghost was now standing, glowering. "He was shot right over there. Some kind of gang thing."

"It wasn't a gang thing," AJ said.

"How do you know? What, are you Bridgeport police?"

"I was. My partner and I answered that call."

"Damn. Really? That's some serious shit. So what did happen? How did he end up getting shot?"

"We don't know."

"Didn't they get the whole thing on video?" The clerk looked up at a camera mounted near the ceiling.

"No. Whoever did the shooting was smart enough to take the tape. So unless your ghost starts talking, we'll never know what happened."

On the other side of the store, the ghost put his hands to his head. "I don't remember." Moaning softly, he stared at AJ with his empty, colorless eyes. "Help me."

"So how come you left the Bridgeport P.D.?" the clerk said.

AJ finally allowed himself to look away from the ghost. "Too many nights like the one I had here."

"Right."

"Let me ask you something," AJ said. "If you think this place is haunted by the ghost of a man who was murdered here, why do you stay?"

"Yeah, well." The clerk smiled. "The boss had such a hard time keeping people that he's paying me double. It's like hazard pay."

"You're not scared?"

"Of the ghost? No. I think it's kind of cool. The customers scare me sometimes. But the ghost—he's dead. What can he do?"

The ghost moved toward the front of the store. Taking a shortcut through the deli case, he was soon behind the clerk. On the counter there, beside the rolls, was the knife that had cut them open. It had a black plastic handle and a serrated edge. The ghost reached for it. The blade wobbled back and forth, like a compass needle trying to find north.

"James," AJ said, with force.

The ghost pulled his hand back.

"What?" the clerk said.

"The guy who died here. Your ghost. His name is James."

The ghost retreated. AJ followed him with his eyes.

"What are you looking at?" the clerk said. "Do you see something?"

AJ put money for his soda on the counter. "If you're so sure he's here, maybe you should try talking to him."

The clerk squinted at AJ but didn't speak or move to take the money.

On his way out, AJ stopped to look back. James was at the counter, swiping at the coins AJ had left there. One slid and fell to the floor, landing at the clerk's feet.

"What the hell?" the clerk said. "James, my man. Chill. If you're going to hang out here, the one thing you can't do is mess with the money." He bent down to find the quarter.

James rose up, leaning over the counter, breaking its plane with his waist.

AJ let the door close behind him. He got in his car. He squeezed the steering wheel tight. "All right," he said. "That's enough ownership for today."

CHAPTER 15

AJ rang Claire's doorbell, waited, then rang it twice more. Nothing. He pounded on the door with his fist. "Hello! Claire!"

"AJ? Is that you?" Ben's voice came from an open window on the second floor.

AJ backed up. Shielding his eyes with a hand, he spotted Ben's bright pink face, well back from the screen. "Hey," he said.

"Claire left early this morning," Ben said. "New York City."

"But her car's here."

"She took a cab to the train," Ben said.

"Why?"

"I guess she was worried about getting a parking spot. I wish I could let you in."

AJ tried the place above the door. There was no key.

"So how'd you make out at the forensics lab? What did the dentist have to say?"

"I didn't talk to him," AJ said. "He was in court."

"What took you so long, then? Did you get lost?"

"I made a couple of stops."

"Stops? Like what?"

"I went to Bridgeport."

"No shit."

"Yeah."

"No shit."

AJ didn't respond this time.

"So what happened? Did you find your other friends from the beyond, or not?"

"One of them."

"You're kidding me!" Ben inched closer to the screen, thought better of it, and backed off. "That's so cool! What did you find out?" He didn't wait for an answer. "I've been thinking of things to ask, like, have they gotten any better at touching stuff? Or being seen?"

"We didn't talk about that."

"Damn. I wish I'd been there. I could have asked the right questions. When you go back—"

"He asked me to help him. I don't know what the hell I can do."

"Oh," Ben said. "Well, what you did, visiting him, talking to him, that's probably the main thing. I bet that went a long way. Just to have someone recognize that you are here. It gets pretty weird."

AJ let his hand drop. "You know I try to get over here as often as I can."

"Yeah, I know," Ben said.

The two men were quiet for a moment.

"Could you just tell Claire?" Ben said.

There was another silence.

"Did you look for the woman in the upstairs hall?"

"Off and on," Ben said. "I haven't seen anything."

"You can't do it off and on. It only takes her a few seconds to pass through. You have to really stake out the hall."

"So I'm supposed to hang around up there all day?"

"What the hell else do you have to do?"

"Nice."

"Sorry." AJ was quiet again.

"I did do something amazing today," Ben said.

"Yeah?"

"I turned the water on. In the kitchen sink."

"Oh, great. You can freak Claire out and empty her well, too."

"It's only a drip," Ben said. "I tried to turn it off again, but couldn't get it. Just say it's a bad washer."

"Didn't I tell you not to mess with her stuff?"

"All right, all right," Ben said. "But listen. I think I figured something out today. I've been trying too hard. You can't force it. You have to just feel it. You know what I mean?"

"No. I don't know what the hell you're talking about."

"When I want to make contact with the physical world. It's like my fastball in high school. If I overthought it, if I tried too hard, it was all over the place. But when I just let go, just threw the ball, then it went right where it was supposed to. Like magic."

"Is that right? I don't remember too much magic from those games."

"Hey, I had a no-hitter my senior year. You don't remember that?"

"I seem to remember hearing about it once or twice, yeah."

"Whatever." Ben looked over AJ's shoulder. "I think I hear Claire's car."

A battered pickup truck with a cap came out of the trees. It rolled slowly up the driveway.

"That's not Claire," Ben said, looking out the window.

"Good call."

The truck stopped and Henry Jacobson got out.

"Mr. Jacobson," AJ said.

"What were you looking at up there? Is there a problem on the roof?"

"No. No problems."

"You've met my son, Ellis." Henry tipped his head to the right.

A man in a dark green work shirt was closing the passenger side door. He rubbed his hands on his jeans. "Hey."

Henry and Ellis came through the weedy yard, two big men, the son a softer, darker version of the father. Ellis reached for AJ's hand. "Nice to see you."

"Is the new owner around?" Henry said. He turned toward Claire's car in the driveway.

"Yeah, I was looking for her, too," AJ said. "Doesn't seem like she's here."

"So you've met her?"

"Yes. Her name's Claire Connor."

Henry looked up at the house, his eyes going from window to window, passing by Ben without hesitation. "Is she going to be here full time or is she just a weekender?"

"I'm not sure what her plans are, exactly. Why do you ask?"

"Since I was the caretaker over here, I know the place inside out."

"Sure."

"It's a handful. She's going to need help. I wonder if she knows that yet."

"So you'd like to continue as the caretaker?"

"Oh, no. I'm too old for that. But Ellis—he could do it. I could train him, give him advice, help him out now and then." Henry glanced at his son.

"I know I've had some trouble," Ellis said, quickly. "But I'm trying to turn things around."

AJ nodded but didn't say anything.

"He's always been willing to work hard," Henry said.

AJ looked at one man, then the other. "You're probably going to have to give Claire time to figure out what help she needs. But I can tell her about your offer."

"Okay." Henry put his hands into the ample pockets of his stained khakis. "So you and Claire are, what, friends? That was quick."

AJ didn't respond.

"One other thing," Henry said. "Jacques Westbury said he left a cane bottom chair here, from the dining room set. He was going to talk to Miss Connor about picking it up sometime. He gave me the others, to repair. I thought maybe since I'm here…"

"I know the one you mean," AJ said. "It was pretty badly broken. She may have already gotten rid of it."

"Was it? Well, I'd like to take a look. There's just that one missing to make the whole set. It'd be nice to have them all. I was going to fix them up, then give them to my daughter as a house-warming gift."

"Maybe it's still around. Let me check the garage." AJ started through the weeds.

Henry moved to follow him, but Ellis grabbed his arm. He waited until AJ was in the driveway, then said, in a low voice, "What the hell is he doing here?"

"I don't know," Henry said. "Maybe because of the Shortman kid, they're keeping an eye on things."

"Goddamn Shortman." Ellis made a face. "He screwed it up for me. That cop's not going to want me working here."

Henry pulled his arm loose from his son's grip. "You made your own problems, Ellis. You've got to take the time and effort now to build your reputation back up. I think AJ will be fair in how he talks to Miss Connor about you. And I'll talk to the realtor, Scott Schwartz. Maybe he'll put in a good word."

AJ tried the garage doors, which didn't budge. "Locked," he yelled across the yard.

Henry led his son toward AJ and their truck. "Thanks anyway," he said, when he was close. With a big smile, Ellis shook AJ's hand for a second time. Then father and son got in the truck and drove away.

AJ walked back to the house.

"What was that all about?" Ben said from the upstairs window.

"Henry Jacobson wants Claire to hire his son as a caretaker."

"Ellis? Hasn't he been in jail a few times?"

"Once that I know of, for larceny. His dad says he's turning his life around."

"Great. You know, we talked to the old man a couple of times about investigating here. He wasn't too friendly."

"Henry's all right. Probably a little territorial about this place."

"I guess," Ben said. "They were talking while you were over at the garage. I couldn't really make out what they were saying, but I think I heard my name."

"I'm not surprised."

"Yeah, I know. I'm getting my fifteen minutes of fame for dying here." He added, as if reading a headline, "Ghost hunter dies in haunted house."

AJ gave him a flat smile.

"I'll be remembered for falling down the stairs," Ben said. "How lame is that?"

"You wouldn't say that if you'd been with me today. There are worse ways to die."

"Yeah? How did he go—the guy you talked to?"

"He was murdered. Shot. We don't know who did it, or why."

"Couldn't he tell you anything about what happened?"

"He still doesn't remember."

"Well, dying like that has got to mess with you," Ben said. "I don't know what my excuse is for not being able to remember what happened to me. It's all still a blank."

There was the sound of a car slowing on the road, then the glint of metal through the trees.

"That's a taxi," AJ said. "This time it is Claire."

"Right. So what are you going to tell her about Ellis? Do you think she should hire him? Give him a second chance?"

AJ watched the cab stop in front of the garage. "Henry, old as he is— I'd hire him in a minute. But Ellis? I wouldn't want him anywhere near this place."

CHAPTER 16

Two cars drove close together down the road to Lords Point. When they crossed the tracks and bore left on Boulder, the early morning fog was suddenly thick and white, so that the whole way along the inlet, the water was just a narrow arc beyond the rocks.

They drove to the end, to Skipper Street, then worked their way back, making half a dozen turns. The clapboard and cedar-shingled houses along both sides were quiet. Here and there a kitchen light glowed. A bike leaned against a tree. A squirrel chased another squirrel across the pavement.

The street made a jog to the right, passed a small park, then jogged again to the left and dead-ended. At the last second, the car in front went right onto a dirt lane. The second car followed. The brake lights flashed red and the cars came to a stop.

"Hope you don't mind that I took the scenic route," Scott Schwartz said, getting out of the lead car. "I wasn't sure you remembered how nice it is down here. Though I guess you couldn't see much this morning."

Jacques Westbury came around the other car, his gray hair fading into the fog, his soft leather shoes making no sound on the damp dirt. "I wondered if you were trying to lose me."

Scott smiled. "It's nice to have a client who's ready to go first thing in the morning. People usually want to do this in the afternoon. I'm an early bird myself." He gestured toward the house. "What do you think?"

Unlike the others they had passed, this one was stark and angular, in the shape of an L. The roof was flat. The long walls were blank.

"It was designed by an architect named Mitchell, who studied with Breuer, at Harvard."

"How much property?"

"That's one of the real pluses. You have a little over five acres. It's deep–there's a lot of land behind the house."

"Isn't there a road back there?"

"Wamphassuc? That's a ways away. You have a good buffer. Plenty of privacy."

When Jacques didn't respond, Scott continued. "As I said, the house is fully furnished. Everything was selected by the architect or with the architect's input. It's really exceptional. Exactly what you're looking for, I'm convinced. You hit the jackpot. C'mon. You'll see." He started toward the door.

Inside, the space was spare, clean and open, bedrooms in one leg, kitchen and living area in the other. While Scott chattered, pointing out fixtures and noteworthy chairs, Jacques followed silently, as if deep in thought.

They went back outside and stood in the little yard, walled on two sides by the house.

"Fantastic, right?" Scott said. "I can't believe this is available just when you happen to be looking for it."

"It is nice. In fact, it's very nice. So why is it available?"

"Actually, they are looking to sell, not rent. But in the meantime, they're anxious to get some income. So they'll take a rental, if they can get a year lease on it. Which I assume is okay with you."

Jacques nodded. "Okay, so why hasn't it sold?"

"There was an incident here that, frankly, scared some buyers off." Scott seemed to be studying the roofline.

"What kind of incident?"

"A death, actually."

"A death," Jacques said. "Come on, Scott. What happened?"

"Okay." Scott crossed his arms. "A couple lived here. No kids. He worked in the city, came home on weekends. One Friday night, his wife ended up dead. Stabbed with a kitchen knife. Turned out later, though the guy had been a big shot banker or something, he was completely bats. He heard a voice that told him what to do. At least, that's what he said in court, and it got him sent to the psychiatric hospital in Middletown."

It was quiet for a long time. The fog muffled any sound from the water or the neighborhood. Jacques took a couple of deep breaths, his broad chest rising and falling.

"I can't believe it," he finally said.

"What?"

"I can't believe you're trying to put me in this house. Did you forget who you're talking to?"

"All right." Scott closed his eyes for a second. "Honestly, I don't have anything else to show you. Anything that is close to what you're looking for. I tried Watch Hill, I tried Saybrook. Even early in the year, we typically only have a couple of rentals that would appeal to you. In a good

84

year. By June, it's just too late to be looking. I'm sorry. And, I had the idea that maybe, in a way, you're the right person for this place."

"In what way, exactly?"

"Maybe you wouldn't scare so easily. Maybe you'd be a little tougher. After what you've been through."

"What you mean is, I have nothing to lose. Everyone already thinks the worst of me. So what if I move into a house where there was a murder?"

Scott shook his head. "That's ancient history, Jacques. There's nothing to be gained by hanging onto it."

Jacques looked back at him but said nothing.

"It's a fantastic place, Jacques. It's everything you asked for—private, furnished, near the water."

"It's a little farther from the water than I wanted to be."

"It's not as far as you think. Let me just get the map."

Jacques followed Scott to his car. Scott spread the stiff paper across the hood.

"It's, what, an eighth of a mile, maybe a quarter, from here to the inlet. An easy walk. Did you talk to Noyes about that boat?"

"Yes," Jacques said without raising his eyes. "It's perfect. I'm getting the title later today."

"See? It's all coming together."

Jacques put his finger on the map. "What's this?"

"Hmmm." Scott bent his face close to the paper. "That's a canal. I didn't know that was there. It comes all the way up to just behind…" He pointed. "To your back yard. Might not be clear, you might need to have some work done, I don't know. Probably. But it sure as hell looks like private access to the water."

Jacques looked past the house into the fog. "Okay, Mr. Schwartz. I think we might have something."

***

Jacques was carrying a suitcase toward the front door when Henry's truck stopped in the driveway.

"Henry," Jacques said, as the old man came stiffly up the walk. "News travels fast in a small town."

"Yes, it does. Unlike me. I thought I'd stop by, see if I could catch you. I'm just on my way to the marine parts store."

"Marine pots?" Jacques looked puzzled. "Oh, *parts*—the marine *parts* store. I guess I haven't been around that accent for a while."

Henry let a grin pass across his lips and disappear. "Guess you're ready for your things."

"I guess I am. Do I need to rent a truck?"

85

"No. I can take care of it. I'll have Ellis help me."

"I'd really appreciate it." Jacques gestured toward the blank right angle of the house. "What do you think?"

Henry rubbed his neck, his bony elbow pointing toward the front door. "It's a little…"

"Modern?"

"Yeah. I guess that's it."

"It's definitely not what I'm used to."

"No," Henry said. "Definitely not."

"It's not exactly a perfect match for my old furniture."

"You said it, not me."

"You want to see the inside?"

"All right," Henry said.

Jacques picked the suitcase up again and opened the door. He showed Henry a kitchen with outdated but top-of-the-line appliances, then a huge living room with a dark slate floor and enormous windows on two sides, furnished with black, rectilinear chairs.

"Impressed?" Jacques said.

"Not sure that's the word."

"You don't have to fake enthusiasm on my account."

Henry didn't acknowledge the joke. "You know the history, right Jacques? You know what happened?"

"Yes. Scott filled me in."

"Then why in hell are you moving here?"

Jacques put his hand on Henry's shoulder. "Come on. I'll show you."

They went out the back door.

Henry let his eyes roam across the curving yard that ended in thick growth. "Private," he said.

"Walk with me." Jacques took off toward the tangle of tall grasses and low scrub.

When the ground grew dark and soft, they stopped.

"You got a waterway here," Henry said.

"Yes, I do. It'll take some work to open it up, but if I chop these plants back, I'll be able to come in here with a small boat."

Henry grunted. "Well, that's funny."

"What do you mean?"

"When I stopped by today, I had in mind to ask you if you needed any help."

"I thought you were retired," Jacques said. "Is everything okay? Do we need to reevaluate your annuity?"

"No. I'm fine. It's Ellis. I was hoping maybe you'd have a job or two for him. He's having a hard time finding work. If he doesn't turn something up soon…"

"I'd want it done right away," Jacques said. "It'd be a nasty job. But I'll pay well."

"Some hard, honest work is just what he needs."

Jacques put his hand on Henry's back. "Okay. It's a deal, then. Let's go inside and we'll hash out the details."

Henry turned toward the house, its right angle, its big, borderless windows. "Let's hash them out right here. I just have one condition."

"Conditions, now?" Jacques said. "Okay, what's the condition?"

Henry stepped away from Jacques's hand. "Just keep Ellis out of that house."

CHAPTER 17

Claire woke to the manic declarations of birds outside her window. Her eyes half-open, she put her hand on the clock, as if to stop an alarm. "Five-fourteen," she said, reading the red numbers. After lying there for a few seconds, she threw off the sheets. "Damn, it's going to be a long day."

She put on paint-spattered shorts and a T-shirt, then went down the stairs, slowly, blinking hard, watching her toes curl over the treads. On the porch, she had a bowl of cereal with a cup of coffee while she flipped through the paper.

She went back upstairs to the freshly painted room. Moving along one wall, she checked the edges at the ceiling and along the shin-high molding. Plastic drop cloths rustled under her bare feet. When she reached the corner, she stood for a second to look out the window at the overgrown yard and the thick woods beyond it.

"I wish I had just one neighbor," she said.

"Right," Ben responded, from the doorway. "This is why AJ has it all wrong. He should tell you about me. We both could use the company."

Claire went back to the removing the tape. When she'd finished, she opened the can of semi-gloss. "Where's that stirrer?"

"It's right behind you," Ben said, moving towards it. There was the slightest brittle rustling from the plastic.

Claire spun around. "Hello?"

They were face to face, Claire and Ben's ghost, close enough that they could have felt each other's breath.

Ben stared back at her, motionless.

"Ah, there it is." Claire reached down and picked up the stirrer. She worked it through the heavy, white paint, knocking it against the can, lifting a chalky smell into the air. After a while, she got down on her hands and knees and started in with the brush, turning the molding from dingy to bright, making little grunting noises as she moved along.

When she had finished one wall, she stood in the center of the room, assessing the result. "It's going to take forever to do this by myself." She checked her watch. "I wonder what time the funeral ends." She moved the can, then dipped her brush. "Sorry, Ben. I didn't mean any disrespect."

"No problem," Ben said.

Claire went back to painting the molding. Ben watched her, commenting on her work, drifting out into the hall now and then. When she was finished, she cleaned the brush in the bathroom across the hall. After coating every inch of exposed skin with sunblock and then insect repellent, she started down the stairs.

Ben followed her. "Where are you going? Don't leave. I like watching you work."

Claire went out the front door and dove into the weeds, yanking them from the ground, tossing them to the side. Soon she had a large pile. She pulled on a tiny sapling that turned out to be the green end of a long root. Defeated, she let it drop. Her hands were raw from the fight. All around her was vegetative chaos.

"This is impossible," she said.

The sun was already hot though it was barely ten o'clock.

She retreated to the kitchen and poured herself a glass of water. When she went outside again, she brought the glass with her, leaving it half full. She began picking flowers and dropping the stems in the water. She picked orange hawkweed and Queen Anne's lace. She bent for dandelions. In the brightest sun, she found escaped rose campion and bee balm.

She placed the glass on the ground, making sure it wouldn't tip, then lay down on her back. The sky was a pale blue with high clouds like long brush strokes. "This is why I bought this place," she said. She stretched her limbs and closed her eyes.

She was asleep when a car, a black European SUV, came out of the trees, kicking up dust. She remained asleep as Jacques Westbury got out of the car and started toward the front door. When she finally woke up, he was standing over her.

"Hi, Claire," he said.

She gasped and sat up, her face reddening.

"Sorry to startle you. I didn't see you there until I was practically on top of you."

She got to her feet. "Mr. Westbury." She took a step backward, toward the house. "Why are you here?"

"Jacques, please," he said. "I brought these for you." He was holding a cardboard tray of violets, starter plants with a few leaves each. "I remember them doing really well along the foundation."

"Thanks." She made no move to take the flowers.

"The back of the house would be better. Too much sun out here."

"Okay. Thanks. That's very thoughtful." She still didn't reach for the tray.

"I actually came over to ask you something," Jacques said. "I left a chair here. A wooden one, missing the caning."

"Right. I remember."

"I was wondering, do you want it? The man who has the others could use it, to complete the set."

"You can have it. But it was broken the night of the...the accident."

"Well, I'll let Henry take a look at it. He's pretty handy." Jacques walked to the step and put the tray down. "I'm so sorry about what happened. That's got to be upsetting for you."

"Yes." Claire shaded her eyes with her hand. "I put the chair in the garage." She let him go ahead of her.

Jacques swung the big garage door open. "There we go," he said, starting for the back wall, where the chair balanced on three good legs. At the last minute, he veered from the chair to a window that looked out on the yard. "Oh. I didn't mean to leave those."

"I'm sorry?" Claire stayed in the sunlight.

"Those pots." He stood by the window for a second, then went to a back door and opened it. "Let me see what we've got. Do you mind?"

Claire hesitated, shook her head, then followed him. Behind the garage, in the weeds beneath the window, was a stack of black metal cages. "What are these things?"

"Lobster pots. This one's an eel pot." Jacques put his hand on it.

"I thought lobster pots were made of wood, sort of rounded on top." Claire made an arc with her hand.

"These metal boxes aren't as pretty to look at, but they work every bit as well. Last longer, too. They belonged to Henry's son, originally. When he got in a little bit of a jam, my father bought them as a favor. The idea was that the boy would buy them back one day. But that never happened." Jacques looked into the weedy grid. "Do you want to keep them? They're still perfectly good."

"What would I do with them?"

"Same thing that we did—catch lobster. Lots of people around here have a few pots for their own use. You like lobster, don't you?"

"I love it."

"I could tell you how to go about setting the pots, if you're interested."

"Oh, I don't know. Maybe."

Jacques crouched down. "That's interesting."

"What is it?"

"Take a look."

Claire joined Jacques beside the pots but remained upright. "I don't see anything."

"There, in the corner." He pointed.

Claire bent closer. "Oh."

Across the wire mesh lay a string of tiny bones—a skeleton so frail that it looked like a quick sketch. It ended in a pockmarked skull.

"A chipmunk, maybe, or a mouse," Jacques said. "The poor thing got in there and couldn't find its way out."

Claire straightened up, frowning.

"Hey, would you mind if I took it—the skeleton?" Jacques said.

"Sure. But why do you want it?"

"I know someone who collects them."

"Skeletons?"

"Yes. Animal remains. I'll need something to transport it. Maybe some cardboard, or even a sheet of paper. Could you—"

"Sure. I'll get you something."

Claire went around the garage to the porch and into the house. When she returned, Jacques had the pot open.

"There's just enough connective tissue to hold the thing together." He took the paper that Claire offered and worked the skeleton onto it.

"Here, I thought you might want to—" Claire held up a plastic food container.

"Thank you." Jacques lowered the paper into the container and pressed the edges of the lid. He carried the container to his SUV. "If you decide you don't want those pots, let me know. It would be a shame to have them just sit there."

"Sure."

"Well, let me get that chair." Jacques went back into the garage and carried the chair to his car. "Thank you so much."

"No problem."

He stood there with his hand on the fender. "Let me show you a good spot for those flowers. We used to have scads of them, when I was a boy."

"Oh, that's all right," she said.

But he was already headed toward the violets. "Do you have a trowel? I could even put them in, right now."

"You really don't have to do that."

"Let me just show you the spot."

He picked up the tray and started through the garage. She trailed after him.

"Right here," he said, stopping just past the back porch. "It seemed to get the right amount of sun." He pushed some weeds aside with his foot. "Look, there are a few hardy survivors. If you cleared these weeds away, and—" He looked down the length of the yard. "You have your work cut out for you. I didn't realize how overgrown it was getting. I guess these flowers only give you more to do."

"It's nice, really," she said, her face relaxing for the first time since she'd awakened in the yard.

Jacques put the tray on the ground, careful to avoid the flowers he had found. "At the end of the house, and then wrapping around, my mother had quite a garden. There must have been hundreds of daffodils. I wonder if there's any sign of them, now."

He waded into the grass, then followed it around the corner, pushing the stems aside. "This grass crowds everything out, doesn't it? Still, I bet there's one of my mother's flowers in here."

Claire began poking around, too, working close to the house. Her foot knocked the frame of a window that was half hidden by the leaves. With a soft squeak, it swung open.

"Crap," she said.

Jacques came over to her. "Oh, my old friend."

"What?" Claire gripped the window, which seemed ready to fall out completely.

"That was my escape route during my youthful rebellious phase. My parents never did find out about it." Jacques knelt down and took the frame in his big hands. "You have to work it into place this way." He squared the window, then slid it backward. When he was done, everything looked precisely and securely in place.

"Thanks," Claire said. "Will it stay?"

"As long as no one messes with it. Caulking might help. If you really want it to be right, you'd have to hire someone. Of course, they'd probably want to sell you all new windows."

"I don't like that being loose," Claire said, frowning.

"I could talk to Henry Jacobson, our old caretaker—the man I'm giving the chair to. He's a master at that sort of thing. One-of-a-kind work that no one does anymore. Anyway, he knows all about this window. He was the only adult who did. He kept my secret for me, God love him. He probably knows exactly how he'd fix it."

"Thanks. I'll have to think about it."

Jacques stepped back. "I found one, by the way."

"What?"

"A daffy." He led her to the spot, then separated the broad leaves from the finer, sharper ones that surrounded it. "My mother would be glad."

He let the weeds swallow the flower up again. "Thanks for indulging me. I've taken up enough of your time."

They went back around the house.

Jacques closed the garage door, then stopped at his car. "I've decided to stay in the area for a while."

"Oh?"

"I'll be renting—something more suited to my current lifestyle. Just as this will suit you, I hope."

He looked at the house. The imposing brown face was sturdy and solid, showing no signs of the neglect that was so evident in the yard.

"Thanks for the violets," Claire said.

"You're very welcome." He opened the car door, then closed it. "Can I ask you for one more thing? Would you have dinner with me? I think of myself as a local, but it turns out that I'm like you—I don't really know anyone in town. And there's a place in Noank that has the best lobster you can find anywhere. Those pots made me think of it."

"Oh, thanks. I don't know. I'm pretty busy here."

"Of course. Well, thanks again. Good luck to you." He got into the car.

Claire watched him drive away down the lane.

When it was quiet again, she went looking for the wildflower bouquet that she'd left in the yard. She carried it inside, placed it on the bottom step, then went up to her bedroom. There, she studied her body in a mirror, tugging her clothes aside.

"What have you been up to?" Ben said, coming into the room. "I've been looking for that other ghost. AJ wants to set me up with her. No luck so far."

Claire inspected her arms.

"You're checking for ticks, aren't you? You know, it really helps if you have someone else to look. If you really want to be thorough."

When Claire twisted the button of her shorts, Ben started to back away. He paused, still in the room. "What the hell," he said. "Being a ghost has to have some perks. AJ will never tell you I'm here, so what difference does it make?"

Claire tugged her shorts down, then kicked them loose from her feet. She examined her bare thighs, at the same time sliding her hands across her skin. Pivoting on tiptoe, she checked her calves. Ben took it all in. When she pinched the elastic of her underwear, though, he withdrew.

"Damn. Once a gentleman, always a gentleman," he said, when he was in the hall. "Maybe I'll be rewarded in heaven. If I ever get there."

He paused, his back to Claire's room, looking at nothing. The house was quiet. The long hallway, cut off from the windows, was dim and still. Then, at the far end of it, a young woman appeared. She came out of the wall, from the smooth and solid plaster, as if stepping through an invisible door.

"Holy shit," Ben said, softly.

She moved toward him, a fixed, almost grim expression on her pretty face.

"Hey," Ben said.

She kept coming. Her dress was long but the full skirts trailing behind her made no sound. Her cheeks and the ruffles of her dress, the hair pulled tight against her scalp and even her eyes were the same luminous gray.

"Hello, miss."

There was a slight hesitation in her advance but she continued. At the last second, Ben slipped out of the way. She passed through the attic door.

"Wait!" Ben said. He followed her, entering the rough room just in time to see her vanish. Then he raced back to Claire, who was buttoning her shorts. "You won't believe it!" he said. "I saw her! The ghost! The stories are true! This place really is haunted!"

CHAPTER 18

Henry was at his workbench, disassembling a chainsaw, when Ellis came out of the gloom of the barn into the shop.

"I was about to go looking for you," Henry said, turning around.

Ellis was scratched and dirty; his hair and clothes dark with sweat. There was blood across the back of his right hand. He leaned against the workbench and let out a long sigh.

"You look a little beat up," Henry said.

"It was tough going, but I got the whole way up one side of the canal."

"You've been at it all this time?"

"Most of it. I took the blades over to Paul's to have them sharpened."

"Was Jacques pleased?"

"He was gone when I quit, but I think he will be. He damn well better be."

"Think you can finish it tomorrow?"

"I'm gonna try. Two days of this will be enough for me."

"I bet it will."

"Did you hear anything from that woman?" Ellis said. "Claire Connor?"

"Not yet."

"I bet good old Officer Bugbee hasn't even mentioned us to her."

Henry put his wrench down. "I've been thinking. None of the guys in town—the carpenters, plumbers, even the landscapers—none of them want the small jobs anymore. I bet you could work every day just taking small jobs."

Ellis swiped a hand across a grimy pant leg. "Not a bad idea. You could line the jobs up and I could knock 'em down."

"There you go."

"And if we wanted a day off to go out in the boat, we'd just take it."

They stood there, backs to the workbench, arms crossed.

"Speaking of the boat," Henry said. "Did you ever put that pot out?"

"Don't think there's much point to that."

"Maybe. But some are saying the lobsters are coming back. If you aren't gonna put it out, maybe I will."

"I sold it," Ellis said, abruptly.

"Sold what. The pot?"

"I was short last month. I got a good price for it."

"For Christ's sakes, Ellis. Who'd you sell it to?"

"Just some guy."

"What guy?"

"What difference does it make?"

"Well, maybe I can get it back."

"No, you can't get it back. God, Dad. It's not the last lobster pot on Earth. It's too damn big for us, anyway. We can get a better one. Listen, I'm beat and I'm starving. I was wondering if you had any more of those ribs."

Henry picked up the wrench again. "Sure, help yourself."

"You coming in?" Ellis started toward the door.

"In a minute."

Henry watched his son's round-shouldered form disappear into shadow. From the dark came the sound of Ellis's shoes scuffing against the damp dirt floor. Then it was quiet. Still, for a long time, Henry stood there, staring into the barn.

CHAPTER 19

Claire was in the shower when the phone rang. Clutching a towel, still dripping, she dashed across the bedroom. She grabbed her shorts from the bed and pulled the phone from the pocket.

"Hello?"

"Hi. It's Melody."

"Oh, hi. How are you doing?"

"I'm okay. It's been kind of a rough day. The funeral was so sad."

"I'm sure. I've been thinking about you." Claire returned to the bathroom, leaving wet footprints.

Ben dashed into the room behind her. "Is that AJ?"

Claire pressed the speaker button and placed the phone on the counter by the sink. Then she began toweling herself dry.

"What did you do with yourself today?" Melody said.

"I weeded. And painted."

"How'd it go?"

"I finished my office. But there's so much to do."

"Would you like some help?"

"Actually, I'm done for today. I have to pick out more paint before I start anywhere else. In fact, I was just going to run out and do that."

"Oh," Melody said.

"How are the guys doing? How'd they handle everything?"

"Sela was real quiet all day. DaSilva's having a rough time. Dewey—have you met him? The retired teacher?"

"Yes."

"He gave a nice little speech," Melody said. "AJ did, too. After the service—I don't know. I couldn't get a read on him. He's holding it all in, I think."

"Strong, silent type."

"Yeah, I guess," Melody said.

"So what are you doing this evening? Are you going to be with them?"

"They invited me to hang out. But I really think it's better for them to be, you know, just the guys. So, I'm sort of at loose ends."

"Oh. Why don't you come over here? We can make it a girls' night."

"I'd love that, Claire."

"Okay."

"How about—"

The words died.

Ben, who had positioned himself outside the bedroom, said, "It's Melody, right? She's coming over."

"I'm losing you," Claire said. She picked up the phone. "This damn battery. I just charged it up this morning."

"I wonder…" Ben said, moving away.

Melody's voice came in fragments. "I said … good?"

"I didn't catch that." Claire pressed the speaker button again and held the phone up to her ear. She spoke a little louder. "Just come over when you can."

"Okay … while … you …"

"I can't hear you. See you soon, I hope." Claire cursed the phone as she put it down again.

***

A citronella candle, the only light on the porch, gave a yellow shine to the women's faces and the wine glasses and the bottles, but let the darkness come close.

"He lives in Maine, now," Claire was saying.

"Do you ever think about calling him?"

"I'm not going to call him. I haven't seen him in two years."

"But you want to call him."

"That's only because I haven't seen him in two years. As soon as I talked to him, I'd remember why I haven't called him."

Ben laughed. He was lingering at the end of the table, slightly luminescent, his colors unaffected by the yellow flame.

"You know," Melody said, "there are interesting men close by. Right here, even."

"You mean AJ."

"Well? I can see that you like him. And why not? He's good looking. He's smart. He's even a cop. A real All-American. What's not to like?"

"He only works part-time as a cop. What's that about?"

"It's temporary. He's only been back in Mystic for a few months. I'm sure he doesn't plan to stay part-time."

"I guess. But he had a full-time job and ran away from it."

"You've actually thought about this, haven't you?"

Claire shrugged.

"Another reason he should come clean," Ben said.

"Remember, there's the family business, the fish market," Melody said. "It's pretty lucrative, from what I can tell. Maybe his plan is to get into that. They call his mother the clam bake queen. You could be the lobster roll princess."

"The duchess of chowder. The contessa of quahogs."

"Right!"

"Seriously," Claire said. "Why aren't *you* interested in him?"

Melody refilled their glasses before answering. "I think if he was older he'd be exactly my type."

Ben drifted closer to the table. "Really, Melody? You like older men? So, that's your thing?"

"How old do you think he is?" Claire said. "Late twenties, right?"

"He's twenty-nine. I know because the guys have been bugging him about turning thirty. He'll be the first of that group."

"Okay," Claire said. "I wouldn't want him to be too much younger than me."

"See, you have your age range, and I have mine. I just think men are more interesting when they're older. They understand what's important in life. They understand me better."

"Are you talking forty or fiftyish, distinguished and successful?" Claire said. "Or wizened old prunes, loaded with cash and looking for a last fling?"

"Thanks, Claire. Do I seem like the Anna Nicole Smith type?"

"Nah. You'd have to bleach your hair."

"I'd have to make a few other changes, too." Melody glanced down.

"Uh huh," Claire said. "Don't older men usually have baggage? You know, ex-wives, children."

"Yeah, that can be part of the bargain. But kids can be fun."

"I guess." Claire looked into her glass. "You know, you would have loved the visitor I had today. He's just the right age for you."

"Yeah? Who's that?"

"Jacques Westbury."

"What?" Ben glowed a little brighter.

"What was he doing here?" Melody said.

"He came to pick up a chair that he'd left behind. And he brought me flowers."

"Really? I didn't see any flowers. Where are they?"

"They're in the back yard. A tray of violets. He even offered to plant them."

"Okay," Melody said, drawing out the word. "That was thoughtful."

"Yeah," Claire said. "He's the complete package. Thoughtful, distinguished looking, successful—"

"Homicidal."

"Hey, nobody's perfect."

"You're right. I'm setting the bar too high. I should call him."

"Not funny," Ben said, as the two women laughed.

"So Melody," Claire said. "Does this age thing explain why you didn't go out with Ben? He was too young?"

Melody stared into a candle flame. "I don't know. Maybe. He was young—twenty-seven, twenty-eight. And he acted young—that whole ghost hunter thing. But he was enthusiastic and funny and sweet, too. Fun to be around. It could be that if he'd had more time, if we'd had more time..." She drained her glass.

"Really?" Ben reached toward her with his tattooed arm.

"He was starting to get through to you," Claire said.

"Maybe. Yeah. I didn't realize it until he was gone."

"Jesus, Melody." Ben ran his hand down her hair.

She shivered.

"You okay?" Claire said.

"I just felt a chill."

"It is getting cool out here."

For a while the only sound was the whirring of the insects in the trees. Melody looked at her watch.

"You know I'm not letting you drive home," Claire said.

"Is your couch available?"

"Of course."

"Might as well finish this off, then," Melody said. She emptied what was left of the second bottle into their glasses.

Some time later, the women went into the house, loose limbed and yawning.

"I'll just stay out of your way," Ben said, remaining on the porch.

Claire fetched a pillow and sheets and they pulled out the sofa bed.

"You want something to sleep in?" Claire said. "Some PJs?"

"No, I'm good."

Melody noticed the bouquet of flowers on the table. "Pretty," she said, lifting the glass.

"Yeah. I picked them in my yard. Just weeds, mostly."

"I love this orange stuff. Hawkweed."

"Me, too," Claire said. "Well, let's get these sheets on."

They worked together, tugging a fitted sheet over the thin mattress, then tucking the top one in.

"I guess I'll head up to bed," Claire said.

Melody followed her into the front hall. "Good night, Claire. Thanks for cheering me up."

"I'm glad you came."

Melody watched Claire climb, then vanish around the turn. There was the sound of a foot knocking against wood.

"Claire, are you okay?"

"Yeah," Claire answered, still out of sight. "I just tripped. These stairs are hard enough when you're sober."

"Tell me about it," Ben said.

"You know, you really should do something there," Melody shouted up. "Put down carpeting, or those grippy treads."

"I know. I think about that every time I come down them. One more project."

"Don't wait until after you've finished the painting—that will take too long. Do it next. I'll help."

"Okay, okay. Don't worry, I'm careful."

In the living room, Melody took off her jeans and stretched out on the edge of the mattress. For a long time, she lay there staring at the flowers.

***

Melody awoke to piercing sunlight and the smell of coffee. Groaning, she buried her face in the pillow.

From the kitchen, there was singing.

Melody rolled onto her back. "Claire, you crazy person!" she shouted.

"What?" Claire came to the doorway. "Sorry about the sun. I need to get some curtains."

Melody opened her eyes halfway. "Nothing like singing and sunshine first thing in the morning."

Claire smiled sheepishly. "Sorry."

"I'm just giving you a hard time." Melody shifted on the pillow. "Oh, that's sweet."

"What's sweet?" Claire said, coming nearer.

"Putting the hawkweed on my pillow." Melody sat up. A single orange flower on a fuzzy stem slipped off the pillowcase and onto the sheet.

"I didn't. You must have put it there before you went to sleep."

"I don't think so. I remember getting into bed and then looking at the flowers. The hawkweed was in the glass."

Claire shook her head. "I think we had a little too much wine last night."

"Yeah," Melody said. She picked up the wilted flower and turned it in her hand. "I guess we did."

CHAPTER 20

"I have some big news, so listen up. Remember what I talked about the other day? A new sister? Well, she's coming. It will be a while, so you have to be patient. It's just like if your mom was pregnant. You'd know that a sister or a brother was on the way, but you'd have a long wait before he or she got there. That's how I think about it.

"Waiting is going to be hard for me, too. We're all going to have to be patient.

"Okay. Let me just shift this a little. There. There we go. I'm glad to be getting some use out of this old bed. It's just the right size.

"What the hell? How did that happen?

"Damn. Excuse me, but damn.

"Where did it go?

"Ah, look. A hole. The fabric is just worn out. I should have replaced this thing a long time ago.

"I'm so sorry.

"I think I know what happened. I was rushed, moving you out of the house. Usually I'm careful, but I had to get out of there in a hurry. You know, haste makes waste.

"I'll just have to go back for it. That's all there is to it. I promise you, no matter what it takes, I'll get your tooth."

CHAPTER 21

Melody went home to get her bathing suit. Claire called AJ. She told him about the plan to spend the day at the beach. "Misquamicut, I think she called it? Do you want to come?"

"I wish I could," he said, over the roar of an air conditioner. "It's great weather for it. Shouldn't be too crowded on a Wednesday, either. But I have to be at the market. They need me all day today."

"Okay," she said. "Next time. Hey, I wonder if you can recommend someone." She told AJ about the broken basement window.

"I could take a crack at it myself. But you'd be better off with the guys my dad has used for years. Donahue and Son. The son does most of the work, now—John. He's excellent. It's a small job, but he'll probably be glad to do it if he thinks there might be more coming. Anyway, tell him that I gave you his name."

"Great. I'll try him."

For a moment there was only the sound of the air conditioning.

"Melody said it was a nice service yesterday," Claire said. "She liked your speech."

"Oh. I'm glad."

Ben, who had been hovering by the porch door, came closer. "I wish you'd put the phone on speaker. AJ gave a speech about me? I would have liked to hear that."

"Well, I should get back to work," AJ said. "There's a lot to do before we open."

"Okay. Talk to you later."

Claire got the number for Donahue and Son from information, then made the call. The cheerful woman who answered promised that someone would be over in the afternoon to take a look.

"John Donahue is the best," Ben said. "You'll be happy with his work."

103

Claire unpacked the last two boxes of cookware and dishes while Ben drifted out to the porch and back.

"I'd help if I could," he said.

Upstairs again, Claire stuffed a bath towel, a suit and some sunscreen into a canvas bag. She hurried down the curved stairs, one hand on the wall, her flip flops slapping against her soles.

"Beach day, huh?" Ben said from behind her. "Boy, I wish I could join you."

Claire went out the door. The latch clicked shut.

"So long. I'll hold down the fort."

***

When Claire returned late in the afternoon, she backed her car toward the front step. Melody parked beside her. Together, they eased something out of the boxy cargo space of Claire's car—a writing desk, with a single drawer in the center and a top that closed over stacked compartments.

"I'm so excited about this," Claire said. "Thanks for showing me that antique store."

"I've always called it a junk shop, but now, I don't know. This is really nice."

They carried the desk across the yard, then worked it through the doorway, tipping it slightly, Claire losing her flip flops. Barefoot, she took the uphill end as they climbed the stairs.

"Welcome back." Ben was waiting at the top. "Something new there?" He dodged out of the way. "Looks like it's not too heavy."

Claire took tiny steps backward. "You okay?"

"Yep," Melody said. "Just keep going."

"No sign of your ghost." Ben followed the women down the hall. "I spent pretty much all day up here, hoping to catch her. She never showed."

Claire and Melody swung the desk into the newly painted room. Claire kicked a plastic drop cloth out of the way. They put the desk down.

"I love the color in here," Melody said. "You guys did a great job."

"Thanks. I'm going to do the hall next." Claire gathered up a drop cloth then carried it out. She put it down by the attic door and began to unfold it, nudging it back against the molding. Melody joined in.

"Thanks," Claire said. "I didn't mean to put you to work."

"No problem."

Looking up from the drop cloth, Claire froze.

The ghost in the long dress was coming toward them, her motion a smooth, unswerving glide.

Ben was right behind her. "You see her, don't you, Claire? Awesome! Talk to her! See if you can get her to respond."

104

"Jesus," Claire said, her eyes big.

The ghost passed by, the wide skirts nearly brushing Claire's leg. Then she vanished into the attic.

"What is it?" Melody said.

Claire pressed her fingers to her brow for a second. "I thought I saw something. It's gone, now. I don't know."

"Isn't she amazing?" Ben said. "Did you get a look at that dress? How old would you say it is, a hundred years? She's this beautiful, hundred-year old girl." He ducked through the attic door.

"Are you okay?" Melody said.

"Yeah."

"What did you see?"

"I'm not sure. A sort of column—more like a ribbon—that was, I don't know, shimmering." Claire held one arm in front of her, snaking it back and forth. "You know the way the air looks over a road on a hot day? It was like that. Only it was moving toward us."

"Wow. I've seen those heat mirages. But never inside."

"Me, either," Claire said. "That was weird. Maybe I was out in the sun too long. Maybe I have sunscreen in my eyes or something."

Ben reappeared from the attic. "Did she notice you? Did you make eye contact?"

Melody touched Claire on the shoulder. "The guys would ask if it was a—"

"No." Claire shook her head. "There's way too much talk about ghosts. It was nothing. I'm fine. Let's move the desk."

"It wasn't nothing," Ben said, following behind as the women returned to the room. "You saw her, Claire. Maybe you have some of AJ's ability."

Each of the women took an end of the desktop. Before they had moved an inch, the doorbell rang.

"Damn." Claire let go.

"Think that's AJ?" Melody said.

"It's too early to be him. Must be the window guy."

"Let's go find out."

"I'm going to stay up here," Ben said. "See if my friend comes back."

When Claire opened the front door there was a stocky man on the front step and a pickup truck in the driveway.

"John Donahue," the man said, extending his freckled hand. "I'm here to look at the window."

"Claire. Claire Connor."

"You want to show me where it is?" John picked up a toolbox.

Claire nodded at Melody, who waited on the stairs. She slipped into her flip flops, then led John around the house, his toolbox rattling with each of his faintly limping steps. Claire directed him to the spot.

"That's a beautiful old window," John said. He trampled the weeds to get a better view.

The white, peeling frame was slightly askew, leaving a gap all along one side.

"Jacques had that in place yesterday," Claire said. "How did it get out again?"

John lifted the window and squared it in the hole. "There's not much holding it. Maybe a strong gust of wind popped it back out."

"So no one's been messing with it?" Claire said.

John saw the concern on her face. "I don't think there's anything to worry about."

"Okay." She forced a smile.

"It's worn, but the wood's still solid. Would you like me to put in a couple of nails to hold things for now?"

"That would be great," Claire said.

John pulled a tape measure from his belt and extended it. Holding the tape to the window, he explained about the shims and the new frame that would be required for the repair. He wrote some numbers on a pad. Then he opened the toolbox and produced a hammer.

"Can you give me a ballpark figure?" Claire said.

"Shouldn't be too bad." He already had one nail in. "Of course, if you want a replacement window, something that would insulate better, that could run you a few hundred to a thousand, depending on what you're looking for." He drove a second nail.

"For now, I just want to fix what I have."

"Sure." After a fourth nail, he stood up. "That should do it until I can get back here."

He put his tools away. They walked back to the driveway. John threw his toolbox into the truck.

"I need to work up the estimate," he said. "I'll give you a call when it's ready." He shook Claire's hand and then drove away.

Claire went back upstairs, past Ben, who was staring at the wall the young ghost had emerged from.

"No more sign of our ghost," he said. "How'd you like Donahue?"

Claire found Melody in the office, admiring the new paint. "The guy seems to know what he's doing."

"John Donahue?" Ben said, joining them. "Oh, yeah. I told you he was the best."

After they had moved the desk to the window, Claire stepped back to look at it. From somewhere below there was a quick series of thumps.

"What was that?" Claire said.

"I heard it, too," Melody said.

"It sounded like something falling."

106

"Maybe it's her," Ben said. "Maybe she's downstairs now."

"Let's go see," Melody said.

On the first floor, the women, with Ben close behind, went from the sparsely furnished living room to the empty dining room, the back stairs, then through the kitchen to the connecting room nearest the garage. They doubled back and tried the little bathroom, then the unused room off the front hall that they had skipped. They saw nothing out of place.

"It must be John, working on that window," Ben said, sounding disappointed. "Why don't I check the basement, just to be sure."

He found the door, tried to grab the knob, swore, then slipped through the wood. He descended the stairs. The big open space was dark and damp, bare except for sump pumps in two corners, a water tank and a furnace up on a slab. The walls were bumpy cement over stone. The only light was from the short windows along the back wall and the two larger windows at the far end. Ben went towards them.

"Yep, just what I thought," he said. "That's what we heard."

The big window on the right, the one that should have been held in place by John Donahue's nails, was gone. Instead of wood and glass there was a hole, a bright rectangle of hazy sky.

Ben moved into the spilling sunlight. "Hey, John. You want to keep it down? You freaked Claire and Melody out when you pulled the window."

He edged closer to the opening. Now he could see a strip of green grass, then the sunlit yard, falling away.

"God, what a beautiful day. Wish I could be out there."

He stared at the bright world through the frame. After a long silence, he raised one hand and then, almost as if he didn't know he was doing it, like someone in a trance, he reached forward. His hand inched closer to the sunlight. He cocked his head one way, then the other. "John? You there?"

He took a half step. His fingers moved into the warm, clear air that seeped through the opening. He turned his hand, as if trying to feel something. He took one more half step.

There was a roar like a sudden gust of wind, and he vanished.

***

He bounced hard against the floor in the front hall, sliding backwards, feet spread. He hit the bottom stair with a thud. "Ow. I'm never going to get used to that." He stood, rubbing his back. "I wasn't even trying to get out that time. Not really."

Claire's voice came from the rear of the house. Ben started toward it. "Claire? The prisoner returns. Not that you missed me."

Claire was in the kitchen, leaning against the counter, talking on the cell phone, her face bright and relaxed.

107

"Okay," Ben said. "Looks like you figured it out while I was gone. John made the noise."

"How are things at the Bay Market?" Claire said.

"AJ!" Ben shouted.

"Under control, finally," AJ said. "Do you want to get some painting done? I'm free."

"Is he coming over?" Ben said.

"Actually," Claire said, "I was just going to ask Melody if she wanted to get something to eat."

Coming in from the porch, Melody shook her head, mouthing, "Work."

"Oh, Melody says she has to work."

"Why don't you come over to the market?" AJ said. "We'll roll out the red carpet for you. Maybe you'll even get a tablecloth."

"That sounds nice."

"You know how to get here?"

"I think so. It's on Route 1, right?"

"The market?" Melody said. "I can give you directions."

"Melody's going to help me," Claire said. "See you in an hour or so?"

"Okay. Bye."

Claire hung up.

"You're bringing AJ back here after dinner, aren't you?" Ben said.

Melody was all smiles. "First date."

"Does dinner at the Bay Market count as a date?" Claire said.

"You can tell me afterwards if it counts."

After Melody was gone, Claire went upstairs to change.

Ben took up his favorite position in the hallway, staring at the smooth wall. "Shit," he said, after a moment. He kept staring at the wall. When Claire reappeared, Ben said, without looking at her, "I think I figured something out. If you can see my ghost girl, then I could have seen her, too—before—you know, when I was alive... I bet that's why I fell. It wasn't just the tricky shape of the treads. It was her. I saw her, was surprised, jumped back and lost my footing. The rest is history."

He pressed forward until his face slipped into the plaster, then pulled back. "I don't blame you, miss. I'm sure you didn't mean it. Right? You weren't trying to kill me."

CHAPTER 22

When her shift was over, Melody left the Dairy and headed up the sidewalk toward the drawbridge. She was holding an ice cream cone. Though the sun was setting, the air was warm, and the ice cream softened quickly, making the second scoop lean to one side. Melody worked to keep ahead of it.

Just before the bridge, she turned right onto a wooden walkway that ran along the river. An old sailboat was moored there. A few shoppers with bags on string handles ambled past it. Further down, coming toward her, a woman walked a small dog, which zigzagged, sniffing every piling and pedestrian.

On the other side of the river was a park lined with benches. On this side there was just one bench, backed up against the wall of a building. A man sat there, looking out at the water. He was well dressed, in a silk shirt, crisp pants and soft leather shoes. He was handsome, with graying hair. He was alone.

Melody took it all in, moving slowly, licking her ice cream. As she neared the bench, so did the woman with the dog. Pulling on the lead, the animal faked right, then went left. Melody swerved to avoid a collision and lost her balance for an instant. Her cone tipped. The top scoop fell. It landed with a sound that was as soft and wet as a kiss.

"Oh my God, I'm so sorry," Melody said.

Jacques Westbury looked up from the glob of ice cream on his shoe. He laughed. "I wish you could see the expression on your face right now."

"Please, here, use my napkin."

"You need that napkin yourself. My shoe is fine."

Melody touched the brown blotch on her shirt. "Damn." She dropped the nearly empty cone into the trash can beside the bench.

"What flavor was that—coffee?" Jacques tapped his toe against the decking.

"Espresso chip. It will stain." Melody had left off dabbing at her shirt and pointed across the river. "There's a little shoe repair place—just over there. We could see if it's open. Maybe they could do something for your shoe."

"I'm sure old Dom closed up shop hours ago. Don't worry about my shoe. It will be fine." He held out his hand. "I'm Jack."

She took it. "Melody."

"That's a nice name. Very...musical." He smiled. "Would you like to try again?"

"Excuse me?"

"That ice cream looked good. Would you like to try another one? My treat."

"Okay. But only if you let me treat you. It's the least I can do."

"Fair enough."

They went back to the Dairy and emerged a short time later with fresh cones.

"They knew you," he said. "You must be a regular."

"I work there."

"No kidding? You're a waitress?"

"You sound surprised."

"I guess I am."

"Good."

"Do you feel like a little stroll? If we walk down Holmes Street there will be fewer tourists to dodge."

"Sure."

They had already started toward the bridge.

"So let me try to guess how you ended up a waitress at the Honey B Dairy," Jacques said after a while. "You came here for something short-term and decided to stay."

"That's right. I—"

"No—I want to get this." He was quiet, then, as if taking the guessing game seriously.

They reached the bridge. Cars hummed across the steel grates. The counterweights hung overhead like enormous, poised hammers.

"You took an internship at the Seaport," Jacques said. "You were supposed to go back to school in the fall but you fell in love with a lobsterman."

"Uh huh. Now while he's out pulling pots I eat ice cream with handsome strangers."

"I'd feel sorry for the guy, but he asked for it when he got involved with a summer girl."

"Spoken like a true local," she said.

110

"So, how'd I do?"

"Well, I do like the Seaport, so I might give you one point. But that's about it."

"Oh. Not so good."

At the intersection on the far side, they turned left, heading upriver.

"So, I guess you'll just have to tell me," he said. "How did you come to our lovely seaside town?"

"My boyfriend took a teaching position at Conn College, and I came with him. While he taught, I worked on a master's in history."

"Seems like a good arrangement."

"Yeah. Except that somewhere in there I realized I'd fallen in love with the area and out of love with him. He left and I stayed."

"So you're on your own now?"

"Yes. I've been solo for about two years." Melody rotated her cone, making a groove with her tongue. "You look surprised."

"Yes. Again. You're just one surprise after another."

They passed a collection of shops, some of them closing for the night.

"Did you finish that degree?" Jacques said.

"No. I may get back to it. I don't know."

"You're still young. You have lots of time."

"Yeah," Melody said. "So what's your story, Jack? You talk like a local but I've never seen you before."

"Well, I was a local. A bona fide native. But I've been away until very recently."

"What brought you back? Is it business? Or did you get homesick?"

"Both. I came back to sell some property. I could have let the lawyers handle it, but I felt a need to see the place one more time. Closure, I guess. I had planned to leave right after the business was done, but… I really do love it here."

He stopped at a stone wall. The river opened up there, wide and peaceful and silver-blue. On the opposite shore, the homes of ship's captains rose, tall and white, topped by widow's walks. On the near side, the seaport museum shipyard, a giant barn-like building, glowed red in the fading sun. All along the shore were the masts of the seaport's vessels— smacks, sloops, schooners and full-rigged ships, and the largest of them, the whaler, the Charles W. Morgan.

"I'll never get tired of this view," Melody said. She worked on her ice cream for a while. "Was your property here in Mystic?"

"No, it was a house in the country."

"So you decided to stay after you sold your house? That's a shame."

"It's fine. My memories there—they weren't all good. And there's nothing that sucks up time and money like a big old house. A young woman from the city bought it. I hope she can handle it."

"A woman from the city?" Melody's eyes narrowed. "Not Claire Connor."

"Yes. Do you know her?"

Melody had stopped eating. Her thumb punched through the cone. "You're Jacques Westbury."

"Yes. My friends call me Jack, but yes. How do you know me?"

"I know Claire. I've heard of you."

"Oh." Jacques took another bite of his ice cream. "Small world."

"Yeah. Small town, anyway." Melody stared at him, her head tilted.

"So tell me what you've heard," Jacques said.

"I've heard quite a story."

"I doubt if any of it will surprise me."

"Why don't you tell me your version," Melody said.

"Okay. But we'd better find another bench. My story will take a little longer to tell than yours did."

CHAPTER 23

AJ lay in his bed, his eyes closed, his chest rising and falling with the practiced rhythm of someone used to being awake when he wanted to be asleep. Sunlight flooded the room. The blanket was on the floor and the twisted sheet covered him only as far as his calves. Buck stood with his snout resting on the mattress, silent, his tail wagging.

"Okay," AJ said, and abruptly sat up.

He stumbled into the living room. After opening the door for the dog, he had a bowl of cereal at the kitchen table, looking out at the water. He let Buck in again, then stretched out on the sofa. With the yellow glow of morning light on the front wall, and Buck on the rug beside him, he fell sound asleep.

Two minutes later, a ringing sound came from the back of the house. AJ reached around blindly, digging between cushions. Finally waking up, he got to his feet and hurried toward the kitchen.

"Hello?" he said, leaning on the counter, where the phone was plugged into the charger.

"AJ? Did I wake you?"

"Chief. No. Maybe. I might have dozed off."

"Sorry. Sorry to bother you. I didn't think it was that early."

"It's all right. I was up." With the phone still at his ear, AJ disconnected the cord. He went to the table and sat down. "What's going on?"

"I have a favor to ask. I wonder if you could round up your friends Sela and DaSilva and come over here."

"Why?"

"I still have Ben's equipment. His parents want nothing to do with it. I'd like to turn it over to them."

"Okay, I'll ask Sela to stop by."

"I'd like it if they both came. And you, too. I need all three of you."

"Yeah? What's up?"

"I'll explain it when you get here."

AJ raked his hair with his fingers, his lips pressed shut.

"See you in an hour or so?" the chief said. "To make up for waking you, I'll be sure there's fresh coffee waiting."

"Chief—"

The phone was dead. AJ sat for a while staring out the window. Then he punched Sela's number.

***

AJ arrived just ahead of the others and led them into the station. They crowded into the chief's office. As promised, there were three cups of coffee on his desk in a cardboard carrier. The two chairs were lined up in front of the desk, facing the combo TV-VCR.

"I picked up some cinnamon rolls, too," the chief said, opening a box. "They're from right down the road. Pretty good, I think."

DaSilva dug into a pastry.

"Is this about the video?" Sela said. His face was dark with two days' worth of stubble. "Because I'm not watching Ben fall down the stairs. No way."

The chief shook his head. "I wouldn't ask that. It is about the video, though. I have a copy on tape, so we can watch it right here. I wanted an expert opinion. For my own satisfaction."

The chief pointed to the chairs, and Sela and DaSilva took them. AJ remained standing, his arms crossed.

"Here," the chief said, reaching across the desk to hand AJ a cup of coffee. "You look like you could use this."

AJ took it without comment.

"Now. I wanted to watch something with you." The chief pressed a button on the remote control. "It's from last Friday night, at the Westbury house. I mean, the Connor house. I'm never going to get used to saying that."

"Chief—" AJ said.

"It's the footage that Sela took." The chief glanced at Sela, who nodded.

DaSilva slid his chair closer to the television, the legs screeching against the floor. "Sorry."

A square, empty room appeared on the screen, in near darkness. The camera panned along one wall, then another.

"Okay," the chief said. "Look close."

The camera had moved on to the last wall. It held steady there. The sound of Sela's gasp came through the speaker.

"Here," the chief said, pressing the *Pause* button on the remote.

In the center of the screen was a faint shape, a wavy disturbance in the air.

"What is that?" the chief said.

DaSilva kept his eyes on the screen. "Can you let it play?"

The chief used the remote again.

The shape hovered, slid away toward the wall, then disappeared.

"Holy shit." DaSilva turned to Sela. "Nice work."

"Yeah?" the chief said. "What are we looking at?"

"Well, it's mobile," DaSilva said. "Seems human in size. Passes through a wall. I'd say that's paranormal."

"Paranormal. You mean it's a ghost?" The chief was reversing the movie, in slow-motion. "It's not something on the lens, or some kind of mist or something?" He looked hard at AJ, who ignored him.

"Can you play it again?" DaSilva said.

They watched the clip a second time, then a third.

"Oh yeah," DaSilva said. "There's definitely something there. We'll have to really analyze it, on our equipment. But this might be one of the best things we've gotten on video. I can't believe Ben's not here to see it."

Sela's gaze was fixed on the TV. He didn't say anything.

"What do you think, AJ?" the chief said. "These guys are the experts."

AJ leaned back against the wall. "I don't know."

"Uh huh." The chief seemed to be waiting for AJ to change his mind. Finally, he said, "Well, I appreciate you guys helping me out. I really do. I've got your equipment for you. I'm sorry I've had it so long. You could have come in sooner to pick it up. I guess I didn't make that clear."

Sela and DaSilva stood. The chief instructed them to stop at the window for the gear. He shook both of their hands. "AJ, I need you to stick around for a second," he said.

"What's up?" AJ said, when the others were gone.

"You still don't want to admit to what you see there, on that tape—or film, or movie, or whatever the damn thing is."

"Is that why you asked me to stay?"

"No." The chief went back behind his desk. "This is from the state lab." He picked up a fax.

"What's it say?"

"'Preliminary results only. Superficial examination of the tooth suggests an adolescent female. Wear pattern indicates orthodontics.'"

"Did Anna Marie wear braces?"

"She did. I checked the file. They came off a few months before she died."

"What about DNA?"

"Not yet. Like I said, this is just the preliminary stuff."

"That'll take God knows how long."

"Well, I'm hoping I can bump it up in the queue a bit."

"You think it's hers. Anna Marie Rose."

Before the chief could answer, a uniformed officer was in the doorway. "Sorry to interrupt, Chief."

"What is it?"

"Something from North Stonington P.D."

The officer passed the chief a single sheet of paper.

Reading, the chief ran his hand across his scalp. "Teenage girl, missing since yesterday." He spun the paper on his desk. "They want us to check the reservoir. I guess she and her boyfriend hang around there a lot."

"You want me to go?"

The chief kept stroking his smooth head with his fingers. "First thing I'm going to do is make a call. I want to talk to Chet over at North Stonington."

"Okay." AJ stood. "Just let me know."

"So you're ready to come back? It hasn't even been a week."

AJ shrugged. "I'm as ready as I'm going to get. What do we do next? About the tooth, I mean."

In response, the chief opened a desk drawer and brought out a manila folder. There was only one thing inside—an 8x10 photograph. It was a generic school portrait, like those taken every year, at every school, of every child. The head tipped slightly, the textured blue background. A pretty teenage girl.

"Look at how confident her smile is," the chief said. "She's not trying to hide those braces." He didn't turn the photograph for AJ to see. He kept staring at it. "And those eyes. They look right through you."

He closed the folder over the photograph, then covered the folder with his hands.

AJ waited.

"What do we do about the tooth?" the chief said. "Until we get the DNA results, we do the only thing we can do. What we've been doing for twenty years. We wait."

CHAPTER 24

Sela and DaSilva sat on a couch in a crowded living room, staring at the flat screen TV mounted on the far wall. They were both wearing headphones.

"Man, you weren't kidding when you said you got something. No audio, but the video is great." DaSilva pressed a key on the laptop computer in front of him and paused the video. "Look. You can almost see an outline."

"Yeah. Right here." Sela's finger traced a shape in the air. He slipped his headphones off and dropped them on the table. "I've got to talk to Melody about this."

"What? Why Melody?"

"If I say anything to Claire, AJ will be pissed. I'll talk to Melody. Let her tell Claire."

"Melody probably won't believe you."

"I have to try. They should be prepared."

"You're right. Claire, anyway. If she runs into this herself, without warning, she'll freak."

Sela stood up.

"I'm going to go through this a few more times," DaSilva said. "Just tell Melody they should call us if they see anything."

"I will." Sela went past the picture window to the front door. Stopping on the little square of shiny flagstone, he turned around. "Hey, don't back it up too far. You don't want to see the first part of this video."

DaSilva held the headphones away from his ears. "Yeah, I know. Ben... I'll be careful."

Sela stepped outside. Ignoring the sidewalk that led to the driveway, he cut across the lawn, jumping the abbreviated split-rail fence to get to his car, which was parked on the gravely edge of the grass. He drove into downtown Mystic, crossing the bridge in bright sunshine. Leaving the car in the parking lot behind the shops, he took the alleyway between buildings, then headed up the sidewalk to the Dairy. As he reached for the door, he saw Melody through the window, delivering a plate of eggs and hash browns to the front table.

"Hey," she said, when he was inside. "There's a sight for sore eyes." She gave him a big smile. Her dark hair was up, hair sticks making a V behind her head. "You want some breakfast? Coffee?"

"I can't stay, actually. I just came to talk for a minute."

"All right. C'mon back to the kitchen."

They went through the swinging doors.

"What's up?" she asked, stopping beside a rack of tall glasses.

"You've been out at the Westbury place with Claire?"

"Sure. Not as much as AJ has, but some. Why?"

"Has Claire mentioned anything about the house? Has she seen anything unusual, or acted uneasy, or——"

"By *anything,* I take it you mean a ghost."

"Yeah." He squeezed the bill of his baseball cap.

"Oh, come on, Dave. I understand that you guys want to keep *Mystic Afterlife* going. Ben would want that, too. But you need to find another location. It's just not fair to Claire."

"You don't understand. The night Ben died, I took some video. I just watched it this morning for the first time. I got something, Melody. It's pretty distinct."

Melody groaned.

"This is real," Sela said. "There's some kind of paranormal activity in that house."

Melody's smile, which had hung on at the corners of her eyes, vanished. She just shook her head.

"I'm serious, Melody. Has she mentioned strange noises, or things moving around, or losing something? Upstairs, most likely."

"No," Melody said, her hand going immediately to her mouth.

"Are you sure?"

Melody let her hand fall. "Look, ever since she moved into that place, you've been pushing these stories on her. How is that helping her? How can she not start seeing things? You know what would help her? Just leave her alone."

"Listen. Whether we talk to her about it or not, she'll probably experience something. The way I see it, we have two choices. We can talk to her now, so that when she does have that first experience, she's ready for it and can handle it. Or we can talk to her after she has that experience, when she calls us in a panic."

"I have to go back to work," Melody said.

"Okay. If anything does happen, if she has any unusual experiences, or problems, will you call me? I really just want to help."

"Sure." Melody went toward the door.

"I wasn't the only one who watched the video," Sela said. "AJ and DaSilva and the police chief all watched it, too."

Melody stopped. "And they all think they saw something?"

"Yeah. Even AJ, though he wouldn't admit it."

Melody looked across the kitchen to where a stocky man in white tended to a griddle. "You know, when I moved here, I thought this was a quiet little town full of regular New Englanders. Salt-of-the-earth types. But I was wrong. It turns out you're all nuts."

CHAPTER 25

"I want to show you the new paint in the upstairs hall," Claire said, as she closed the front door.

"I'd like to see it." Though Melody was closer to the stairs, she hesitated, her hands clasped in front of her.

"I'll follow you," Claire said.

"Okay." Melody started up, moving deliberately, her hand on the banister as they went around the turn. When she reached the last step, she stayed there. She leaned into the hall. "This is great." She looked back and forth. "It's so much brighter."

"Thanks." Claire craned her neck to see past Melody. "Doesn't the color change the whole feel of things?"

"It does," Melody said. She stayed planted on the top step, blocking Claire's way.

"I'm just glad that you're done," Ben said, coming out of the first bedroom. "I don't want you scaring off my new friend."

"Have you seen any more of that shimmer?" Melody said.

From behind, Claire touched Melody's shoulder. "No, nothing. I really think I had sunscreen in my eyes."

"Yeah, I'm sure you're right." Melody finally moved up.

Once in the hall, Claire began folding a drop cloth. "We were at it until two a.m."

"Really? I guess it took a long time because of all the doors."

"All the doors and all the talking," Ben said.

"We got a late start."

"Ah. So did your dinner at the Bay Market count as a first date?"

"It kind of did feel like a date, yeah."

"Okay! How did it go?"

"I had a really good time." Claire gave the plastic one more fold, a faint

120

smile on her lips. "I met his parents, which doesn't usually happen on a first date."

"Aren't they nice? They're probably thrilled to see him socializing. He's been kind of withdrawn since he came back from Bridgeport."

"You got that right," Ben said. "He used to be a lot of fun."

"Does he ever talk about what happened there?"

"Not to me," Melody said. "Maybe Ben knew."

"Are you kidding?" Ben said. "He never told me anything. Even now that I am one, he still doesn't want to talk to me about ghosts."

"Are you going to see him today?" Melody said.

"He's coming over later. He has to help his parents at the market first." Claire tossed the drop cloth into a room.

"So, your first date. That's big news." Melody started down the stairs. "I have some news, too."

"Yeah? What is it?"

"I want you to keep an open mind," Melody said.

"Okay. Why?"

"Promise?"

"Melody."

She was quiet until they reached the front hall. Ben stayed behind, on the stairs.

"Last night after work I was trying to walk and eat ice cream at the same time—never a good idea for me—and I managed to dump my cone right onto this guy's shoe. I was so embarrassed. I mean, the shoes probably cost more than my car. But he was really nice about it. He even offered to buy me a new cone. We went back to the Dairy, got some ice cream, and then ended up talking for a couple of hours."

"You couldn't have planned that better." Claire stood with her hand on the banister.

"It does sound like a scam, doesn't it? I mean, I did notice him sitting there. But I swear, the ice cream was a complete accident."

"Hey, I believe you."

Melody made a face.

"So are you going to see him again?"

"He's supposed to call me tonight about dinner."

"Very good. I have to ask—is he, you know, distinguished and successful?"

"Yes and yes. But you really mean, is he older?" Melody let her smile grow. "He's the perfect age."

"Geezer," Ben said.

"So tell me about this guy. Where's he from? What's he do?"

"Right now, he's just planning to be here for the summer. But he said he might decide to stay longer."

"Must be nice to have that flexibility."

"You're not exactly punching a time clock yourself."

"True. My little vacation is about up, though. I'm going to have to start writing again soon. So what does this guy do?"

"There are some family businesses he's involved in."

"Involved in, meaning, he's the owner."

"Board member, I think."

"Very nice. So he's, like, *independently* distinguished and successful."

Melody acknowledged this with a quick smile.

"Freeloader," Ben said.

"And is there the baggage that we talked about?"

"No."

"No?" Claire said. "Like, nothing?"

"Not even a carry-on. He's never been married. He has no children. He's not in a relationship."

"Geez. That's good, I guess."

"You guess? How could it not be good?"

"Well, you have to wonder how someone gets to be his age... I mean, why hasn't he ever been married?"

"He's never met the right person."

"He said that?"

"Yes."

"Well, okay," Claire said. "So, does he have a name?"

"You promised to keep an open mind."

"About his name? What, is it Santa Claus or something?"

Melody crossed her arms. "It's Jacques Westbury."

"No way," Ben said. He faded backward, disappearing in stages as the risers claimed his legs, his waist, his chest and then the stunned expression on his face.

"Oh, Melody," Claire said. "I don't know."

"Open mind, remember? We had a long conversation. I told him what I'd heard and he told me his side of the story. He says he had nothing to do with what happened to that girl. He knew her. He was teaching her to sail. And maybe she had a little thing for him. But there was nothing funny going on."

"And you believe him?"

Melody bit her lip. "Yeah. I think I do."

Ben pushed into the open. "Don't fall for that shit, Melody! He's lying."

"You've talked to him, Claire," Melody said. "Does he seem like a bad person to you?"

"I've only seen him a couple of times," Claire said. "We barely spoke at the closing. The other day, when he was here, it was—I don't know, awkward. Weird."

"What do you mean? Why was it weird?"

"Because he's a pedophile and a killer," Ben said.

"I'm not sure. He got the chair from the garage. Then he wouldn't leave. He went behind the garage to look at some lobster pots that were left back there. He had to show me where to plant the violets. He started looking for his mother's daffodils. We found the broken window, and he told me all about how he used to climb out of it as a kid. It was just…weird. He obviously wanted to hang around. I couldn't tell if he wanted to hang around the house or me."

"Creep," Ben said.

"He's friendly," Melody said. "Did you think of that? It's only weird if you believe those stories about him."

"He asked me out to dinner. He said he knew a lobster place."

Melody walked away toward the living room.

"I just don't want you to get hurt," Claire said, following.

Melody went around the end table, stopping on the other side of it, as if to put it between her and Claire. It held a loose bouquet of wild flowers and flowering weeds, in a vase.

"Are you thinking hurt emotionally or hurt physically?" Melody said.

"In any way. Please think about this."

"She's right, Melody," Ben said, having joined them. He grasped unsuccessfully at a flower.

"My instincts about people have always been good," Melody said. "I don't think I'm wrong about him."

"But what if you are?" Claire raised her hands as if in defeat. "Okay, okay. Just take it slow. Don't go anywhere, you know, secluded, with him."

Melody rolled her eyes. "I can look out for myself. You know they never even charged him with anything, Claire? There's no evidence. What we've been hearing from the guys it's—it's like one of their ghost stories. A local legend."

"So if he calls you—"

"If he calls me and asks me out, I'll probably go."

"Damn it, Melody!" Ben clenched his teeth, his right hand making a fist. He took an angry swing at the vase. And he made contact. His shining, pink fingers didn't slice harmlessly through the rounded glass— they caught, held, and sent the whole thing crashing to the floor.

"What the hell?" Claire said. "What just happened?"

Melody was staring at the broken vase, dumbstruck.

"Holy shit," Ben said.

"It's okay," Claire said. "It was a cheap vase."

Melody was still staring at the mess. "I didn't do it. The vase just moved. You didn't see?"

"No, I didn't. One second." Claire dashed toward the kitchen. "I have to mop up the water before it stains the floor."

"Sorry," Ben said, turning his hand in front of him as if it had just then appeared at the end of his arm. "That was a total accident. I didn't think I could do that."

"Never mind the floor." Melody was moving around the table, giving it a wide berth. "Let's go outside."

"Melody, it's okay," Ben said. "It's just me. Shit. I'm really sorry."

"Outside?" Claire shouted, from the next room. "Why? I have to clean up the mess."

"C'mon, Claire." Melody stayed by the front door. When Claire returned with a towel and a plastic wastebasket, Melody grabbed her arm. "Let's go."

"One second." Claire scooped up the scattered stems and broken glass and dumped them in the wastebasket. After dropping the towel on the wet floor, she stepped on it, then picked it up. "All right."

"Don't go outside," Ben said. "Or at least leave the door open, so I can hear."

But they closed the front door behind them. Melody didn't stop until she was standing in the weeds a few feet from the house.

"What's going on?" Claire said. "You seem freaked out."

"I wasn't going to say anything, because I thought it was just the usual... But now..."

"What are you talking about? You weren't going to say anything about what?"

"Dave—Sela—came to see me this morning. The night Ben died, when all of them were here, I guess he wandered around with Ben's video camera."

"Ben was dead and he was filming?"

"He didn't know Ben was dead. It was—I'm not sure about all that. Anyway, he took some video upstairs. He just watched it for the first time this morning. He says he saw something on the video. A ghost."

Claire looked back toward the house. For a long time, she seemed to be studying the doors and windows. In a pane on the first floor, Ben's face glowed.

"Don't you think those guys just see what they want to see?" Claire said.

"I know. But he was very serious, very concerned, when he talked to me. Completely convinced that he had caught a ghost on film. He said the other guys saw it, too—DaSilva, AJ, even the police chief. I mean, I blew him off, just like you. But now—"

"What do you mean, now? Now that a vase slipped off of the table? You must have bumped it. Or I did."

"No one bumped the table. The vase didn't slip off. That's what I'm trying to tell you. I was looking right at it. It moved. It slid. That's why it fell."

"Maybe the table's slanted. It's an old house. I'm sure the floors—"

"Claire! Jesus Christ. It wasn't a slanted floor. The vase was sitting there, solid, and then it moved. Fast. Like it was being pushed."

Claire shook her head slowly.

"Dave wanted to know if you had seen anything strange," Melody said. "He said if you haven't, you probably will. I told him you hadn't seen anything. But really, there was something."

Claire just looked at her.

"That thing, that shimmer you saw in the hallway."

"Melody. It was... There was something in my eyes."

"Yeah? And the flower on my pillow?"

"We'd had an awful lot to drink. We probably just didn't remember putting the flower there."

"That's what we told ourselves. But I don't know anymore. In fact, I'm really pretty sure the flower was in the glass when I went to sleep."

Claire remained quiet, watching Melody's face.

"When Dave caught it on film," Melody said, "the ghost was upstairs."

"Upstairs in the hall?"

"Yeah. Where you saw that shimmer."

"Crap." Claire let her hand drop. "You think I did see something?"

This time they both turned and looked toward the windows. Ben's mournful face stared back.

"Dave said to call him if you had any problems," Melody said. "If anything strange happened. I think this definitely qualifies."

"I don't know, Melody. Is this just crazy?"

"Maybe if he comes over, talks to us, goes around with his cameras and stuff... Maybe he can explain everything. On the show, sometimes they find a rational explanation for things that seemed supernatural."

"Do they?" Claire held the towel up as if just remembering it. A green, wilting stem clung to it, and a shiver of glass, which flashed in the sun. "Okay," she said. "Okay. Let's call him."

CHAPTER 26

Claire and Melody waited by the garage as Sela parked his car.

"I got here as fast as I could," he said, through the open window. "DaSilva and Dewey should be right behind me."

"Are you okay with that, Claire?" Melody said, in a soft voice. "With the other guys being here?"

Claire hesitated. "I guess I was hoping to keep this quiet."

"I'm sorry, I should have talked to you first," Sela said. "If you don't want the whole team… But they'll keep it private. You can count on that."

There was an engine sound, then a sedan appeared from behind the lichen-spattered trees. When it stopped, Sela went immediately to the driver's side.

After a few minutes, Dewey stood up from the car. He forced a smile. "When I offered to help you, the other day, I wasn't expecting this."

"That makes two of us," Claire said.

"Hi, Claire. Hi, Melody." DaSilva came around from the other side of the car. He wore a black T-shirt with the stenciled letters *M.A.* over a winged skull.

"Hi." Claire eyed the shirt for a moment. "Okay, so what happens now?"

"Why don't you show us where the vase fell," Sela said. He did his high-stepping, tick-avoiding walk through the weeds as he followed Claire to the front door.

"Sorry," Claire said, catching the tail end of the performance. "I have to get someone out here to mow."

"Don't mind him," DaSilva said.

As Claire opened the door, Ben swooped into the hall. "Guys! Holy shit! I've been trying to get you out here. AJ has been such a jerk about it." He dodged out of the way as the group continued on to the living room.

126

"So, how cool is this? You're investigating this house, and you're looking for me."

"It was right here," Claire said. "I guess that's kind of obvious." She stared at the wastebasket full of flowers and broken glass.

"We were just standing here talking," Melody said, "and the vase slid off this table. Claire didn't see it happen, but I did. The thing moved like it was being pushed."

DaSilva crouched down to examine the rubble in the wastebasket. "Sounds like a hostile gesture. We might be talking demonic."

"Shut up, DaSilva," Ben said.

Sela shook his head. "You know what Ben would say about that."

DaSilva nodded. "Shut up, DaSilva."

"Exactly."

"Ben wasn't into the whole demon aspect of the paranormal," Melody said.

"And he definitely wasn't into scaring the client," Sela said. "Have you had any other experiences?"

"Tell him what happened upstairs," Melody said.

Claire described seeing the shimmer in the hallway.

"So Melody, you saw it, too?" Sela said.

"No," she said. "But there was something else that I did see." She told them about finding a flower on her pillow.

"You had to know that was me," Ben said. "Right?"

"So maybe we're dealing with a poltergeist," DaSilva said. "It's manipulating physical objects."

"Poltergeist?" Ben said. "That's way too Hollywood for me. The thing with the flower was kind of dramatic, though, wasn't it? I hope you appreciate how hard that was. It took me all night."

Sela turned around in place, inspecting the room as if he were a potential buyer. "Anything else?" he said. "Have you heard any strange noises, or had things go missing?"

"Or maybe experienced odd sensations?" DaSilva said. "Like there was a presence in the house? Like you were being watched?"

"You make it sound so creepy," Ben said. "A *presence*."

"Well, I was uncomfortable being here at first," Claire said. "But that was just getting used to living out here in the country. None of my stuff has been moved around. And noises? There are the usual creaks and groans of an old house. Yesterday, Melody and I did hear a bang, like something fell. We looked around but couldn't find anything."

"You checked the whole house?" Dewey said.

"Well, on this floor," Claire said. "It sounded like it came from down here."

"Jesus," Ben said. "It was just John, working on the window."

DaSilva was squatting again, aiming the camera.

Ben leaned in close. "Nice. Is that new? How many megapixels is it?"

"Damn," DaSilva said. "The battery on this thing is half gone. I just charged it."

"Let me see." Sela took the camera for a second, then passed it back to DaSilva. "Claire, have you had any problems with batteries? Like on your cell phone, or flashlights?"

"Yeah, I have, actually. My phone has been bad for a while, but lately I can't get it to hold a charge at all. Why?"

DaSilva stopped fiddling with the camera. "Ghosts draw whatever energy they can from their surroundings to manifest themselves. They can drain batteries—though it's usually not that quick."

"Hey, sorry," Ben said. "If I'm doing it, it's a total accident." He backed up. "Maybe it's not me draining the batteries. I'm not exactly manifesting myself. My friend, though—she has been showing off. That's got to take a lot of energy."

Sela pulled a phone from his pocket. "I'm down to two bars. I think, if it's okay with you, Claire, we should go ahead and get started. While we still have battery power. Let's hit it with everything—EVP, EMF, video."

"I have my KII meter," Dewey said. "I'd really like to try it."

"Dewey," Ben said, "stick to the historical stuff. You know I don't believe in those things. It's way too easy to get a false reading. I guess now that I'm gone, you think you can get away with it. Sela, tell him."

The three men went out. Claire and Melody stayed behind in the living room, their backs to the window.

"They seem to know what they're doing," Claire said.

"They do."

"That's weird about the batteries."

"Yeah, it is."

Claire picked up a stray shard of glass. She dropped it in the wastebasket. "They really believe in this stuff."

"They really do."

"Just wait," Ben said. "I bet you will, too."

Sela returned, carrying a duffel bag that had been printed, like DaSilva's T-shirt, with the letters *M A*.

As Dewey came in behind him, he was talking on the cell phone. "Okay. All right. All right." He ended the call. "Bad timing."

"What's wrong?" DaSilva said, following him in.

"A girl from North Stonington has gone missing. The cops got a tip that she's up at Pachaug. They're rounding up all the guys from the fire department for a search party."

"There's not a lot of daylight left," Sela said.

"I guess they have an idea of where she is. With enough guys out there beating the bushes, they figure we can find her before sundown."

"How old is she?" Claire said. "The missing girl?"

"I'm not sure. Fifteen, sixteen."

"I hope she's okay," Melody said. "I've heard there have been some shady characters up there."

"Really?" Claire said. "Pachaug State Forest? That's one of the places my realtor told me I should check out."

"Oh, it's beautiful," Sela said. "But we get people growing pot up there. Some of them are serious types. You wouldn't want to mess with them. We just have to hope that she didn't."

"I better get going." Dewey left his bag in the hallway. "There's a camera and the KII meter in here. Maybe I can come back after the search wraps up."

"Why don't you give me a call first?" Sela said. "See if we're still here."

"Good luck," DaSilva said.

"Thanks." Dewey paused in the doorway. "I hope we both find something."

After Dewey left, Sela and DaSilva looked sideways at each other.

"This is when Ben would start barking out orders," DaSilva said.

"C'mon, guys," Ben said. "Obviously you want to start in the living room, where the most recent activity has been."

Sela carried the bigger bag into the center of the room. "Well, this is where things seem to be happening."

"Attaboy," Ben said.

"You don't have to wait until it gets dark?" Claire said. "On the show, it seemed like it was always nighttime when you investigated."

"You've seen the show?" DaSilva beamed at her.

Sela unzipped the bag. "Ben always said that ghost stories are better at night. But you can investigate anytime."

"I trained you well," Ben said.

DaSilva opened Dewey's bag and produced a sleek video camera.

"Dave," Sela said, "why don't you point that toward the table? Claire, do you have another vase or something we can borrow?"

"You want to recreate the scenario," DaSilva said. "Good idea."

Ben took up a position behind Sela, against the wall. "You don't need it, but I like it."

"I have a big pitcher," Claire said. "Would that work?"

"That will be fine," Sela said.

"Is there anything I can do?" Melody said.

"Sure," Sela said. "You can take some temperature readings." He pulled a pistol-style thermal scanner from the bag, then attached a metal wand to the grip. "Just point this ahead of you as you move around the room. Squeeze this trigger to get a reading here. What you're looking for is cold spots."

"And what do I do if I find a cold spot?"

"Just let us know."

"Don't worry, I'll stay out of your way," Ben said. "I've scared you enough."

Melody took the scanner. "If only Ben could see me now."

"Yeah, if only," Ben said.

Claire came in with the pitcher. "What if Ben *can* see you?"

Everyone stopped what they were doing.

"I knew I liked you," Ben said.

DaSilva and Sela looked at each other. "Nah," DaSilva said.

"It couldn't be Ben," Sela said.

"Why not?" Claire put the pitcher on the table. "I mean, if it is a ghost, why couldn't it be his ghost? He did die here."

"Ben wouldn't stick around," DaSilva said. "With all the time he spent studying the afterlife, he'd be ready for it. Ready to move on. And he doesn't have any attachment to this place. A ghost that haunts this house would have some reason to be here, some connection."

"Right," Sela said. "Besides, there have been stories about activity in this place forever, way before Ben—"

"I don't think there'd be room here for him, even if he wanted to stay." DaSilva had gone back to extending the legs of a tripod.

"Room?" Claire said. "What do you mean?"

"Ghosts can be territorial."

"Hey, we're all friends here," Ben said. "I mean, I want to be friends."

Sela set a small rectangular device on the table.

"What is that?" Claire said. "An MP3 player?"

"It's a digital audio recorder. Sometimes it will pick up sounds, voices, that we weren't able to hear. We call them—"

"EVPs," Melody said. "Electronic voice phenomenon."

"That's right," Sela said, surprised.

"Hey, I was paying attention when Ben used to ramble on about this stuff."

"You just made my day," Ben said.

"Where do you want to put this?" DaSilva lifted something from Dewey's bag.

"That looks like a stud finder," Claire said.

"I wish it was," Ben said. "Because it would definitely find me. Ha ha."

"It's a KII meter," Sela said. "Similar idea to a stud finder. We may be able to use it to communicate with the spirit."

DaSilva placed the meter on the television stand.

"Guys and their gadgets," Melody said. "Why don't you just try talking to it?"

"I will," Sela said. "When you finish that side of the room, you can sit down. Everyone. Once things have been still for a moment, I'll try to make contact."

Claire, Melody and DaSilva took the sofa.

"Hello," Sela said, still standing by the table, facing the empty center of the room. "My name's Dave." He spoke slowly, as if to someone who barely knew the language. "We're not here to harm you. We'd just like to talk, or communicate in some way. If you speak, we may be able to hear you with this." He picked up the digital audio recorder. "You may be able to make the lights flash on that box near the television, and make yourself known to us."

"God, Sela," Ben said. "We're dead here, not stupid." He moved closer to the table. "Let's see if we can get an EVP first." He bent toward the recorder. "Testing one, two, three. This is Benjamin Shortman. Welcome to my afterlife."

"We had one flash!" DaSilva looked past Ben to the KII meter.

"Jesus Christ," Ben said. "I'm over here. I told you, those things are worthless."

"Can you light that again?" Sela said.

"Okay. If that's how you want to do it." Ben crossed the room, stopping a few feet from the meter. He waved his hand. No light. He closed the distance and waved again. Nothing. He continued right up to the device. The full arc of lights turned a bright green.

"Holy shit," Sela and DaSilva said, in unison.

"How about that," Ben said. "It does work."

Sela motioned to the others to be quiet. "Can you make the lights flash again?"

Ben had moved to the side. "I guess it doesn't matter if I stand right in front of the thing. It's not like I block your view." He slid back to his former position. The lights went on and stayed on.

DaSilva laughed. "Nice."

"Now is when you ask me a question, Sela," Ben said.

"We should ask it something," Sela said.

"Right." DaSilva's knees bounced up and down. "Can you make the lights flash two more times?"

"Jesus. That's your question?" Ben pulled back, then went forward, back, then forward. The lights responded.

Melody grabbed Claire's hand.

Sela stepped a little closer to the meter. "Did you knock the flowers off the table?"

"Now you're thinking." Ben made the lights flash once.

"Tell it to flash once for *Yes*, two for *No*," DaSilva said.

"I wish you would stop with the *it*," Ben said. "That hurts." He moved away from the device, then approached it, then moved away. The lights flashed once. "This is like a goddamn interpretive dance."

"Yes," DaSilva said.

"Did you break the vase because you're angry?" Sela said. "Or were you just trying to get our attention?"

"What the hell am I supposed to do with that, Sela?" Ben said.

"I guess I need to rephrase that as a *Yes* or *No* question."

"Ask it if it wants to be left alone," Melody said.

Sela shook his head. "That may not be a good idea."

"Are you kidding? You just got here." Ben had already flashed the lights twice.

"Are you answering *No* to that question?" Sela said.

Ben moved in, then away. The lights blinked once.

"Does that mean *Yes*, you were saying *No*?" DaSilva said. "Or *Yes*, you want to be left alone?"

"Oh, for Christ's sake." Carefully waving one hand, Ben made the lights blink a rhythm—*shave and a haircut, two bits.*

"Whoa," Melody said.

"Awesome!" DaSilva said. "Can you do that again?"

"Sure. And I can do this, too!" Ben did a crude soft shoe in front of the KII meter. The lights flashed enthusiastically.

"Ask it something else," DaSilva said, when the meter had gone dark.

Groaning with frustration, Ben bent down in front of the meter and opened his mouth, as if he were ready to swallow the thing whole. All of the lights blinked green.

"Okay," Sela said. "What do we want to find out?"

"Are you Ben Shortman?" Claire said.

"Wait, wait!" Ben backed away from the meter. "I want to answer that one!" The lights winked, then went out. He moved close and the lights turned on.

"What was that?" Sela said. "Was that two blinks?"

"It was one blink! Jesus Christ! It was a *Yes*!" Ben backed up again.

There was a knock at the front door.

"Please be AJ," Claire said, getting up.

When she opened the front door, he was there on the step. He had fresh flowers in one hand and Buck's collar in the other.

"Hi," Claire said, relief spreading across her face. "Am I glad to see you."

"What's going on?"

"Something happened. Come in, I'll explain."

Buck reached toward Claire with his sharp nose.

"I should leave Buck outside." AJ kept a tight grip on the dog's collar.

"AJ," Melody said, coming into the hall. "You brought flowers." To

Claire, she added, "Did you tell him?"

"Tell me what?"

"Just come in." Claire tugged on AJ's elbow, bringing him across the threshold.

Melody reached for the bouquet. "Let me take those. They're so nice. Lilies and wildflowers."

"Is that Sela's car outside?" His hand still on the dog's collar, AJ edged past Claire and into the living room. "What the hell is going on?"

The answers came at once in an unintelligible mix.

"This is why I tried to call you."

"AJ! They know I'm here!"

"There's real activity, AJ. Look at the KII meter."

"Something pushed a vase off the table," DaSilva said, last to speak and first to be heard. "That's what started it all."

"Me!" Ben shouted. "I pushed the vase. Tell them it was me!"

AJ scowled at Ben, then seemed to catch his mistake. He flinched, looking off balance. In that moment, sensing an opportunity, Buck pulled free. He dashed into the living room.

"Buck!" Ben opened his arms. "How are you, boy? I bet you can see me."

The dog hesitated, pointing Ben's way like an arrow on a bowstring.

"Buck," AJ said. "Stay."

"It's all right," Claire said. "There's nothing in here he can break."

Melody returned with the pitcher, which held the flowers now. "Don't worry. He's well behaved." She put the pitcher on the table. "Beautiful."

Ben crouched down. "Bucky boy." He motioned to the dog. "Come to Papa."

"Stay," AJ said. "Stay, Buck."

"Come on, Buck," Ben said. "Let's run." Ben zipped across the floor toward the dog, passed it, then circled around and headed back.

The dog's eyes followed him. Every muscle in his canine body was wound tight.

"Buck." AJ reached for the dog as Ben made another circuit, faster this time, dodging the obstacles.

The dog couldn't fight it any longer. He leapt, crossing half the room before anyone could take a breath. Ben laughed, banking his turn as he and the dog reversed direction.

"Buck!" AJ yelled.

Ben and the dog raced around the room.

"Wow," DaSilva said. "I've never seen him act like this."

"I got ya, I got ya," Ben called, chasing and being chased as the dog lapped him.

AJ made a grab for Buck's collar but missed. The dog and the ghost made another loop. Buck swerved expertly to avoid the table, but Ben was not so skilled—or maybe this time he didn't bother. He went directly at it. As he passed through the wooden top, he dragged the pitcher with him. It raced the length of the table, then shot forward, throwing its contents into the air. Crashing to the floor, the pitcher cracked from base to lip.

Claire let out a shriek.

"Oh my God," Melody said.

"I saw that," Claire said. "This time I saw it."

"Is the camera on?" Sela yelled.

Ben stopped near the television and surveyed the mess. "Sorry. Two in one day."

The dog jumped beside him, barking. The lights of the KII meter made a green smile.

"There's something here," Sela said. "And I don't think it's happy."

"Come on, AJ," Ben said. "They'll have to believe you now."

AJ snapped his fingers. "Buck. Come here, boy."

The dog continued to bark, though his tail wagged.

Ben took a swipe at the KII meter. It made a slow half turn. He laughed. "I think I'm getting the hang of this."

"Let's get out of here," Claire said. She was already heading for the door.

AJ reached for her arm. "Wait. It's okay."

"No. Sela's right. There's something here. And it's angry."

"It's not angry," AJ said. "It's just a pain in the ass."

"What do you mean?" Claire stopped trying to pull away. "What are you talking about?"

"*It* is Ben," AJ said. "And he's right over there."

CHAPTER 27

The only sound in the room was the dog's barking. Ben ran his hand across Buck's head. The dog whimpered, then fell silent.

"AJ?" Claire looked from AJ to the KII meter. "What do you mean he's right over there?"

"Yeah," Sela said. "What the fuck, AJ?"

"You mean you can sense his presence?" DaSilva said.

"Or can you actually see him?" Sela said.

"AJ. Don't chicken out now."

"I can see him," AJ said. "He's next to the television."

"Holy shit. Are you sure it's Ben?" DaSilva said. "What does he look like—a cloud, a shadow?"

"He looks like Ben. Only a little more colorful."

Sela picked up the thermal scanner. He went forward, slowly, holding the device in front of him. On the television stand, the lights of the KII meter still made a curve.

"Are you getting variation?" DaSilva said.

"Not much. A couple of degrees."

By now the wand was practically in Ben's chest.

"Jesus. Give a ghost some space." Ben stepped aside.

"Grab Dewey's camera," Sela said. "See if you can get something with it."

"Right, right." DaSilva began frantically unscrewing the camera from the tripod.

"There's no hurry. I'm not going anywhere."

DaSilva lifted the camera. "AJ, help with the aim."

"You're doing fine," AJ said.

"Calm down, Dave. I'll make it easy for you." Ben put himself in front of the lens and struck a pose—arms crossed, chin tilted forward.

"Do you believe this?" Claire sought out Melody's eyes, but Melody was watching AJ intently.

After a few seconds, DaSilva reviewed the video. "Nothing. Maybe it will show up when we see it on the monitor."

"Damn," Ben said. "I'm going to have to figure out how she does it."

Melody was still staring at AJ. "Is this the first time you've seen him?"

"Tell them the whole deal," Ben said. "You're not doing yourself any favors by clamming up now."

As Ben was speaking, the dog left him and went to AJ. He sat at his master's feet, like he, too, was waiting for an answer.

"It's not the first time. I've been seeing him since that first night I stayed here."

"Really?" Claire's eyebrows, already raised, went up another notch. "So those times I thought you were talking to yourself—"

"Whoa," Sela said. "You can talk to him?"

"He's not so good at listening," Ben said, "but we can talk."

DaSilva aimed the camera again. "Do you mean like *talk*? Have a conversation?"

"Just like I'm talking to you," AJ said.

"Damn," DaSilva said. "We feel like we're doing really good if we get three words we can barely make out."

Sela pointed at AJ with the thermal scanner. "You asshole. I can't believe you didn't tell us."

"I'm telling you now."

"Well, you took your sweet time."

"You think it seems like a long time," Ben said. "Try being on my side of it."

AJ ran his hand through his hair. "I didn't tell you because it sounds crazy. It *is* crazy. I kind of wanted to stay out of the psych ward."

"Your closest friends are paranormal investigators, you jerk," Sela said. "Did you think we wouldn't believe you?"

"Right. Like you believed that guy who showed up to help you investigate the Provincetown lighthouse—the guy who said he could see ghosts? What was his name? You all laughed at him. You still talk about what a weirdo the guy was."

"His name was Chip," DaSilva said, "but Ben called him Small, because there was no way he was a medium."

"Okay, so it's not very funny. Sue me."

"You didn't meet him, AJ," Sela said. "You would have thought he was a loon, too."

"Maybe. But the point is, even you guys have a hard time with it, when someone says they have that ability. If you haven't experienced it yourself..."

136

"We don't think you're crazy," Melody said, "but it is a lot to take in."

DaSilva had been following the conversation with the camera. Now he let it drop. "I bet Claire wants proof. The homeowner always wants proof."

"Proof?" Ben said. "The vase! The pitcher! The fucking KII meter! What the hell do you want?"

"We have the video that I took," Sela said. "We can all see that. AJ, is that Ben, on the video?"

"Oh, man," Ben said. "Let's not drag her into this."

The dog fell heavily to his side and stretched out his legs, groaning quietly.

"I got it," Ben said. "AJ, you can tell them why I knocked the vase off the table."

AJ just looked at him.

Ben continued. "Melody met Jacques Westbury last night. She told Claire she might go out to dinner with him. When I heard that, I took a swing at the vase. And I actually connected. The thing went flying."

"Jacques Westbury?" AJ said. "Melody, are you serious?"

"What?" she said. "What are you talking about?"

"Ben knocked the vase off the table when you said you were going out with Jacques Westbury?"

"Melody, is that true?" Sela said. "Westbury? The guy's probably a murderer. Not to mention that he must be, like, ninety years old. What the hell are you thinking?"

"Maybe she's thinking he's ninety years old and loaded," DaSilva said.

"That is so insulting." Melody closed her eyes. "I can't believe you said that."

"Did he see you two having ice cream?" There was an edge in Claire's voice. "AJ, is that where this is coming from? Did you see Melody and Jacques?"

"No, I didn't see them. I don't know what you're talking about."

"So you really want me to believe that Ben told you. Just now."

AJ didn't answer.

Claire picked up the audio recorder from the table and stared at it. "Do you have the house bugged, or something? Have you been spying on me?"

"Claire," Melody said. "You don't mean that."

"They've got all the right equipment." Claire held up the audio recorder as exhibit A. "And AJ's been in here pretty much every day. By himself, a lot of the time."

"You think he would do that? Bug your house? And anyway, how could he have rigged all the other stuff—the vase, and the pitcher and that meter thing?"

"I don't know." Claire inspected the recorder.

"Well, I do know," Melody said. "You can trust AJ. You can trust all of them."

"Yeah? Maybe you're not such a good judge of character."

Melody stood silent for a moment, taking that in. "You know what? Maybe I should go."

"I'm the one who should go," AJ said.

"Isn't that for Claire to decide?" DaSilva finally lowered the camera.

"Hang on, guys," Ben said. "Nobody needs to go anywhere."

Claire was shaking her head rapidly. "I'm sorry, but this is too much. Melody, I didn't mean it."

"It's all right."

Claire started toward the kitchen. "I need some air."

AJ backed out of her way. "Claire. Let me explain."

"She doesn't need an explanation. She needs more proof." Ben reached for her as she went by. His hand passed through her arm.

Quickening her step, Claire disappeared. There was the sound of the porch door banging closed.

"Are you happy now?" AJ said to Ben. "Did you see the look on her face? That look is why I haven't said anything until now. That look says it all."

"She'll come around. Go talk to her."

"Are you talking to Ben now?" DaSilva said. "Where exactly is he?"

"Please." AJ raised his hands in front of him. "Everybody just stay put."

"Tell the guys to watch the KII meter," Ben said. "While you're talking to Claire, we'll try that again."

"You tell them," AJ said over his shoulder, heading quickly toward the porch.

He found Claire in the narrow back yard, staring into the trees. "Are you okay?"

"No. I've been trying to calm myself down. It's not working very well."

"Do you want the guys to leave?"

Claire didn't answer.

"Do you want me to leave?"

"Actually, I was thinking that I should leave and the rest of you should stay."

"I'm so sorry, Claire. I know this is crazy."

"This is beyond crazy. I have two choices here. Either you're a deranged stalker who has wired my house, or you have supernatural powers that enable you to communicate with the dead."

"Which way are you leaning?"

She looked at him for the first time since he'd come outside. "Let me ask you this. The first night you volunteered to stay—was that because you

138

thought Ben was here?"

"I didn't know. I wanted to find out, yeah."

"So that's why you offered to help me paint—it gave you an excuse to be here."

"No. That's not the only reason."

Her intense blue eyes were still fixed on him. "Why would he stay here?"

"You mean stay in this world? I don't know. I don't know how it works. All I know is that he can't leave your house. He has tried."

Claire faced the trees again. "I saw something yesterday. Upstairs, in the hall. It was like a shimmer. Was that Ben?"

"I don't think so."

"Why? If you can see him, maybe I can, too."

"No, Claire. I really don't think so."

"No? Why not?"

AJ let out a slow breath. Finally, he said, "He's been around you, around both of us, a lot. You've never seen him."

"Oh, God." Claire crossed her arms, then pulled them tight around herself. "So what did I see?"

"I don't know. I wasn't there."

"Well, what do you think I saw? Is there…something else?"

No answer.

"AJ."

"There's a woman."

"You mean, a ghost. A woman's ghost."

"Yes. I've seen her, and so has Ben. She doesn't talk. I don't know what's up with her, yet. I'm sure she's harmless."

"Harmless? Shit. I wasn't even thinking about that. But since you put the idea out there, how can you know?"

"She's obviously been around a while. By the way she's dressed, I'd say over a hundred years. People say they've seen a ghost here, but nobody's ever had any problems with it."

Claire was quiet for a long time. "Why isn't this freaking you out? I feel like I'm losing my mind."

"I've had some time to get used to it. This ability or whatever didn't start here."

"You've been seeing ghosts all of your life."

"Most of it."

"You mean, like, constantly," she said. "Everywhere you go."

"So you believe me?"

"I'm trying."

He nodded. "I've seen a few over the years. It was pretty rare, until Bridgeport. That place was a nightmare."

"So it does freak you out." Claire seemed reassured by that thought. "It freaked you out enough for you to quit your job."

"It was more than that. I couldn't do my job. I almost got my partner killed."

Claire watched him for a while without saying anything. "What happened?"

AJ closed his eyes but didn't answer.

"Come on, AJ. I think you owe it to me."

He glanced at her, then looked away. "We responded to a domestic disturbance. When we announced ourselves, there was no answer, so we went in. The place was all busted up. We found the victim in the master bedroom, on the floor. Someone had smashed a mirror, just demolished it, on her. She was naked, covered in blood, and her skin was all ripped apart, with broken glass sticking out everywhere.

"My partner started checking her for a pulse. It was my job to keep watch, because whoever had done this might still be around. But with this goddamn talent I have, I was the worst lookout in the world. Because the woman's ghost was there, too. I tried to ignore her, just do my job, like Tony or any other cop would do. But the ghost looked at me, and, even though I knew better, I looked back at her. The second we made eye contact, she started screaming."

"Screaming? At you?"

"Yeah. You've never heard a scream like that. It was the most desperate terror and the most violent rage, mixed together. It was all that was left of her, and it just came pouring out. The sound just grabbed me, right where I stood. It was like… Have you ever jumped into freezing water and had that feeling of cold clamping down on you, squeezing the air out of you?"

Claire nodded.

"It was like that, only ten times over. So, when I should have been taking in the whole scene, listening for telltale sounds, staying alert to any sign of the killer's presence, I was doing only one thing—trying to block out that voice. Finally, even with Tony right there, I had to do something. I got out the words, 'Ma'am, it's all right.' I was hoping that Tony would think I was talking to the woman on the floor, as if she might still make it. I said it again. The ghost only screamed louder."

"Oh, AJ. I'm so sorry."

"No. That's not it. See, while I was playing ghost whisperer, I missed the fact that the boyfriend was now standing in the doorway to the bathroom, pointing a gun at my partner. Luckily, Tony wasn't half deaf with the screams, like me. He heard something—the creak of a hinge or a floorboard—and just in time he ducked out of the way. The bullet went right where he had been. I took the guy down, but only after I almost cost my partner his life."

Claire touched his hand.

"After that, I had no choice but to quit. My partner tried to tell me that it was all right. We'd gotten the bad guy, and we'd both gotten out of there alive. But he didn't know. I couldn't tell him the truth."

"That's awful." Claire pulled her hand back. "But now you're on the Stonington police force. Aren't you afraid of the same thing happening here? People die in Stonington, too."

"Sure. But it seems that they only become ghosts when they die suddenly or violently. We don't get too much of that here. And I'm on my own—no partner. I can only endanger myself."

Their eyes met and held for a long moment.

"Do they all scream like that woman?" Claire said. "Did Ben scream at you?"

"Let's walk." AJ started across the yard. Claire joined him. They picked their way through the weeds, past the tray of violets.

"By the time I saw Ben, he had calmed down. The others, in Bridgeport, didn't all scream. But a lot of them, seemed—I don't know—crazy."

"You mean frightened, panicked?"

"More than that. They weren't like Ben. Even if I'd been alone with them, I don't think I could have talked to them. It was like something was really wrong. Some basic part of them was missing."

"But Ben seems okay? You can talk to him?"

"So far."

"Why do you say so far? Are you worried that he'll end up like the other ghosts you saw?"

"Yeah, I am. I mean, he's trapped in the house. He can't communicate with anyone except me. He can't touch anything, really—"

"He did today."

"I guess he did. Once in a while, somehow... But most of the time, he's...a ghost. It's like he's not gone, but he's not here, either. I know what that would do to me."

Claire searched his face. "Yeah, I think you do know. So, what, it's your job to keep him sane?"

"Maybe. Keep him sane, keep myself sane. I tried ignoring this ability I have. I tried running away from it. Now, with Ben here, I can't do either." AJ stopped walking.

They stood there quietly, at the end of the house. The sun had dropped below the trees, and there were long shadows across the weedy grass.

"This other ghost," Claire said, "upstairs. Do you think she's crazy?"

"She's doing the same thing over and over. She doesn't seem aware of anything around her. That's crazy, don't you think?"

A floodlight that was mounted on the corner of the house blinked on.

AJ turned toward it. "What is that?"

"It's one of those dusk-to-dawn lights. It's wasted, way down here. Where I need it is on the garage."

"No, I mean that thing on the ground by the house."

"Oh." Claire was already moving toward the white shape that was half hidden by the grass. "It's the window. That's weird. The guy nailed it in. I saw him do it."

AJ knelt down when they reached the cellar window. He lifted it up. "The nails are still there. But they're bent. This pane is broken." He touched the sharp edge carefully. Turning to the foundation, he ran a hand around the empty rectangle.

"So someone pulled the window loose and broke into the house?"

AJ had picked up a shard of glass and was studying it. "No. I think you have it backwards."

"What do you mean?"

"They didn't break into the house, Claire. They broke out of it."

CHAPTER 28

"Ben? Are you here?" Sela peered across the living room as if into a fog.

"Wait, wait." Ben raced toward the KII meter. It blinked.

"Make sure you get this," Sela said, looking at DaSilva.

"Yeah. Maybe if I keep my distance the battery will hold out." Aiming the camera at the meter, DaSilva retreated almost to the front hall.

"So, Ben, are you okay?" Sela said.

"Am I okay? What the fuck? I'm dead." Ben waved his hand at the meter again, making the light blink once. "Whatever."

"Why is he still here?" Melody said. "I thought you guys were sure he'd move on."

DaSilva kept the camera to his eye. "Unfinished business?"

"We could try asking him," Sela said.

"No, wait. I want to ask him something." DaSilva leaned out from behind the camera. "Ben, did Jacques Westbury kill that girl?"

"Dave!" Melody said, "that's out of line."

Ben jumped back from the meter as if to make sure it wouldn't flash. "How the hell would I know? What do you think, all us dead folks are hanging out at Claire's house talking about how we died?"

"That's not necessarily a *Yes* or *No* question," Sela said.

"Sure it is," DaSilva said. "Either he killed her or he didn't."

"But what does Ben blink if he doesn't know?"

"Oh, right. Okay. Ben, is the girl here? Have you talked to her?"

"One at a time," Sela said.

"It doesn't matter." Ben made the meter blink twice. "It's a *No* for both."

DaSilva swung the camera toward the others, then back to the KII meter. "Ben, do you remember dying?"

143

"Jesus!" Melody moved in front of the camera. "Why would you ask him that?"

"Always the master of tact," Sela said.

"Not a thing." Ben blinked *No*.

"You fell down the stairs," DaSilva continued, waving Melody out of the way. "It's on video. Do you want—"

Melody stepped in front of him again. "Stop! What is wrong with you? We should be trying to help him. Ben, do you need something from us? Can I do anything for you?"

"Damn, Melody," Ben said. "There was a time when I would have killed for you to ask that question. It's a little late now. Dave was going to ask me if I wanted to see the video. That's the question I want to answer." He looked at Melody, his voice and the meter both silent. Finally, he waved his hand once.

"*Yes*," Melody said. "That's a *Yes*. He wants something. How do we figure out what it is?"

"Twenty questions," Sela said. "Is it bigger than a breadbox?"

"Oh, Jesus Christ," Ben said.

"Morse code." DaSilva lowered the camera.

"What?"

"We could use Morse code to communicate."

"Okay, yeah," Sela said. "But who the hell knows Morse code?"

"I learned some of it a couple of days ago for a thing with Dewey's scouts. Here." He pulled a card from his wallet. "Dewey gave us these cheat sheets."

"Ben," Melody said, "do you know Morse code?"

"Sorry, I'm a little weak on my telegraph skills." Ben waved twice.

"I could write it out for Ben," DaSilva said.

"I think there's paper in the kitchen." Melody left the room. She came back a minute later carrying a tablet and a ballpoint pen.

DaSilva had put the camera on the tripod. He sat on the couch and copied out a chart of the alphabet.

"Now we're talking," Ben said, having come close to watch.

When he finished, DaSilva tore the sheet from the tablet and put it on the floor by the meter.

Can you see that, Ben?" Sela said.

"Awesome." Ben blinked the light once.

"Hot shit," Sela said. "Okay. Now, what do you want? What can we do for you?"

Ben waved his hand quickly three times, then held his hand in front of the meter, making the lights stay on.

"Dot, dot, dot, dash," DaSilva said. "That's a V."

"Good." Ben waved his hand twice.

144

"Was that *No*?" Melody said. "It's not a V?"

"I think that was dot, dot," DaSilva said. "For the letter I."

"Right you are." Ben continued his little dance.

"Dash, dash, dot. That's a G," DaSilva said.

"No! That was a D, God damn it. Dash, dot, dot." Shaking his head, Ben blinked the light once more.

"E," DaSilva said.

"At least you got that one right." Ben made the three dashes for the O, then pulled his hands back.

"V, I, G, E, O. *Vigeo*," DaSilva said. "Sounds Italian."

Ben groaned.

"No, it's *video*," Sela said.

"Thank God," Ben said. "Someone with some sense."

"Video?" Melody said. "Dave, are you still filming?"

"He wants to watch the video, from that night," DaSilva said. "That's what I was trying to tell you before."

Sela looked from the meter to the empty space beside it. "Ben, is that what you mean? You want to watch the video?"

"Yes! Finally." Ben waved once.

"I don't believe it," Melody said. "Who would want to watch themselves die?"

"It's still on the camera," DaSilva said. "We can play it right here." He went to a bag in the hallway and came back with a cable. "This should give us a really nice picture." He connected the camera to the television. "Better than our monitor."

The big LCD screen lit up.

DaSilva worked the buttons on the camera. "You want to see the whole thing, from the beginning, right?"

Ben signaled *Yes*.

"I don't think you should do this," Melody said.

DaSilva had already pressed the *Play* button. "Maybe it will help him. Maybe then he can move on."

"Ben, do you want to move on?" Sela said.

Ben reached for the meter, then pulled his hand back.

Sudden and loud, Ben's voice filled the room. "Ben Shortman. Approaching the Westbury house."

"Whoa." DaSilva grabbed the remote control. "That's kind of weird." He lowered the volume.

On the screen, the *No Trespassing* sign appeared from the darkness. There was Ben's recorded voice again. "Guess I'll have to edit that out." The camera entered the house, swung through the kitchen, with its dark, lurking cabinets, and moved on to the hallway. It found the stairs. Ben explained his intention to check out the second floor, urging his friends to come soon. When he'd set the camera on the chair, pointing upstairs, he said, "This is so cool, guys. Be back in a few minutes."

Ben's ghost smiled. "I really should have waited for you. I guess I was just too excited. From what AJ said, I didn't even use the still camera, after I put the video camera down. Pretty sloppy technique."

On the screen, Ben climbed out of sight. Then, the empty stairs, in shadow.

"I'm not watching this." Melody faced the window.

DaSilva blew air between clenched teeth but kept his eyes fixed on the television.

It showed Ben coming down the stairs. He stopped, turned around and went back up again.

"This must be where she surprised me," Ben said. "It's too bad I didn't have a camera in my hands at that point."

There was just the stairs, rising into oblivion.

"What was that?" Ben said, pointing. "Back it up. Back it up. Fuck." He went to the KII meter and set the lights going.

"What's up?" Sela said. "You want us to stop?"

DaSilva pressed the *Pause* button.

Ben frantically began to spell out his message. He'd gotten only as far as *BAC,* with DaSilva calling out the letters, when Sela guessed what he was trying to say.

"Back it up," he told DaSilva. "Go slow. He can flash the lights to tell you to pause on something."

DaSilva reversed the video as far as Ben descending the stairs. Ben made the meter flash.

"Okay, okay." DaSilva let the film advance.

On the screen, Ben came down the stairs, then went up again.

"What's going on?" AJ came into the living room. "What are you watching?"

DaSilva hit *Pause.*

"They're watching the video," Melody said. "Ben's—his last night."

"AJ, I saw something," Ben said.

Claire appeared behind AJ. "Melody, will you come with me?"

"Sure." Melody sounded relieved.

"Is Claire all right?" Ben said.

"Not really." AJ turned to the others. "Look, you guys need to pack up."

"She wants us out of here?" Sela said.

"Wait, AJ," Ben said. "First, you have to see something."

"I don't want to watch that again."

"You have to. It's important."

AJ took a deep breath and crossed the room. "Play it."

DaSilva started the movie again. They all watched the empty stairs.

"What was that?" Sela said.

"Attaboy." Ben lit up the meter. "Did you see it, AJ?"

AJ didn't answer.

"That didn't show up on our monitor," Sela said. "You need this big screen."

"Let's watch it again." DaSilva backed it up.

"Right here." Sela pointed.

On the television, Ben descended, turned around, then climbed out of view. A moment later, at the top of the frame, the shadow brightened for an instant.

"That is definitely a flash," Ben said. "It's obscured by the turn, but—"

"I think that's a camera flash," Sela said. "So Ben did have his still camera."

"Bingo. I must have pulled it out of my pocket when I reached the hall. I guess I saw my ghostly friend and used it on her."

"Okay," DaSilva said, "so what was he taking pictures of?"

"The same thing that I caught with the video camera," Sela said. "The ghost. But it's weird. That camera was never found. The chief even asked us about it."

DaSilva's heel tapped against the floor. "Well, if we don't have it, and the chief doesn't have it, where is it?"

"Good fucking question," Sela said.

AJ shook his head, an unhappy expression on his face. "I'll check with the hospital. It probably got left there. That happens once in a while."

"Right," Sela said. "Good."

While they talked, the movie continued to play. Ben crashed down the stairs, sending the camera flying and creating cinematic chaos. Then, all was calm again. There was only Ben's face, huge and close, his empty eyes staring at nothing.

"God damn," Sela said. "Turn that off."

The screen went black. DaSilva put the remote down.

"Okay, guys," AJ said. "You've got to clear out."

"What's up?" Ben said.

"It looks like somebody's been in the house."

"What?" Sela said. "Someone broke in?"

"Think it's Westbury?" DaSilva said. "Did Claire have the locks changed?"

"I need to ask you not to talk about this with anyone," AJ said. "You got that, DaSilva?"

"Yeah. I'm not a total idiot."

"What are you going to do, AJ?" Sela said.

"Talk to the chief."

"You're not leaving her alone, are you?" Sela pointed toward the ceiling.

"She won't be staying here."

"She'll probably have a *For Sale* sign up by breakfast," DaSilva said.

"Can you blame her?" Sela had already pulled the cable that connected the camera to the television.

DaSilva went to the nearest bag. He placed the camera in it.

"Tell her we're sorry about all of this, and we'll do anything to help." Sela collapsed the tripod.

"I'll tell her," AJ said.

Ben watched his friends work. They were quick and efficient. "Do they really have to go?"

Within a couple of minutes, the guys had packed up their gear and were on their way out.

Sela stopped at the door. "Ben." He hesitated. "Good to see—or, talk—" He paused again. "Good to just know."

"Come back soon," Ben said.

"Bye, Ben." DaSilva waved. "Hang in there."

As the door was closing, Claire and Melody came down the stairs.

"Are you all set?" AJ said.

"Yeah." Claire carried a small bag.

"I'm going to need a minute. Is that all right?"

"Take as long as you want."

"I'll turn off the lights and lock up."

"For what it's worth," Claire said.

"Will you call me, let me know you're set for the night?"

"Sure." Claire's lips made a thin smile.

"Okay."

Melody mouthed "Bye," but let Claire go out ahead of her. "I'll make sure she calls."

"Thanks," AJ said.

"Don't worry. She seems to have a stubborn streak. She's not giving up."

AJ hesitated at the open door, then went out onto the step. He watched the women walk away.

When she reached her car, Claire looked back at the house. "So much for belonging here," she said.

Melody opened the door of her car. "You're going to follow me?"

Claire nodded.

AJ watched them drive away. Then he went back inside. "That was a nice stunt," he said. "You and Buck."

At the sound of his name, the greyhound, who had been sleeping in the middle of the living room floor, got up and went to AJ.

"So?" Ben said. "Are you going to tell me what's going on? What makes you say someone's been in the house?"

AJ described the window lying on the grass, the broken pane, the crooked nails.

"We heard a noise," Ben said. "I thought it was John, working on the window."

"Claire told me about the noise. She said John had already left. I think what you heard was the window being struck from inside, then falling out of the frame."

"So if I had gotten down there sooner—"

"You were in the basement? Did you see anything?"

"No. That's what I'm saying. We wasted a lot of time looking around the first floor. By the time I got down there, whoever broke out would have been long gone. Then, I got too close to the window and…"

AJ nodded.

"How'd they get in, without me seeing them?" Ben said.

"The only thing I can figure is that they came in the same way. They either saw the window was loose, or maybe they already knew about it."

"Okay. But still, why didn't I see them, once they were in the house?"

"They never made it out of the basement. Claire came home and John showed up to work on the window. They were stuck down there. When John left, they knocked the window out and ran off."

"That's fucked up."

The two of them were quiet for a while.

"So are you going to call the hospital?" Ben said. "Get that camera back?"

"Yeah, about that." AJ scanned the floor at the foot of the stairs. "I don't think the camera's at the hospital."

"But you said—"

"I was just saying that to stall the guys." He went up a few stairs.

"Oh." Ben looked up at him. "What are you doing?"

"Trying to figure out what exactly did happen. You still don't remember anything?"

"Not about that part of it, no."

"If you dropped the camera…" AJ shook his head "There's just nowhere it could have fallen that it would be hidden. Claire would have seen it, or I would have, or you, or the chief. It's just not here."

"So what the hell happened to it?"

"I can think of one explanation. But I don't like it very much."

"Yeah? What's that?"

"You have the camera, you take a picture, and then you come rolling down the stairs, with no camera. In fact, the camera is never seen again."

"Right, the camera's missing. So?"

"Maybe the camera's missing because someone was up there, in the hallway."

"My friend the ghost was up there. That's what I keep saying."

"No. Not the ghost. Someone who has the camera. Someone who took it from you."

"Oh, shit."

"Yeah. I don't think you fell down the stairs, Ben. I think you were pushed."

CHAPTER 29

AJ stared at the hole in the foundation, the cell phone in his hand. He pressed the buttons to make a call.

The chief answered on the first ring. "AJ. What's up?"

"Hi, Chief. I'm over at Claire Connor's. It looks like there was a break-in."

"Have you called it in to the station? We'll want a detective over there. It'd be Wheeler tonight."

AJ stared off across the tall grass, more a clearing than a yard, its size becoming less certain as the sunlight faded. "It's complicated," he said. "I'd like to talk to you first."

"What do you mean, it's complicated?"

"The video, Chief. We watched Ben's video again. We saw something—something we hadn't noticed before."

"When I watched the video, the only thing I noticed was that ghost you claimed not to see. And who's *we*?"

"I'm not talking about the ghost. It looks like someone was in the house the night that Ben died. Chief, we can call Wheeler. But I'd really appreciate it if you could come over here first."

"Sit tight. I'll be there in fifteen."

"Thanks." AJ snapped the phone closed and slipped it in his pocket. He went back along the house. At the tray of violets, he paused.

"Jacques Westbury brought those," Ben said, from the porch.

AJ looked up, startled. "I didn't know you were there."

Ben was just a faint outline behind the screen.

"Sorry. I thought you couldn't miss me, with my glow..." He looked down at himself. "Though it does seem to be dimmer, doesn't it?"

"Claire told me about Jacques's visit," AJ said. "I don't think she planned on saying anything. She was forced into it when we found the

151

window."

"She probably didn't want to worry you."

"Yeah, I know. I can't really complain, with all the things I tried to hide from her. I didn't want her to know the stories about this place, or about Westbury. Or about you. I thought I was protecting her. It seems stupid now."

"You'll get no argument from me."

AJ made a face but didn't defend himself. "The chief's coming over."

"Good. What did you tell him?"

"Just that there was a break-in."

"But you are going to tell him, right?"

"I don't know."

"He's a good friend, a mentor, even. He'll believe you, AJ."

"He might, he might not. Either way, it's the end of my career."

"No way. You're a good cop. And you could be even better if—"

"Don't even start," AJ said, cutting him off.

"Okay. Okay."

"Just keep quiet while the chief is here. I don't need any distractions."

"I'll be as silent as the grave."

***

AJ met Chief Brown in the driveway.

"Where's Ms. Connor?"

"She left with Melody."

"Probably a good idea. So you've got evidence of a break-in?"

They walked around the front of the house, Ben shadowing them inside, moving from window to window.

The chief pointed his flashlight at the gaping hole in the foundation. "Everything's the way you found it?"

"Well, my fingerprints are on the glass, and on one of the nails. But I put it all back where I found it."

The chief nodded. "The window was definitely forced."

"Forced out, though, chief. You can see how the wood's splintered, the bent nails, and the way the broken glass fell. This came out with one violent shove."

"Okay. How does someone shove a window right out of the wall?"

AJ related what Claire had told him, about Jacques Westbury's visit, Jacques's story about using the window when he was a teenager, and then John Donahue coming to the house and tapping a couple of nails in to hold the window in place. The chief raised his eyebrows at Jacques's name but let AJ continue. "From what she said, I think Claire and Melody heard the window being pushed out. They were on the second floor. I guess it sounded like it came from the first floor. They didn't see anything, because they didn't look in the basement, or outside."

As the chief listened, he worked the beam of the flashlight around the window. "What's your theory about why someone would be breaking out of the house?"

"I think they got into the house right before Donahue arrived. Claire came back around the same time. So, they were trapped in the basement. They waited until Donahue left, and Claire was upstairs, then they knocked the window out and made a run for it."

The chief switched off his flashlight. "Talk about lousy timing, huh? Breaking into an empty house just before everyone descends on the place."

"Yeah."

"So if this is how they got out, how'd they get in?"

"There's no sign of forced entry anywhere else," AJ said. "I think they used the window to get in, too—just like Jacques Westbury used to."

"Okay. But I think we can eliminate Jacques. Why would he tell Claire about his personal trick window, then turn around and use it himself? Let alone, why would he break into a house that he just sold?"

"I don't know. Maybe he left something behind that he didn't mean to."

"I like the way you're thinking. But you know it's much more likely just kids. A couple of times, when the house was empty, we chased some teenagers out of here. Maybe they didn't know someone had moved in. Or maybe they thought they'd find some booze or something."

"Yeah."

"Have you called Wheeler yet?"

When AJ shook his head, the chief pulled a phone from his pocket, punched a number and had a quick conversation. He put his phone back in his pocket. "Wheeler will be here in a few minutes. How about inside? Anything disturbed or missing?"

"No. Doesn't appear to be."

"Can we get in?"

They used the porch door. Ben was right on deck, greeting the chief with a big grin. "Chief! Good to see you!"

AJ gave Ben a tight shake of the head.

If the chief noticed it, he didn't let on. "Pretty nice table and chairs for a porch," he said, sliding his fingers across the table top.

"They're going inside, as soon as the dining room's painted."

"She'd better hop to it. We get a thunderstorm—"

"I know."

"Which way to the basement?"

AJ led the way through the kitchen to the basement door. The chief already had a latex glove on one hand. He swung the door open, then hit the wall switch. His shoes fell heavily, making the open treads bounce. By the third step, the air had gone damp and cool.

"So what's this about the video?" the chief said. "You said you saw something?"

"Yeah." AJ kept his hands to his sides, careful not to touch the railing. "Right after Ben goes upstairs the second time, or I guess it's the third time—right before he falls, you can see a camera flash, at the top of the frame."

"A flash? I never saw a flash."

"None of us did, until we played it on Claire's television."

"You guys should have an HD TV at the station, for police work," Ben said, following behind. "Of course, it helps to have an expert looking at it, too. If I do say so myself."

At the bottom of the stairs, the chief swept the uneven foundation with his flashlight. "Who else was watching the video?"

"Sela, DaSilva and Melody," AJ said.

"Yeah? Why the crowd? What was going on?"

"We saw a flash. It looks like Ben did have that still camera, after all. So the question is, where is it?"

The chief turned the flashlight on AJ. "You have a theory about this, too."

"I think Ben surprised someone, maybe someone who, more than most, had some reason to not want to be caught here. Someone who grabbed the camera and shoved Ben down the stairs."

"I've been thinking about that," Ben said, coming around to AJ's side. "If I was murdered—that would explain why I'm here."

AJ glanced in Ben's direction.

The chief's eyes narrowed. "You okay?"

AJ nodded.

The chief aimed his beam toward the far wall. He started toward the empty rectangle. Through it, a patch of sky was visible.

The chief's light went from the window frame to the floor below it, where there was a concrete block. "Our man may have put that block there, used it as a step."

"Yeah," AJ said.

"Were the guys doing one of their paranormal investigations?" the chief said. "Is that why they were here?"

"Something like that."

"It couldn't have been your idea. Did Claire call them? Did she have some kind of a—"

"Melody called them. She and Claire saw something, earlier in the day."

"I guess I'm not surprised."

"Look, Roland. I know you find this all very interesting, but let's not get sidetracked. I think Ben may have been murdered."

"You might be right. But I don't think that looking into the other goings on in this house is getting sidetracked."

"Way to go, Chief," Ben said. "I knew you were a good man."

AJ flicked his hand in Ben's direction.

When he saw that the chief had been watching, AJ said, "The open window's letting mosquitoes in. I had one buzzing in my ear."

"Very funny," Ben said.

The chief studied the air around AJ's head, as if trying to find the insect. Then he turned to the window again. "Not much to fingerprint here. We can try the frame." He pointed at it with the flashlight. "All right. Let's go on up."

The chief led the way to the porch. "So, what do we have—a recent break-in, another break-in, a possible murder and some kind of paranormal goings on. Is it all connected?" He sat down at the table

AJ, who had gone to the door, backed up.

The chief held up his right hand, which was still gloved. He peeled off the glove and stuffed it into a pocket. "I think I told you I had a friend who had a special ability for the paranormal."

"Can we focus on the crimes, Chief? Break-ins? Murder?"

"He didn't like the word *ghosts*, though," the chief said. "He called them *frights*. Said that described them better."

"Hey," Ben said. "Thanks a lot."

"He had a really hard time with it. Nowadays, a certain kind of person capitalizes on that kind of thing. They get their own TV show. They become celebrities. Back then, that wasn't an option."

"Chief," AJ said, "I really don't see what—"

"Did you ever wonder why your Uncle Gus took off for Alaska?"

"What?"

"Uncle Gus?" Ben said. "So that's where the *Augustus* comes from, huh, AJ?"

"Your Uncle Gus. That's who we're talking about."

"I've never heard that he…" AJ stopped.

The chief clasped his hands in front of him. "You never heard it before because your grandfather hushed it up."

"But Uncle Gus told you."

"Yeah. He'd seen a couple of those frights. There was one out at Pachaug he'd even talked to. But instead of feeling like he had a talent, Gus felt the whole thing was a terrible weight, a burden."

"Because he knew that no one would believe him."

"That was part of it. But beyond that, it just plain scared the shit out of him. You know that line from the Bible—'I walk through the valley of the shadow of death?' He said once that he wasn't walking through that valley, he was living in it. That he just wanted to get back into the sunlight. When he got up the courage to go to his father for help, what he got instead was a threat to be locked up in a mental hospital. That's when he talked to me, told me everything."

"And you believed him."

"We'd been best friends from grade school right on through. There wasn't any question of believing him." The chief gave AJ a hard look. "You remind me a lot of Gus."

"Yeah, I've heard that before. I guess it's the chin."

"I'm not talking about your chin. I think you know that."

"He's onto you, AJ," Ben said.

AJ leaned back against a post. He didn't respond to either comment.

"You've got that same thing that Gus had," the chief said. "You look—well, *haunted* is the only word."

"Oh, for Christ's sake," AJ said.

"If you're dealing with the same thing, then I can help you."

AJ straightened up again. "Chief, we've got work to do here."

"That's exactly what I'm talking about. Putting the talent to work. On the job."

"If you want that kind of talent, why don't you call Uncle Gus?"

"Well... When I was working the Anna Marie Rose case, I did call your uncle. I asked him to come back, see if he could use his ability somehow, to get information that I couldn't get."

"But he didn't want any part of it."

"That's right. He said he was just getting his business going up there. He couldn't leave. But that was an excuse, I think. For the first time in a long time, he was happy. He'd found his peace."

"Exactly," AJ said, with a faint smile. "He just wanted to be left alone."

"But you, AJ—you're not happy. It doesn't take a special talent to see that."

AJ looked out at the trees. "I'm happy enough."

"Okay, look," the chief said. "Let me put it to you this way. If you're going to work for me, then you need to be honest with me."

"There you go, AJ," Ben said. "He's not giving you any choice."

AJ didn't respond for a long while. He just stared out through the screen. Finally he said, "I've been thinking maybe I shouldn't work for you, or for any other police chief."

The chief sat back in his chair. "Why? You think this is so difficult? You know I've had guys with alcohol problems, with addiction problems. I've been able to help them work through it. I've never just thrown someone away."

"There's no twelve-step program for what you're talking about."

"AJ," Ben said, moving toward him, "the chief wants to help you."

"That was a bad analogy," the chief said. "This isn't a sickness. It's an ability. A talent. It could do a lot of good."

"You know he's right," Ben said.

AJ shot Ben a look.

The chief was watching. "He's here, isn't he? Ben Shortman."

AJ stared ahead, his arms crossed.

"That's a simple question," Ben said. He tried to put his hand on AJ's shoulder.

AJ tilted his head toward the ceiling. For a long time, he stayed that way, looking up at the painted slats.

"AJ," Ben said.

"Okay." AJ faced the room again. "Okay. Yes. He's here."

"AJ! I wish I could kiss you!"

The chief only nodded, looking unsurprised, as if this were the most ordinary conversation in the world. "That's good."

"That's good?" AJ said.

"So you do have the talent. Now let's see if we can use it. Can you communicate with Ben? Can he tell us anything?"

"I can talk to him. But no, he can't help."

"I can help!" Ben's glow seemed to gain a little wattage. "Give me something to do!"

"He doesn't remember what happened to him," AJ said. "He didn't see the break-in, and he's not in communication with any other spirits who know anything."

"I'm going to remember," Ben said. "I just have to keep trying."

The chief's eyes went back and forth across the room. "Is Ben all right?"

"Why does everyone ask that? I'm not all right. I'm dead."

"He's dead, Chief," AJ said.

"Guess that was a stupid question."

"Duh," Ben said.

"He appreciates your concern," AJ said.

"Who else knows about him? The guys? Claire?"

"Yes."

"They know about you, too?"

"With what went on today, I had no choice."

There was the hiss and pop of tires on the driveway.

"That's got to be Wheeler," the chief said.

"Chief," AJ said, "Claire and Melody and the guys know, and now you know. But at least to start, can we keep this—my talent or whatever you call it—quiet from the rest of the department?"

"Absolutely."

A car door slammed shut.

"Okay," the chief said. "Let's get to work."

***

Wheeler's car pulled away, leaving AJ and the chief alone in the yard.

"I should lock up." AJ didn't move. "So, Chief, if whoever broke in here was after something, but they never made it out of the basement…"

"Yeah?"

"They might try again."

"If they wanted something badly enough. You're right. They might try again. We could get lucky."

"What do you mean?" AJ said. "How would that be lucky?"

"Because we'll be waiting for them."

CHAPTER 30

"Can you listen up for a second? I want to tell you something. I've been thinking about it pretty much non-stop for the past couple of days, and I've made up my mind. It's too crowded here, too bright, too busy. This isn't a long-term solution for us. Particularly with another one on the way, right?

"So, you're moving back.

"Don't get too excited yet. You should know that it won't happen right away. I have a plan, have it pretty much all thought through, but... Things will take some time.

"I'm always asking you for patience, aren't I? Well, patience is not just a virtue, as they say, it is the most important virtue. I learned that again the other day, when I got stuck in that dank basement. I was a prisoner there, while that woman not only had the run of the place, but was busy trying to see to it that we were shut out for good. It's just not right. That place was ours for so long.

"I realized something, while I was waiting in the basement. It won't be enough to scare that woman into moving out. There would be stories about the place that would keep some buyers away for a while. But we've seen how that works. Eventually, someone would come along who hadn't heard the stories, or who didn't believe. We'd be right back where we started.

"So, it's not just about getting her out of the house. It's about getting her out in the right way. If we want to do something that lasts, it's got to be dramatic. We've got to make that house unsellable. We've got to see to it that no one wants to live there ever again."

CHAPTER 31

Claire moved her face closer to the bubbled glass and looked out at the sound. "This house is amazing," she said. "You know what? I actually feel safe."

"Yeah, me, too," Melody said. "It's like we're in some kind of high-class witness protection program."

"Exactly. I'm so lucky to know you, Melody. And it's so lucky that you know someone who is so generous with her house."

"It's amazing the people you meet serving coffee at the Honey B Dairy."

"I guess this makes up for the bad tippers."

"I had two people at the counter. One left me a dime and the other left me holding the keys to this place."

"How long will she be gone?"

"She'll be sailing for at least two more weeks, depending on the winds, I guess."

"Must be nice."

"Yeah, but doesn't it sound dull, compared to what we've been through?"

Claire smiled but said nothing.

"C'mon," Melody said. "I have something to show you. I've saved the best for last."

They crossed the room, zigzagging through wingback chairs, passing a case that displayed spyglasses and scrimshaw, and, instantly changing centuries, entered a kitchen of shiny stainless steel and granite.

"This way." Melody made a left turn.

Claire followed her. "Whoa," she said, backing up, taking in the sight—wine bottles floor to ceiling, a fusillade of tilted corks. "I've seen stores with less."

"Isn't it great? Diane said I could help myself."

Claire dragged a finger across the embossed foils. "Too bad I don't know enough to pick the most expensive bottle."

"Well, the *most* expensive are here." Melody went to the end of the wine rack, where there was a tall cabinet. "And, unfortunately, it's locked. So, we'll have to make do."

"Okay. I'll try."

"This should help," Melody said. She continued past the wine cabinet to a freezer. "Drum roll, please." She pulled on the handle. The seal gave, noiselessly, and the bulbs blinked on.

"Oh my God."

The freezer was filled, top to bottom, with neatly stacked cartons of ice cream.

"This is how they build walls in Candyland," Claire said.

"So, the question is," Melody said, "do we start with ice cream or wine?"

"That is a tough choice."

"I should warn you that they have all the makings for sundaes in the refrigerator."

"Okay, then. Sundaes it is."

A few minutes later they were sitting at the island in the kitchen with their spoons and their heaping bowls.

"This is all my fault," Melody said.

"Fault? That we're eating sundaes in one of the nicest houses in Mystic?"

"You know what I mean. I shouldn't have said anything about ghosts. I shouldn't have called Dave. If I'd kept quiet, you'd be having a nice evening with AJ right now."

"Melody, I have ghosts in my house. Nothing you did or didn't say can change that fact."

"So you're ready to accept that? Ghosts?"

"I don't think I have a choice. You were a skeptic, too, and now you believe. Right?"

"Yeah. But I've spent a lot of time with Ben and the guys. It's all they talk about. It wasn't that hard for me to make the leap." Melody paused. The freezer hummed. "What about AJ? Do you believe him?"

Claire poked at her ice cream, pushing a maraschino cherry deeper into it. "I don't think he bugged the house. I feel bad that I said that."

"It didn't look like your reaction surprised him."

"I know. That makes it worse. You've known him for a while—has he ever seemed, I don't know, delusional?"

"No, no. Withdrawn, a little sad, maybe. Tired. Not delusional."

"Right. And Melody, I do trust your judgment. I didn't mean what I said."

"Okay. Remember that when Jack calls."

They concentrated on their sundaes.

"So," Claire said, "if we're going to accept the existence of ghosts, what else do we have to reconsider?"

"I've always liked the idea of angels."

"Yeah, but with angels come demons."

"Right, there's a trade-off. How about fairies?"

"Fairies are nice," Claire said. "And gnomes."

"Leprechauns," Melody said. "But only the cute ones, with the big shoes and the pot of gold."

"The Jersey Devil."

"What, a hockey player?"

"No, the monster. He lives in the Pine Barrens in New Jersey."

"Okay, sure." Melody licked her spoon. "USOs."

"You mean UFOs?"

"No. Unidentified submerged objects."

"Now you're just making stuff up."

"I'm not, I swear. You really need to watch more cable TV, Claire. You're missing out."

"I had no idea."

They dug into their ice cream in silence.

"You reset the alarm, right?" Claire said.

"Yep. Nobody's getting in here without half the state knowing it. I set off the alarm one night. It's got this booming male voice. Really wild."

They were down to the last, marbled spoonfuls of ice cream and topping.

"Is that what I need—an alarm?" Claire said. "My house was going to be my peaceful, safe haven. What a joke."

"Well, I guess this isn't helping." Melody scraped the bowl. "Maybe we should move on to the wine."

"I should call AJ first. He thinks I'm at your place." Claire let her spoon drop. "Oh, God. My sister."

"Shit. She was supposed to come this weekend, right?"

"Yeah. When we talked about all of the problems there'd be with a big, old house, crime scene tape and paranormal activity weren't even on the list."

"She'll probably want to go after the real estate agent."

"I don't know what I'm going to tell her."

"If you want privacy, the master bedroom's just down the hall. There's even a balcony, with a great view."

"Thanks. Thanks for everything."

"Then you'll be ready for some wine?"

"Absolutely. Lots. Pick out something good." Claire had her cell phone in her hand. "The balcony is this way?"

"Down and to the left."

When Claire was gone, Melody put the bowls in the sink and ran water. She watched the stream turn white and race down the drain. Then she crossed the room to the wine pantry. She pressed her palm against a cork. She pulled out another bottle, examined the label, then slid it back into place. "Where do I start?" she said.

From the kitchen, there was a ringing sound. Melody went toward it. She found her big, orchid-colored bag and unzipped a central compartment. Already smiling, she raised the phone to her ear. "Hi, Jack," she said. "I was just thinking about you."

CHAPTER 32

In the early morning chill, AJ walked away from Claire's house, along the tree line, the weeds dotting his jeans with dew as he passed. Birds dipped across the ragged yard—sparrows and flycatchers with long tails and cardinals red as beating hearts. The woods to his right were still deep in shade, and the silvery green lichen on the gray trunks and stones almost glowed.

There was a break in the trees—a narrow lane, unused for many years, littered with leaves and fallen branches and roofed over by oaks and maples. AJ stood there as if considering taking that path, or trying to imagine where it came out. From the other side of the house there was the thud of a car door. He headed back.

The chief was standing on the front step. His starched uniform emphasized the roundness of his belly. "Morning," he said.

"Hi, Chief."

"You out looking at the window again?"

"I was just walking the property. There's an old farming road down there. I don't know where it goes. Our guy could have used it to get to the house without being seen."

"Okay. That's another thing we need to check out." The chief gestured toward the closed door. "Have you talked to Ben? Has he remembered anything since yesterday?"

AJ reached for the handle and swung the door open.

Ben was a foot back on the other side. "Somebody needs to cut down on the donuts, huh, AJ?"

"Ben says hi," AJ said over his shoulder. Then, "The chief wants to know if you've remembered anything."

Ben shook his head. "I still don't. I've been trying really hard. I spent half the night trying to recreate the scene, you know, to see if I could jog

164

my memory. Up and down the stairs, pretending to hold the camera. I'm exhausted today. Look, I mean—" He held out an arm, "I even look tired, right? Aren't I—I don't know—duller or something?"

"What did he say?" the chief asked.

"He still doesn't remember anything. He's working at it, though."

"Tell him thanks," the chief said. "I appreciate it."

"You just did."

"I'm going to get it," Ben said. "I know I am."

"AJ," the chief said, "did you talk to Claire last night?"

"Yeah. She should be here soon."

"How's she holding up?"

"She's struggling. I wish she dealt with this as easily as you do."

"It wasn't always easy for me. Remember, you're not the first person I've known who could see the dead. You've got to be patient with her. She'll come around."

"I hope so." AJ glanced at Ben, who shrugged apologetically. "She's planning to go back to New York City today. I guess she has some things she has to do there, anyway, meetings with her publisher or something. She'll be gone today and tomorrow, at least."

"Did you mention the fingerprints?"

"She was going to stop at the station on the way here."

"Good."

"I'd give you mine, you know, but—" Ben turned both palms up.

"Here she comes now," AJ said, nodding toward the driveway.

Claire's car stopped by the garage and she got out. As she approached the step, she held up her hand to show a finger still dark with ink.

"Thanks," the chief said. "That will be a big help."

She stepped past the chief and put her hand on AJ's arm. "Hi."

A smile seemed to spring loose across his face. "Hi. You okay?"

"Not yet. Unless there's anything else you want me to do, I'd like to go pack."

"Okay. Don't forget the charger for your phone."

"I never go anywhere without it."

They paused, looking at each other, but didn't say any more.

Ben backed away as she came at him. "Good morning, Claire. Look, I feel bad about this. I didn't mean to haunt your house, you know? I don't want you to feel like you can't live here. I can stay out of your way. And I hope we can be friends."

Claire started up the stairs.

There was the sound of another car in the driveway. Soon Sela was coming toward the house with a duffle bag, high-stepping it through the weeds. "You should bring a mower out here, AJ," he said.

"Ticks," AJ said to the chief.

"I have a cousin who got Lyme," the chief said. "The antibiotics did the trick for him. I guess he was lucky."

Sela worked his way around an especially leafy plant, as if it might jump him.

"As soon as I get a chance, I'll mow," AJ said. "But I'm going to be kind of busy. That's why you're here."

"I know." Sela was looking down at his ankles, turning them one way than another.

"You poor bastard," Ben said from the doorway. "This place is like your worst nightmare, isn't it?"

AJ squelched a smile.

Sela looked from him to the door. "Hi, Ben."

"Hey, Sela," Ben said. "Isn't it cool to be involved in this investigation? It was my idea to use the cameras."

"Thanks for helping us out, Dave," the chief said. "And so early, too." He shook Sela's hand. "Did you see Detective Wheeler?"

"Yeah. DaSilva did, too. We both did the fingerprinting thing."

"Great."

"Should I start setting up the cameras?"

"Claire's upstairs," AJ said. "Let's wait until she leaves."

The chief helped Sela lower the duffle bag onto the step. "So, did AJ explain what we're after?"

"Yeah. Basic surveillance. You think someone has been in here a couple of times. If he comes back, you want to catch him on video."

"Exactly," the chief said. "Can you do that?"

"Well, it's pretty much what I always do. Except that this time you're trying to catch live people rather than dead ones."

"One other difference," the chief said. "The cameras have to be hidden. It doesn't do us any good to catch someone breaking in if they see the camera and destroy it. Or steal it."

"Believe me, I don't want that, either."

"You don't have any of those pinhole cameras?"

"No. But I think I can deal with it."

"I'm going to be on watch inside," Ben said.

"And as I understand it," the chief said, "they're not trap cameras— motion-sensitive. We have to just let them run."

"That's right," Sela said. "When we use them for paranormal investigation, we want to get everything. We can't depend on motion to set them off."

"How long a recording can you get?" the chief said.

"I have the old camera that uses mini cassettes," Sela said. "Six hours, tops. But then I have the two cameras with hard drives. They'll get seven and eight hours of high quality, twenty to thirty hours max. And I brought the laptop, so you can offload and start over. I went through the process with AJ."

"I'll make sure he gets it right," Ben said.

"We brought the department's camera, too," the chief said. "It uses the tapes. If you want it."

There were footsteps on the stairs and Claire came into view. She had changed into black jeans and a knit top. A scarf was looped around her neck, and a soft suitcase hung from her shoulder.

"I'm ready to go," she said. "Hi, Dave."

He smiled back at her.

"I'll be in touch," the chief said.

"Okay. Goodbye, everyone."

"I'll walk you to the car," AJ said.

They went through the grass. She put her bag in the back seat.

"I'll call as soon as we learn anything," AJ said.

"Just call, even if there's nothing. Okay?"

"I will."

She made a quick move forward and put her arms around him.

He allowed himself to lean into her, to take a single deep breath through her hair. Then he watched her drive away.

Sela was on the porch when AJ found him, standing on a chair, positioning a camera to point across the room toward the door. "This little built-in shelf is perfect," he said. "And these things from the kitchen…" He arranged two silver tins so that the lens just fit between them.

"That's not bad," the chief said.

"Not bad at all," Ben said.

Sela stepped down. "Okay. So I need to cover the front door and the basement window. That leaves me with the room that connects to the garage—it has doors front and back, and one to the garage. I'll put a camera in that room to cover all three."

"All right," AJ said. "When I come back to switch them out, we might want to move one up to the attic."

"Why the attic?"

AJ and the chief exchanged a glance.

"He doesn't know about the tooth?" Ben said.

"It's just another place we want to cover," AJ said.

"Whatever you say." Sela stepped to the side to check the tins from a different angle. "I'll take the other HD camera to the basement. I hope I can plug it in down there." He went toward the front hall, where he had left the duffel bag.

"What are the chances we'll get something?" AJ said, when Sela was gone. "It seems too easy."

"Maybe we'll get lucky," the chief said. "We're due. Chet called me this

167

morning—my counterpart in North Stonington. He's starting to really worry about this missing girl. When she's gone missing before, she's always turned up the next day, all apologetic. So, already this is different. She didn't take anything with her, according to her parents. No clothes. No make-up."

"Shit." AJ ran his hand through his hair, leaving it temporarily in spikes. "Where was she last seen?"

"She left a friend's house on Jerry Browne Road the day she disappeared. She was going to meet up with a boyfriend at the reservoir and then head up to Pachaug State Forest. They talked to him. First, he said that she never showed, then he changed his story and said they went up there and had a fight. He left her there, he said, at a picnic area at Green Falls."

"Do you think he did something to her?"

"Chet doesn't think so. He knows the boy."

"So they searched Pachaug, right? They didn't find anything?"

"Nothing. They're going up again today, with dogs."

"Maybe I should take a look around," AJ said.

"That's what I'm thinking."

"What, because you can see ghosts?" Ben left the hidden camera and came over to them. "Jesus, AJ. I wish I could help. If you had been straight with me a long time ago, you'd have a lot more practice doing this kind of thing."

"It's all right, Ben," AJ said.

"You know Pachaug is one of the most haunted places around. We've been up there a bunch of times for the show. You should be prepared to see something."

AJ just looked back at him.

The chief followed the direction of AJ's eyes. "I've wanted to ask you, AJ," he said. "That shape that Sela got on the video. Is that Ben?"

"No. It's a woman. Judging from her clothes, I'd say she died at least a hundred years ago."

"Interesting. I wonder what happened to her." The chief bit his lip. "Well, that's long before the Westburys were in this house. We can't think about that right now."

Sela reappeared with a video camera and an extension cord. "Which way to the basement?"

AJ showed him, then returned to the porch.

The chief let Sela's footsteps fade away. "I did some checking into who we might be looking for, if it was kids. Didn't really get anywhere. I'm thinking you should try Dewey Allan, see if he's heard anything about any of the locals. He's still in touch with the high school crowd, right?"

"He has that scouting crew, yeah."

"Okay, good. Talk to him. See if he has an idea."

Sela was on his way up the stairs again. He stuck his head into the porch. "I need something to hide the gear."

"There might be boxes in the garage," AJ said. "But wait—do you have Dewey's number on your cell phone?"

"Sure." Sela handed AJ his phone, then left through the kitchen.

AJ added Dewey's number to his phone.

After a while, the front door opened again. "I found some empty boxes," Sela called out. There was the sound of cardboard getting wedged in the narrow space by the basement door. "It's okay, I got it."

When Sela was gone again, the chief said, "I'm going to Meridan. Taking Dr. Umble out to lunch. He's got a weakness for the cheddar bacon dogs at Lulu's."

"So you're using a hot dog to speed up our investigation? Will that work?"

"I don't know. He really loves those hot dogs."

"Good luck with that."

"When Sela's done," the chief said, "we should all take off, let things quiet down here."

"I'll drive over to Pachaug. Maybe I can get a look before the weekend campers start arriving."

"Good. Good."

Sela clomped back up the stairs, sounding worn out by his third trip. "That's the last camera. Now what do we do?"

"We've dropped our trap into the water," the chief said. "Now we see what walks into it."

CHAPTER 33

The lot by the picnic area was empty as AJ pulled in. He sat for a minute, studying the photo that the chief had given him, the same one that had been passed out to the search party. It showed a girl with bleached blonde hair and a delicate hoop through her lip. He got out of the Jeep. "C'mon, boy," he said.

Buck bounded across the tarmac. They took a sandy, root-crossed path toward the water. There were picnic tables in a little clearing, then a strip of beach and the swimming area marked off by ropes. It was deserted. There was no smell of charcoal, no plastic cups in primary colors, no rattle of ice in a cooler, no voice summoning children to a meal.

AJ looked under the nearest table. He kicked at a discarded wrapper. "Is anyone here? Leah? I want to help you."

Turning, he saw gray trunks and leaves, yellow green in the morning sun. A squirrel chided something, maybe Buck, from a nearby branch.

AJ went to the next table and circled it, saying Leah's name. He kept on like that, one table after the other. When he encountered even the barest suggestion of a path, he tried it. He saw nothing but the packed earth and the trees, heard nothing but birds and the leaves whispering in a breeze and his own voice calling out for the girl. Now and then, Buck checked in with him, appearing suddenly out of the brush, racing past.

Finished with the tables, he walked along the edge of the water, checking for any sign. He wound around the lake, sometimes following an informal, stony path. When he reached the paved road, a marked and maintained trail led off into the woods. He took it. As he walked, the sun got stronger, reaching deeper into the trees. He started to feel hot. He went back to the road, tried another tail, then backtracked to the road again. He walked the loop road through the campground. There were a few cars

170

backed in, a few tents, a few families sitting around smoky fires. Most of the sites were empty. He checked each of these—the picnic table, the improvised shortcuts to other sites or to the road. After the last campsite, he circled back to the picnic area. Leaning against a table, he looked at his watch. He'd been at it a couple of hours already.

From somewhere in the woods ahead of him, there was a piercing, desperate scream.

He ran after it. "Hey!" he shouted. He crashed through the undergrowth. "Hey!"

The screaming had stopped, and he stopped running. He was breathing hard.

"Police!" he shouted.

The scream came again—a woman, maybe a girl, giving full-throated voice to fear. From the right, this time. He ran toward the sound. "Police! Stay where you are!"

The scream came again, but behind him. Then, before he could change direction, it came from the left.

"Hey!" AJ tried to follow the sound. "I'm here to help!"

From some distance away, there was a rustling of leaves, then a clawing sound, growing louder, something approaching at speed.

"Hello!" AJ said.

The sound got louder. It was closing in.

"Hey!"

The greyhound burst out from the underbrush. He ran past AJ and away again. AJ went after him. Somewhere ahead, the dog barked. AJ rounded a large rock, and there was Buck, standing taut and alert. Backed up against the rock was a woman in a brown skirt, beads at her waist and around her neck, looping across her breasts. She turned and faded into the rock. The last things to go were her moccasins and her long dark braid.

Buck and AJ stared where the woman had been. Then Buck came over to his master and stood with his flank against AJ's leg. The two of them watched the rock. There were no more screams. No sounds of any kind. The birds and the squirrels and the leaves were silent.

AJ patted the dog's head. "I don't know about you, but I've had enough of this place. Let's get the hell out of here."

When he looked up, AJ saw a figure, not ten feet away. A man—pale, blue, tattered. Their eyes met.

"Gus?" the man said. Then his mouth clamped shut, his face went blank, and he vanished.

***

AJ pulled off of Flanders Road onto the shoulder. Ahead of him,

Dewey was perched on a stone wall. He was eating a sandwich and looking out at a cemetery, where teenagers were scattered, some holding clipboards, others pressing tracing paper against worn headstones. The scouts were dressed for the summer day in shorts and T-shirts, the girls in camisoles, and, next to the dull monuments, their skin seemed to glow.

AJ left his window down a couple of inches. "You stay put," he said to Buck, who sat panting in the passenger seat.

Dewey turned toward him. "Hey, AJ. What's up?"

"Hi, Dewey."

"Want a sandwich? There are extras in the cooler."

"No, thanks. I'm fine." AJ stayed on the road.

"Okay." Dewey took another bite.

"Can we walk a little?"

Dewey wrapped the sandwich up again, then hopped to his feet. "Hey guys," he shouted. "I'll be back in a minute."

A couple of the scouts waved. Dewey and AJ headed down the narrow road.

"What do you need to talk to me about?" Dewey said.

AJ didn't answer right away. Dewey's sandals slapped against the pavement.

"Have you heard anything about kids breaking into houses?" AJ said, finally.

"No. These kids wouldn't do that, AJ. They're all pretty straight."

"I know. But I thought maybe they'd hear something. It's amazing what people tell each other on Facebook. I'm not talking about hardcore burglary—just kids messing around, maybe on a dare."

"Sorry, I don't know anything. What's going on? Do I need to start locking my doors?"

"You should always lock your doors."

Dewey slowed, then looked back toward the cemetery. "Actually, the other night, a couple of the girls were talking about some new summer boys who showed up down on Lord's Point. How cute they were. The guys were saying those boys were bad news. I just figured they were jealous, but maybe there's more to it."

"Do you think you could get some names for me?"

Dewey touched his ponytail. "Sure."

They started back.

"How's Claire doing?" Dewey said.

"She's fine."

They walked in silence, looking ahead to the cemetery and the scouts, some of them busy with their work, others joking across the gravestones.

"I know you guys were there yesterday," AJ said, as he approached his Jeep. "At Claire's."

"Oh. I didn't know what you'd heard, or what you'd think about the whole thing. I had to leave early." He hesitated, then went on, his eyes lighting up. "Do you know if they found anything? I haven't talked to the guys yet. I was thinking how cool it would be to get back in there with the scouts. Teach them about paranormal investigation and history at the same time. Maybe we could even trade Claire for the use of the house—do some chores, cut the grass, maybe."

"Dewey." AJ opened the door. Buck watched him from the passenger seat "Look, don't bother Claire with any of that right now, okay? Don't even ask. If you want the scouts to see ghosts, try Pachaug. You can camp up there, tell ghost stories by the fire, the whole deal." He got into the front seat and rolled the window all the way down. "Sorry. It's been a rough week. You'll call me if you get a name, right?"

"Yeah, yeah, sure. No problem."

"Thanks." AJ turned the Jeep around. In the rearview mirror, he saw Dewey sit on the stone wall, study the crust of his sandwich, then toss it into the weeds.

***

After dropping Buck off at home, AJ went straight to the office in the back of the police station. Chief Brown was putting his signature to something while news played on his little television. He shoved the paper aside but let the news continue. "So, how'd you make out?"

"I just spoke to Dewey. The kids have been talking about some boys down on Lord's Point that may be trouble. He's going to try and get names for me." He sat in one of the plastic chairs. "That guy—I don't know about him."

"Why?"

"He was talking about taking the scouts into Claire's house to do an investigation."

"He's always been like that, AJ. A little overenthusiastic. You reined him in, I hope."

"Oh, yeah."

"So what about Pachaug? Did you see anything?"

"No sign of the girl."

"Where all did you look? Did you stick to where she was last seen?"

"I used that as the starting point, but I checked the whole area—the edge of the pond, the trailheads nearby, even the campsites. I was pretty thorough."

Neither man spoke for a while. The chief seemed to be looking into the infinite distance between his desk and the television. "It was worth a shot, anyway," he finally said. "You ever hear the stories about that place?

About Pachaug? It's supposed to have been haunted for a long time."

"Is there something you want to ask me, chief?"

"Well, you didn't see the girl's ghost, but did you—"

"Yeah. The stories are true. I saw a ghost. In fact, I saw two."

The chief's eyes widened briefly. "But you didn't get anything from them?"

"No, I didn't get anything. I didn't exactly conduct an interview."

"Okay. All right. Maybe next time you can take me up there."

"Next time? I guess so. Sure. You don't think you'll see them?"

"No. But it would still be interesting."

"If you say so." AJ stood up. "How was your lunch with Dr. Umble?"

The chief rubbed his belly and grimaced.

"That good, huh?"

"Next time I'll just give him a cash bribe."

"Did you get anything, besides indigestion?"

"He said he'd try to move the tooth up the queue. But he's really overloaded. It looks like there's a serial killer working up in the Quiet Corner."

"Not so quiet, I guess."

The conversation died for a moment.

"Maybe we need to go some other route," AJ said.

"That's what I thought, too. So I stopped in to see Julia Samuels on my way back here. She was the housekeeper for the Westburys for over thirty years."

"Did you learn anything?"

"I learned that she may be a tiny woman, at eighty-two, frail as a bird, but she has a memory like an elephant."

"That's the kind of memory you want."

"She didn't remember anyone losing a tooth on the attic stairs. She said the Westburys weren't big on having visitors. Jacques rarely had friends over. When he got older, he was out of the house all the time, at the club, sailing. Mrs. Westbury's sister would come once in a while. She had twin boys."

"Maybe it happened after the Westburys, then. Maybe one of the kids who broke into the house over the years."

"Yeah, could be. Unfortunately, we don't have any names. Even when we caught someone there, we just sent them off with a lecture. Unlike that Julia Samuels woman, I don't have a memory like an elephant. I'm going to talk to Romano when he comes in, see if he has anything to add."

AJ nodded unenthusiastically. "I'm going over to Claire's house and deal with the cameras."

"All right. And listen," the chief added, stopping AJ in the doorway, "don't be discouraged. This ability of yours—it's going to pay off. I'm sure of it."

CHAPTER 34

"Ben, where are you?"

AJ dropped the door key into his pocket and continued into the house. He retrieved two video cassettes from the hall closet, then went onto the porch. "Ben?" he said again, looking around.

He pulled a chair over to the high shelf and replaced the tape in the camera that was hidden behind the tins. Retracing his steps, he veered into the living room, where there was a camera on a table, obscured by a straw hat and a vase. He swapped the nearly used tape with the blank. Carrying that camera and the two used cassettes, he climbed the stairs, watching the treads on the turn.

Ben was at the far end of the hall, near the attic door. "AJ. You just missed it."

"What's going on?"

"It's unbelievable. I got through to her. She definitely heard me. I think she saw me, too."

"Did she say anything?"

"No, but she looked like she wanted to, right before she disappeared through this door. Next time I want to be waiting for her on the other side of the door, in the attic. I think if I can get her at just the right instant, I can reach her."

"I was going to put this camera up there." AJ pointed toward the door.

"Oh, don't. It might scare her off."

"Ben, do you remember what we're trying to do here? This is important."

"Yeah, yeah. I remember. Can't you set the camera up in the hall? I mean, nobody's going to get to the attic without passing by here."

"It's kind of hard to hide a camera in an empty hallway."

"Just put a chair out here, put the camera on it, and toss a drop cloth over the whole thing."

"That might work." AJ went down to the porch and returned with a wooden chair. "You know you were supposed to be keeping watch downstairs. How much time did you spend up here waiting for your lovely lady ghost?"

"She is lovely." Ben's eyes closed for a second. "I don't know how long I was up here. I guess I lost track of time. Did you swap the tapes in the two older cameras?"

"Yeah. I'll take them to my house and see what we got."

"I wish you could watch them here, so I could see, too. Remember what happened with my video—I was the only one who noticed the flash. But there's no VCR."

"I can't be spending time here, anyway, if we're going to catch something." AJ arranged a drop cloth on the chair, leaving a gap for the lens, which was aimed at the stairs. "I should go. I'll be back later this afternoon to change the tapes again. I guess it will be time to reset the other cameras, too."

"Right," Ben said. "That's a little more complicated. Bring Sela."

AJ paused at the top of the stairs. "I'll see you in a while. Say hi to your friend for me."

"Okay. Maybe I'll have a message from her when you come back."

Before leaving the house, AJ looped around and went down to the basement. It was quiet and dark. The boxes Sela had carried down were stacked against one wall. The window was right where it was supposed to be.

***

When AJ pulled into his own driveway, Sela was waiting there, music blaring from the open windows of his car.

"Good song," AJ said, coming over, the videotapes in his hand. "Claire was playing this the other day. When we painted."

"Really? I like her more all the time." Sela shut off the sound and opened the door. "I hope you two are going to be able to fix things between you."

AJ ignored that. "I got the tapes," he said, holding them up.

They went inside. Sela slid one of the little tapes into an adapter, then slid that into the VCR.

"I can't believe we're going to watch, what, twelve hours of video," AJ said.

"Since we're looking for a flesh-and-blood person, I think we can speed it up. Compared to looking for a ghost, this should be a piece of cake."

"Good."

"Did you guys find out anything today?" Sela said. "Do you have any ideas about who we might see?"

"I guess a couple of summer kids landed with a bad reputation. Could be them."

"All that money and what they come up with for entertainment is B and E. I hope we nail their asses."

AJ brought a couple of sodas in from the kitchen. They settled onto the couch. AJ held up the remote. "Here goes." He switched on the television and started the tape.

They were looking down and across the porch toward the screen door, and beyond it, the yard.

"Not a bad angle," Sela said. "The glare on the screen makes it hard to see past it, though."

"If he comes in the door, we'll see him just fine."

The television showed the shiny surface of the table, the rectangles of the door, the metal screen making a blurred haze of sunlight.

"Fast forward?" AJ said.

"Do it."

AJ pressed the button. The player whined.

The image was the same—the table, the screen door, the bright, blurred yard.

AJ and Sela stared at the television, sipping their drinks carefully so that they never had to look away. They watched the rectangles of the screen door and the polished dining room table.

"God, Dave," AJ said after a while. "Is this what you guys do? I have new respect for you. I think I'd go crazy."

"Yeah, and it's been, what, three minutes? You'd never make it on our team."

They were quiet, focused on the image, which bumped ever so slightly, as if it were outside the window of a smooth, speeding train.

The table. The screen door. The yard.

AJ sank back into the cushions, then thought better of it and sat upright again.

Asleep by the front door, the dog moaned and kicked his legs.

After a while, AJ stood up. He tried that position, occasionally wagging his head back and forth..

"You're pathetic," Sela said. "Good thing you don't have a desk job."

AJ sat down.

Table.

Door.

Yard.

They finished their drinks. AJ's eyelids slid lower, bounced up again, then closed. Sela nudged him awake.

Table table table.

Door door door.

Yard yard yard.

AJ yawned.

"You know, I got this," Sela said. "If you want to lie down."

"I'm fine." AJ opened his eyes wide.

Table door yard door table yard table yard yard. Table.

AJ titled back again.

Taaaaable.

Dooooorrrrr.

Yyyyaaarrddd.

Sela elbowed AJ hard in the ribs. "Wake up! We've got somebody!"

"What is it?"

"Take a look." Sela restarted the film.

A figure stood at the screen door. He was wearing a cap that hid his face.

AJ moved closer to the television. "That damn cap. Back it up. Maybe we can catch something as he walks to the door."

Sela rewound the tape. They watched the man come from the direction of the garage. He was half hidden by the sheen of the screen door.

"Well, we know it's not bored rich kids," Sela said.

"You can't see his face at all," AJ said. "He's wearing a windbreaker and khakis."

"He's carrying something. Cages, maybe. They look almost like lobster pots. Oversized lobster pots."

"Right. That's what they are. Claire said she had some behind the garage."

"So what the hell? He's stealing her lobster pots?"

The man dropped the pots. He stepped forward and peered through the screen, his cupped hands obscuring his face. Then he turned, picked up the pots and went around the porch, moving out of the frame.

"Damn," AJ said.

"Let me try it again." Sela replayed the segment.

"Freeze it," AJ said, when the man stood at the screen. "What's that writing, on the cap? Something *club*."

"Quanaduck Club," Sela said. "It's the Quanaduck Yacht Club. That narrows it down, doesn't it?"

"Yes, indeed it does."

"What does Jacques Westbury look like? Is this him?"

"I don't know," AJ said. "I've never seen him, either. I mean, I've seen pictures of him, but they were probably all from twenty years ago. I don't know if I'd recognize him now. And with what we got here, I couldn't even tell this guy's age."

"Maybe there's more," Sela said. "Maybe he came back." Sela fast-forwarded through the rest of the tape. More table, door and yard. "We killed one," he said. He got up to start the other tape.

"That's from the camera that was on the front door," AJ said. "If he started out in the back, I'm pretty sure he didn't come in that way."

"You want to watch it or not?" .

"Go ahead." AJ left Sela to it while he made a couple of sandwiches. He put them on the coffee table. They ate with their eyes on the screen. The six panels of the door never changed.

"Well, that's not going to win any Academy Awards," AJ said.

"Maybe with the right soundtrack," Sela said. "What now?"

"Now we go to the chief."

***

"How are you making out with the surveillance cameras?" the chief said, when AJ appeared in his doorway. "I see you brought help."

"Hi, Chief," Sela said.

AJ held up the tapes. "I have something I want you to see."

After AJ explained what they had on the tape, the chief came around from behind his desk and leaned out of his door. "Manzella!" he shouted. Pulling his head back into the room, he added, "He did security part-time at the Quanaduck right up until he made detective. Maybe he'll notice something."

Officer Manzella joined them in crowding around the television. He had silver hair and a straight back and a neat mustache that was still dark. "What are we looking at?"

"We got this from the Wes—the Connor house," the chief said.

They watched the figure come to the porch door.

"Quanaduck," Manzella said, gesturing toward the television. "I can't see the guy's face, so I can't tell you who that is, if that's what you're after. I do recognize the cap, though."

"Well, yeah, we recognize the cap," Sela said. "It says Quanaduck right on it."

Manzella shot Sela a look. "More than that. First of all, it's red. That means it's not a regular member's cap, it's an instructor's cap. They run a good program down there, using those little JY-15s."

"How many instructors do they have?" the chief said.

"I don't know. A good number. What with part-timers, maybe a half dozen or so. The staff turns over every few years. Which brings me to the second thing. The style of the cap. That changes every couple of years, too. This one here's an old design. I'm guessing it goes back ten, fifteen years."

180

"Westbury would have belonged to that club twenty years ago," AJ said. "Could the cap be that old?"

Manzella shrugged. "Yeah, maybe."

"I think it's time I had a talk with Mr. Westbury," the chief said.

"Shouldn't we wait until we have more?" AJ said. "I don't want to scare him off. There are two cameras I haven't checked yet. Maybe we got a better shot."

The chief shook his head. "You check those cameras. But Jacques isn't going anywhere. He bought himself a nice boat and is renting a house. You know where he's renting?"

AJ shook his head.

"That place down on Lord's Point where there was a murder a few years back. The guy stabbed his wife."

"He didn't just stab her," Manzella said. "He made a pin cushion out of her."

"That's right," the chief said. "It was awful. What kind of man rents a place with that kind of history? It's sort of—"

"In your face," Sela said.

"Okay, yeah," the chief said. "I was thinking ghoulish." He pointed the remote at the television, switching it back to the news. Firemen stood in the glare of a burning building. For a while, the only sound was the reporter's voice coming through the little speakers.

"Is there any way we can confirm the age of that cap?" the chief said, his eyes coming back to the room.

"Sure," Manzella said. "They have the whole collection in a case at the club."

"Okay. Go to it." When Manzella was gone, the chief added, "Good work, AJ. Still, all we got there is trespassing. Some minor theft, if he's taking those lobster pots without Claire's permission. She didn't tell Jacques or anyone else he could have them, right?"

"Not as far as I know."

"What about Ben? Did you talk to him? Did he see anything?"

AJ puffed his cheeks. "Nothing."

"All right. Plain old detective work, then. There's nothing wrong with that." The chief tapped AJ on the back. "You keep going with the cameras. I'll go talk to my friend Mr. Westbury."

CHAPTER 35

Chief Brown crept down the narrow street, ready for anything. For good reason. Twice, young boys on bikes darted out in front of him. At the last intersection, he turned away from the neighborhood. With another turn, he left it completely behind. When he had finally stopped his patrol car in the driveway, he sat for a long time, staring across the trim grass at the barren walls of the isolated house.

"God, I hate this place," he said under his breath.

He walked to the front door. No bell. He banged a couple of times with his fist. The response was more silence. He went around the left side of the house. The end wall was inset and nothing but glass. Looking in, he saw square black chairs on a vast slate floor. Against one wall, out of place, was a worn, brown trunk, marked, since that day in Henry's barn, with a long strip of blue painter's tape.

There was the whine of a motor from behind the house. The chief went toward it, into the back yard. Before long he was standing at the edge of a waterway. A small boat with an outboard motor came into view.

Jacques Westbury steered the boat toward the chief without acknowledging him. He cut the engine and let the hull run aground. As he dragged the boat further ashore, the chief helped him.

"Hello, Officer Brown," Jacques said. He reached back into the boat and tossed an anchor into the mud. "I mean, Chief Brown. I hear you've been promoted."

"That's kind of old news, Jacques. You've been away too long."

"Too long, or not long enough?"

"Guess that depends on who you ask."

"Okay, Chief. I don't see a welcome basket, so I'm guessing you're not here just to chat. Something happen that I should know about?"

"I'm afraid so. There've been some problems at your old house. I'd like to ask you some questions."

"Well, it's not my house anymore, so they're not my problems." Jacques was wearing a cap with a long bill. He shifted it on his head, revealing and then hiding again fine, gray hair darkened by sweat.

The chief, feeling his shoes sinking into the soft dirt, raised one foot and examined it. He took a step back toward the house. "Have you been there since the closing?"

"I'm sure Claire told you I was. I'd left a chair that I decided I wanted. So I stopped by to see if she wouldn't mind letting me take it."

"You showed her a basement window that was loose."

"I didn't need to show it to her. She found it herself. I only recommended that she get it fixed."

"You said you used to sneak in and out of the house that way."

"Yes, I did. I was feeling a little nostalgic, I guess."

"Who else knew about that window?"

"I have no idea. Probably half the teenagers in town, back then."

"Is that the only time you've been there?"

"Yes."

"You sure? Maybe there was something else you forgot, something else you went back for."

"Oh, I see. So there was a burglary. Someone used that window to get into the house, and you think it was me. Come on, Chief. I haven't crawled through a basement window, or any other window, in a long, long time."

The chief studied Jacques's face, then looked past him to the boat. There was a coil of black rope near the bow. "Is that sink rope?" the chief said. "The kind that you tie between lobster pots?"

"Yes."

"You going to be doing some lobster fishing?"

"I might set a few pots."

"Looks like a lot of rope."

Jacques gave the boat another tug.

"Where are your pots?"

"I don't have them yet."

"I see. Just the rope."

"Yes."

"You know, Claire had some lobster pots at the house, too. I guess that's another thing you left behind."

"That's right. I talked to her about them."

"You haven't been back there to see about taking a couple of those off her hands?"

"No, Chief, I haven't. What exactly happened at her house, anyway?"

The chief ignored the question. "So you're staying the whole summer?"

"Maybe longer."

"Then why sell the house?"

"It was time for me to move on. I'm sure you understand why."

"You like this place better."

"No, not really. But there wasn't a lot to choose from. I like the access to the water. So, I'm making do."

"The murder that happened here—makes you feel right at home."

A ruddy color flooded Jacques's cheeks. He gave the boat another tug. "Is there a point to this?"

"How about the yacht club? Is it time for you to move on from the yacht club, too? Or did you rejoin?"

"The Quanaduck? I haven't been back there, no."

"You were an instructor at the Quanaduck, weren't you?"

"Yes, a long time ago. Chief, what's this all about?"

The chief hooked one thumb on his heavy black belt. "A man wearing a Quanaduck Club cap was seen skulking around Ms. Connor's house. Our detective says it was an old instructor's cap, from about twenty years ago. Which means back in your day."

"So naturally you think of me, even though there must be half a dozen, maybe two dozen, men and women with those caps."

"Do you still have yours?"

"Actually, I did, until recently. But it went into a box of clothing I donated to the Salvation Army when I cleared out the house."

"Really? When did you make that donation?"

"I'm not sure. It's been pretty hectic. You know, Carl Foley's still in town. I ran into him the other day. He was an instructor back then, too. You could ask him if he has his cap."

"Thanks for the tip."

"Anytime, Chief. Now, if you'll excuse me, I have nothing in particular to do."

"Must be nice for you. Talk to you again soon, I hope."

The chief left Jacques standing by his boat. He crossed the yard again. As he passed the house, his pale reflection followed him in the glass.

CHAPTER 36

Jacques came into the huge room, buttoning a crisp shirt over his chest. Though the floor was hard stone, his shoes made no sound. He wound his way through the furniture and stopped at the old trunk. Crouching, he snapped open the latch. He reached inside and brought out a small, plastic container.

He went out the front door to his car. After navigating the neighborhood streets to Route 1, he headed north up the shoreline. Before long, he turned left, away from the water. He drove through rocky woods divided by stone walls. He passed clusters of houses, then woods, then houses again.

He slowed and pulled into Henry Jacobson's driveway. On his left was the barn. On his right was the ranch house, a porch running the length of it.

He went to the front door of the house and knocked. After a moment, the door opened, in stages, first a crack wide enough for a single eye, then the width of a face in shadow.

"Hi, Jacques," Henry said. "Good to see you." He opened the door a little wider and stepped through it.

"I hope you don't mind me stopping by unannounced."

Henry closed the door behind him. He was wearing a brown T-shirt that stretched tight over his big frame. "Is it about Ellis? Did he do okay?"

"Oh, he did a great job. The canal is in fine shape. I've been using it."

"All right. He always did know how to work when the work was in front of him. If you've got anything else to do…"

"I will at some point. You know who you should talk to is Claire Connor. That place—well, I don't have to tell you. It can keep someone like Ellis busy. In fact, I know she's got something right now—that old basement window. She discovered it while I was over there and wants to fix it. I mentioned your name. I could find an excuse to talk to her again, put in a good word."

"Huh." Henry rubbed his chin and looked away. "Thanks, but that's all right."

"Okay," Jacques said, looking puzzled.

"I meant to tell you. My daughter really appreciated the furniture. She said to be sure and thank you."

"Glad to hear that," Jacques said. "I brought the last chair. It's in pretty bad shape, but I figure if anyone can repair it, you can."

"You have it with you? Let's take a look."

They crossed the driveway. The hatch of Jacques's SUV swung up with the hiss of hydraulics.

Henry leaned into the cargo space. "I think it's salvageable."

"Careful. There's not much holding it together. Here." Jacques got in front of Henry and slipped both hands under the chair. He stood up, cradling the thing as if it were an injured child.

"Let's take it to the barn," Henry said.

"There's something else on the passenger seat for you. Take a look."

Henry went around the vehicle and came back with the plastic container.

"Open it," Jacques said.

Henry pried the lid free.

"I don't know if you do anymore, but I remember you used to collect skulls and things. I thought you might like that. Looks like maybe a mouse—"

"Chipmunk." Henry looked into the container at the frail skeleton, the ribs as thin as jewelry wire. "That is something. Near perfect. Thanks."

"You must have a sizeable collection by now, if you've kept at it."

"I do. Let's go on to the barn. You'll see."

Jacques followed Henry to the door. The old man drew back the heavy latch and then put his shoulder to the wood. The door slid aside slowly.

"I was wondering if you still had those boxes of clothes I left," Jacques said. "The old shirts and the like?"

"I dropped them off at the Salvation Army right away. That kind of thing sits out here for more than a day and I'd have critters setting up housekeeping in it."

"So you didn't want any of it?"

"I got enough clothes."

"Yeah, I'm sure you do," Jacques said.

"You looking for something in particular?"

"I could use a few things to wear when I'm working in the yard."

"You're doing yard work now?"

"Well, what else am I going to do all day?"

"I'm sure I don't know."

"Oh, well." Jacques looked around the dark space where his furniture had once been collected. "Where do you want the chair?"

"This way. I have my shop over here." He swung open a door in the rough wooden wall.

They stepped up into a long, narrow room with a plywood floor, shelves along one side and a tool-strewn workbench with saws hanging behind it. In the far corner was a keg-sized woodstove.

"Nice setup," Jacques said, lowering the chair carefully.

Henry went to the shelves.

Jacques followed him. "Ah, so here's your little natural history museum."

"It's a regular Peabody."

"That's at Yale, right?"

"Yeah. I go down there once a year." Making room, Henry shifted an object to the side—a deer skull, with gaping eyeholes. "I never get tired of it. My parents took me the fist time when I was just five or six. I saw those dinosaurs in the great hall, and I was set. That's what started me collecting. Of course, I don't have fossils, I have bones and other remains. Animals of the modern age." Henry looked back and forth between the space he had cleared and the plastic box.

"Maybe you should just keep it in the container."

"Okay, thanks. That'd be easiest, for now." Henry slid his new acquisition into place.

"So what is all this? Can you give me the tour?"

Henry started at one end of the long shelf. "Squirrel, complete. Raccoon skull. Hawk wing. Possum foot. You can guess what this is, by the teeth."

"Got to be a beaver."

"That's right. Looks like it's made for cutting, doesn't it?"

"It does," Jacques said. "I bet there's a story about each of these animals, and what happened to them."

"I guess. I don't think much about that. I just like the objects."

"How did you come to find so many?"

"You wander around enough, like I do, you come across things. And people bring things to me that they've found, like you did. My son has a knack for it—you know, sharp eyes. Anything Ellis finds, he brings to me. The hawk, though—" he put his hand on the feathers "—that just fell out of the sky, dead. Landed on the pavement as I was driving down Flanders Road. Like it had a heart attack in mid-air. Strangest thing."

"That is strange."

"Nests, down at this end. Robin, flycatcher and my favorite." Henry held up a twig to which was attached a tiny, nearly closed bowl covered with curled bits of lichen. "Hummingbird."

"Wow, that's something."

"Yeah. Held together with spider web. The hummingbirds tear webs apart and use them to build these things. Once in a while they get caught doing it."

"What did you do to your hand?" Jacques pointed at a long scrape that went from the knuckle of Henry's index finger back toward his wrist.

Henry put the twig back on the shelf. "Cut it on something at the dump. That's what I get for trying to pick there, since it's against the rules anymore." He lifted a long, translucent ribbon. "Black snake. Got this right here in the barn."

"Now you tell me," Jacques said. He bent to the lowest shelf. There was a long bone there, blunt at one end, with a rounded spur almost like a handle at the other. "This is pretty big. What animal is it from?"

"I haven't been able to figure that one out, yet."

Jacques straightened, a slight grimace belying the smoothness of the motion. "Quite a collection."

"It's just something I fool around with. Ellis and me."

"Did you ever call Claire Connor about those lobster pots? I bet she'd let you have them."

"Not yet." Henry squinted at Jacques. "I just can't get used to someone else being in that house. It doesn't seem to be bothering you half as much as it is me."

"I feel relieved, mostly."

"I can understand that." Henry had cupped one hand in the other, as if to protect the wound. "Did you decide about the boat?"

"They're bringing it up tonight. It's a beauty. You'll have to come see it. I'll take you out."

"That'd be real nice. I haven't been out in a fine sailboat in—well, since your dad died."

Jacques put his hand on Henry's shoulder. The two men were quiet for a moment.

"Since you're back on the water," Henry said, "maybe you should take those pots from Ms. Connor."

Jacques seemed to be considering the idea. "No. I know how much you and your family love lobster. Anyway, those pots are too big for me. Maybe I'll get myself a smaller one. Bachelor size."

"Suit yourself."

"Well, I'd better get going. Good luck with that chair."

"I think I might need it. It got pretty banged up, somehow. Good luck with your boat."

They went back through the door. Henry stayed there while Jacques turned his SUV around. As Jacques drove away, a gray tiger cat appeared from the shadows and rubbed against Henry's leg.

"What's he up to, girl?" Henry said. "Thinks he's so smooth, so smart." He headed across the cement-hard driveway, the cat following him, its tail straight up. After he'd closed the front door behind him, Henry lifted a brick-red cap from a peg on the wall there. He looked at it, as if reading the lettering stitched in gold thread—*Quanaduck Club*.

The cat was at his feet, rubbing against his ankles, purring.

Henry walked as far as the kitchen, where there was a steel trash can with a pedal. He put his foot on the little half circle, raising the lid. He dropped the cap. Then he let the lid fall shut.

CHAPTER 37

AJ and Sela stood over the stack of lobster pots behind Claire's garage. The bottom row was half submerged in the grass.

"First he breaks into the basement," AJ said. "Then he comes back and takes a couple lobster pots. It doesn't make any sense. What's he up to?"

"Those are some big freakin' pots." Sela bent to peer into one. "Look at this parlor. I could fit in there. Jesus."

"I don't know why anyone would want to take these things, the way lobster fishing is now."

"Yeah, there aren't many people setting traps anymore. Since the die-off began in, what, '99?" Sela straightened up. "What's the catch in the sound now, 150,000 pounds? When it used to be millions? Everyone knows it's because of the methoprene in the water. But no one will do anything about it."

AJ took a few steps past the pots, his head down.

Sela followed him. "This is when you find something, right? A shoe print or a glove or something."

"You watch too much television." AJ gave up looking in the grass and started back toward the porch.

"Did you find anything?" Ben said from the other side of the screen.

"You'd never believe it," AJ said. "There was a glove back there."

"He's just yanking my chain." Sela followed AJ into the porch. A laptop computer was open on the table, connected to a video camera. Sela tapped the keyboard. "Okay. All the video's loaded onto here." He closed the lid and disconnected the cable. "Do you want to set the cameras up again?"

"Yeah," AJ said. "I want to try to get a good look at this guy. I'd like to see his smiling face."

"There's going to be a lot of video to watch, if we keep shooting," Sela said. "We're not going to be able to keep up with it."

"He's right, AJ," Ben said, from over Sela's shoulder. "When we do an investigation—I mean, when I used to—we'd take maybe twenty hours of video. It's bad enough going through that. Anyway, you don't even need the cameras. If anything happens, I'll see it."

"Not if you're trying to keep watch in the upstairs hallway. You can't be everywhere at once."

Ben shrugged. "That's true."

"What about the upstairs hallway?" Sela said.

"Ben's been trying to catch the ghost you saw upstairs."

"I like that. A ghost hunting a ghost."

AJ looked out across the back yard, past the tray of violets, to the corner of the house and down the weedy open space beyond. Clouds had moved in over the trees. "A storm's coming. I should check with Claire, see if she wants me to get this table inside." He pulled the cell phone from his pocket and worked the keypad with his thumbs.

"When's Claire coming back, anyway?" Sela said.

"She's not," Ben said, "as long as the house is full of video cameras."

AJ snapped the phone closed. "I don't think it's the cameras that she's avoiding."

"Oh, that's great. It's my fault." Ben glared at AJ for a moment. "Okay. Maybe it is. What exactly do you want me to do? You know I'd leave here in a second if I could."

"Calm down, Ben. I was talking about me, not you."

"Sorry. What, you think she's avoiding you?"

AJ didn't answer.

"That sucks," Ben said. "She just needs time. About the cameras, though—if you set them up again, just don't put one in the upstairs hall, okay? I think it scares my friend. I was so close to actually communicating with her, but since you put the camera there, she hasn't been back."

"Ben, this is important."

"What are you guys talking about?" Sela said. "What's important?"

"Ben thinks the cameras scare that other ghost away. He wants to try to communicate with her."

"Oh." Sela scanned the room. "Ben, that thing upstairs—it's a residual haunt, isn't it? There's no intelligence there. It's like an echo. You're not going to be able to talk to it. I mean, you're the one who taught me about this stuff."

"She's not just an echo," Ben said. "Maybe the whole theory of residual haunts is wrong. There is intelligence. I can see it in her eyes. In fact, there's something very special about her. I think... I think I'm in love with her." He looked surprised to be saying those words.

"You're kidding me," AJ said.

"What?" Sela said.

"Ben's interested in the ghost."

"Of course," Sela said. "Talking to a ghost—that was always his dream."

"No, I mean, he's *interested* in her. Actually, he said he's in love with her, but that just seemed too ridiculous to repeat."

"Oh, Jesus." Sela blew air through his teeth. "Ben, is this a thing with you? The woman you can't have? You kept after Melody all that time, when it was obvious that you weren't getting anywhere. That was sad, but this—this is just crazy. I mean, Melody was an unattainable woman, but at least she was an *actual woman*. This ghost you think you're in love with, can she even talk?"

"Go fuck yourself," Ben said.

AJ shook his head.

"Uh huh." Sela rubbed the whiskers on his chin. "So if you can't talk to her, exactly what kind of connection do you have? Can you touch her?"

"I don't know."

"He doesn't know," AJ said.

Sela was focused on the space where he guessed Ben was. "I never thought about this before. Ghosts have a hard time touching things, but what happens when two ghosts come in contact with each other?"

"I said I don't know," Ben said.

AJ shrugged.

"Well, what happens when you touch yourself?"

Ben rolled his eyes. "Of course I can touch myself." He patted his stomach.

"What did he say?" Sela turned to AJ. "Can he?"

"Yes, he can touch himself. You want to warn him about going blind or should I?"

"Ben," Sela said, "have you tried touching her? You've got to do that. See what happens."

From across the lawn, there was a low, resolute rumble. The three men all looked toward it. The dark clouds covered half the sky.

"Did Claire text you back?" Sela said. "About moving the table?"

AJ checked his phone. "No." He put the phone back in his pocket, then began pulling chairs away from the table. "Let's get this inside. Then we'll head over to my house and watch the video."

"What about the cameras?" Sela said. "Do you still want to set 'em up again?"

"Please, don't." Ben slipped into the table to put himself directly in front of AJ. "Look, forget about my thing with her. My ghost friend might know something. Like who was in the basement and the yard. Or what happened to me. She might even know about that girl—Anna Marie Rose.

I think I can talk to her, AJ. Just let me try."

AJ stared back at Ben, silent.

"You know the chief would want me to try to talk to her," Ben said. "Hell, he would want *you* to try to talk to her. But if you won't do it—"

At this, AJ laughed. "C'mon, Sela. Let's move the table and then get the hell out of here."

"So, no more cameras?"

"No. Like you said, we have a lot of video already. Anyway, we don't want to screw up Ben's love life."

CHAPTER 38

Listen up. I know it's early, but I didn't think you'd mind. It's not like I'm waking you. People like to say, 'I'll sleep when I'm dead,' but, really, only the living sleep, right?

Anyway. I made a promise that we'd move back to the house. I hope you understand, this thing I have to do, this thing with Claire, it's complicated. For one thing, it's tough getting her alone. Her friends are in and out of there all the time, and there's no predicting when. Melody is a special problem. She even stays overnight sometimes.

So, this is what I've been faced with—trying to plan for an unpredictable situation, trying to be ready for anything. Finally, this morning, I had a very important realization. It's not enough to be ready for anything. You have to be ready to do anything.

I am.

What I'm trying to say is that after today, you won't have to wait much longer.

Well, the sun's coming up. Even if things go exactly as I hope they will, I'm going to be a busy man. I'd better get started.

CHAPTER 39

"Leave that here," Jacques said, putting out his hand to stop her.

"Why?"

"Because no one brings a purse on a sailboat. Especially that purse."

Melody let the strap of the bright orchid bag fall back onto the chair. "I bring it everywhere. I'll be lost without it."

"Baby," Jacques said, his voice all swagger, "you'll never be lost with me at the helm."

"Oh, brother." Melody rolled her eyes.

Jacques laughed.

She reached into her bag. "I'll just grab my phone."

"No phones," Jacques said. "Definitely no phones. Look, I'll leave mine, too." He placed a square device next to the bag.

"What if there's an emergency?"

"The boat has a radio. C'mon. Where's my spontaneous, adventurous Melody?" Taking her hand, he led her from the big living room through the dimly lit kitchen to a door that opened onto the back yard. "Your generation is much too dependent on technology."

"Please don't start with the *your generation* crap." Melody stepped out into the early morning. "It's not a generational thing, it's a class thing. My boat barely has oars. I forgot that your boat would have a radio. Let alone all the other bells and whistles you take for granted."

They started across the lawn. The clouds glowed red ahead of them.

"Okay," he said. "When we're out in your boat, you can bring your phone, and that giant purse. But you'll have to do the rowing."

"Why? Do you have a bad shoulder?" She rubbed his back.

"My shoulders are fine. Like you said, it's a class thing."

"How's that?"

"My class doesn't row."

She stopped rubbing and smacked him.

When they reached the canal, he helped her into the motorboat that was beached there. He shoved the boat backward into the water. As he sat down next to her, she put her hand on his knee.

He pulled on the starter rope and the engine came to life. They began to move through the tight channel. It was just wide enough. The tall stalks of the marsh plants whispered against the sides of the boat; they bent overhead, casting shadows. A wet leaf swept across the bow, catching Melody on the cheek, making her squeal.

"Sorry," Jacques said. "I'm going to need to get Ellis back out here."

The boat went slower, creeping along. The passage shrank, the plants closed in, the bow parting them with a dry, crackling sound. Jacques cut the engine and tipped the propeller out of the water. It seemed that they would disappear into the tangle and be swallowed by it.

"Jacques," Melody said, shifting back on the seat.

Suddenly, the bottom dropped away and a bright expanse of water opened up in front of them. Jacques let the small boat glide quietly into the lagoon.

"Here we are," Jacques said.

A dozen sailboats were moored in water that was like polished stone under the overcast sky.

"It's so still," Melody said. "I guess I won't be getting a sailing lesson today."

"No, not today." Jacques's mouth tightened. He reached to pull the cord again.

"Wait!" Melody said.

"What's wrong?"

"I want to guess which boat is yours. It will be too easy if you're heading right to it."

Jacques let go of the cord.

"That one. The blue one." She pointed.

"Which blue one? There are two blue boats out there."

"Turquoise, I mean. Farthest out. I'd bet money on it."

Jacques shook his head. He started the motor and aimed the bow in a different direction. The sailboat in front of them now was small, with a dull red hull and a short mast.

"Oh," Melody said, disappointed.

But as they drew close to the red boat, Jacques steered them around it, until they were heading toward Melody's pick—a sleek thirty-foot sloop near the mouth of the cove.

"I knew it," she said.

"How did you guess?"

"The only thing in the house that you bought for yourself was a turquoise vase. And I noticed two new shirts that color hanging in your closet. I think you're decorating and dressing to match your boat. Which is kind of cute."

"You have me all figured out, don't you? You missed your calling. You should be a detective."

"Coming from you, I'll take that as an insult."

"No, no. You could change my mind about the police. If it were you coming around to hassle me, I'd look forward to it."

"Jacques," Melody said, looking concerned, "has someone from the police been hassling you?"

His jaw clenched hard for a moment before he answered. "I'm sorry I brought it up. Let's just say that Chief Brown is a very persistent man."

They closed on the sailboat with no more conversation. When they were anchored alongside, Jacques brushed a loose strand of hair away from Melody's eyes. "I'll give you the tour," he said, his face relaxed again. "Then we can see about breakfast."

They climbed aboard. He led her down the companionway steps. The first stop was the compact luxury of the galley—reddish teak, black speckled countertops. Jacques produced a large silver kettle from behind a latched door. He put it on the stove. "What do you think?"

"This is nicer than my kitchen at home." Melody let her fingers slide across the wood. "So you really think we'll find someone willing to sell us a lobster right out of the trap? I've never heard of anyone doing that."

"When I was growing up that's how we always bought our lobster—never from the market."

"So there really are people catching lobster here in Stonington? I thought we got all our lobster from Maine."

"You'd be surprised how many people set traps right in the shallow water. Recreational lobsterman, or small-timers trying to make a few bucks. River rats, we used to call them."

Melody centered the heavy kettle on the burner. "Still, it seems like we'll have to be awfully lucky to come across someone just as they're pulling up their pots."

"Why all the negativity? You don't trust me to know what I'm doing?"

She cocked her head, regarding him. "If I didn't trust you, would I be out here?"

He smiled. "Let's finish the tour." He showed her the table in the main cabin, where they would eat, the compact head, the forward V-berth that was all bed.

She lay back on the mattress, looking up at the complex puzzle of wood and portlights. "So where do we look, anyway, to find a lobster—out in the sound? Or do we stay in close to the shore? Will it take a long time?"

He leaned over her, pinning one hand. "Are you that hungry?"

"I guess I am. Every time I think about a lobster omelet, my mouth starts to water."

"Well, we'd better get going, then. I can't have you drooling all over my new sheets."

Back on the deck, Jacques took the helm. They motored out of the cove into gray, empty water.

"I don't see any boats." Melody stood at Jacques's elbow, squinting into the breeze. "We're going to be all alone out there. Maybe we're too early. Especially on a gloomy day like this."

"We're not too early. And a few clouds shouldn't matter."

"I don't even see any lobster buoys. Wouldn't you see them, if there were pots here?"

Jacques looked at her quizzically. "I thought you trusted me to know what I'm doing."

Melody found a pair of binoculars stowed by the wheel and scanned the water in all directions. "Look, here comes someone."

Jacques reached for the binoculars. "I don't believe it," he said, after a minute of studying a boat that was as battered as an old shoe. "That looks like Joe Bacchiocchi."

"Will he have lobsters?"

"He might, but they won't do us any good. Joe was—I guess he still is—the local lobster pot watch dog and thief all rolled into one. God, he must be well into his eighties by now."

"He steals lobsters? Why doesn't he get into trouble?"

"His regular patrol kept the more serious poachers away. Everyone considered the few lobsters he took to be fair payment for services rendered." Jacques handed the binoculars back to Melody. He kept the course out into the sound.

"I think he's stopped," Melody said after a while. "Maybe he found a pot. Though I didn't see a buoy there."

"Could be a ghost pot."

"What's a ghost pot?"

"A pot that's been abandoned. Sometimes it's just been tossed overboard. Sometimes the line's been cut by a boat propeller."

Melody lowered the binoculars. "Wonder why they call them ghost pots? It sounds like they're for catching ghosts."

"Pots for catching ghosts? That's a bizarre idea." Jacques turned to her with a wry smile. "You have an interesting imagination. Scary, but interesting."

"Should we go check it out?"

"No."

"Why not? If it's a ghost pot, it doesn't belong to anyone. Maybe Mr. Bacchiocchi will share if he finds something."

"Not with me. I won't count Joe as someone happy to see me back in town." Jacques stared ahead toward the red clouds.

Melody studied him without saying anything. Then she looked off the stern again. "He's pulling something up. I think it's a lobster pot. A really big one."

Jacques throttled the engine back and looked over his shoulder.

"Another boat's coming over," Melody said. "Damn. They're in the way. Now I can't see the pot."

A sharp sound cut across the water—a human voice.

Melody grabbed Jacques's arm. "Did you hear that? That was a scream. From the other boat. Something's wrong."

Jacques watched for a moment more. "There was probably a spider crab in the pot. They'll make anybody scream." He faced the wheel again and pushed the throttle.

"Can we go back?"

"Whatever it is, Joe's not going to take help from me. Come on, do you want that lobster or not?"

"Yeah. Yeah, I do," Melody said. But she continued to watch the other boats until they were just shadows on the horizon.

CHAPTER 40

AJ woke on his couch, upright, fully clothed. Morning light already flooded the living room. Buck stood at the front door, on alert, his nose pressed to the crack. There was a knock on the door. Then footsteps. Then, at the big picture window, there was Claire. She waved. AJ got to his feet, crossed the floor and pulled on the knob, sending the dog backward.

"Hi," she said. "Sorry to wake you."

"No, that's fine. Come in."

She slipped out of her muddy sandals. A smile flickered across her face. "Is that Dave Sela's car outside?"

"Yeah. I guess he's still here. DaSilva, too."

"So that's why you were on the couch?"

"Yeah."

"Sorry I didn't get back to you last night," she said. "Your text..."

"That's okay. We moved your table inside."

"Good. Thank you." Claire clasped her hands, then let go. "I have some things I want to talk to you about. But I wanted to do it face to face."

"Yeah, I—"

Upstairs, a door closed. Then Sela's voice came down. "Hurry up, will ya."

"Okay, okay."

There was the rapid thudding of feet on the stairs and Sela came into view. Seeing Claire, he stopped short. DaSilva ran into him from behind, almost knocking him over.

"Jesus, DaSilva, slow down."

"Hurry up, slow down. Make up your—Claire!"

"Hi, guys," she said.

DaSilva squeezed past Sela into the room. "We didn't know if you were coming back."

AJ shot him a look.

DaSilva grinned at him. "Don't worry about the video, AJ. We watched the rest after you went to sleep. There was nothing."

"Thanks," AJ said. "I'll repay you with coffee."

"You paid last night, with beer," Sela said. "The empties are in the sink." He scratched his stubble, which was closing in on being a beard. "Anyway, we have to get to the market. There's another big event this week. Some kind of planning thing for the Blessing of the Fleet. Lots of prep work to do."

"With everything going on, I can't believe we're spending the day picking lobster meat from the shell. You sure you don't need us, AJ? I could round up my cousins to fill in at the market."

Sela gave DaSilva's arm a tug. "Come on. AJ doesn't need us right now."

"But—"

"Bye, guys," AJ said.

The two Daves headed for the door.

"See you later," Sela said.

DaSilva waved, and they went out.

As if suddenly aware of his slept-in clothes, AJ pulled at his T-shirt. "Well, do you want some coffee? I have eggs. I could make eggs."

"Actually, I brought pastry." Claire raised a plastic bag that was dangling from one hand.

"Great."

They moved to the kitchen. AJ busied himself with putting grounds in the coffee maker and setting the table by the window with mugs, sugar, silverware, plates.

"Nice touch," she said, watching him make diagonal folds in the paper napkins.

"Habit. I've been on too many catering jobs."

When he went for the plastic bag that she had put on the counter, she grabbed it away from him. "Wait."

"Yeah?"

"There are a couple of things I really need to talk to you about."

"Okay. But maybe some coffee first?" He inspected the level in the glass pot. "It would clear our heads. My head, anyway." He faced her again, his hands gripping the counter behind him.

"You're stalling."

"Okay," he said. "Maybe I am. Go ahead. Tell me what you need to tell me."

Claire ran a hand through her hair, which gleamed in the pale light of early sunrise. "I spent all night—and I mean all night—I didn't sleep—trying to wrap my head around everything that's happened. I still don't know how I feel. But I do know one thing—I can't stay in that house."

"Right. No one expects you to stay. Are you going to talk to Schwartz?"

"Schwartz? The realtor? No. You didn't let me finish. I'm not selling the house. But I can't stay there while I sort things out."

"Sort things out how?"

"I need to know who was in my house and why. I'm counting on the Stonington P.D. to help me with that."

"We're working on it."

"Any progress?" Her blue eyes searched his face.

"Some. We need more time."

"Okay," she said. "I want to put in a good alarm system."

"I can get you a name."

She nodded.

It was quiet, other than the coffee dripping down into the pot and a mourning dove calling outside.

"Then there's Ben and that other ghost. I know Ben's your good friend, AJ. But how would you feel about helping him—both of them—to move on?"

AJ shifted from one foot to the other. "Yeah. I'm sure that would be the best thing. But that's more the guys' line of work."

"Right. I'll need their help."

"And what if they can't help you?"

"I don't know." Claire tucked her hair behind her ears. "Maybe I could learn to live in a haunted house. Apparently people do." She edged back a little, crossed her arms in front of her, seeming for the first time unsure of herself. "I'm going to find a place to stay up here. So I can keep working on things. Keep myself present in the house, maintain my territory. I understand that's important with this kind of thing."

"Maintain your territory?" AJ relaxed his grip on the counter. "How many hours did you spend on the Internet to find that?"

"I was serious when I said I didn't sleep."

"I guess you were." His smile faded slowly. "You know you can stay here."

"That's the other thing," she said.

"What?"

She stepped forward, closing the distance between them. He put his arms around her, pulled her in, felt the curve of her back, the soft finery of her hair. He kissed her.

"Is there anything else I should know about you?" she said. "Are there any other special talents or abilities?"

"Could be."

"Mind reading? Spoon bending?"

"I was going in a different direction."

He drew her close again. He kissed her neck, her throat, the hollow there between curved bones. He was undoing a button at her collar when she reached past him for the pastry bag. "Maybe we should have some breakfast now."

Pushing the bag out of her reach, he kissed her again.

She laughed. "I thought you wanted breakfast. Coffee, to clear your head."

"My head's perfectly clear."

"I'm thinking breakfast in bed."

"Oh," he said. "Maybe you're the mind reader." Then, as easily as she plucked the bag from the counter, he took her in his arms, lifting her.

Before he could take a step, his cell phone rang.

"That can wait," he said.

He touched her cheek, her nose, her eyebrows with his lips.

The phone rang again, and again.

"Damn." He lowered Claire gently to the floor, then fished the phone from his pocket. "Chief?"

"AJ, I'm at Westbury's house. The place he's renting. No one's answering the doorbell, but I can see a bag inside. A woman's purse. It's a big, purple thing. I remember from when she was at the station that Melody Johnson had one like that."

"I know they met recently, and she was talking about seeing him. I was hoping she'd change her mind. Guess she didn't."

The chief grunted. "Any chance it's someone else's bag? I mean, is that a popular style now?"

AJ turned to Claire. "Are big, purple bags in style?"

"Purple bags? What?"

"Like Melody's. You know, purses."

"Oh. The orchid bag. No. That's just Melody."

"No, Chief. I guess they're not in style."

"Was that Claire? Is she with you?"

"Yeah."

"She must have the number for Melody's cell phone. Tell her to call it."

"Okay." AJ looked at Claire. "Can you call Melody? Her cell phone?"

Claire produced her phone from the purse on the counter. She worked the keypad. "It's ringing."

"She's calling now, Chief."

"Yeah. I can hear it. The phone's in that purple bag. It's Melody's." The chief swore under his breath. "Hold on. I'm getting a call from the station. I'll call you back."

AJ closed his phone.

"Who was that?" Claire said.

"The chief's at Jacques's house. Melody's purse is inside. He heard her phone ringing when you called."

"Oh." She frowned. "Why was the chief at Jacques's house?"

AJ's phone, still in his hand, rang again. He opened it.

"AJ," the chief said. "I need you to meet me at Garbo's dock, in the Borough. You know, where Garbo's used to be."

"What's going on?"

"Old Bacchi, doing his morning rounds out by Lord's Point—he pulled up a body."

"Jesus."

"I'm standing on Westbury's launch right now. That little motorboat he's using is gone. I guess Melody went with him. This is a helluva start to the day, isn't it? Get down to the dock, all right? I'll see you in a few."

"I'm on my way." AJ headed out of the kitchen, already throwing off his shirt.

"What is it?" Claire followed him up the stairs, stopping at the open door of his bedroom, where his pants lay in a heap. "AJ?"

He didn't respond. He was pulling on a pair of jeans that was already fitted with a belt and a holster that rode high on the hip. When he came back into the hall, he was zipping up a windbreaker. He pressed a key into her hand. "This is to the front door. If you decide to go out, just let Buck in before you leave."

"AJ. Is it Melody?"

"No. I'm sure she's fine." AJ gave Claire's arm a quick squeeze, then rushed past her and down the stairs. "Keep your phone on, okay?" He let Buck out.

Claire caught up with him. They kissed there by the open door. "Be careful," she said. From the big window, she watched AJ pull away, accelerating quickly as he hit the road. His Jeep raced up Mistuxet and disappeared. Then everything was perfectly still, except for the greyhound, running crazy circles around the lawn.

CHAPTER 41

Alone in the big house, Ben slipped into the empty bedroom at the top of the stairs. "I need to talk to you," he said, to the painted plaster, to the air. "I waited for you all night, and I'll wait all day if I have to. Please, just show yourself." After a moment, he went into the hall again. "C'mon. I got AJ to remove the camera. I did that for you." He headed for the attic door, watching it. Nothing moved. "Damn," he said. He turned around.

In that instant, the young woman stepped out of the wall. She came toward him. Despite her stiff, full dress, she was silent.

Ben positioned himself to block the way, feet apart, arms crossed, like a brightly glowing bouncer. "Stop!" he said. "You see me. I know you do. You have to see me."

The woman advanced on him. Her hair was pulled back in a tight bun. Her face was fixed, determined.

"Listen," Ben pleaded. "Please stop."

For a moment, the woman continued, but then, when she was right in front of him, not two feet away, she did as he had asked—she stopped.

"I knew it!" Ben said. "You're not an echo."

The woman looked at the floor.

"Sorry. That was rude. Let me start over. Hello. My name is Ben."

The woman lifted her head, focusing on him gradually, as if having to think about working the muscles.

"You can see me," Ben said. "Please, tell me your name."

The woman seemed to take in Ben and her surroundings for the first time.

"You've been…gone…a while," Ben said. "But I think this is your home."

A frown wrinkled the smooth skin. Her lips twitched but produced no sound.

"It's been a long time since you talked to anyone," Ben said. "But I'm sure you can if you just try. Please try."

"Comfort." Her voice was creaky as a dry hinge.

"Comfort," Ben repeated. "What do you mean?"

"I need comfort." She sounded stronger this time.

"Oh. That I understand. Really, I do."

She stared at him with brimming, blue eyes. Then, suddenly, she began to fade. The color drained from her face, her hair, her clothes. In seconds she went from pale to translucent. Then she was as Claire had seen her— just a subtle shiver in the air.

"No," Ben said. "Don't go." He reached toward her. "Take my hand."

But she was gone.

CHAPTER 42

An ambulance beat AJ to the scene. When he arrived, it was already backed up in the little alleyway that ended in the dock, lights flashing. The chief's car was there, too. Police tape had been strung between two pilings, and there were already a few onlookers, treating the tape like a velvet rope at a premiere. AJ slipped under it.

"What's going on down there?" a man shouted after him.

AJ kept going. There was the smell of the worst possible low tide. Ahead of him was Bacchiocchi, a wiry man with bright white hair that pointed in every direction. He was standing by himself, looking longingly at a fishing boat that, like him, was undersized but tough. On the other side of the dock, the chief was talking to a middle-aged couple who wore bright polo shirts and sported deep tans. The two guys from the ambulance stood together, smoking. In the middle of all of this was something covered with a tarp—a low, rectangular shape.

The chief left the couple and came towards AJ.

"Jesus, AJ," he said, when they were close. "What a fucking mess."

AJ looked toward the tarp. "Is it her? The missing girl?"

"Leah. I'm sure it's her. The height and weight are right, the hair."

"I have the photo in my glove compartment, if you want to compare—"

"I don't think that will help." The chief stared back at AJ, a grim expression on his wide face. "Is she here? You know—"

"Her ghost? No. Not so far."

"Okay." The chief crouched down by the tarp. "Prepare yourself. I don't know what all you had to deal with down in Bridgeport. But I doubt you ever came across this." He grabbed a corner and pulled back the tarp, lifting it, careful to block the view of the onlookers at the end of the dock.

The shape under the tarp was a black metal cage—a lobster pot. Inside the pot was a body. AJ saw feet, then naked, pale, hairless legs. A female pelvis. Then a torso. All of it an inhuman color and grotesquely swollen.

The chief paused with the end of the pot still covered. He straightened up. "Something got to her, AJ. Crabs, maybe fish. God knows what. It's awful."

"All right."

The chief pulled the tarp back the rest of the way. What AJ saw then was not a face but a cluster of wounds. At the tattered edge of one gash was a little gold ring. "Jesus, Roland." AJ raised his arm as if blocking a blow.

"Her parents are going to have to ID her." The chief looked like he might be sick. "Can you imagine anything on Earth that's worse than that? Coming to the morgue to ID this child?"

AJ didn't say anything. For a while he didn't make another move. Then, keeping his arm raised, he worked his way around the pot.

"There's no tag on the pot, if that's what you're looking for," the chief said.

"Right." AJ let his hand fall. "This thing may be distinctive enough. I've only ever seen a pot this big once."

"At the Westbury house." The chief didn't even try to correct the name this time. The pot was from the Westbury house, not the Connor house. The chief covered the pot again. "We are going to get the bastard this time. He's not running away to France."

"We still don't really have anything on him."

"We got him on video stealing a pot exactly like this one."

"All we have on video is a cap—"

"Which Manzella confirmed was his—"

"It could be his. It's the right age, that's all. Roland—"

"All right, all right. I know we still have to do the leg work. And we will. By the book. We'll get a warrant, we'll search his house and we'll find the fucking cap. And God knows what else. I'm just saying, AJ, I know we got him. I can feel it. Are you telling me that you can't?"

AJ didn't respond right away. "This isn't one of the pots on the video."

"What are you talking about? It sure as hell is. It's the same gigantic goddamn pot. You just said so yourself."

"Right. It may have come from behind Jacques's garage. But I'm sure the doc will tell us that this body's been underwater for a while, since before we got that video of the guy stealing the pots."

"Okay. But it's the same guy stealing the same damn pots. He's stealing more pots because... Jesus Christ. There are going to be more bodies."

AJ left the chief and walked away down the dock, past the boaters who looked after him with lost expressions, past one bristling white yacht after another. He went all the way to the end. He stared out at the sound, squinting into the diffuse, gray light.

The chief caught up with him.

"I hope you're wrong, Chief," AJ said. "Because if you're right, then our killer's out there right now, with Melody."

CHAPTER 43

Claire drove up the hill past the marine supply store and followed the long curve to the supermarket. She was easing into a parking space when the clouds let loose.

"Shit," she said, as she killed the engine. She sat for a minute watching the water roll down the windshield. From the purse beside her she produced a notebook. She opened it, then slid a pencil from the spiral binding. She wrote *Bread*. She paused, the pencil ready on the next line. The rain pounded on the metal roof.

Three loud raps broke through the din, making Claire jump. A man in a hood peered through the passenger side window. Dewey Allan. He waved with a weak smile.

Claire pressed the button to open the lock.

"Sorry to startle you." He slipped through the door, already shedding his thin jacket. A folded newspaper dropped out from under it.

"I didn't notice you," she said. "I guess I was deep in thought."

"Writer's block?" Dewey gestured toward the notebook on her lap.

"Pretty bad when I can't even come up with a shopping list."

"Here's an idea—take-out."

Claire smiled.

"I'm parked at the far end of the lot," Dewey said. "It was just sprinkling when I started back to my car. Then, boom, this monsoon." He twisted to inspect the cushion behind him. "I hope I don't get your seat wet."

"Don't worry about the car. A little water won't hurt it."

Dewey folded his jacket on his lap. "Hey, I'm sorry I didn't make it back to your house the other night, to help the guys—"

"That's okay. How did your search go? You were looking for a girl who's missing, right?"

"We didn't find anything. It's a shame." Dewey pressed his lips together. "So have you had any more activity at your house?"

"Supernatural, you mean? No."

"Of course, unless you have equipment, you can't really be sure."

"Maybe I should get one of those meters."

"A KII meter? You could borrow mine."

"Don't you need it?"

"I'm not sure how much investigating we'll be doing, with Ben gone."

"Right. I'm sorry."

Dewey looked down at his newspaper for a moment. "So, what do you think—do you want to try it? The meter?"

Claire wagged her head as if tossing the idea back and forth. "Maybe that would be good."

A smile flashed across Dewey's narrow face. "I wish I had the thing with me. I could show you how to use it right now."

"Does Dave Sela still have it?"

"No, it's at my house. I could pick it up, then swing by your place."

"Yeah," Claire said. "But I don't know when I'm going to be home. I have errands to run."

"Me, too. Maybe I'll just throw it in my car and try to catch you whenever—if not today, then some other day."

"Okay. If I'm not there, you could just leave it by the front door."

"Sure..." Dewey hesitated. "It's not difficult to use, but there are a few tricks. It really would be better if I could show you."

"Oh. Well, I hope you catch me at home."

"Yeah."

They both looked out at the rain.

"I wish I was one of those clever people who keeps an umbrella in the car," Claire said.

"And here I am a scout leader. I guess I'm not such a great role model for *Be Prepared.*"

"I'm sure this won't last. It looks like one of those brief but intense showers."

"You might be right." Dewey slipped into his jacket again. "But I think I'll make a run for it."

"Good luck. I'm going to try to finish this list."

Dewey tugged his jacket up over his ears, then slipped the newspaper under it. "See you soon."

Claire watched him race across the parking lot, looking long-necked and headless, splashing with each stride.

CHAPTER 44

"Please," Ben said. "I can help you." He went to the attic door and pushed his head through it. "Where are you?" He pulled back into the hallway. "I mean, what's this fading in and out stuff? Do you go somewhere? Or do you just, you know, cease to be for a while? Like when I try to leave this house?" He moved slowly toward the stairs. "Are you stuck in this place, too? At least this is your house, right? I just happened to die here." He held his hand up to the wall, his fingertips dipping in and out of it as he went. "How do you stand it? Being here but not really being here. This body that's not really a body. No blood, no skin. I can't touch anything, most of the time. And even when I can, I don't *feel* it. It's like a magnet pushing another magnet. No contact. No one except AJ can see me or hear me." He was at the other end of the hall, now, near where he had seen the ghost appear before. "AJ and you. I know you can hear me. Come on, show yourself. Talk to me. We can help each other."

He stared at the wall.

Suddenly she was there, behind him. He seemed to feel her presence before he saw her. "Jesus, you could scare someone half to death," he said. "If they were alive to begin with."

"Forgive me. I didn't intend…" Her voice was soft but there was strength in it, this time.

"It's fine." Ben gave her a big smile. "I'm just glad you came back."

Her young eyes were piercing and distant at the same time.

"My name's Ben. I don't know if you heard me before. What's your name?"

"Elizabeth."

"Elizabeth. That's beautiful. I think we can help each other. When you disappeared, before, I was trying to take your hand. Will you take my hand?" He reached out, his palm up.

She lifted her arm from her side. She placed her thin fingers on his. They both stood staring at their hands.

"I can feel it," he said. "I can feel your hand."

She looked away.

"I want to help you," Ben said. "You said you need comfort. Well, you can have the comfort of my company for as long as we're here."

The ghost's face seemed to grow still paler; her smile drooped. "You misunderstand me. I need to find Comfort. They say I'm not to have her, but—"

"Her?"

"Comfort Bloodgood. My daughter. She was taken from me. I need to find her."

"Oh. Maybe I—"

"I must find her." Elizabeth let go of Ben's hand. She went past him, quickly, moving toward the attic.

"Elizabeth, wait," Ben said.

But she had reached the door and disappeared.

CHAPTER 45

AJ moved the yellow tape out of the way, letting the ambulance back toward the tarp. At the last minute, the chief came lumbering up the dock and slapped the side of the vehicle. He spoke with the driver through the window. The ambulance made two points of a three-point turn, ending up broadside to the tarp, closing off the view from the alley. There were groans from the crowd that had gathered there.

"What's going on?" AJ said.

Officer Manzella, still wearing his raincoat, though the rain shower had stopped, took the tape from AJ's hand. "Better go find out."

AJ chased after the chief, who was heading back down the dock. "Hey, Chief. We're not taking the body to the morgue?"

"Not yet."

"There's nothing left to do here, Chief. Anyway, Manzella can cover it. Once they take the body, we can head over to Jacques's house. I want to be waiting for him when he comes in."

"If you want to talk to Jacques, you'll stay." The chief gestured toward the breakwater that separated the sound from the low, gray sky. There, a sailboat was heading into shore. "They finally raised him on the radio. He's coming to us."

"Holy shit." AJ squinted into the distance. "Melody..."

"They spoke to her, too. She's fine."

AJ let out a long breath. "So he's not trying to run. What do you think that means?"

"I don't know. Maybe he thinks he's untouchable."

"I can see why he would think that."

"Sure," the chief said. "I hope that's what he's thinking. I hope he keeps on thinking it, right up until we lock him up for good."

214

"What's this about?" Jacques said, as he hit the dock. He turned to help Melody.

"That's Bacchiocchi's boat, right?" She pointed. "I knew it." She took Jacques's hand and stepped across the gap.

"Knew what?" the chief said.

"That it wasn't just a spider crab." She stole a look at Jacques. "Bacchiocchi pulled a lobster pot out of the water and then someone screamed. Someone from another boat."

"Officer Bugbee," the chief said, "how about you stay here with Ms. Johnson and get her story. I'll talk to Mr. Westbury."

"What's going on?" Melody said. "What was in that pot that Bacchiocchi pulled up?"

"Mr. Westbury," the chief said, gesturing toward the tarp. "After you."

"AJ?" Melody said.

AJ was silent until the other men had walked away up the dock. "Do you have any idea how worried we were?"

"We who? You and the chief?"

"Me and Claire. You should call her."

"When did you talk to Claire?"

"I saw her this morning. She's back. So tell me what happened. What did you see?"

"I've pretty much told you everything. Bacchiocchi pulled a lobster pot out of the water just as another boat was coming up to him. Someone in that boat screamed. That's all I know. We were pretty far away. I was using binoculars."

"You didn't try to get closer to see what was going on?"

"Jacques said it was probably just a spider crab." Melody looked past AJ. "The chief's not going to learn anything from him. He was busy steering his boat. Jesus, is that the pot that Bacchiocchi pulled up, that thing under the tarp?" She started toward it.

"Melody!" AJ reached for her arm.

Standing on the tarp, the chief was saying, "You want to take a seat?" He motioned toward the long, squared-off shape under the canvas. "A big guy your age, probably his knees aren't what they used to be. Take a load off."

"No thanks," Jacques said. "It looks a little damp."

"All right."

"Are you going to tell me what this is about?" Jacques's face was scrunched up as if he were being stung by the strong smell of briny decay. "What's under the tarp?"

"It's a lobster pot. Big, isn't it? Ever seen one that size? Oh, that's right, you have. Behind your old garage there's a whole stack of them just like this one."

Jacques put a hand to his nose.

"Tell you what," the chief said. "How about you take a look, see if you recognize anything. The pot, or what's inside." He took the edge of the tarp on the side opposite Jacques and began to drag it back. He watched Jacques's face. He pulled it up over the pot. The pale, greenish, swollen legs came into view, then the soft, naked hips.

"Jesus," Jacques said, turning away.

The chief kept pulling until the whole pot was exposed. From inside, the girl's empty eye sockets stared upward.

"Come on, take a look," the chief said.

Jacques was facing the sound. He was swallowing hard. "Who is that? What happened to her?"

"Ever seen this pot before?"

"The pot? Who cares about the goddamn pot?"

"I do," the chief said. "I'm asking you if it looks familiar."

Jacques glanced down quickly. He made a sound like he'd been punched in the gut. "I don't know," he said after a while. "It's a lobster pot. You want me to say it's like the pots at Claire Connor's house."

"Right. The house belongs to Claire now, and the pots do, too. But that doesn't mean you don't have a couple. You remember stopping by her house? Posing for the camera with a lobster pot in each hand? Showing off that vintage cap from the yacht club? I guess you plan on getting into the lobstering business. Funny time for that, with everyone else getting out of it." The chief pulled the tarp back across the body.

Jacques stepped away from the tarp. He stood there looking at the boats, biting down on his lower lip. "I think I can explain what you saw on the video. That cap."

"Feel free," the chief said.

"I left some old clothes, along with some furniture, with the caretaker— the man who used to be our caretaker. There was a cap in with those clothes."

"What, you just remembered this? Since the last time I talked to you?"

Jacques didn't respond.

"Henry Jacobsen," the chief said. "So you're saying it was him wearing your cap in the video."

"No," Jacques said. "He told me that he took the whole lot to the Salvation Army. Anyone could have that cap now."

AJ had let Melody go. She ran up the dock. "What was that? What was in the pot?"

The chief didn't respond for a moment. "A body. A girl we've been looking for."

"Oh, my God." Melody put a hand over her mouth. The smell seemed to hit her at the same time as the news. She took a step back. "How would a girl end up in a lobster pot?"

"I have no idea," the chief said. "I was hoping Jacques could help me with that."

"Why would he know anything about it?"

Jacques shook his head, ever so slightly, as if he weren't responding to Melody's question, but to a question he had asked himself. "Strange," he said.

"That's one word for it," the chief said.

"I'm reminded of something, from a long time ago. Henry has a son, Ellis. I grew up with him. He was almost like a part of the family."

"What about him?"

"My family sent him to Pine Point, with me. He was in my class there."

"Okay," the chief said. "Why are you remembering him all of a sudden?"

"Our senior year, in biology class, we had to do a project. You could choose any topic, then do a presentation about it. Ellis did what he called an experiment in forensics."

The others waited.

"He got a hold of some animal carcasses and put them in a couple of lobster pots that he lowered into the sound. He checked on them every day, logging the progress of the decomposition. He took pictures, too. Polaroids. It was the most gruesome thing I've ever seen in my life. Until today."

"What kind of animal carcasses?" the chief said.

"I think it was a raccoon that he said was roadkill, and a pig's head that he got from the butcher. And some kind of a leg. I guess from a deer."

"Does Ellis still live around here?" Melody said.

"Yes," Jacques said. "He's been doing some work for me. And…"

"What?" the chief said.

"After you grilled me the other day, I went to Henry's to ask him about the cap." Jacques studiously avoided the chief's scowl, keeping his eyes on Melody. "He took me into the barn, where he has a collection of animal remains. He said something about Ellis, something about how Ellis helps him build the collection. I can't remember exactly."

"What kind of animal remains are in this collection?" the chief said.

"Skulls and nests, that kind of thing. There was one large bone that seemed kind of—I don't know."

"Kind of what?"

"I'm not exactly an expert on bones. I don't know what kind of animal could leave a long bone like that, except a human."

The chief cursed under his breath.

Jacques finally looked at him. "Wait, I remember what Henry said. He said Ellis has the knack."

"The knack?"

"The knack for finding things. Things for the collection."

The chief swore again. "Come on, AJ." He started toward the street.

"Excuse me?" Jacques called from behind him. "Are we done? May I go?"

The chief stopped. "Sure, go. But that means go home. Stick around. It doesn't mean take off for France."

As they passed the ambulance, the chief paused to give instructions to the driver. Then he told Manzella to wrap things up once the body was on its way to the morgue.

"So that's it?" AJ said, as they continued on to the chief's car. "You're done with Jacques? What happened to the search warrant? To nailing him, by the book?"

"We're still going to do all of that." The chief opened his door. "But it's not going to be on this case."

"So you believe Jacques's story?" AJ said. "The cap, the science project?"

"Maybe. I watched him as I uncovered the pot. That look on his face—he doesn't know anything about this murder."

"You sure he didn't just fake it? If he's a psycho—"

"I interviewed Jacques nineteen years ago, about Anna Marie, remember? I saw the guilt all over his face, then. That's how I know he's our guy for that one. So unless he's spent all these years taking acting lessons, then, no, he wasn't faking today."

"You really think it could be Ellis?"

The chief got in the car and opened the window. "What do you know about him?"

"I was at Claire's the other day when he stopped by with his dad. They were hoping Claire would take him on as a caretaker. He's been in some minor trouble. Right after I came back here, I stopped him for driving erratically. Gave him a breathalyzer test. He passed. He's kind of different. But I wouldn't have pegged him for a murderer."

The chief looked past AJ to the crowd. "Do you know everyone you see out there?"

AJ followed his gaze. "I know some of the names, but I guess I don't really know them."

"Me, either, AJ." The chief faced forward again. "Get in the car. I want to talk to Ellis before he hears about Bacchiocchi pulling up the pot. We're going to find out just how well you had him pegged."

CHAPTER 46

She went slowly up the lane toward her house, easing into the dark trees. The rain had paused but thunder boomed beyond the woods. As she approached the garage, she ducked her head to get a view of the house. Lightning cracked over the roof. She pulled all the way up to the edge of the weedy lawn. Grabbing her overnight bag, she dashed through the wet plants to the front door.

"Crap," she said, pausing on the step. "Looks like Dewey hasn't been here yet."

When she was inside she closed the door behind her and leaned against it.

From upstairs came the voices that she couldn't hear.

"Maybe that's AJ," Ben said. "You need to meet him. Come on."

"You believe your friend can help me?" Elizabeth said.

"I'm sure of it. He'll track down your daughter, find out what happened to her, after you, after they—"

"But my relations were scattered across many states. It would take too much travel, too many letters. It's too much to ask."

Ben smiled. "This kind of thing isn't as hard as it used to be." He rounded the turn in the stairs. When he saw Claire, he stopped. "Oh. It's Claire."

"She can't see you or hear you?" Elizabeth said.

"No. But I'm not so sure about you. I think she saw you in the hallway once." He started down again. "Maybe just go slow."

Claire locked the front door. Then she headed toward the stairs.

"Shit." Ben retreated, half disappearing into the wall.

Elizabeth was slower to react. As Claire hurried by, her arm passed through Elizabeth's fingers. Claire stopped. She smoothed the

219

goosebumps that had appeared on her skin. "Ben?"

Two steps down, Ben peeked out from the plaster. "This is so frustrating."

"Should I try to make her see me?" Elizabeth had turned sideways to avoid merging her arm with Claire's hip.

"No," Ben said, "not while she's on the stairs. She already looks nervous. I don't want anyone else taking a fall."

Claire continued up, then on to her bedroom. She put her bag on the bed. "I wish I had that KII meter."

"Me, too," Ben said from the doorway.

"Wait." Claire produced a cell phone from her purse. "Perfect. Fully charged." She put it down on the bureau. "Okay, Ben. It's not as good as that meter, but it might work, at least to let me know that you're here." She stepped away. "So. Try to run down my battery."

"I like the way you're thinking." Ben went into the room. "Elizabeth, you can help me. Let's both put our hands on the phone."

Elizabeth remained behind, looking puzzled.

"This thing that Claire just placed on the dresser. We need to put our hands on it."

"Why?"

"It will show her that we're here." He was already at the dresser, his hand covering the phone.

"I don't understand," Elizabeth said, but she joined him. She lowered her hand onto his.

He smiled at her.

"Is it working?" Elizabeth said.

"I think so. Can you feel it? A little charge, a kind of tingle?"

She blushed a brighter blue but didn't speak.

"Let's check." Ben pulled his hand away and inspected the tiny screen. "Oh, yeah. Come on. A little more."

Ben stacked his hands on the phone. Elizabeth slid her tapered fingers across his knuckles.

"Okay, let's see what's happening." Claire reached for the phone.

The ghosts pulled back.

"Holy shit," Claire said, when she saw the little empty rectangle. "Well, okay. It works. I guess you're here, Ben." She scanned the room. "Good. Creepy, but good."

"Gee, thanks," Ben said.

"I just came to pick up a few things," Claire said. "I'm staying at AJ's."

"All right, AJ," Ben said.

"I may be getting a KII meter from Dewey. Then, we can actually communicate."

"That's great!" Ben said.

"So, I guess I should call AJ." As Claire punched the number, the screen cleared suddenly, then went dark. "Shit. The battery just died. I guess we went too far. Where's my charger?" She searched the outer pockets of her overnight bag, then her purse. "Crap." She unzipped the bag and sifted through the clothes. "Crap, crap, crap."

"Sorry," Ben said. "I guess we don't know our own strength." He squeezed Elizabeth's hand. "I told her she should get a land line."

Claire stood up from the bag. "Well, I guess I need to add a charger to my list." She checked her watch. "If Dewey stops by, I can use his phone."

From outside, there was the sound of a car door.

"Ah," Claire said, "speak of the devil."

CHAPTER 47

They started with the house, a dingy little ranch behind vine-drenched stone walls. The chief knocked on the door. When there was no answer, he tried the detached garage and the back yard. They were standing in the beat-down grass when the clouds opened up. "Perfect," the chief said.

Dripping, their clothes dark, they got back in the car.

"Maybe Ellis is at his dad's house," AJ said.

The whole way there, the rain continued. Henry's house was as trim as his son's was shabby. There was no answer at the front door. They dashed back across the softening dirt and tried the barn door. It slid open.

"Chief," AJ said, "this isn't exactly by the book."

"What am I, a goddamn librarian?" The chief went inside.

They stood there listening to the rain pound the roof, breathing air that was thick with the smells of old hay and sodden dirt. When his eyes had adjusted, AJ pointed to a door in the wall. They went through it. A light already burning showed the workbench and, beyond it, the shelves displaying the relics. Like respectful museum-goers, the two men moved slowly past the collection, studying without touching. Grunting, the chief squatted to see the bottom shelf.

"I don't see the large bone that Jacques talked about," the chief said, when they had reached the end.

"Me, either. Maybe he didn't mean for Jacques to see that bone. Maybe he's got it tucked away someplace now."

"Maybe."

The chief retraced his steps. He let his eyes run over the pitted and tool-strewn workbench and the toothed blades hanging behind it.

"What are you looking for, Chief?" AJ said.

"The things they want to hide from us. Like that bone."

"Right. Anyone who's hiding something is probably up to no good."

The chief let out a breath. "I used to think like that, when I was a new cop. But you should know better than most that it's not that simple. Everyone's got something they want to hide. Dark things, sometimes. Strange things. Everyone, even the good guys. It's a cop's job to see that stuff. In fact, once you're on this job for a while, you can't *not* see it. Once that light clicks on, AJ, you won't be able to turn it off."

AJ watched the chief for a long while without saying anything. The chief went back to studying the tools—old fashioned implements of stained wood and tarnished steel. Claw hammers, levels like little pointed speed boats, block-headed mallets, a crooked brace and bit. One thing right in front stood out—it was colorful, round, soft and new.

"Painter's tape," AJ said. "When I went to help Claire paint her house, she couldn't find her tape. She wouldn't let me start painting until I proved to her that I could do a straight line by hand."

"My wife's the same way. It's got to be perfect."

"Funny, there aren't any other painting supplies here. Brushes, rollers, that kind of thing."

"True."

AJ reached for the tape, but pulled his hand back. "I bet the last time Claire's house was painted, Henry did it. He was the caretaker there for a long, long time. After all those years... I mean, you take care of a place for that long, you end up feeling like it's yours. Then this strange woman moves in... I wonder how he felt about that."

"What are you getting at?" the chief said.

"I don't know." AJ leaned over the tape, moved his head side to side. "I bet Henry knew about that trick window."

"I'm sure he did. Probably knows everything there is to know about that house."

"What if he was using that window to, you know, check in on his old place, the place that he still thought of as his own? You see that sometimes—people going back to visit houses they've left, treating them like they still belonged there."

"You do," the chief said.

"What if it was Henry who was in the house the night that Ben was over there? What if it was Henry who knocked him down the stairs?"

The chief was quiet for a moment. "Ben still doesn't remember anything from that night?"

"No. But maybe he doesn't need to. Maybe this roll of tape is our answer. We could run this back to the station, check it for Claire's fingerprints."

"You think this is the same roll of tape that Claire was missing? Henry took it?"

AJ shook his head. "You're right. That's crazy."

The chief went to the shelf. He stood in front of the nests and bones. "Maybe, maybe not," he said. "After seeing a dead girl in a lobster pot, I have a whole new definition of crazy."

CHAPTER 48

"And he arrives," Elizabeth said. She had taken Ben's hand again.

"What?"

"Speak of the devil and he arrives. Don't you know that saying?"

"Oh. I guess I've never heard the second part." He tugged on her hand. "Let's go downstairs. I want to hear what Dewey tells her about the KII meter."

They found Claire and Dewey in the living room. Dewey was holding a duffle bag. He had changed clothes since meeting Claire in the supermarket parking lot, and he looked as if he had shaved and showered, too. He smelled faintly of cologne.

"I like rainy days," Claire said. "I've done some of my best writing on rainy days."

"Right, I can understand that," Dewey said. "I don't know, maybe I need to start over. Try writing something different."

"Maybe you should try fiction."

"Maybe. I've always liked ghost stories."

"That would be perfect for you."

"You know, you're right. Or what about a non-fiction ghost story? If I could make contact here in this house, use the KII meter to communicate with the ghost, and tell his story... I could be a ghost writer for a ghost."

"That would be unique."

"Yeah." Dewey smiled. "Well, we should get started." He went to the near wall and set the duffle bag down. Something inside it clanked heavily.

Ben and Elizabeth watched from the stairs.

"That man is one of the previous owners," Elizabeth said.

"No," Ben said. "He does research for me. I guess he's branching out."

Dewey opened the zipper of the bag and removed something, then closed the zipper again. "I picked up a couple of new meters. One really isn't enough."

"You didn't have to do that," Claire said.

Elizabeth was frowning, her eyes unfocused, as if she were straining to remember something. "He has been here before."

"He was here the other day with the guys," Ben said, glancing at Elizabeth but then watching Dewey tear open the packaging. "Wonder where he got that meter? Is someone carrying them locally?"

"Before that," Elizabeth said. "He has spent time here."

Ben touched her arm. "You know, your memory may be a little fuzzy."

"No," she said, pulling away. "I'm absolutely sure. I remember his voice."

"Okay. Who was he talking to?"

Elizabeth was headed for the duffle bag.

"Elizabeth," Ben called after her.

Dewey passed a meter to Claire, then went back to the duffle bag. "I've been wanting to get more into the technical end of the investigations. And this will be so much better for you. Instead of moving one meter around all the time, you can just set these up and leave them."

"That will work better." Claire turned the device around in her hand. She traced the bead-like lights with her fingertips.

Dewey slid the zipper and produced another meter.

Elizabeth peered into the bag. "Ben, does this man raise pigs?"

"What? No. He's a retired history teacher."

Dewey pulled another meter from the bag.

"How many of those did you buy?" Claire said.

"Five." Dewey put the last on the floor. "So that's five new ones plus my old one." He pulled a large pack of 9-volt batteries from the bag.

"That's a lot of batteries. At least let me pay for them."

"It's no problem."

"Okay. But I'll replace them all when I return the meters. They won't last in this house."

"You might be right." Dewey tugged the zipper back across the bag. "Do we have time to set all of these meters up? I'm sorry, I didn't even ask if you have plans."

"No, that's fine. I'm going to AJ's, but he's tied up with some police business. So I'm not in a huge hurry."

"So you and AJ...." Dewey let that hang in the air for a while. "Well, good. We can really think this through, then. Maybe we can even test them out, see if we can stir up some activity."

"I'm not sure I want to go out of my way to stir things up."

"Oops. Sorry. I forget that not everyone is as comfortable with the dead as I am."

"Comfortable with the dead," Elizabeth repeated, looking up from the duffle bag. "I remember him saying that."

Ben had caught up to her. "Why did you ask me if he raises pigs?"

"There's a knife in the bag. My father had a knife like that. He used it for only one thing—to slaughter the pigs."

"What?" Ben bent down and stared into the short opening that remained at the end of the zipper. "That's a nasty looking knife. Why the hell would he have a knife?" He looked at Dewey, his eyes narrowing. "Elizabeth, I need you to remember when you saw him. I need you to try really hard to get your memories of him in order."

"It's so difficult, Ben. The days all blend together."

"Just try, for me. Try to work back from when Claire moved in."

Claire and Dewey were at the couch, now, installing batteries in the meters. Dewey said, "Certain electronic devices will give you a false reading if they're too close to the meter. Cell phones, for example. Or walkie talkies."

"No problem there," Claire said. "My cell phone's dead. And I haven't owned a walkie talkie since I was ten."

"Okay. Why don't we put a meter in here, and one in the kitchen. Then we'll have to think about the upstairs."

"I wouldn't mind having one in my office."

"And your bedroom, right?"

"I'd almost rather not. I'd probably never fall asleep."

"You could set one up there, but turn it off when you went to bed."

"That's true," Claire said.

"I also brought some little notebooks. I thought maybe we'd put one by each meter. You could make a note each time there's activity. That could help establish a pattern."

"All right," Claire said, unenthusiastically.

Still holding a meter, Dewey returned to the duffle bag.

"Back up," Ben said, pulling at Elizabeth's arm. "I don't want that meter to light up. If he thinks there's something paranormal, he'll want to do a full-scale investigation."

They gave Dewey some space. He took a stack of small notebooks and a box of pencils from the bag. He reached in one more time, then quickly slipped something small and dark into his pocket. He closed the zipper again. "I'm going to set this meter up in the kitchen."

"What was that he tucked away in his pocket?" Elizabeth said.

"I don't know," Ben said. "But he seemed to be trying to hide it. Can you remember anything more? When did you see him?"

"I remember Claire. She hung little squares of color on the wall."

"Okay, good. What about Dewey?"

"I remember a night of loud noises and lights, people shouting."

"That's probably the night I was here. Do you remember me from that night?"

She sighed. "I'm sorry." Her eyelids lowered.

"But he was here?" Ben said.

Elizabeth seemed almost in a trance. "I remember something. I can't tell you when it happened, or even how many times it happened. I remember Dewey going up the stairs—the attic stairs. He was alone. But he'd sit in the attic, talking."

"Trying to engage, or provoke," Ben said, quietly, to himself.

"What?"

"It's a technique that ghost hunters use, in an investigation. They try to get a reaction from the entity."

Having come back into the living room, Dewey led Claire up the stairs. He held a meter in front of him, as if it were a compass pointing the way.

"We should follow them," Elizabeth said, moving to the front hall.

Ben took her arm. "Wait. Not too close. We have to stay away from the meter."

They looked up from the bottom of the stairs.

Dewey reached the turn, then paused. "So do you think about it every time you come up the stairs?"

"You mean, what happened to Ben?" Claire said.

"Yeah."

"I try not to."

"Maybe it was your ghost that did it. You know, pushed him down the stairs."

"What do you mean? The police said it was an accident."

Dewey laughed. "Yeah, well, I'm sure Chief Brown isn't looking to have another unsolved murder on his record." He climbed the last couple of steps. "Which room is your bedroom?"

"Last door on the right."

When Claire had disappeared, Ben let go of Elizabeth's arm. She started up ahead of him. From somewhere above, there was a brief buzzing sound, then a loud thud.

"What the hell?" Ben said.

Elizabeth reached the top first. Ben was still rounding the turn when Dewey shot out of Claire's room and came flying down the hall. He was on Elizabeth before she could react. For an instant, he obliterated her. He paused, then, sweeping his hands in front of him as if clearing a spider web. When he looked up again, he and Ben were face to face.

"Weird," Dewey said. He took off again, blasting through Ben, thumping down the stairs.

Ben remained frozen. "Oh my God."

"What is it?" Elizabeth said.

"I remember. I remember that night." He tipped to the side, his shoulder sinking into the wall. "I was at the top of the stairs when I saw something—it was you. I snapped off a couple of pictures. Then Dewey came out of the dark. He ran right through you, like he did just now. He grabbed my camera, then he pushed me. I lost my balance. I fell, started rolling and couldn't stop. I don't remember hitting the bottom." Ben righted himself, pulling out of the plaster. "He killed me. Dewey killed me."

"I don't remember any of that, Ben." Elizabeth looked down the hall. "We must check on Claire." She didn't wait for him, but raced to Claire's room. "Come quickly!" she shouted from the doorway.

Ben joined her. Claire lay motionless on the floor beside her bed.

"What did he do to her?" Elizabeth said. "Is she all right?"

Ben tried to lay a hand on Claire's wrist, then her neck. His fingers blurred and sank into the skin. "Damn it!" He put his ear to her chest. "She's breathing."

"Listen," Elizabeth said, touching Ben on the shoulder. "He's coming back."

Dewey burst into the room. He was wearing latex gloves. He had long tie-wraps in one hand and the duffle in the other. He went straight to Claire.

"No!" Ben shouted, trying to grab the tie-wraps. His hands came up empty. "Fuck this! Fuck this! Fuck being a ghost!"

Working like a rodeo cowboy, Dewey secured Claire's hands and feet.

"There must be something." Ben spied the KII meter on the bed. "C'mon. At least we can distract him." He rushed to the meter, waving his hands. The lights flashed crazily.

Unaware of the little show, Dewey pulled a roll of duct tape from the duffle. "Sorry to do this. I just don't want the distraction." He tore off a long piece and covered Claire's mouth with it, lapping it well down her cheeks on either side. He observed her for a second, slid his fingers from the slick tape to the soft, pale skin.

Ben was grasping at the tie wraps again. "Elizabeth, help me. We have to try."

She worked at Claire's feet while Ben tried the hands. Claire was coming to, moving in uncoordinated jerks. Ben's hands chased the quivering ends of the tie-wraps. Finally, he pulled back. He screamed in an agony of frustration and fear.

"I'm going to try to make him see me," Elizabeth said. She went toward Dewey, who was digging in the duffle bag.

"Yeah. Maybe you can scare him," Ben said. "Scare him to death."

Dewey produced a compact white cube from the duffle bag. He tore off the plastic wrap, then pulled at the cube, unfolding an arm, then a leg, gradually turning it into a coverall.

"Look at me," Elizabeth said over and over, her starched skirt swaying back and forth. "Over here."

But Dewey was focused on his work. He shook the coverall out and slipped into it. When Elizabeth moved to stop him, her arms outstretched, he passed through her, without pause. He reached into the duffle again. This time, he brought out the knife.

"Elizabeth, go downstairs," Ben said.

She stopped her dancing. She stared at Dewey and the long blade.

"Go!" Ben said.

She fled the room.

Claire had struggled to her knees. Dewey knocked her down again, then straddled her. "Sorry about this," he said. "I have to make it messy." He pulled her hair away from her temple. Shouting into the tape, Claire whipped her head back and forth. Dewey pinned her with one hand, bearing down until she was still. Then he calmly swept the knife across her scalp.

From behind, Ben charged, screaming. His arms passed through Dewey's head. Dewey paused for a second, closing his eyes, hard, like someone fighting off a headache. He opened his eyes again and watched the red line swell across the white skin. "There we go," he said.

Dewey lifted Claire, being sure to tip her so that her head was low. She tried to roll, to kick, but he gripped her tight. Dripping her blood, they went into the hall. He struggled with the knob of the attic door but managed to turn it without losing his load. He lurched up the stairs. At the top, he lowered Claire clumsily. The instant she hit the plywood, her legs, her arms, her mouth, all fought against their restraints.

"Claire, Claire," Dewey said, leaning over her. She stopped moving. A few strands of her blonde hair had gotten stuck in the bloody wound and he freed them carefully with his fingers. "I don't have anything against you, not really. I just need this house. For my family."

She began to struggle again.

"See, to prove there are no hard feelings," he said, a hard edge in his voice now, "I'll make it easier for you to stay still." He had a compact stun gun in his hand, a rectangular unit no larger than a pack of cigarettes. He pressed it against her neck. There was a buzzing sound. Claire jerked and went limp.

Dewey headed down the stairs again. Ben jabbed at him, uselessly, as they passed each other.

"Claire," Ben said, moving to her. Her blood seeped across the plywood, painting the grain. "Can you hear me? Claire! Claire!"

Dewey was back already, taking the steps two at a time, carrying the big duffle bag. He began unpacking things—a heavy rope, a fat, rusty hook. He tossed the rope over a beam and tied it to itself, then looped the hook through.

"Fuck you!" Ben shouted, struggling to grasp the knot. "You fucking fuck! I'm going to kill you!" He tried pushing the hook back through the loop. It swayed but didn't come free.

Dewey centered the rope on the beam so that the hook was directly over the stairs. He tied a thinner, cotton rope, softened and stained as if it had been an outdoor clothesline all summer, around Claire's ankles. Then he grabbed her by the knees, and, showing strain for the first time, lifted the rope over the hook. Cupping her head, he carried it down a couple of steps, then let go. Claire swung freely, upside down. Her shirt fell away from her waist; her blonde hair made a curtain around her head. The bright red flow from her scalp began in earnest.

Dewey checked his work, taking deep breaths, his white coveralls marked with scarlet. He hurried away down the hall, leaving Ben trying to staunch the bleeding with his vaporous palms and fingers.

Dewey continued down to the kitchen. Slipping into the room behind him, Elizabeth watched Dewey root around in the cupboards, saw him pull out a large pot. As he stood up, she went to the KII meter on the counter and waved her hands in front of it. The green lights flashed. "It works," she said.

Dewey's eyes found the meter.

Elizabeth continued to flash the lights. "Now you see me."

"What the hell?" Dewey said. "Who's here?"

Elizabeth hesitated.

Dewey shook his head, then hurried up the stairs, his ponytail swinging behind him.

As Dewey came down the hall, carrying the pot, Ben reached for the open attic door. His hand passed through the wood. He left the attic and tried pushing the door from the other side. He only melted into it. With one last desperate lunge, he sent the door swinging. Slowly, almost lazily, it closed. The latch clicked.

Dewey stopped. He stared at the door. He raised the pot in front of him.

"That got your attention," Ben said.

Dewey detoured into the bedroom. He went to the meter on the bed.

Flying past him, Ben waved frantically.

The lights flickered.

"What the hell?" Dewey backed away. "Is someone here? Is someone here in this house?"

Ben flashed the lights.

Elizabeth had come to the doorway. "Keep doing that, Ben," she said. "He's frightened."

"Can you make the lights stop?" Dewey said.

Ben pulled back. The little beads winked out.

"Damn." Dewey pulled the pot tight to his chest.

Ben backed away still further from the meter. The lights stayed dark.

Dewey squinted hard at the little gray device on the bed. "Ben? Is it you?"

"Hurry, flash the lights," Elizabeth said.

Ben moved toward the meter.

"You know you can't stop me," Dewey said.

Ben hesitated. "He's right. We can't stop him."

"Ben?" Dewey said. "It is you, isn't it?"

"Answer him," Elizabeth said.

But Ben only raised his hand, signaling, *Wait*.

"All right. Not Ben." Dewey took a deep breath. His eyes jumped back and forth. "Do I know you?"

Ben reached out and swept a hand past the meter. The lights traced a bright green arc.

When Dewey spoke again, his voice was low, almost a whisper. "Anna Marie?"

"Holy shit," Ben said. He waved both hands this time. The lights went crazy.

"Oh my God," Dewey said. The pot dropped against his thigh. "Is it really you? Are you here?"

From Ben, one quick flash of the lights.

The pot slipped free of Dewey's fingers, clanged to the floor and spun noisily.

"I—I don't understand," Dewey said, when it was quiet again. "I thought—you were with me—with your bones…"

Ben was still.

"You stayed behind. Why? The tooth—is it because of the tooth?"

Ben flashed the lights again. "It was hers," he said. "I knew it."

"I'm sorry," Dewey said. "There were people in the house. We had to get out of here fast. The bag—I didn't know that it had a hole." For a long time, Dewey seemed to be hunting for something in the empty air in front of him. He stepped toward the meter. "I've been so stupid. We can communicate with this meter. I should have tried it before. I let myself be swayed by Ben. He didn't have much use for them. The fool."

"Asshole."

Dewey stared at the meter, which was dark. "Are you still here?"

Ben quickly flashed the lights.

"I have to ask—are you angry at me?"

"Yes!" Ben flashed the lights.

"I don't blame you." Dewey closed his eyes for a second. "It's not just the tooth, is it?"

"Hell, no," Ben said, blinking the lights.

"We've never been able to talk about what happened. I've talked to you, but I never knew if you were listening. And I could never hear *you*. You know that I didn't mean to hurt you. That it was an accident."

"No I don't," Ben said. "Why don't you explain it to me."

"Do you remember that day?" Dewey said.

Ben pulled back and let the lights stay dark.

Dewey touched the elastic that bound his hair. "I remember it like it was yesterday. I was out for a walk on the Indian trail. I found you there, where it comes close to Jacques's yard. You were watching his house, watching for him. It made me sick to see you there."

Ben didn't move.

"I was so tired of it all. Did you even know how much I cared for you?"

Ben was a statue.

"I didn't think so. Why else would I mentor your club, and supervise that stupid play you were in? It was to be near you. But you only cared about Jacques. That day on the trail, I tried to tell you that you were making a fool of yourself. You just rolled your eyes. I grabbed your arm, to try to get you to listen to me. When you pulled away, you stumbled and you fell. You landed hard on a rock, right here." He touched his temple. "In these woods, you're guaranteed to hit a rock, aren't you? I carried you all the way back to my house. I thought I could save you. But by the time I got home, it was too late. Too late even to call for an ambulance. I could only hold you, be with you for the little time you had left."

"You bastard," Ben said.

"I'm so sorry, Anna Marie. But you do know what I've done for you, since then, right? I gave you companions. Your dog. And now a sister, Leah. But you haven't met her yet, have you?"

Ben didn't respond.

After watching the dark lights for a long time, Dewey said, "Now that you see what I'm doing here, today, you understand how far I'll go for you. When I'm done, and the story gets out, no one will ever want to live in this house. We can have the place to ourselves." He kept his eyes on the meter. "Are you still here? Are you listening?"

Ben signaled that he was.

"Good. So. I have work to do. I have to finish this job. You should stay away. I'm doing this for you, but I don't think you'll want to watch." Dewey reached for the pot.

"No!" Ben sent the lights into a frenzy.

Dewey ignored them. He walked out into the hall.

"Damn!" Ben said. "I only made things worse." He grabbed Elizabeth's hand. "Maybe we can't stop him. But we have to try."

They didn't bother going around Dewey this time. Their linked arms bisected his waist. "Are you ready for this?" Ben said. Elizabeth nodded. They passed through the door into the attic.

At the sight of Claire, awake again and wriggling mutely above a growing slick of blood, Elizabeth stopped dead. Her hand went to her mouth. She was standing like that when the door opened.

Dewey was holding the pot at his hip. He put his foot on the first step, but then paused, his head cocked to the side. Still carrying the pot, he backed up and closed the door.

"What's he doing now?" Ben said.

"Maybe he's afraid to come up," Elizabeth said. "You really frightened him. Who was he talking to? Who is Anna Marie?"

"It's a long story. Not now."

Claire was concentrating all of her energy on pulling at the tie-wrap that bound her hands.

"How can we get her down?" Elizabeth said. "And this bleeding…" She tried to press her hand against Claire's wound. The blood slipped through her fingers.

Ben put his hand on the spot. The red seeped into his palm. "Shit. If I wanted to shove her a little, I might be able to do that. But to keep pressure… I can't." He looked from the blood to the hook dangling from the beam to the tie-wraps on Claire's hands, to the tape on her mouth. Groaning, he balled his fists tight.

"Wait," Elizabeth said, touching his hand. "Do you hear something? Downstairs."

"Yeah, I do. Claire, we'll be right back."

The two ghosts passed through the door and hurried down the hall. Dewey was gone. He'd left the coveralls and the pot at the top of the stairs..

AJ's voice came up from the entryway. "Well, I need to get to the station. Tell Claire I was here, all right? And tell her to charge her phone."

Racing toward the sound, Ben yelled, "AJ, watch out! He's a killer! He has Claire upstairs. Hurry!" He arrived on the landing just in time to see Dewey jump AJ from behind. They fell to the floor, Dewey on top.

"AJ!" Ben said. He tried a big right hook at Dewey's head.

Dewey reached into his pocket and rolled away. AJ was getting to his feet when Dewey pressed his hand against AJ's neck. The stun gun buzzed, and AJ collapsed to the floor. Breathing hard, Dewey stood up. He gave AJ another long burst.

"I have to stop this now," Ben said. He raced up the stairs.

Elizabeth, who had paused partway down, hiked her skirts and went ahead of him. "What are we going to do?"

Ben looked at the bunched-up coveralls and the pot. "I have an idea.

When I say so, start going down the hall, just like you've done a million times before."

Dewey came scrambling around the turn.

"You ready?" Ben said.

Elizabeth nodded.

Dewey was on the last step.

"Go," Ben said.

Elizabeth began to move toward the attic.

Dewey was in the hall. He stopped abruptly, squinting, trying to focus, trying to find a shape in what he saw. "Anna Marie? Is that you?"

Elizabeth hesitated.

"Keep going," Ben said.

Instead, she turned. She fixed her stare on Dewey as if to burn all the way through. And then she came at him.

"Anna Marie," Dewey said, backing up. "What do you want?"

Behind him, Ben swiped at the pot. His hand passed through it. The pot didn't budge. "You can do this," he said.

Dewey took another step back.

Ben swept his hand in front of him. This time, he made just enough contact to nudge the pot. It slid into Dewey's path. Dewey stumbled, twisted to see what was in his way, and completely lost his balance. With the pot tangled up in his legs, Dewey crashed down the stairs, ricocheting around the turn, his feet flailing behind him. One foot found the sweet spot between balusters. As the rest of his body continued down, there was a wet, cracking sound. Dewey landed at the bottom, stunned, grimacing in pain.

Ben raced downstairs. He leaned over AJ. "Hey. Come on, wake up."

AJ's eyes opened. He saw Dewey on the floor. "What the—"

"Claire needs you," Ben said.

"Where is she?" AJ stood, his legs still wobbly.

"The attic."

"Who are you talking to?" Dewey said through gritted teeth. He tried to gather himself, put his feet under him, but screamed in pain.

"Let's go," Ben said. "Dewey's not going anywhere."

"I can make sure of that." AJ dragged Dewey to the door. From behind his back, he produced a pair of handcuffs. "Watch him for me," he said, when Dewey was cuffed to the knob. He reached into Dewey's pocket and pulled out the stun gun. "You could have warned me about this."

"What?" Dewey said.

"Sorry," Ben said.

AJ ran up the stairs.

Elizabeth was waiting in the hallway. "She's badly hurt. You must get

235

her down."

"Show me."

He followed Elizabeth to the door and flung it open. Claire hung there, limp, pale, her blood making a sluggish waterfall that dropped to the next step. With a pocket knife, AJ cut the tie-wrap that bound her hands. Then, circling her with his arms, he lifted her ankles up over the hook. She braced herself as he lowered her to the stairs, her palm landing in her blood. AJ helped her sit up. He peeled the tape from her mouth. Sobbing, she leaned into him. He put one arm around her and with the other, pressed the gash on her head.

She struggled to stand. "We have to get out of here. Dewey—"

"It's all right. He can't hurt you now."

She looked up at him woozily. "He was going to kill me. You saved my life, AJ."

"Not me. It was Ben and his friend, Elizabeth. They're the ones who saved you."

"Are they—" Claire eyes swept the room.

"I'll tell you all about it, later."

"Okay. And you can tell them something, for me."

"Sure."

"Tell them I'm glad they're here. Tell them they can stay as long as they want."

CHAPTER 49

The EMT rolled the gurney toward a waiting ambulance. Dewey, strapped tight to the pad, stared up at the dark sky. Wheeler followed along beside him. Nearby, the chief spoke through the window of a squad car. Manzella sat behind the wheel, gripping it tight, as if he couldn't wait to drive away.

"Wheeler's going to ride with him," the chief said. "Once you get to the hospital, I want both of you to stick with him every minute. As much as they'll let you. Anything he says, you write it down."

"Okay, chief."

"Looks like they're ready to go," the chief said. "Keep me updated." He stepped back, clearing the way for Manzella to follow the ambulance down the lane. He continued on to a second ambulance, parked closer to the house. AJ was half in the open bay, watching an EMT pull a wide bandage across Claire's wound. The chief motioned to AJ, who left his post, reluctantly.

The chief put his hand on AJ's shoulder. "She'll be okay."

"I know. She lost some blood. But mostly, she had the shit scared out of her."

"You look like you did, too."

AJ didn't say anything.

The EMTs arranged a cushion behind Claire's head, propping it up.

"So Dewey is our guy?" the chief said. "For Ben, for Leah, and for Anna Marie? All of them?"

"Yeah. Ben heard him talking. They won't be able to use it in court, but—"

"Don't worry. We're going to put him away forever."

AJ seemed to savor that. "I guess he said some things to Claire, too. Something about there being a family."

"What do you mean? What family?"

"I think he meant he was creating a family. Of ghosts."

"Jesus," the chief said. "This just keeps getting weirder."

A car pulled to a stop in front of the garage. It caught the shifting lights of the emergency vehicles.

"Great," the chief said. "Who's this?"

"That's Sela's car," AJ said.

The chief went to the driver's side. Sela had already rolled down the window. DaSilva was beside him.

"Hey, guys," the chief said. "Now's not the best time for a visit."

DaSilva bent toward the chief. "We saw an ambulance leaving. Did something happen to Claire?"

"She's fine. She needs to be checked out at the hospital. AJ's going with her. Why don't you two head over there. They're going to need a ride home. AJ can explain everything."

"What happened?" Sela said.

"Go on," the chief said. "You need to get out of the way."

Sela turned the car around.

The chief went back to the ambulance. "Your buddies are going to meet you at the hospital."

"Okay," AJ said. "You're not coming?"

"I'm going to catch up with Dewey first."

Inside the brightly lit ambulance, the EMT motioned to AJ, who climbed in and went to Claire's side. The instant the doors were closed, the ambulance was moving.

***

"How is she?" the chief said as he entered the waiting room.

"All right." AJ was standing, though all the chairs were empty. "They're stitching her up now."

"She'll probably have a hell of a scar."

"I'm more concerned with her emotional state. She just keeps staring into space."

"Does she have any family around here?"

"A sister in Massachusetts. She's on her way."

"Great. Best thing for her," the chief said. "That was some good work, AJ. She's lucky to have you on her side. So is the Stonington P.D."

"It was Ben. He took care of Dewey. I didn't do much more than call it in."

"No kidding? Well, good job calling it in, then. Ben still can't work a phone, right? So, he needed you for that."

AJ only shook his head.

238

"It sounds to me like you worked together. Like I've been saying, your peculiar talent is going to be useful. It's going to make you one very unique cop."

"We'll see."

"They're prepping Dewey now for surgery on his ankle," the chief said. "I left Manzella with him."

"Did he talk to you?"

"Me, Manzella, the nurses, anyone who'd listen. He couldn't spill it fast enough." The chief sat heavily in one of the thinly padded chairs. "I still can't believe that we have the guy who killed Anna Marie Rose. That it's over."

"It is over, Chief."

They were quiet for a long while. The television mounted in the corner played the news at a whisper.

"Ben said he was obsessed with her," AJ said. "That he's been carrying her remains around all this time."

"That's right. He had them at his house at first. Then, after the Westburys left, he moved them up to the attic of that house. He figured we wouldn't look there again. It was all about the girl's ghost, though. He thought the ghost was connected to the bones. He thought he was taking care of her. The night that Ben died, investigating Claire's house, Dewey was trying to retrieve the bones before Claire moved in."

"Yeah. Ben finally remembered what happened that night."

"So he remembered Dewey grabbing the camera?" the chief said. "Dewey still has it. I guess the last picture on it is the one that Ben took of him, right before he pushed Ben down the stairs."

AJ let out a quick breath. "Dewey and Ben were friends for a long time—years. How could Dewey do that?"

The chief didn't answer.

"Did Dewey say anything about the other girl? Leah?" AJ said.

"Oh, yeah. He got the idea to put her in the lobster pot from one of those CSI shows. He bought the pot from Ellis. Dewey thought he was making a companion for Anna Marie's ghost—a sister. In his mind, he was making a family."

"That is one sick man. And we never saw it. When I think of all the kids he's worked with—"

Sela and DaSilva came into the room. DaSilva carried a tray of coffees in paper cups. He looked as if he'd already had three himself. "How's Claire?" he said.

"Okay," AJ said. "Getting some stitches."

"Is it true?" DaSilva said. "The cafeteria's buzzing. Did Dewey kill those girls? The one from twenty years ago, and the one who just went missing? I can't believe it."

There were voices in the hall, then Claire was in the doorway, looking pale and moving gingerly. She carried a sheaf of papers in one hand. There was a thick pressure bandage on her head.

AJ went to her. He put his arms around her. "You okay?"

"Yeah."

"Are you ready to leave? You can wait for your sister at my house."

"Do I need to make a statement or something?"

The chief was on his feet again. "That can wait until morning."

"No, I want to do it now."

"Claire," AJ said. "I'm not so sure that's a good idea."

"And reliving the whole thing tomorrow morning is?"

Before AJ could respond, Melody and Jacques appeared behind Claire. The two women hugged.

"Are you all right?" Melody said. "We stopped at your house and saw the police. They said you were at the hospital. That's all they would tell us. I was so worried."

"I'm okay. Or, I will be."

"A TV news crew followed us here, in one of those satellite trucks. They came for you, didn't they?"

"Oh, God," Claire said. "Did they?"

The chief went to the window and looked down at the parking lot. "AJ, why don't you get Claire out of here. Maybe we'll get lucky and the reporters will look for Dewey first."

"Dewey?" Melody said. "What does he have to do with this?"

"We'll see you at the station," AJ said. "Sela, can you give us a ride?"

"You bet," Sela said. "Come on, DaSilva."

They headed for the exit.

"Claire," Melody shouted after them. "Call me if you need anything!"

Claire waved. Then they were gone.

Jacques and Melody stood in the hall, looking into the waiting room, where the chief nodded at them, silent. After a while, the chief grabbed two of the white paper cups from the tray. "Coffee?"

"Thanks," Jacques said. "But I think we'll be going."

"Your choice. But you may want to stick around."

Jacques cheeks were instantly red. "Surely you're not going to accuse me this time? I don't even know what happened. Did someone break into the house again?"

"Hold on," the chief said. "It's actually the opposite of what you're thinking."

"What do you mean?"

"Nineteen years ago, you left here with a lot of people thinking you were a murderer. Me included. In just a minute, I'm going to clear your name."

A smile spread slowly across Jacques's face. He took the coffee that the chief was still holding up for him. "Okay. This I've got to see."

CHAPTER 50

AJ leaned back against the Jeep and watched the greyhound sprint across the yard. Chasing some imaginary prey, Buck faked left, then veered right and disappeared behind the house. AJ called after him, "Buck! Come on boy!" He was following the dog, clapping, when Claire's car came to a stop in the driveway. AJ met her as she was just stepping onto the gravel. They kissed there, her arms around his neck.

"It's nice to have you back," he said.

"Nice to be back." She hadn't yet let go of him. "You'll have to come with me next time."

"Yeah, maybe I will."

Buck, having completed his circuit, shoved his slim nose between them. Claire backed away, laughing. She scratched the greyhound behind his ears.

"So the book signing went well?" AJ said.

"Yeah. Great turnout. I practically had to ice my hand afterward." Claire made a writing motion in the air.

"I bet you did. Who wouldn't want your autograph?"

"Well, I'm a little more famous, now, with everything that happened here."

"That's one positive, at least."

She shook her head but smiled. "The exciting thing, though, is what I found on the way out of Baltimore."

"Ah, so you did stop to do research on Comfort Bloodgood."

"Yes, and I'm so glad I did. It was amazing, AJ. It turns out that Elizabeth's aunt and uncle were prominent citizens in the little town I stopped in, Havre de Grace. They raised Comfort as their daughter. There was nothing secret about her. So, the historical society had all kinds of information. I have photographs of all of them. There are even a couple of Comfort's children."

"Did you find out any more about Elizabeth? What happened to her?"

"I was able to piece some of it together, from letters. Elizabeth was unmarried and pregnant when she moved to Stonington. The man everyone here in town thought was her husband was in fact her brother—the husband thing was a ruse to keep up appearances. When Elizabeth died, her father took the baby down to the aunt in Havre de Grace. The brother took off, the father traveled west, and the family lost track of both of them. Or, I did, anyway."

"Comfort had quite a beginning. So you don't know anything about how Elizabeth died?"

"I do, actually. Just a few weeks after giving birth, she fell down the stairs."

"So the story is true. Was there any suspicion—"

"I found one letter written by the aunt in Havre de Grace. She had her doubts about the fall being an accident. I guess Elizabeth's brother wasn't too happy with pretending to be a husband and father, and there was lots of arguing leading up to Comfort's birth. He threatened her, AJ."

"So she might have been pushed. Just like Ben. That could explain why she has no memory of her death."

"I guess."

Claire and AJ both watched the dog, who had resumed his laps.

"Either way," AJ said, "that's a sad story to have to tell Elizabeth."

"I'm going to focus on Comfort and the good life that she lived."

"Sounds like a plan."

"There's something else, AJ. You know I've said that I felt like I belonged in my house, since the first time that I saw it?"

"Yeah."

"Comfort had seven children. Her youngest girl, Mary Charlotte, married Elisha Connor."

"Connor? Are you related?"

"Not by blood. But our families are connected."

"Are you sure?"

"My father has been working on the Connor genealogy. Mary Charlotte is on his chart—the names, dates, everything matches."

"Wow. That's…"

"Kind of freaky?"

"Yeah."

They were quiet for a moment. A seagull cried overhead.

"I'm ready to head over to the house," Claire said.

"All right, then, let's go." AJ called Buck, who responded eagerly.

"Maybe we should leave Buck here," Claire said.

"But Ben's always so glad to see him."

"I know, but the way Ben gets Buck going… If I'm going to have these papers spread out…"

"Right." AJ let the dog into the house, then got into the passenger seat of Claire's car. They started down Mistuxet.

"Any new developments with Dewey?" Claire said after a while. "Has he admitted to any other murders?"

"No, and we haven't found any more bones on his property. Just the two skeletons, in the greenhouse—Anna Marie's and the dog's."

"You still haven't made contact with the ghosts of either of the girls?"

"No." AJ watched Claire as she watched the road. She lifted a hand from the steering wheel, then slid it under the hair at her temple, where the stitches had left a faint, broken line.

"So where's the stuff on Comfort?" he said.

"It's all in that case in the back."

AJ twisted in his seat. "Guess I'll have to wait till we get there."

"Yeah. Elizabeth really should see it first, anyway."

"Fair enough. We should call Melody. She'll want to be there for this."

"Oh, I forgot to tell you. I did call her," Claire said. "The offer Jacques made on the house on Wamphassuc Point? It was accepted. They're going to spend the day celebrating by looking at furniture and paint chips."

"Uh oh. Are we going to get drafted to paint?"

"We might." She laughed. "Then again, I don't think Jacques's exactly a do-it-yourselfer."

"You might be right."

They drove through the rocky woods. Claire took the lane into the trees, kicking up dust. She parked by the garage.

"I wish I could see how Elizabeth reacts," Claire said. "You have to tell me everything she says, okay?"

"I will. Ben, too. This will mean a lot to him."

"Yeah." Claire looked through her window at the imposing brown house.

"Are you ready?" AJ said.

She nodded but still didn't open her door.

"I know this is hard," he said.

"It's not just what happened to me." Claire closed her eyes for a second. "I had this dream last night. I came back here. Ben and Elizabeth were in the dining room, setting the table. There were only two places—no room for me."

AJ took Claire's hand. "This is your house. You said you belong here. It's going to be fine."

"Yeah, you're right." Claire released her seatbelt and got out of the car. She retrieved the case from the back seat.

They went to the front door, across weeds that had been cut to approximate a lawn.

"Hey!" AJ called when they had stepped inside. "Ben! Elizabeth!" There was no reply.

"I hope we're not interrupting anything," Claire said.

"Like what? What would they be doing?"

Claire tilted her head at him, a slight smile on her lips.

"What? Oh." AJ laughed. "Do you think that's possible?"

They both looked up the stairs.

"It's a little stale in here," AJ said. "How about some fresh air."

"I'm going to set up on the dining room table," Claire said.

When Ben came down the stairs, AJ was in the living room, working on a sticky window.

"Hey, AJ. Did you come by yourself?"

"Claire's here. She has something for Elizabeth, about her family."

"Fantastic. I'll go get her."

"What's this about my family?" Elizabeth appeared on the stairs. Her hair hung in disarray about her shoulders.

"Hi," AJ said. "Your bun..." He reached behind his head. "I didn't know you could..."

Elizabeth gathered her hair in one hand.

"Anyway, Claire's in the dining room," AJ said. "Go see."

Claire was busy arranging photocopies on the big table. There were solemn portraits, old newspaper clippings and letters in dark cursive. At one end of the table, two pieces of paper placed together showed a hand-drawn family tree.

"Oh, my," Elizabeth said, swerving around the table. "What is all of this?"

"Elizabeth wants to know what you have here," AJ said.

"It's the history of your relatives in Maryland," Claire said. "Really, it's your daughter's history."

"Comfort?" Elizabeth said.

"Can you show her a picture of Comfort?" AJ said.

"Here." Claire plucked a photograph from the table. "Comfort as a new mother, holding her own beautiful daughter."

Elizabeth reached for the paper, but let her hand fall.

"Now that you've seen her," Claire said, "you should know your granddaughter's name. It's your name. Elizabeth. Comfort obviously knew about you."

Elizabeth's hands had covered her face. A tear rolled off her cheek and vanished.

"There's one other thing." Claire put her finger on the large and many-branched family tree. "This is your granddaughter, Mary Charlotte." She moved her finger to the far bottom of the page. "And this is me."

Elizabeth's disappearing tears continued to flow. Claire looked at AJ, who nodded.

"Why don't I show you what's here," Claire said. "Piece by piece."

It took some time, with AJ acting as the go-between and Elizabeth requiring frequent stops to digest it all.

"Thank you, Claire," Elizabeth managed to say, when they had finished. "This is so wonderful. It's beyond wonderful. All these long years, I've been afraid that my daughter, my family, wouldn't accept me, that they wouldn't even know who I was. I'm not afraid anymore. For that, I can't possibly thank you enough."

After AJ had repeated those words, Claire took his arm. "Why don't we give her some more time to look this over."

"Good idea."

They went back through the front hall and outside.

"That was a nice thing that you did," AJ said.

"Yeah," Claire said. "I filled in some of the gaps for her." She continued to her car. "Now I have something to show you." She opened the trunk.

"Please don't tell me you have a *For Sale* sign back there."

"No," she said, reaching in. "It's not a *For Sale* sign. Geez."

She carried a cardboard tube around to the front of the car, slid a roll of paper from the tube, then spread it on the hood.

"What is that?" AJ said.

"An architect friend drew these up for me."

AJ came around and helped to hold down one side of the paper.

"These are plans to redo the stairs," Claire said. "Make them safer."

"I like that. What's the second sheet?"

"This is a plan for opening up the attic." She pointed at the drawing. "I'll change the stairs going up. Then, if I raise the roofline, I can make one big open room. There will be windows all along this wall, and over here, built-in shelves and storage. On this side, I'll have a custom-made writing station."

"Well, all right. Seems kind of permanent."

Claire kept her eyes on the plans. "It's a big job, but if I give up my apartment in the city, I should be able to save up enough."

AJ let go of the paper and put his arms around Claire. She pressed against him as the paper curled up on itself. They stood for a long time with their arms around each other, the sun warm on their skin.

"We should tell Ben and Elizabeth," AJ said. "They'll be relieved."

"Let me bring the plans in to show them."

She gathered up the roll of paper and they went back to the house.

"Hey, guys," AJ called from the front hall. "We have something else you should see." He reached the dining room first. "They're not here."

"Maybe the porch?"

As she went through the kitchen, Claire watched the KII meter on the counter. The lights were dead.

"They're not there, either," AJ said, looking out the back door. "Must be upstairs. I'll go get them."

He circled around to the landing, then went up. "Ben!" he shouted, going room to room. Claire joined him, a KII meter in her hand. After two more passes through the bedrooms, AJ tried the attic. It was empty, too. He went back down. He closed the attic door and for a long moment, stared at the place in the wall where Elizabeth had appeared.

Claire raised the meter. The lights stayed dark. "Is it my imagination, or does the house feel different?" she said.

"It's not your imagination. It feels—I don't know—empty." AJ grazed the wall with his fingers.

"Ben can't leave the house, right? He tried and he couldn't. But Elizabeth has."

"Well, Ben thinks she never really left. She just faded out sometimes. Lack of interest, he said."

"But now—they're really not here."

"Seems that way."

Claire put a hand on AJ's arm. "Do you think they'll be back?"

"I know what Sela and DaSilva would say. They've moved on. Those things you showed Elizabeth…maybe they freed her from whatever was keeping her here. And it seems like Ben went with her."

Claire watched AJ for a while, watched his eyelids drop and pause and leave a damp shine.

AJ cleared his throat. "That dream you had… Maybe Ben and Elizabeth were setting the table for us."

They stood in the quiet hall, keeping the silence.

"This is a good thing, AJ," Claire said. "You didn't want Ben trapped here. Either of them."

"Yeah. Yeah, it is a good thing."

"And Ben finally got the girl."

AJ smiled. "Apparently."

Claire switched off the meter. She looked up and down the hall again. "So, we're really alone."

"Yeah."

"You know this is the first time we've been alone in this house."

"I guess you're right." AJ put his arms around her. "All alone," he said. "Let's see how that feels."

Janis Bogue, a native of Stonington, Connecticut, and William Keller are married and have two daughters. They live in Woodstock, New York, where they are at work on the next AJ Bugbee mystery.

Visit them on Facebook at
http://www.facebook.com/authorJanisBogueAndWilliamKeller